The Young Stag

Book V – Islands in the Mist

J.M. Hofer

ISBN-13: 9798600796966

The Young Stag
J.M. Hofer

Synopsis of Book IV, Into the Shadows

Din Scathach

Alt Clud
STRATHCLYDE   GODODDIN

ULAID   Caer Ligualid

                                R
                                H
Amergin's Order   Ynys Manau   E
                                G
                                H
Knockma   E
                                D

            GWYNEDD
            Dinas Emrys
            Mynyth Aur   S
                          Viroconium   A
                                          X
Maes Gwythno   O
                                          N   S
                                          S   A
                                                 X
            DYFED   O
                          GWENT   N
                   Caer Leon   Caer Mincip   S
            GLWYWISING
                                 Caer Lundein

            Ynys Wydryn   Ambrius
            DUMNONIA   SAXONS
       Din Tagell   Exeter

                                        ARMORICA

Isle of Ynys Wydryn
Affalon / Avalon / Glastonbury

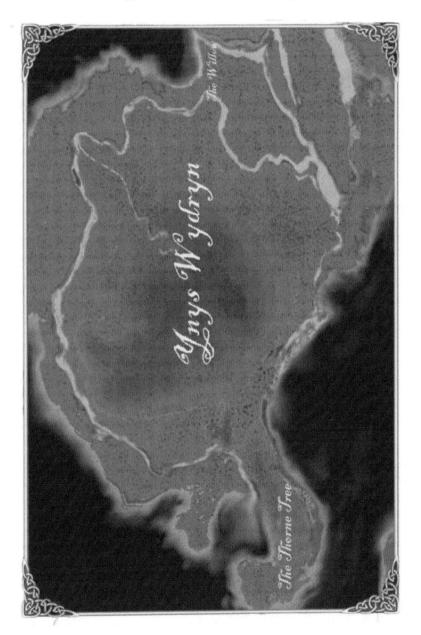

Dear Reader,

Islands in the Mist is a multi-generational epic spanning several volumes. As it can be difficult to remember all that has happened from one book to the next, I've added a synopsis at the beginning of each volume that summarizes the one prior. I hope this serves to enhance your enjoyment of the series and wish you happy reading.

J.M. Hofer

Synopsis of Book IV, Into the Shadows:

Taliesin the Bard is released from Myrthin's enchantment by a small girl who calls him Father. She leads his spirit back to his physical body which lies concealed in a crystal cave on the island of Affalon. He awakens unaware of how much time has passed in the mortal world. Fearing that Nimue, Mistress of Affalon, may have colluded with the archdruid Myrthin to secure his imprisonment, he flees to Caer Leon seeking the counsel of his former lord and patron, Uthyr Pendragon.

Arhianna the Firebrand and her estranged Jute husband, Jørren, dramatically reunited after months of separation, have reconciled and settled in Arhianna's home village of Mynyth Aur. Jørren is restless and soon insists on rejoining his clan, whom he led north to escape the wrath of his sworn earl, Hengist, after refusing to take part in a plot to slaughter their unarmed enemies. Arhianna regrets abandoning her husband for his assumed participation in the devious plot, and agrees now to go North with him in search of his people.

Soon after setting off on their journey, Arhianna realizes she is pregnant. She remembers nothing of her time with the Daoine Sidhe in Knockma or her romance with Taliesin (Book III), so she naturally believes Jørren is the father. The prospect of a child quickly heals their marriage, but it comes with an unexpected price — Arhianna discovers she can no longer wield her Firebrand.

Meanwhile, Igerna, Arhianna's closest friend, struggles with pregnancy woes of her own. Recently widowed and now queen to Uthyr Pendragon, she is unsure of who — or what — fathered the child she carries. She fears her child may have been conceived prior to marrying Uthyr, fathered by a creature disguised as her former husband, Gorlois (Book III). Unlike Igerna, we know the imposter was her current husband, Uthyr Pendragon, who duped her with the help of Myrthin's powerful sorcery. Igerna, however, yet remains in the dark. What manner of creature made love to her, murdered her true husband, Gorlois, and fled? Worse, what manner of creature might she be carrying in her womb?

Igerna's secret becomes unbearable. With Taliesin gone, she confides in Myrthin, whom she believes will sympathize with her suspicion that she may be carrying the child of a nature spirit or sea god. Myrthin, who knows the truth, encourages her to confide in Uthyr, assuring her she has nothing to fear. Igerna remains unconvinced.

Nimue, sworn to deliver Arhianna's child to the Sidhe king and queen of Knockma, searches for her quarry in the mortal world. She travels to Mynyth Aur looking for Arhianna but is told by Lucia that Arhianna recently departed for the northern kingdoms, forcing Nimue to resume her search. She resents the bargain she struck to deliver Arhianna's child to Knockma in exchange for Taliesin's release, but is determined to do whatever she must to secure her true love's freedom.

Back in Mynyth Aur, Bran struggles with chronic pain and a waxing addiction to a powerful medicinal mixture provided by Myrthin. Arawn, Bran's overlord since Book I, witnesses his struggle and offers him a position of power in the Underworld. Bran refuses, determined to hold on, having recently become a grandfather. Neither Bran nor Lucia feel ready for him to leave the mortal world yet.

Arhianna and Jørren arrive at a Saxon settlement in the North where they have a fateful encounter with a man named Earl Ingvar. Ingvar accuses Jørren of being an oath breaker and fatally stabs him. Arhianna, unable to summon her Firebrand, is taken prisoner. She discovers Ingvar has taken over Jørren's settlement and enslaved her former clanswomen. She is thrown into slavery alongside them but is shunned; the women blame her for their misfortune, believing if she had not abandoned them or convinced Jørren to disobey Hengist, all would be well. Their only hope is that Ragna, Jørren's mother, who managed to escape their fate, will return with help.

Taliesin arrives at Mynyth Aur eager to see Arhianna but is crushed to learn she has departed with Jørren. He laments that she must remember nothing of their romance in Knockma; or, worse, that she does remember, but has chosen Jørren over him. He tells Lucia that Myrthin is to blame for the long sleep he and Arhianna suffered, and to be wary of him. Concerned, Lucia tells Taliesin about Nimue's recent visit to Mynyth Aur and her desire to determine Arhianna's whereabouts. Taliesin can no longer deny Nimue's betrayal. He shares his suspicions with Lucia and makes her promise to stay in Mynyth Aur while he seeks out Arhianna to warn her.

Taliesin heads north to the hall of King Urien and tells him he is seeking someone in nearby Saxon territory, but, out of caution, does not reveal who. Urien, who greatly admires Taliesin's genius as a bard, makes him a bargain: a guide, dogs and provisions for his quest if he agrees to be his Pen Bairth for a year. Taliesin accepts, and Urien appoints a sour giant named Gawyr as his guide.

Gawyr soon finds out Arhianna has been taken captive by Ingvar. He urges Taliesin to give up his search, saying if Arhianna isn't dead already, she surely wishes she were. Taliesin refuses and instead doubles his efforts.

Nimue arrives in Urien's hall soon after Taliesin departs. She asks about Arhianna but discovers she is not there, nor has she been, recently. Dismayed, Nimue asks Urien to send out a search party, saying Arhianna set out for his hall weeks ago and may have met with misfortune. Urien complies, disturbed by the idea of an ally's daughter coming to harm in his kingdom. Nimue, content to have Urien's men do the searching for her, easily charms Urien into inviting her to stay until Arhianna is found.

As Gawyr presaged, Arhianna suffers terrible abuse at the hands of Ingvar and his men. She prays to her patroness, the goddess Freya, offering her the child in her belly in exchange for the return of her Firebrand, but her prayers go unanswered. Convinced Freya has forsaken her, Arhianna prays instead to Morrigan, war goddess of her own people. Under her influence, Arhianna's hunger for revenge grows, as do her supernatural abilities, but, alas, not her Firebrand.

Ragna is successful in finding help. She returns with a fierce band of warriors who liberate the women from their captors. Most of the men are slain but a few escape, Ingvar among them. Scáthach pledges to deal with them and bids the women take the village back for their own. Arhianna is horrified by the idea of staying there. She asks Scáthach if she can join her clan, determined to learn to fight as they do. Scáthach quickly sees she's pregnant and refuses, asking which of the dead bastards was the father. Arhianna proudly announces, "none of them," revealing, in front of her mother-in-law, Ragna, that Jørren is the father of her child. She then deals Ragna subsequent blows of hope and despair by recalling her reunion with Jørren, how they came north to rejoin the settlement, and his tragic murder at the hands of Ingvar. Ragna is heartbroken by her son's death but finds solace in the prospect of a grandson.

When Scáthach and her warriors prepare to leave, Arhianna again entreats Scáthach to allow her to join them. Ragna steps forward in protest, insisting to Scáthach that Arhianna does not know what she is asking. Scáthach ignores her pleas and asks to see Arhianna's palms. After examining them, she reconsiders her decision and grants Arhianna's wish. Ragna is horrified. She begs Arhianna not to go, but Arhianna is resolute and departs.

It is not long before Arhianna regrets her decision, for she is not accepted by these women, either. None of them approve of Scáthach's decision to allow her to join them, least of all Scáthach's daughter, Uathach. Arhianna feels drawn ever deeper into the dark presence of Morrigan, finding the power of the goddess intoxicating. Arhianna swears that if her babe survives, she will name the child Morrigan, after her new patroness.

Shortly before arriving at the fortress of Dun Scáthach, Arhianna falls behind on a disorienting stretch of land called the Plain of Misfortune. No one in the party waits or turns back for her, leaving her to fend for herself in a hostile land. She eventually finds her way across the plain to the fortress but cannot find a way up its treacherous mountain perch. Weeks pass, until Arhianna resigns herself to the fact that no help is coming.

Gawyr and Taliesin continue their search for Arhianna, at last arriving at what they believe to be Ingvar's settlement. Out of caution, Taliesin visits the village by shapeshifting into a dog and discovers, to his joy, that Ragna is in charge. He returns to the village as himself accompanied by Gawyr, where he learns Arhianna has eluded him again, having left with Scáthach. Taliesin pledges to Ragna he will do all he can to bring her back.

Meanwhile, Arhianna struggles to survive as winter approaches. She eventually finds her way to a grotto with signs of an entrance into the mountain that she suspects leads to the fortress. She attempts to swim to it but is swept up by the riptide and loses consciousness. She awakens to find herself in the grotto with her rescuer—a selkie who warns her not to enter the "house of blood." He invites her to live with his people instead, where she and her "pup" will be safe. Arhianna refuses. He warns her if she stays, both she and her child will die.

After weeks without any news, Lucia grows anxious about Arhianna. She and Bran sail north to Alt Clud on the Ceffyl Dwr with Tegid, Ula and Creirwy. They discover Urien is already searching for Arhianna, thanks to Nimue, who is out riding in the woods when they arrive. Eager to confront her, Lucia rides out to find her.

Nimue, meanwhile, is approached in the forest by her estranged brother, Maelwys, whom she hasn't seen in many years. Maelwys warns her not to return to Urien's hall, assuring her he knows where Arhianna is. He offers to help her fulfill her obligation to Oonagh and Finbheara, if only she will allow him back into Affalon. Nimue reluctantly agrees but warns him her mistress, Arianrhod, has the final say on the matter. Placated, Maelwys leads Lucia astray in the woods.

Taliesin and Gawyr arrive at Dun Scáthach, where Taliesin prays his search for Arhianna will end. With Taliesin's help, Gawyr climbs the Giant's Ladder to the top of the mountain and crosses the Bridge of Leaping into the fortress, earning him respect among the warriors and the privilege of training among them. He asks Scáthach about Arhianna and is told she is alive and in good health, but that she is pledged to the order and cannot be disturbed.

Taliesin waits for Gawyr's return by the seashore, where he sings to pass the time. This summons the attention of a great many selkies, one of whom happens to be his foster mother, Ula, come to visit her clan while the Ceffyl Dwr is docked in nearby Alt Clud. Taliesin tells her he must get into the fortress. In an effort to help, Ula introduces him to the same selkie who rescued Arhianna from drowning. We find out he is her son by Taliesin's foster father, Elffin. Taliesin is outraged and heart-broken that Ula kept such a secret from Elffin, but after a few days, he forgives her and embraces his newfound brother. He gives him a name to use among men: Arvel.

Arhianna gives birth to a daughter in the shelter of the grotto. Scáthach, at last, appears to her, saying she has now earned the right to train among her warriors, but only if she gives her child to the selkies to foster. Arhianna protests but Scáthach is resolute, saying she cannot be both mother and warrior. She assures her when her daughter is older, she, too, can train among the order, and reach the potential Arhianna's maternal ancestors squandered. When Arhianna protests, Scáthach warns her that the Daoine Sidhe are seeking her child, and that only within her territory will she and her child remain safe. Arhianna does not know who the Daoine Sidhe are or why they want her child, for she still has no memory of Knockma, but she chooses to trust Scáthach. She hands her baby over, resolving to become so fierce a warrior and sorceress that she will be able to protect her child herself and fetch her back from the selkies.

Taliesin hears Arhianna's labor cries on the wind and finds his way to the grotto. There he encounters Scáthach, who somehow, seems to know much about him. He asks to see Arhianna, but Scáthach refuses, saying once an apprentice begins her training, she may see no one. Ula appears holding Arhianna's newborn child. Taliesin proclaims himself the child's father, again begging to see Arhianna. Scáthach refuses. She issues him the same warnings she gave Arhianna and departs.

Taliesin, Ula and Arvel row the baby to Selkie Isle. Taliesin has misgivings about Scáthach's intentions, and takes it upon himself to devise a plan, recalling Cerridwen's advice to have his daughter fostered "beneath the dragon's wing." Instead of leaving her in care of the selkies, he asks Ula to swim her to Caer Leon (Uthyr Pendragon's fortress) by way of the sea inside her sealskin, knowing the Sidhe will have no chance of tracking her. Ula accepts.

Taliesin travels overland to Caer Leon with Arvel and Gawyr, hoping to mislead the Sidhe. Nimue, who is in the area, senses his presence and follows her heart to where he is, insisting to Maelwys that she must. Taliesin has a confrontation with Maelwys that ends with Taliesin driving a dagger into his heart. Nimue begs Taliesin to forgive her, pleading her love for him as the cause of her treachery, but Taliesin rejects her.

Ula uses all her strength to get to Caer Leon, enduring rough seas and ruthless predators. Taliesin is waiting for her when she arrives. She delivers the child safely into Taliesin's hands and, mortally fatigued by her efforts, swims out to sea for the last time.

Taliesin visits Igerna, knowing she is on the verge of childbirth. He asks her to foster his daughter as twin to her own child to save her from the Sidhe. For the love Igerna bears both Taliesin and Arhianna, she agrees. Taliesin's plan works, and the entire kingdom believes Uthyr Pendragon's queen has given birth to twins: Arthur and Morgen.

Igerna must now carry the burden of keeping yet another secret from her husband. She confides in Taliesin about her first; that of not knowing who fathered Arthur. Taliesin, like Myrthin, urges her to tell Uthyr at least this secret, taking heart that both babes were born of magic. Igerna finally confesses her misgivings to Uthyr. He, in turn, makes his own confession: that of deceiving her with Myrthin's help, revealing that he is, indeed, the father of her child (or children, as he now believes). Igerna feels enraged that Uthyr has allowed her to grapple with her guilt for so long but knows she cannot rebuke him too much; they have both deceived each other, and she would yet have to, for many years to come. She does, however, insist that Myrthin be banished from court and Taliesin put in his place. Uthyr, eager to please her, agrees.

Back in Mynyth Aur, Bran's pain continues to diminish him. Arawn begins coming to him nightly, sharing wisdom and prophecy. One fateful night, he leads him to the sacred grove, where Cerridwen awaits. She bids Bran look into her cauldron. In its depths, he sees visions of the tenuous future of Brython, the horrible things Arhianna has suffered, and an infant he does not recognize. Cerridwen cannot, or will not, explain the visions, but promises if he were to accept Arawn's offer, he would have both the answers he seeks and the power he has lost in the mortal world. Weary of being a burden and eager to regain the ability to help those he loves, Bran accepts Arawn's offer. With Gareth now an able chieftain, Bran knows the Oaks will be in good hands.

After a night of beautiful farewells to his wife and brethren, Bran leaves them behind to embrace his new role in the Underworld.

So ends Book IV.

Now, on with the story...

Arhianna

CHAPTER ONE
Dun Scáthach

Arhianna woke for the third time that night, teeth chattering in protest against the wind blowing through her chamber. She hugged her wolf pelt closer, coiling herself as tightly as she could against its molesting chill. All the chambers in Scáthach's fortress stood open to the sea below and the training ring within. They were unfurnished, unadorned, and without doors—a stone beehive, crawling with lethal denizens.

It was not long before the rude blush of dawn joined forces with the wind to torment her. She moaned in surrender to the morning, struggling to ignore the injuries she had sustained the day prior as she sat up and turned her face toward its cruel light. She crossed her legs and settled into her devotions, driving her pain away with her chanting.

She had greeted every sunrise since her arrival with praise and prayers for Morrigan, asking she continue to bless her with strength and courage for as long as she deemed her worthy. Every morning, Morrigan's black wings rose up behind her in response. *I am with you.* In that moment, all the misery of the past day and night dissipated. In its place flowed a fierce resolve, driving her to leap from her chamber and face her training anew.

Then came the morning meal, such as it was. Nuts, berries and a mysterious hot brew Niamh the cook made. No one knew what was in it. It tasted like dirt and bark, and—some swore—stag's blood, but lent an energy and clarity of focus that meant less injuries than there might be otherwise. Over the moons, Arhianna developed a taste for it that had become a morning craving. It called to her now, twisting in between her mantras like ivy. She ignored the growling of her stomach through the rest of her repetitions and then stood up to wash.

Outside the warriors' chambers were ledges of ancient bedrock, riddled with bowl-shaped pockets that collected rainwater. She went out and splashed her face, bracing herself against the cold shock. Icy drops fell from her forehead back into the pool as she watched the weak light of dawn play upon the ripples of the water. She bent down again and poured water over her smooth head, fingering the long rough scab from the graze she had suffered the week before,

1

compliments of Uathach. *That'll leave a scar,* she noted. She sat up and sunk her fingers into the bowl of deer tallow Niamh had given her, and smeared a generous amount along the length of the wound, hoping to speed its healing. Her thick hair would have provided protection, in this instance, but the benefits of having nothing for the other warriors to grab her by made keeping it short the better choice. She had shaved it off the day she arrived and had not let it grow into more than a copper shadow ever since.

She heard the others waking and washing, mingled with the clanging of breakfast pots and weapons being readied for the day. She stood up and went to join the others in the hall.

"Ready for me to kick that beautiful arse o' yers agin, today, *macushla*?" Aengus murmured as she passed by.

Arhianna had been disappointed to discover there were men training at Dun Scáthach. She had hoped it would be only women. Many were sons of Scáthach's female warriors who had been in training from the time they could hold a weapon, but they were not the only men there. Anyone who could scale the mountain and best Uathach on the Bridge of Leaping—also called the Pupil's Bridge, among other more colorful names—earned the right to train at Dun Scáthach as well. Aengus was such a man.

"You may have an easy time of it." She scowled. "Raise your arms, and I might faint straight away from the stench. Why don't you take mercy on us all and bathe?"

"An' why would I do that?"

Arhianna shook her head as she ladled herself a large bowl of Niamh's brew and sat down across from him.

His eyes danced at her, crow's feet crinkling beneath his copse of dark curls. "Gods, yer a beauty, Ronin," he whispered, bending his head toward her. "If we survive this place, I'm takin' ye home with me—an' don't worry—I'll wash fer ye ev'ry morn' an' put on a fancy tunic—set ye te swoonin'…"

She glared at him. "I'd sooner put a dagger through my eye." She meant it. *No man will ever touch me again.*

He raised a bushy brow and sat back, clucking his tongue. "That's a shame." He drank down his brew and let out a long sigh.

2

"Such pretty blue jewels they are—clear as the sky on a bright summer morn'." He winked at her, stood up and walked out, his bulk swaggering from side to side like a prize bull.

Arhianna leaned over her hot bowl and let its steam warm her face. *I swear to Morrigan, I'll beat that smirk off his face today. Him, and all the rest of them.* She gripped her bowl tightly, picturing her staff slamming into his jaw.

"Ronin!" she heard Scáthach scold over her shoulder.

Arhianna looked down and realized her brew was boiling. She took her hands away from it and chided herself, glancing around at the others to see if they had noticed. Only Hedrek was staring. *No matter there. He never says anything.*

Ever since her Firebrand had returned, she struggled to keep it under control. It was far harder to manage than it had been before, because she felt angry all the time. Flames seemed ever ready to leap from her fingers.

"Be more careful," Scáthach warned on her way out of the hall, signaling breakfast was over. The warriors stood up and followed her outside into the training ring. Someone was already there, however, standing in the center like a pillar from a Roman temple.

"Bloody hell!" Aengus blurted. "An' here I thought *you* were a giant!" He elbowed Hedrek in the side. "Where the hell'dya think *he* came from?"

Hedrek's copper mustache curled skyward from under his scowl. "Gods, Aengus—do ye ever shut up?" He lumbered down the thick stairs into the ring, shaking his head as he went.

Arhianna followed, eager to see the giant close up.

"What's your hurry, little Ronin?" a voice cried.

Arhianna turned to see Uathach on her heels. "You don't get whipped enough every day? You're certainly no match for that one. Why don't you go live with the selkies and your wee one? You're just going to get yourself killed if you stay here. You should leave, before you end up a cripple, like Niamh."

Anger coursed toward Arhianna's fingers, threatening to burst into flame. *Bitch!* She clenched her fists, attempting to thwart her fury. *I could burn you to ash if I wanted to.*

She could, she knew, but she would not. She knew if she wanted to become a warrior worthy of such a gift, she had to learn to fight without it. She had lost her Firebrand before, which meant she could

3

lose it again. To depend on it was foolish. *More than foolish.* She had lost her husband learning that lesson. Besides, Uathach's comments stung because they rang true. Arhianna had been beaten every day of her training and had yet to win a single match against anyone. Uathach was ever quick to remind her it was because she did not belong there; she had not bested her on the Bridge of Leaping or scaled the walls to the fortress. And yet, Scáthach had allowed her to train with the clan anyway.

"We've been holding back to save your face, lass. It's all you'll have out there." Uathach shoved her aside, leapt down into the ring, and strode with the power of a stallion to where her mother stood beside the giant in the center of the ring.

Arhianna regarded her fellow men and women-at-arms. Every one of them looked fierce, scarred and muscular—body and mind forged by hardship and battle. *Not me. What misery have I known, except what has befallen me this past year?* She glanced down at her pale skin and slight build. *She's right—I'm no match for them. Not even if I were to train the rest of my life. They wield sword and spear the way Taliesin plays his harp—like they were born to it. I should have stayed with Ragna. I could have sent for Seren or sought someone to train me there. I'd be holding my daughter right now.* She choked up and clenched her fists again.

"Warriors!" Scáthach cried from beneath the shadow of the giant's frame. "This is Gawyr nam Fiannaidh, descended from the great Fomoiri across the sea. Does anyone doubt me?"

Aengus tossed his chin in Gawyr's direction, threw his arms apart like two enormous temple doors and shrugged his shoulders. "I don't doubt it, but I'll bring ye down just the same, big man!"

Hedrek rolled his eyes, glancing over his shoulder at Arhianna before shaking his head.

"Very well, Aengus, as you're so eager this morning." Scáthach pulled her leather bag of rune-bones from her belt and held it open in front of him. "See what the fates have to say about it."

Aengus pulled a bone from the bag, looked at its symbol, and held it aloft. "Duir!" he roared, then pounded his chest with his fist.

Scáthach held the bag out for the woman standing next to him, who chose and announced her symbol. On and on it went, around the circle. Those who held matching runes at the end would train together for the length of the morning.

4

Uathach reached in and pulled one out. Her eyes lit up as she read its symbol. She held it up between thumb and forefinger, displaying its slanted lines. "Straif!" she bellowed.

Arhianna wrung her hands in anticipation of her turn. *Ugh. Please, let it not be Straif today.* She was in no state of mind to face Uathach.

A few more warriors pulled their runes. None chose Straif. Soon, it was her turn. Though there were five warriors left to choose after her, somehow, she knew the one she would pull out, no matter how many of the runes she fingered within the bag. Ever since the dreadful day of Jørren's murder, it seemed to her the gods heard all her prayers backwards, for they routinely seemed to give her the opposite of what she asked for. She felt no surprise when she looked down and saw slanted lines in her palm. She held up her rune and shot Uathach a look of fierce defiance. "Straif!"

Uathach glared back at her, grinning with malice.

Arhianna struggled to keep her face as smooth as slate. She summoned her courage and anger, and they ran to her side like two faithful hounds. *Don't let her see your dread. You can defeat her. Remember, you've fought wolves.* She glimpsed a dark flash of black feathers from of the corner of her eye as she stoked her courage.

The bones were all returned to the bag, and then Scáthach pulled one out to determine who would train first. Again, Arhianna knew what it would be. She threw her shoulders back and clenched her fists, determined to endure whatever the morning had in store for her. She met Uathach's eyes and moved forward to meet her in the ring.

Scáthach pulled a bone from another bag that would determine which weapons they were to practice with. Arhianna dared not wish for anything in particular.

"Staves!" Scáthach announced.

Arhianna and Uathach went to the wall, chose their weapons, and returned to the ring. Arhianna was on the ground before she had a chance to strike one blow. She scrambled to her feet, her blood rising at Uathach's arrogant grin. "Go home, have some more Saxon bastards. At least we know you can do that."

Arhianna felt the flames within her fingers humming like taut bowstrings, ready to lash out at her enemy. She refused them their freedom. Instead, she lunged with her staff and missed. The price was

5

another blow, this time to the kidneys. She cried out and fell to her knees, rolling to the side to miss yet another merciless strike. Uathach's staff hit the ground beside her, sending a cloud of dust into the air. Arhianna jumped up and struck her in the back of the head, sending her reeling forward, but instead of ending up face first in the dirt, as Arhianna had hoped, she somersaulted out of the fall and whirled around with a heart-stopping battle cry. The next blow caught Arhianna in the back of the legs, sweeping her off her feet. She fell flat on her back and felt the wind leave her lungs. She stared up at the sky, blue one moment, filled with Uathach's face the next. She felt Uathach's staff crush her windpipe.

"Enough!" Scáthach cried. "Victory to Uathach!" Uathach released the pressure from her throat and stood up, still wearing her nasty grin.

Arhianna rolled over and pressed herself up on her elbows, struggling to breathe. She got to her feet, returned her staff to the wall, and moved to the side of the ring. One of Scáthach's servants offered her water. She drank it slowly, washing down the dust she had inhaled.

Match after match, Arhianna watched closely how and why the victors won. Long before she was ready, it was time to face Uathach again. This time, with knives. Arhianna reached down and gripped the hilt of her dagger. She closed her eyes. *Morrigan! Help me defeat her!* Again, her determination rose. She opened her eyes and felt Morrigan's black wings rise behind her. Her skin and dagger blade steamed in the cold sea air. But she did not care. *I'm tired of hiding it. Let them see. Let them all see!*

When Uathach lunged for her, she unleashed a stream of fire down her arm to her dagger, engulfing it in flames. Uathach's shock gave her the few seconds she needed to deliver a well-placed kick to the chest that sent her stumbling backward. She seized the opportunity she had created like a starved animal, leaping onto Uathach and putting the hot blade to her throat. Uathach cried out.

"Ronin!" Scáthach ran over and yanked her off Uathach. "What are you doing?" An angry long burn from her knife edge was already blistering across Uathach's neck.

Arhianna felt better than she had in weeks. She seethed her answer through clenched teeth. *"Winning."*

6

So went the morning of the ninety-ninth day of Arhianna's training at Dun Scáthach. Overcoming Uathach was the only taste of victory she had managed to seize in all that time, and it felt good. *I'll pay for it, but I don't care.* She had not been able to tolerate the thought of another beating by Uathach.

Scáthach had sent her from the ring for what she had done, so she went to the only other place she could—her chamber. To wander the tunnels of the mountain and fortress without permission was forbidden.

She went out to the deepest pool on the stone ledge, washed her wounds, and then stared at her reflection in the bloody water for a long time, watching it settle into stillness as the water calmed. Once it had, her heart leapt at the sight of black wings rising behind her. She held her breath, waiting to see if Morrigan would show her face; but saw nothing but her wings arched up behind her.

"Ronin." Scáthach's voice startled her out of her trance. "You broke our agreement."

Arhianna felt a surge of indignance, and the wings behind her stretched out wide and strong. Emboldened, she turned around and shot her eyes like darts into Scáthach's face. "To hell with our agreement."

Scáthach remained calm. "If you will not keep it, you must leave."

Arhianna stared at her. "Fighting is not my gift. You know what my gift is. You said you'd teach me to use it, but you haven't! Instead, you send me into the ring every day to get beaten by your warriors, endure injury after injury, and give me no training on how to fight back—it's not so different from being a slave to Ingvar and his men!"

Scáthach's beautiful features twisted into a terrible scowl. "If that's what you think, then you truly don't belong here at all."

Arhianna swallowed hard. *I shouldn't have said that.*

"You'll find no pity here. Keep our agreement or leave." She turned to go, but then stopped and looked back. "If you do choose to leave, beware—the Daoine Sídhe roam the borders of my land, and they want your daughter. Take her with you, and you'll have a changeling in your arms by morning."

7

Arhianna had grown up hearing plenty of stories about changelings—the Sídhe would take a child they fancied in the night and swap it for one of their own, charmed to look like the one they had stolen. "I don't understand. Why do they want her?" Arhianna's voice cracked. "How do they even know about her?"

Scáthach shrugged. "The Daoine Sídhe see many things we cannot. I know your daughter is meant for great things—greater than I've ever seen in any child's birthing water before. Who knows? Perhaps being taken by the Sídhe is a part of her destiny."

"No!" Arhianna blurted, shaking her head. "No, they'll not have her!"

"You won't have a choice. You're no match for them as you are."

"Then how long before I am? I can't stay here training for moons on end—she'll forget me—and then what? To what end is all this suffering and humiliation?" Arhianna's stomach tightened into knots. "It'll be for nothing!"

Scáthach's expression remained smooth as marble. "It could be days, moons, or years—that all depends on you. But you must decide by dawn if you're staying or leaving. I'll not grant you a second chance." She turned and left.

Arhianna watched her disappear into the shadows of the fortress and then turned her eyes toward Selkie Island. The sunset blazed in wide flaming colors behind it, making it stand out more than usual. She could make out several small columns of smoke curling into the air and pictured her daughter being nursed beside one of their fires. *Which one?* Her throat choked. *Morrigan, show me my daughter.* She looked down into the bloody pool, now turning purple in the twilight, hoping to see Morrigan's black wings once more. Nothing came forth. Arhianna refused to give up. She stared into the pool repeating her request, until night spread across the sky and smothered her reflection.

Arhianna still did not move. She sat staring out at Selkie Island, all through the night, under the limpid watch of the stars. Scáthach's words came to mind: "To be triumphant, one must always know what one is fighting for."

There's only one thing in the world I'm fighting for. And if she forgets me, there's nothing. I can't stay here for years—and that's how long it will take for me to best the likes of any warrior here. She swallowed hard. *We must find refuge, Daughter. Somehow, we must get to the Isle of the*

Sisterhood. *Elayn will take us in, and I can train to be a Sister. The Fae wouldn't dare touch us there. And there won't be any men to touch us, either.* She shuddered as the dark thoughts of what Ingvar's men did to her came rolling in like black, choking clouds, sending burning surges of panic through her chest. *No, no, no*—she pushed the images from her mind, desperately trying to think of nothing, mumbling a mantra to crowd them out of her mind—*Morrigan, Morrigan, Morrigan,* she whispered, invoking her patron goddess.

Eventually, the now familiar black wings rose up behind her and folded around her shoulders, blocking out the panic and filling her with strength. She took a deep breath and sighed with relief. *Thank you.*

She felt confident Morrigan would protect her on her journey, and she resolved to take her chances. *I'll ask Scáthach for an arsenal of iron weapons and talismans against the Fae, go get my daughter, and make my way south.*

Arhianna left her chamber at the first hint of dawn the next morning, resolved to tell Scáthach her plan. She was the first to rise. She jumped down into the ring and made her way toward the hall where the warriors took their meals. She had taken only a few steps when a huge dark figure emerged from the shadows to her right and approached. *The giant.* She froze in her tracks, unable to pick out any features within the moving shadow except for the flash of a dagger. Its silver blade gleamed out at her despite the darkness. She pulled out her own blade and widened her stance. "Stay where you are!"

The giant put his hands up. The gleaming blade went with them. "I'm sorry, didn't mean to scare you," he whispered. "Please, I've got something for you—I swore I'd put it into your hands as soon as I got here." He held out his weapon.

She ventured closer and discovered the giant was not holding a dagger at all, but rather a thing as far from it as could be—a feather. She felt drawn in by its intricate beauty. Every strand in the feather seemed to have liquid starlight flowing down it, pulling the eye inward and holding it in a trance. "What kind of bird did *that* come from?"

"Don't know. But Taliesin insisted I give it to you."

9

"Taliesin?" Arhianna's heart took off like a startled bird. "Where is he?"

"Don't know that either." Gawyr held the feather out again, his eyes sweeping the ring. "Please, before anyone sees us. He said no one else could know about it. You must hide it."

Ah, more secrets. Seems I'm to forever be poisoned with secrets.

CHAPTER TWO
Arianrhod's Feather

Arhianna reached out and pinched the feather's quill between her fingers. The moment she touched it, her body lurched, as if she were standing on the deck of a moving ship instead of solid ground. The sparring ring began turning around her, and the heavens swirled open. She stumbled from the vertigo and felt Gawyr's rough warm hands take hold of her arms to steady her. She took a few clumsy steps in the direction of her chamber but then felt her spirit being pulled out of her body through the top of her head. She looked down just in time to see her body crumple to the ground. She watched Gawyr scoop her up in his arms and look around in alarm, his brow grooved with worry. He skirted the ring under the cover of the night's fading shadows, reached her chamber, and carried her in.

Arhianna then looked skyward, no longer concerned with her body or what was happening below. She desired nothing more than to soar up into the spiral above her and fly where it beckoned. She vaulted into the heavens like a bird of prey, a pair of powerful black wings at the edge of her vision. She felt fearless knowing Morrigan was with her.

The wings carried her up through a thick cold layer of clouds into a brilliant world of pure sunlight. Stretched out below her rolled a billowing sea of white, obscuring all the ugliness and violence beneath. *No wonder the gods forget about us. From here, it's easy to forget the horrors that lie below and the ones who create them.* She flew higher, breaking through one glorious layer of light after another, until all the colors ignited into a cosmic blue fire and burned out. Then, the true splendor began. All around her, suspended in an eternal deep silence, blazed a turning wheel of stars. In the center of it all stood a woman in robes of ether, hands stretched out over millions of galaxies.

Arhianna flew toward the goddess, like a tiny black moth toward a towering silver elm in the night. She alighted on the edge of one of her fingernails. The finger moved toward one of the trillions of spiraling spokes emanating from the center of the wheel. Arhianna watched for some time, hesitating to set her feet upon it, but at last summoned her courage and stepped onto its luminous thread.

In that moment, up and down ceased to exist. Small swirling galaxies floated toward her like lazy clouds pushed by a timeless, galactic breeze. As they neared, they swirled with more force, expanding and spinning around her in a storm of lightning and stardust. She struggled to grasp the thread, but it was no use. She had no choice but to surrender.

And everything stopped.

She opened her eyes to see her hands pressed against a large stone, as if she intended to push it over. *Where am I?* She looked around and discovered Taliesin standing beside her. Her heart leapt. She reached over to touch his hand, but it dissipated into stardust. *It's a dream. Only a memory. And yet, I can move through it…*She looked around again and recognized where she was. *We're on top of Killaraus.* She left herself standing at the stone and wandered around, exploring her memory. Behind a tree, she spied Myrthin chanting in their direction, his eyes wide and unblinking, staring at the two of them with unknown intention. She watched helplessly as she and Taliesin fell to the ground like sheaves of culled barley.

A cloud of black hate flowed from her chest and snaked its way toward Myrthin. *It was you! You did this to us! You cursed us with the long sleep!* She ran to where he squatted and attempted to slap his face, but it did not hit flesh. He, too, was formed of nothing but stardust.

Yet—the stone was solid! Nothing else had kept its form when she reached out to touch it—not the trees, not Taliesin, not Myrthin— nothing. *But the stone was solid.* Intrigued, she went back and pressed her palms into the stone again, but this time, she found she could not pull them away. The dark wings behind her flapped in a panic, like a bird caught in a snare. Again, she had no choice but to surrender to the energy that pulled at her. When the vertigo finally stopped, she found herself standing on a path that led to a cathedral of trees.

I know this place, too. I've been here before. She knew, somehow, that if she followed the path, it would take her to a glorious courtyard where there would be feasting and dancing—and that Taliesin would be there, playing his harp and singing for her. She smiled, suddenly overwhelmed with love for him. *I've been here! I've dreamed of this place!* She walked along the path toward the trees, eager to see the courtyard once more.

With each step her eagerness grew, and she broke into a run, fearing the cathedral might disappear before she reached it. Every stride brought a new memory—dancing with Taliesin, riding horses with Taliesin, drinking honey wine with Taliesin—but then came flashes of memories that shocked her. She remembered kisses and caresses between them. She suddenly felt his hands and lips on her body, as if he were making love to her right there, upon the path. Stunned, she stumbled from the path and wandered into the woods, dizzy with excitement and confusion. She wandered through a thickening carpet of ferns, moss and flowers, until she came to the edge of a stream with a clearing on the other side.

Familiar voices floated in and out, tangled in the breeze. She crossed the stream for a closer look, but her foot slipped on a mossy rock, causing her to reach out and grab a tree trunk to keep from falling. When she regained her footing and looked up, her eyes fell upon a nude couple making love in the clearing. With a shock, she gasped, recognizing her own copper curls spilled out upon the blanket of crushed grass.

The next moment, she was beneath Taliesin's body, her arms wrapped around him instead of the tree. She felt his heaviness upon her and breathed in the scent of his skin. It triggered a flood of new memories that sent her reeling in their wake.

How could I have forgotten? Her entire being cringed with nostalgic pain, overwhelmed with deep love for him. In that moment, she woke from what remained of the darkness her mind had labored beneath for moons.

"Oh, gods, Taliesin—she's yours! She's yours!" she whispered to him, but his eyes were from the past, and though they were gazing down at her full of love, she knew he could not hear her now. He was but an echo of the past, like all the rest. She was granted only a moment more before he, too, turned to stardust, along with the trees around her and the earth beneath her. Only one thing remained—a face. A face that had been hidden by the now transparent grasses, spying on their lovemaking; a face she knew belonged to Oonagh, Queen of Knockma.

In a wild burst of fury, Arhianna surged to her feet, her entire body aflame, and snatched the queen by her shoulders. "Hear my oath, Queen of the Daoine Sídhe! You'll never have her! Never!"

The apparition of Oonagh smiled and flashed its wicked green eyes at her before it, too, dissipated, leaving Arhianna aloft in the swirling heavens, fists clenched and flaming with rage.

13

Arhianna awoke in her chamber. She felt animal skins wrapped around her. *Strange. Who did this?* She sat up and squinted at the light outside, attempting to determine the time of day. Her muscles cried out in protest as she got to her feet and walked out on the ledge. Birdsong and a blush from the east confirmed it was dawn. Seeing the last of the stars sent her hand seeking the feather. It lay tucked beneath her tunic strap. She ran her thumb and forefinger along its silver edges, and everything came flooding back—her encounter with Gawyr in the ring, the strange flight through the cosmos, and all the shocking visions that had followed. Shaken, she knelt in front of one of the pools and splashed cold water on her face. Gasping from its bracing shock, she slaked her intense thirst, staring at the hazy outline of Selkie Island on the horizon as the water dripped down her face like icy tears. She pictured her daughter cradled in the arms of a selkie, suckling at her breast.

No—our daughter, she corrected herself. *Taliesin, you must help me. I can't protect her on my own. I need you.* Again, her hand strayed to the feather, remembering the giant who had given it to her. *I must talk to him.*

Eager for answers, she stood up too fast, and a wave of dizziness overtook her. She sank to her knees until it passed. *I need food.* She made her way to the feasting hall, expecting to see the rest of the warriors but, to her surprise, found only Niamh. She seemed intent on her work, whispering to herself in hushed tones as she dropped herbs into a cauldron hanging over a low cookfire. Hearing her enter, she looked up.

"Ronin! At last, you've awoken!" She walked over and looked her up and down, squinting with concern.

At last? Arhianna's stomach sank, unable to avoid thinking of the moment her mother had told her she had been asleep for ten moons. "How long have I been asleep?"

"Today would have been the ninth day. I couldn't figure it out. You had no fever and no serious wounds. You simply wouldn't wake. I thought someone might have cursed you." She frowned. "Certainly wouldn't put it past Uathach." She shook her head and pointed to a low stool by the cookfire. "Sit down. You must eat something."

Niamh had been one of Scáthach's best warriors in her younger days but had lost the lower half of her left leg in a skirmish with one of the sky tribes, which is what the warriors of Dun Scáthach called the Picts. Determined to overcome her misfortune, she crafted herself a leg from ash wood. She now walked with nothing more than a slight limp but could not fight the way she used to. Now, she served the clan as a cook and healer. She had tended many of Arhianna's wounds over the past three moons.

"Great Mother. Nine days?" Arhianna felt ashamed. *Uathach will never let me live this down.* "Where is everyone?"

"Gone east to aid Edor of Gododdin. All except Uathach and the giant. He refused to leave until you recovered." She narrowed her eyes on Arhianna. "Why's that, then? How do you know him?"

Arhianna shook her head. "I don't. But he knows someone dear to me." She found it strange that of all the warriors in the entire clan, the two who remained were the ones she most and least wanted to speak with.

"Well, he'll be pleased you've awoken." Niamh ladled her out some broth and set it in front of her.

"When will the others return?"

"Not sure. Could be moons."

"And what are we to do until then?" Footsteps at the end of the hall caused Arhianna to turn her head. The sight of Uathach made her cringe.

"I'll tell you, whelp," Uathach answered, striding toward her. "Now that you're done with your nap, you can train with me. And if you try any tricks like last time, I'll kill you. Why don't we start now?" She kicked the stool out from underneath Arhianna and would have struck her, were it not for Niamh, who blocked Uathach's blow and caught Arhianna in the small of her back with her wooden leg, preventing her from falling into the cookfire. "*Not* in my kitchen!" she growled at Uathach, eyes flashing. She pointed her spoon in the direction of the ring. "Take it out there!"

Uathach sneered at Arhianna. "Come on, then, little Ronin. Unless you've decided to be a kitchen maid instead?" She walked out, twirling a pair of daggers around her fingers with blurring speed. The sound of the blades set Arhianna's teeth on edge.

Niamh righted the stool, and Arhianna stooped to pick up the broken pieces of the bowl she had dropped. Thankfully, she had finished her broth, otherwise she would have suffered the humiliation of her breakfast spilling down her chest in addition to her shame.

Niamh shook her head. "That woman hates you. I don't know why, but she does. You need to learn faster if you're going to train with her, or you'll have every bone in your body broken before the clan comes back."

"I'm doing my best," Arhianna offered, her voice weak.

"Well, if that's your best, you'd better give up your training and become a kitchen maid, as she said," Niamh barked. She threw the pieces of broken pottery into the fire. "I'm sorry, Ronin, but you make the same mistakes over and over. Are you even trying when you're out there?"

"I said, I'm *doing* my best!" Arhianna shot back, teeth clenched. *I'm just not a warrior, like Father or Gareth or Seren. I'm just not.* Her eyes fell upon Niamh's wooden leg. A wave of regret came over her. "I'm sorry. Would you help me? Train, that is?"

Niamh furrowed her brow. "As if I had the time."

"Please? The clan's gone...you don't need to cook for more than a few now. And besides, I'll help you—I'll do whatever you ask. In fact—" Arhianna had a thought. "I'll tell Uathach I've decided to work in the kitchen with you until the clan gets back. We can train when she goes hunting."

Niamh shook her head. "You know she'll never let you live it down. If you refuse to train with her now and try to go back in the ring later, she'll destroy you."

"Not if I'm ready. You can help me—I know you can—I just need someone to help me understand what I'm doing wrong."

"Understanding is one thing. Overcoming is another."

Arhianna sighed. "Do you think I can do it or not?"

"There's where your problem lies, lass." Niamh shook her head. "Don't you see? It doesn't matter what *I* think. Doesn't matter a damn bit." She raised her brows in Arhianna's direction, scolding her with wide eyes. "*You* must believe you can do it, and never doubt it for a moment." She turned back to her work. "And that's your first lesson. Think on it. We start tomorrow."

CHAPTER THREE
The Great Chamber

"Damn the gods, lass! Don't be so hesitant!"

Arhianna lay flat on her back, the wind knocked out of her, looking up at Niamh's scowl. She felt a familiar surge of anger fill her breast but did her best to route it into productive action. She jumped up, resolved. "Let me try again."

"Fine. Once more, but that's it—we need to start the evening meal."

The sound of feet landing on gravel cut their conversation short. Arhianna whirled around to see Uathach standing behind her, arms crossed. "So, little Ronin's training with a cripple, now, is she? Let's see how that's helped her." She kicked Arhianna in the back of the knee, knocking her off balance.

Arhianna looked at Niamh in dismay, but Niamh's face remained stern and impartial. Arhianna knew she had no choice but to fight. She turned to face Uathach and settled into her stance, spear ready, every muscle taut with anticipation.

Uathach attacked with unrelenting force. Arhianna managed to block a few more of her blows than usual. Even so, it was less than a minute before she took a hit to the nose and Uathach threw her to the ground. She opened her eyes to see Uathach's sneer blocking out the sky, her spear pointed at her throat. "Go home, little Ronin. Before you become a cripple yourself."

Niamh stepped forward and took hold of Uathach's spear, opening her mouth to say something. Uathach whirled around and slammed its rod against Niamh's chest, sending her sprawling. "Don't meddle!"

Arhianna did not fail to seize the opportunity to get off the ground and recover her weapon. The moment she stood up, blood flowed from her nose down over her throbbing lips and chin.

Uathach lunged at her, causing a surge of adrenalin, but then calmly stepped back and chuckled. "No. Niamh's right. That's all for today." She motioned behind her. "The real warriors are hungry." Arhianna followed her gesture and saw the giant standing at the edge of the ring. She immediately forgot her anger, wondering how long he had been there watching them. *I must speak with him!*

17

But this hope, too, Uathach snatched away. "Gawyr and I are going ranging tonight. Something's out there killing all our deer, and it's not the wolves." She looked back and forth between Arhianna and Niamh. "It's too bad we're the only warriors here. We could use some help."

Niamh ignored the insult. "Then we'd best get you fed. Forgive the delay, Lady Uathach." She looked at Arhianna. "Let's go, Ronin."

Smoldering inside, Arhianna followed her to the kitchen. Niamh pointed to a pile of turnips and onions on the table. "Cut those up, and get them in the pot."

Arhianna attacked the pile with her knife, chopping more vigorously than she needed to. Niamh took down a plucked chicken that had been hanging by its feet from the ceiling. It was soon in the pot as well.

After Arhianna finished chopping vegetables, she sat down by the hearth to bake bread. It was one of her new duties before every meal. She slid disk after disk of flattened dough into the fire, drawing warmth and comfort from the flames. Their bright dance calmed her nerves and stoked her resolve. *One day, Great Morrigan, with your help, I'll be a fierce warrior. As great as my father.* She felt movement behind her and looked up to see long shadows of enormous wings stretching along the walls toward the ceiling, dancing in the firelight. Her heart leapt. *As great as my father.* Her throat choked up as she thought of how safe she used to feel wrapped up in his arms. *I miss you, Father. I miss you so much.* She wiped away the tears that had managed to leak from her eyes. *I want to come home, but I can't. Not yet. Not without my daughter.*

Uathach and Gawyr had not returned by the following morning, nor the next, nor the morning after that.

Arhianna rose at dawn on the fourth morning since their departure to find the kitchen empty. She searched the fortress until she found Niamh on the far side of the bridge. She stood staring down at the wide plain below, arms folded and brow furrowed.

"Do you think they're in trouble?"

Niamh did not turn her head. Her gaze remained fixed on the land below. "I know they are. Something dark roams the plain, but I don't know what it is."

Arhianna's stomach clenched. *If anything happens to that giant, I'll never find Taliesin.* Her hand reached for the silver feather beneath her tunic. The moment she touched it, her heart swelled with courage. "Then we must go and help them."

Niamh turned to look at her, a rare but faint smile upon her lips. "At last, you're beginning to act like a warrior."

The next morning, Arhianna found Niamh in the kitchen, mumbling under her breath, as was her habit, filling a satchel with herbs and other strange items from her apothecary. She seemed so intent on her work, Arhianna chose not to greet her, sitting down to watch instead.

Once satisfied with the contents, Niamh slung the strap of the satchel over her head and across her chest and knelt on the floor. She flipped back a length of material hanging from the bottom shelf of her apothecary, reached in and yanked out one end of a wooden box nearly as long as a coffin. She looked up and beckoned to Arhianna. "Come help me with this."

Arhianna's curiosity swelled. She had always assumed there was nothing but cooking pots and crockery behind that drape.

"Grab the other end, and help me pull it out."

Arhianna did as she was told. Once they had succeeded in sliding the box out, Niamh pulled out her large ring of keys, found the one she was looking for, unlocked the box and raised the lid.

Arhianna felt disappointed. Inside were nothing but ordinary-looking swords, daggers and axes. "Why keep these here, instead of out on the wall with the rest?"

Niamh raised her brows. "Why indeed?"

Arhianna shrugged and crouched down for a closer look. "Are they special, somehow?"

"You're smarter than they think." Niamh winked at her and pulled out a sheath and dagger. "This should work well for you. Good at close range."

Arhianna took the dagger and chided herself, realizing her initial assessment had been hasty. She had spent enough hours in the forge

19

to know an exceptional blade when she saw one. Upon closer examination, she saw script had been written upon it, but it was too tiny for her to make out. She looked up at Niamh. "This is fine work."

Niamh gave her a nod. "Like I said, you're smarter than they think."

"What does the inscription say?"

"Words of protection. Victory over your enemies. Things of that sort." She dove back into the box and fished out a good number of arrows with fine tips and handed those to Arhianna as well. "Put those in your quiver."

For herself, Niamh chose both a dagger and a sword, then closed and locked the box. Together they pushed the box back beneath the shelf. Then, Niamh stood up and grabbed a spear with an ornate staff out of a dark corner in the back of the kitchen. A veil of disturbed cobwebs floated into the air.

Niamh raised her chin in Arhianna's direction. "Ready?"

"Ready." Arhianna followed her out of the fortress and across the bridge. She felt shocked when Niamh suddenly swung herself under the bridge into Uathach's cave. "We're going that way?"

"We are. Come on."

Arhianna swung under the bridge and took Niamh's outstretched hand. She felt uneasy stepping into Uathach's quarters, which seemed about as warm and welcoming as Uathach herself. Furnishings consisted of nothing more than a stool by the fire and a stiff-looking pallet without furs or blankets. Skulls were stacked along the walls from floor to ceiling. Arhianna shuddered. "Who were they?"

"Enemies. Men and women who tried to breach Dun Scáthach."

Arhianna's gaze flowed over the perfect rows of skulls. *And these are but a few of her victories. There are surely countless more rolling around in the sea beneath the bridge.* She reached out and touched one of them, tracing its high cheekbones and wide teeth with the tips of her fingers.

Niamh took two torches off the wall. She dipped them in a bucket that stood at the entrance to a dark passageway at the rear of the cave and began rifling through her fire pouch. "Damn the gods— I've lost my flint. Look around, there should be one over there by the firepit."

Arhianna came over and took a torch out of the bucket. "That won't be needed." She set it aflame and handed it to Niamh. "Now that it's just you and I, I don't want us to keep any secrets from one another." She took out the other torch and did the same with it.

Niamh stared at her a moment, torchlight flickering on the surface of her green eyes. "Does anyone else here know you're a Firebrand?"

Arhianna nodded. "Scáthach. I swore to her I wouldn't use it in training. But we're not in training now, are we?"

Niamh raised her brows. "I wouldn't say that, exactly. There's no telling how this will go. It may end up being more training than either of us have bargained for. I only hope we can find them before it's too late. And…" she trailed off, apparently thinking the better of whatever it was she had been about to say. "Never mind. Let's go. We're wasting time." Niamh held her torch aloft and plunged into the inky depths of the corridor ahead.

Arhianna rushed in after her, eager to see what secrets the mountain held. "Where does this lead?"

Niamh's voice echoed back to her through the tunnel. "Through the catacombs to the Great Chamber. There, it splits into several passageways."

"So, there's more than one way into the fortress."

"Oh, far more."

Arhianna felt like a fool, thinking of the countless hours she had spent scouring the foothills for trails or hidden entrances. "I must be blind. I searched for moons and found no way in except the grotto. And even that led to a dead end."

Niamh laughed. "Ronin, for a lass like you to have found a way in at all means you've earned the right to be here."

Arhianna scoffed. "Uathach doesn't think so."

Niamh huffed. "Uathach is here to forge warriors. Don't waste time feeling sorry for yourself. It'll get you nowhere."

Niamh's comment hit home and stung, prompting Arhianna to change the subject. "How long will it take us to get through the mountain?"

"Most of the morning. We've got to keep moving. I've no intention of venturing out onto the plain on foot, so we need time to fetch ourselves some horses from the meadow before nightfall."

21

Arhianna remembered the plain well and was not keen to see it again. It was where Scáthach and her women had left her behind. The bitterness of it returned, foul and strong, souring her stomach. True, their abandonment had made her stronger, but she could just as easily have been killed. *And my daughter would never have been born.*

The sound of something scurrying away from the light broke her thoughts. She looked for its source, but nothing moved except the torchlight flickering on the walls of the passage. She noticed a series of niches up ahead in the corridor, stretching as far as the light could reach. She peered into them as they walked by. A skull had been placed in the center of each one, surrounded by bones arranged in intricate patterns, emanating outward like rays of the sun. "Who were these people?"

"This mountain holds the bones of at least ten generations of warriors, all of whom were born and trained here."

"Who put them here—in this way?"

"Whomever they gave the honor to when they earned the title of Warrior. Sometimes a sister, sometimes a daughter, sometimes Scáthach herself."

"So, all of Scáthach's warriors who die in battle are laid to rest in here?"

"Oh no. Only the ones who were born, raised and trained here."

"What do you do with the rest?"

"We return them to their families, if they yet have family. If not, we burn them and let the winds carry them wherever they wish to go."

Arhianna liked that idea far better than moldering in the catacombs. She glanced again at the parade of skulls staring out at her as she passed. "I suppose my daughter could be buried here someday. She was born within the mountain."

Niamh nodded. "She could, if she chooses to become a warrior and dies with honor. But that's a path she may not wish to take."

Arhianna thought of her daughter lying in that cold dark place without her. She shuddered, dismissing the thought. *I'll never let that happen.* "What about you, Niamh? Were you born in the mountain?"

Niamh shook her head, causing her long blonde braid to flash in the torchlight. "No."

She offered no further information, so Arhianna pressed her. "How long have you been here, then? How did you get into the fortress? Did you fight Uathach on the bridge?"

Niamh remained silent a moment before replying, the step of her wooden leg and hissing of the torches the only sounds in the passageway. At last she spoke. "I've been here as long as I can remember. Scáthach found me screaming in the grotto when I was but a few moons old."

Arhianna's mind whirled with possibilities of how and why Niamh's mother had abandoned her, but she voiced none of them. "Who raised you, then? The selkies?"

"No. Scáthach herself. She'd given birth to Uathach a moon before, so she had milk to nurse us both. Why she chose not to give us to the selkies—me, especially—I don't know, and I've never asked. Perhaps the burden of raising us is why she forbids it now."

"So, it was fate, I suppose," Arhianna murmured, almost to herself. They walked on for a long spell, each in their silent world, until Arhianna noticed a change in the temperature and the scent of the air. She filled her lungs, revived by the fresh salty breeze.

"Smell that?" Niamh asked, a smile in her voice. "The Great Chamber's just ahead."

"What's the Great Chamber?"

"A resting place for all the past and future mistresses of Dun Scáthach."

"What do you mean, all? Have there been others?"

Niamh laughed. "Of course! Does Scáthach look like she's a few hundred years old?"

"Well, no. I thought maybe…I don't know. Maybe she possessed some kind of magic to keep the Crone at bay."

"And why would a woman wish to do that? So she can watch her lovers and children die, over and over, for eternity? How much would you have a woman suffer? Besides, a life without the deep wisdom of the Crone years is a life half-lived."

Arhianna supposed she was right. The terrible power of the Crone was both feared and revered more than the other faces the Great Mother wore. "So, there have been other mistresses, then."

"There have. Eight lie here in the Great Chamber. The Scáthach we serve is the ninth. Our mistress changes with the times, forever strong."

"Then one day, the Scáthach we know will lie here as well."

"When her time comes. And she, in turn, will pass her strength, wisdom and title on to the fiercest of her female warriors."

Arhianna knew what that meant. *Uathach will one day rule Dun Scáthach.* As much as she resented Uathach, she could not help but respect her. Save Scáthach herself, she was, without a doubt, the fiercest warrior among them.

Niamh continued. "The Great Chamber is where we go to honor them all. The spirit of Scáthach can be called upon in times of need and is ever ready to give advice."

Within a few minutes, the passage opened up. Light poured in from a wide opening in the side of the mountain. Arhianna squinted and blinked until her eyes adjusted. Once they did, she marveled at what she saw.

The ceiling of the chamber rose at least twenty feet in some places. An altar carved from green serpentine marble stood in the center. Eight stone sarcophagi surrounded it like the spokes of a wheel, the feet of each facing inward, so that if their inhabitants were to wake and sit up, they would all face one another. On top of each tomb lay a weapon, presumably the favorite of the deceased; some bore swords, others, spears or bows. One of the sarcophagi was much taller and longer than the others, bearing a weapon Arhianna had never seen before. "That's her, isn't it? The first?"

"It is. She was said to be seven feet tall."

"What weapon is that?"

"One of her own design. The *Gáe Bulg.*"

Arhianna moved in for a closer look. The vicious-looking spear had several barbs. She traced her finger across them and found they were still as sharp as needles.

"The only way to remove that weapon from a body is to cut it out."

Arhianna cringed. Many things had been placed on top of the lid around the nasty weapon—mugs of ale, bowls of bread and dried fruit, chunks of amber, jewelry, daggers, arrowheads. Some were a bit more gruesome—the bones of enemies, perhaps. A few dried umbilical cords.

"We leave her all manner of offerings."

Arhianna studied the massive tomb, walking around it with the softness of a cat. Tucked in alongside it lay a smaller tomb. The likeness of a young man dressed for battle had been carved into its lid, his hands folded across his chest. A gold ring had been placed on one of his fingers. She reached out to touch it and then hesitated. "Who was this?"

Niamh sighed. "There lies Connla, beloved son of Scáthach and the great Cú Chulainn. Like Uathach and myself, he was nursed and raised within the walls of Dun Scáthach, training for battle as soon as he could walk."

"I didn't know Scáthach and Cú Chulainn had a son. Why have I never heard of him?"

"That's a story for another time. Such sorrow should not be released in a place of rest." Niamh pulled a candle out of her pouch, lit it with her torch, melted a pool of wax on the forehead of Scáthach and set the candle into it. She rested her hands on either side of it and closed her eyes. "Great Scáthach, help me find Uathach and her companion, Gawyr the Giant. If they be in danger, grant me the strength to assist them and the courage to face my death, if that is the Great Mother's will." She opened her eyes and looked over at Arhianna. "You must choose your own words, if you wish to pray to Scáthach. I'll wait for you over there, in the corner of Morrigan's Eye." Niamh walked toward the wide cave opening and stood on its ledge, gazing out at whatever lay beyond, tendrils of her fine hair floating on the breeze.

Arhianna longed to see the view for herself but felt compelled to pray, as Niamh had done. She looked at the many offerings in dismay. *I have nothing to offer. Not even a candle to light.*

As if it had heard her thoughts, she felt the quill of the feather in her tunic poke her breast. Her instinct told her not to part with it. *I may forget my past again. Then, how will I remember?* Yet, she was wise enough to know that without sacrificing something she valued, her prayer would not carry any weight. She reached into her tunic and pulled the feather out. It gleamed like moonlight, iridescent and glorious. It took all her will to lay it down. "Great Scáthach, this feather will show you all my memories, and through them, you will see the faces of my enemies. I ask you to guide me, along with your patroness, Morrigan, against our enemies; that I might use all the strength I have to aid both your daughter and mine."

Arhianna felt a familiar surge of power, accompanied by the shadow of wings around her. She smiled. *I've been heard.*

25

She stepped away from the sarcophagus and turned to see Niamh staring at her, face as white as the light behind her. "Great Mother," she whispered, eyes wide.

"What?" Arhianna felt frightened. She looked behind her but saw nothing. "What is it?"

"I've never seen shadow-wings that large before!"

Arhianna felt thrilled. "You see her, too?"

"What do you mean, her?"

"Morrigan!"

Niamh shook her head, a deep furrow in her brow. "I see no one with you."

"But—you just said you can see her wings."

Niamh nodded. "Oh, I can—I see wings, lass—but they belong to you."

CHAPTER FOUR
Shadow-wings

Arhianna stared at Niamh in disbelief. "They're mine?"

The Great Chamber grew quieter around her, as if all the mistresses of Dun Scáthach were watching and listening. She reached behind her, feeling for evidence of what Niamh had told her. "The wings are mine?" She closed her eyes and tried to move them, but it was an unnatural feeling; it was not the same as moving one's arms or legs.

"They are, lass. By the grace of Morrigan, you've grown shadow-wings. The largest I've ever seen."

Arhianna shook her head. "I don't understand. What are shadow-wings?"

"The old stories speak of them growing from a deep and terrible desire for revenge or escape." Niamh ventured closer, her eyes wandering over an area a few feet over Arhianna's head. "I've seen them a few times before, on some of the women who've come here. They're Morrigan's most powerful gift. But, like any power, they can become a curse if not used wisely."

Arhianna's blood ran cold. "How?"

Niamh took her torch down from the sconce she had set it in. "I'll tell you, but we must keep moving."

Arhianna took down her torch as well and followed Niamh out of the chamber into one of the dark passageways on the other side. There were three. Niamh took the one furthest to the right.

"Where do the other passages lead?"

"This one leads to the grazing fields near the plain, where the horses roam. The one to the left leads to the grotto you know, and the one in the center leads down to the boneyard."

Arhianna winced. "The boneyard?"

"It's down by the sea on the north side of the mountain, where those defeated by the Defender of the Bridge have fallen to their deaths. Uathach uses it to recover their skulls and add them to her wall."

Arhianna asked no more questions about the passages. "Tell me about the wings, now."

Niamh looked back at her a moment. "Come walk beside me. This passage is wider than the others. We use it to bring up animals and supplies."

Arhianna quickened her pace and moved along beside her. Niamh glanced above Arhianna's head, as if checking to see if her wings were still there. Satisfied one way or the other, she continued, "Shadow-wings grant your soul the power to fly to other realms, including the Underworld, and to speak to those who dwell there."

Arhianna felt a jolt of excitement. "Do you mean I can speak to anyone who has died?"

"Not anyone—only those in the Underworld. But make no mistake, lass—that's a power many covet."

"Why?"

"Some of those souls have been there since the time of Babylon. They wield unimaginable knowledge and power. All realms have kings and queens, and the Underworld is no exception. It's home to perhaps the most corrupt and cunning souls imaginable."

Arhianna's mind fed on the possibilities. *Surely there are souls there more powerful than Oonagh or Finbheara—ancient beings who would know how to defeat them.* "And you're telling me I can fly there and speak with them?"

Niamh turned her head and looked her in the eye. "You can. But I must warn you, the Underworld is nothing like the Summerlands or even the Otherworld—the souls who dwell there crave fame, power, revenge or pleasure so deeply that they can neither see nor find the Summerlands; they long only to return to the living, chained to our world by their passion for the things they crave. Hungry to experience the world again, they will try and tempt you with their knowledge."

"What kind of knowledge?"

"Advice on matters of love and war, or they might share ancient spells and curses. Sometimes, however, a Shadowmaster—someone with shadow-wings—requests a service from them instead."

"Like what?"

Niamh shrugged. "To spy on an enemy or a lover, terrorize a person to madness, haunt someone's lands or castle…these are but a few."

"And what do they ask in return?"

28

Niamh gave her a weak smile. "I'm glad you understand there's always a price to pay for such favors. In return, they will demand you fly them out of the Underworld and into ours."

"And once they're here? Then what?"

"Here they stay, for as long as they can outwit Arawn and his hounds. Some have gotten quite good at it, from what I understand."

"And what happens if Arawn finds them again?"

"You mean when." Niamh corrected. "He takes them back to the Underworld. If, by the grace of the Great Mother, they happen to be light enough to walk across the Lake of the Dead into the Summerlands, they will at last enter its golden fields, but that rarely happens. The truly sad thing is they could rise up out of the lake themselves, if they could only overcome their guilt and hatred. Or whatever dark burden they are carrying that keeps them too heavy to rise."

Arhianna felt a rush of power. *They're my wings—all this time, they've been mine! And I could have been using them.*

Like a spider weaving a web, Arhianna could not help but think of Ingvar and how satisfying it would be to find him, torment him as ruthlessly as he had tormented her and the women of her clan, and then kill him in the most painful, humiliating way possible. She felt her wings stiffen and spread out in response, stretching to their full span.

Niamh must have sensed something, for she turned and looked at the space behind Arhianna. What she saw caused her to stop in her tracks and grip Arhianna by the shoulders. "Listen to me, Ronin— I tell you of these powers because I want you to be prepared, but such bargains are dangerous. You don't want to deal with the souls in the Underworld except in the most desperate of circumstances. Many who end up in the Underworld were once shadow-masters themselves. If you're not careful, that will be your fate."

Arhianna wriggled out of her grip. "Understood. Thank you for the warning." Yet she thought of nothing else for the rest of the descent.

Arhianna and Niamh emerged from the mountain some miles upriver, not far from where Arhianna had shot her first deer. She

29

recognized the widening and thinning of the river and the tracks up and down its banks where the animals came to drink. She stared at the entrance into the mountain, unable to understand how she could have missed it. Granted, it was well-concealed, a narrow s-shaped passage, that, when looked at straight on, seemed completely solid, but she could not help feeling angry and foolish. *I sat in those bushes for hours. I was so close! Mere feet away, and I never saw it.*

Niamh bent to fill her goatskin and then splashed across the shallow river. "Hurry! We need to find horses before nightfall." Even with her wooden leg, Niamh set a strong pace. It was not long before she pointed out some horses, grazing in the distance on the plain. "Out there. See them?"

Arhianna nodded. "I do."

"Let's go." Niamh strode in their direction, pulling out her rope and preparing a bridle. "Follow my lead."

Arhianna smiled, realizing no one at Dun Scáthach had any idea what an accomplished horsewoman she was. She had spent nearly every afternoon of her childhood riding and passed countless hours in the stables. She sized up each of the horses and chose one of the mares. She soon had her eating an apple from her hand, making it easy for her to slip the bridle around her head. She turned to see how Niamh was faring. She had not made as wise a choice. "Some of these horses haven't been ridden in some time," she observed. "Like the one you're trying to rope."

Niamh frowned. "I'm certain the others took the best horses to Gododdin. We're stuck with the ones they couldn't rope or didn't want."

"That doesn't mean there aren't any good horses here." Arhianna pointed to a mare a bit further off. "Like that one. She's a much better choice." Arhianna came over and reached for Niamh's rope. "May I?"

Niamh shrugged and handed it over. Arhianna worked her same magic on the second horse and led her back to Niamh.

Niamh chuckled. "Well-done, Ronin. We've got a few hours of light left, thanks to you. Let's make the most of them."

"What's our plan?"

"Ride across the plain until we meet up with the river again and follow it until the sun sets. They've been gone for days—so unless they immediately met with trouble, they're sure to have camped

30

somewhere. With any luck, we'll find tracks to follow. I just hope their trail isn't too cold by now." She looked up at the sky and scowled at the gathering storm clouds. "And we'd best pray to the Mother not to send any rain before we have a chance to find something."

"Let's move, then." Arhianna leapt onto her mare and gave her a nudge with her heels. She rode side-by-side with Niamh, fearful she might somehow be left behind on the plain again. She did not trust the strange magic surrounding Scáthach's fortress. She relaxed only when the plain began to give way to foothills. They soon reached a ridge that afforded a good view, and Niamh once more looked up at the sky with dismay. "Sun'll be setting soon." She pointed to a gorge between the mountains rising up before them. "We need to get in there before it does. There's a camp we often use. Good fishing, good shelter, and we'll be safe from what roams the plain."

Arhianna glanced behind her and scanned the landscape, her heart beating faster. She had heard stories about the Plain Wraiths. Warriors who were foolish enough to end up out on the plain at night sometimes encountered them. Those unfortunate souls invariably spent a harrowing night being tormented and led miles off course. Though they did not, or perhaps could not, kill someone directly, they often led them to their deaths. "You mean the Plain Wraiths?"

"Among other things."

They traveled faster, the fading sun spurring them on, following a tributary away from the river up into the narrow gap between two mountain peaks. Once within it, the temperature dropped considerably. The smell of pine filled the air, wafting fresh over the tumbling water as they rode alongside it. Despite Niamh's comment of night-roaming predators, Arhianna felt safe, like a child in the wrinkled arms of her grandmother.

It was well after dusk before Niamh stopped and got off her horse. "We're here."

Arhianna dismounted and followed her into a clearing where a waterfall cascaded into a small pool. They tied their horses to the trunks of two tenacious pines growing beside the water. Their trunks had twisted away from the place their seedlings had taken root in an effort to warm their limbs in the sun each day. There was a wide sandbank surrounding the pool, indicating there were times when the water level rose much higher. A smooth rock ledge stretched out over

31

their heads and curved down to meet the sandbank, forming an enormous arch-shaped hollow.

Niamh bent down to inspect a few charred logs within a ring of stones. There was a pile of chopped firewood beside it and a few stumps around its perimeter. "Well, someone was here in the last few days."

The sun had set, so Arhianna lit a lantern and walked about. She spied a net and a few fishing lines hanging from a tree limb near the pool. "And it looks like they may return."

Niamh came over and inspected Arhianna's discovery, fingering one of the fishhooks with a glazed look in her eyes. "Perhaps, but that seems almost too fortunate." She took Arhianna's lantern and held it up, turning in a circle, scanning their surroundings. After a few revolutions, she shook her head and lowered it again. "Let's get some sleep. It's too dark for anything else." She led the way back to the fire ring and began building a pyramid of kindling.

"No, let me. See to the horses. They've not been fed yet." Arhianna took over and had a fire blazing in a mere moment. She sat down on one of the stumps with relief. Fatigue crept into her muscles as she watched the luminous white froth churning in the pool at the bottom of the waterfall.

Niamh soon came and joined her. She opened her satchel and handed her one of the disks of bread she had baked the night before. "Eat this and get some sleep. You're going to fall off that stump."

Arhianna took the bread, ate half, and put the other half in her pocket. She lay down on the ground beside the fire and rested her head upon her pack. She was nearly asleep when she heard a man's voice cry into the camp, "Ho, sisters of Scáthach!"

CHAPTER FIVE
Uathach's Rescue

"Who's there?" Niamh had her bow trained on the dark shadow lurking at the edge of the camp. Arhianna prepared to engulf him in flames. "Name yourself!"

"Gawyr! It's Gawyr! Don't shoot!"

Niamh let out a sigh of relief. "Great Mother, you gave me a fright."

"I'm sorry." Gawyr lumbered out of the trees, ducked under the ledge and crouched down by the fire. "Finding the two of you is the only luck I've had in days…Uathach's been taken captive."

"What?" Niamh scowled. "Impossible. None of the sky tribes are stupid enough to touch her and risk war with the House of Scáthach!"

Gawyr shook his head. "Not the sky tribes. They looked Saxon. I'd planned to come back and fetch you from the fortress, but then I saw your tracks. You saved me the rest of the trip." He settled himself the rest of the way onto the ground. "You don't have any food or ale to spare, do you?"

"Of course," Arhianna said. She passed him her flask and satchel. "Not enough to satisfy someone your size, I'm sure, but it's something."

"Thank you." Gawyr ate a piece of bread and washed it down with ale. "We roamed up and down the river a few days watching the deer, waiting to see who or what was hunting them down. Nothing happened the first night, but on the second, around twilight, we saw them take one. We tracked the hunters, hoping to find out where they were camped, but a storm rolled in. The sky clouded over, got purple and angry-looking, and the wind picked up something fierce. Then a mist rolled toward us from the horizon—strangest thing I've ever seen—like an ocean wave coming out of the hills, flooding the plain. Uathach knew it was trouble. She jumped on her horse and told me to run, but we couldn't outrun it. It overtook us. The fog was so thick, I couldn't see a thing. Heard Plain Wraiths hissing in the mist around me, like I'd stumbled into a nest of adders. I called out for Uathach, but she didn't—or, couldn't—answer me. All I managed to do was attract more unwanted attention." He reached down and gripped the hilt of his sword, pulled it out of its sheath and lay it across his knees.

33

"If it weren't for this sword, I'd be a dead man, rotting somewhere out there on that plain."

Niamh's eyes widened. "*Sídhebane?*" She leaned in for a closer look, her face twisting with suspicion. "But, that's Scáthach's sword…why do you have it?"

"She gave it to me before I escorted Master Taliesin back to Rheged. Said there were Dark Sídhe roaming about and that I'd need it. Didn't realize she gave me her own weapon. Or how right she was."

Arhianna grew more anxious. "So, what happened to Uathach?" She felt surprised by the urgency she felt to help her.

Gawyr held up a hand to calm her. "I wanted to run after her—but I couldn't do anything until the mist cleared. I've heard enough tales about people ending up miles off course that I didn't dare try to travel through the mist. So, though it nearly killed me to sit there, that's what I did, 'til it cleared and I could see the land again. I didn't stop running 'til I found them."

"And?" This time it was Niamh who prompted him.

"And I found her lashed to a tree in a camp of Saxons. She sent me away, saying they had a powerful mage with them, so I came to find you. Save Scáthach herself, everyone knows you're the most powerful witch at Dun Scáthach." Then he turned toward Arhianna. "Taliesin told me of your gift as well."

Arhianna felt surprised. "He did?"

"Said you're a Firebrand. Is that true?"

Arhianna nodded. "It is."

Gawyr grinned. "Then the bastards'll burn tomorrow morning. Come on," he urged, "got to get to their camp before daybreak. There's enough moonlight to make our way there." He rose like a mountain come to life, pressing his meaty hands into his lower back with a groan that seemed to shake the leaves on the trees. He walked about the camp, inspecting the small stores of supplies that were there with a frown. "Any more weapons or food?"

Niamh shook her head and held up another ration of bread to him. "Not that I know of."

He took the bread and shoved an entire disk between his yellow teeth.

"How many are there?" Niamh asked, gathering her things into a bundle.

34

"About thirty or forty, I think."

Niamh shook her head. "This may not be easy."

"With a witch, a Firebrand and a giant?" Gawyr laughed. "It'll be over in a minute!"

Arhianna formed flames at the tips of her fingers to reassure herself she still possessed her gift, then hitched her pack higher on her shoulder. "What's our plan?"

Gawyr shrugged. "You burn 'em, we kill 'em." He motioned to their packs. "Let me carry those. Least I can do."

The women gratefully surrendered their loads. He bundled them up with the rest of the supplies and tossed the whole lot over his shoulder as if it were no heavier than a bag of chicken feathers. Niamh mounted her horse and led the way out of the gorge, Arhianna close behind her, and Gawyr brought up the rear, keeping an eye on all that lay ahead over the treetops.

Niamh called back. "Tell us everything you can remember about these men—especially the mage. What of him? What did he look like?"

Gawyr recounted what he could remember as they traveled down the pass and skirted the plain, moving away from its borders whenever they spotted a pocket of mist. "Don't want to be anywhere near those damn things," Gawyr growled. "But there's no other way through." He picked up the pace, striding ahead of them. "Run those horses, if you have to. Don't let that mist drift any closer to us. It'll be another few miles."

Arhianna kept a watchful eye on the mist. After a few miles, as promised, Gawyr led them in a new direction, away from the plain and into hilly terrain that rolled into the northeast. The trees thickened around them so much that Gawyr had to occasionally stop and climb a hill to determine where they were, but he always returned sure of his direction. "We're almost there."

"Good, because it's nearly dawn."

"Or bad," Arhianna pointed out, "because we still don't have a plan."

"How many are we dealing with, again?" Niamh asked Gawyr.

"I saw no more than forty."

Niamh wrinkled her brow. "Are you sure that's all?"

"No."

35

"Fine. We hope for the best." Niamh looked over at Arhianna. "You free Uathach and get her a weapon. Then she, Gawyr and I will carve the bastards up, and you burn everything to the ground. That's the plan."

"Got it." Arhianna nodded.

"Good. Let's go." Niamh motioned to Gawyr, who took the lead. The three of them continued on. Within the hour, he stopped and pointed out horse and foot tracks. "We're close," he said in a low voice. "Camp's about a half-mile up ahead."

Niamh dismounted. "We'll go on foot from here." She glanced up at Gawyr. "You stay here. We'll go and see how many there are."

Gawyr scowled. "No! I'll go."

"But you'll be seen!" Niamh protested.

"No, I won't. I did it before, I can do it again."

"You were lucky—that's all. Why take the risk?"

"She's right," Arhianna interjected, glancing up at Gawyr. "You should stay here. And so should you, Niamh. You can't run fast enough if they spot you." She dismounted and tied her horse to a tree. "I'll go. I must have eavesdropped on a thousand council meetings as a child. Never got caught once."

Niamh and Gawyr looked at one another, perhaps waiting for the other to protest, and Arhianna took advantage of their hesitation. "I'll be back soon." She strode off down the trail before they could say anything, following the tracks with what little light was left of the day.

After a quarter of an hour, she began to hear voices. She moved toward them until she caught a glimpse of a campfire's light through the trees. *Please, no hounds,* she prayed. She had not seen any evidence of dogs on the trail but still felt anxious. She got as close as she dared and slipped up into a tree. The canopy overhead was just the way she liked it—dense and continuous, one tree's limbs intertwined with the next. As children, she, Gareth and Taliesin used to clamber around the treetops of the Sacred Grove for hours, seeing how far they could venture from tree to tree without coming down. They had gotten so skilled at it they could traverse nearly the entire grove in such a way.

Like a prowling cat, she moved across the canopy toward the voices, until she could clearly see a circle of six men around a fire. She leaned into the trunk of the oak she was in and listened to their conversation from above. *Saxons indeed,* she realized quickly. *Gawyr was right. But what are they doing all the way out here?*

One man's voice overpowered all the others, clearly the result of too much ale. He stood up and pointed in her direction, causing her heart to jump. "I say we teach the bitch a lesson and send her home to her mother in pieces."

"Don't touch her. Ingvar'll have your head!"

Ingvar? Could it be? The sound of his name ignited fury in Arhianna's heart. It traveled through her veins like lightning until every muscle in her body tensed with rage. It took all her will to keep her flames in check. *Dare I hope it's him?*

The drunk man stood up and walked toward her tree, causing her heart to slam against her ribcage. He moved beneath the limb she stood on and spoke. "She was with them that night they came and raided the village. I remember her ugly face."

She knew now, without a doubt. These were Ingvar's men. Arhianna changed position just in time to see the man bend down and grab Uathach by her wrists, but she did not yield. She yanked them away, rolled onto her back and launched her feet into his chest with a fierce cry, sending him toppling backward into the campfire. He rose up yelling, smacking at his tunic to put out the sparks. The other men laughed at their companion, not moving an inch to help him. Once he recovered, he turned on Uathach with a vengeance. He lurched his leg back to kick her, but even with her hands and feet bound he was no match for her. She maneuvered out of the way and deflected his blow with her feet, knocking him off balance. He toppled to the ground again.

The men howled with laughter now, incensing their foolish kinsman to rage. He pulled his sword from its scabbard and lunged toward Uathach.

"No!" one of the men cried, at last jumping up from his haunches. He grabbed his companion's arm. "You can't kill her!"

The others were quick to respond, eyes darting like flies between each other and Uathach.

"We won't kill her," another said, standing up. "But it's been weeks since I had a woman. Though this one looks more like a man. We'd better find out first, eh?"

37

The drunk man sheathed his sword and spit on Uathach. The rest of the men rose up in unison and moved toward her like a pack of wolves, eyes glittering with malice.

The sight of them descending on Uathach filled Arhianna with a searing fury. Yanked back to her vilest memory, she found herself trapped in Ingvar's hall, held down while his men took turns having their way with her. She felt her shadow-wings rise in response to her rage, arching behind her, as if offering her a way to flee her memories. Though she was a good twenty feet in the air, she leapt from the tree without hesitation. She sailed to the ground as silent and deadly as an owl and unleashed an inferno on Uathach's attackers.

Satisfaction flooded her body as their cries of agony filled the air. They burned like victims in a wickerman on Samhain, screaming and flailing around the grove in a drunken dance of pain.

Arhianna cut Uathach's bonds and took the bow and quiver from her shoulders. "Here." She offered them to Uathach. "Finish them."

"No." Uathach shook her head. "Let them burn." If she had felt any shock at the display of Arhianna's power, she did not reveal it.

Arhianna nodded in agreement. "As you wish." She stood next to Uathach and watched, reigniting any flames the men managed to put out, listening to their pitiful cries with deep and disturbing satisfaction. It was not long before Gawyr and Niamh appeared, swords drawn, to finish them off.

When it was done, Uathach turned away in a huff and began pacing the camp, cursing under her breath. "The rest of those bloody bastards are on their way to take the fortress with their damn mage. This bunch were going to take me to Gododdin as a hostage to force Lot's hand."

"Then we must stop them!" Arhianna looked back toward the fortress, wondering how they could have missed encountering the rest of the Saxons.

Niamh cleaned and sheathed her sword. "Even if they make it across the plain, it'll take them weeks to find a way inside the mountain—if they can find one at all."

Uathach stopped pacing. "They know about the entrance below the Giant's Ladder. I don't know how, but they do. And I fear they have a mage with them. We have to get inside the fortress before they do."

Gawyr raised his bushy brows. "And if they beat us to it?"

Uathach chose one of the Saxon horses and began tying her things on its saddle. "Then we'll have to hide in the tunnels and ambush them, one by one, until every one of their bloody skulls is stacked against my wall."

Gawyr looked at her with one eye squinted. "And the mage?"

"Scáthach's magick is strong," Niamh said with a reassuring nod. "It's protected the fortress for centuries. The mage's power will wane within its walls."

"Let's hope so." Uathach swung herself up onto the horse she had chosen. "We've wasted enough time. Let's go."

She led the way along the winding trail through the foothills, avoiding the white expanse of the plain where they could easily be spotted by the enemy.

"Keep an eye on that plain, Giant!" Uathach called out to Gawyr. "You see anything, you say something!"

Gawyr responded with an affirmative grunt. His height afforded him a long, unimpeded view over the brush-crowned, undulating hilltops between them and the waste. He let out a low grumble, from time to time, and muttered about a misty cloud or swirl of dust moving their direction, but they were not set upon.

Arhianna frequently looked back for his dark form. She felt increasingly anxious that she would turn around and find him gone. Somehow, she felt he was the only person in her life she could trust. Even Niamh, whom she had grown to admire, seemed to have dark secrets she held close.

They pushed the horses as far as they dared, navigating the tangled trails as best they could in the fading light of day. All seemed resigned to Uathach's plan, but Arhianna suspected everyone, including Uathach herself, was thinking of all the ways it could go wrong.

For Arhianna, the only thing she feared was at last having the chance to kill Ingvar and failing. *Such a thing would be more than I could bear, Morrigan. I pray you'll be by my side when the time comes.*

She felt her invisible wings stiffen and stretch up into the falling night.

39

CHAPTER SIX
The Defense of Dun Scáthach

Uathach surged ahead once the trail widened and flattened out, leaving the rest of them to follow in her wake. By late afternoon, they reached the wide, shallow place in the river where Arhianna had shot her first deer—the one she had nearly paid for with her life.

"Gawyr and I will guard the bridge," Uathach turned and announced. "If they're inside, they'll never make it out alive. If they're still outside, they'll never get in. I'll go up through the mountain." She looked up at Gawyr. "You take the Giant's Staircase. You've done it before. You can do it again."

Gawyr did not look eager to do it again, but he did not protest.

"You two," Uathach said, turning to Niamh and Arhianna, "go fetch the selkies. Bring them up through the grotto. You should know that part of the mountain well enough, Ronin."

Arhianna could not decide if her comment was an insult or not, but decided it must be. *Even after what I did for her.*

"Wait until dawn," she continued. "Soon after, you'll hear my signal, and then we send these dogs to hell." She tossed Niamh the keys for the gates Arhianna had spent hours trying to pick the lock of.

"We'll be ready," Niamh declared, hooking the keys onto her belt.

The pairs separated, each intent on carrying out their part of the plan. For the hour that followed, two things consumed Arhianna's thoughts: her chance to finally take the revenge she had so long desired against Ingvar, and seeing her daughter on Selkie Isle.

After they traveled along the river for some time, the trees gave way to brush, and the brush to pebbles, and the pebbles to the wide sand beach that stretched to the edge of the cold, grey sea.

Niamh pointed to a thin cleft in the side of the mountain and changed direction. "This way."

Arhianna did not scold herself for failing to find this passage into the grotto, because she never would have fit through it with child. It was a narrow squeeze, barely wide enough to pass through near the ground, and clearly only possible at low tide. It led into the mountain and opened into a series of caverns carved out by the sea. They came to a set of gates she did not recognize. Niamh took the keys from her belt and unlocked them. They passed through, wound

40

around several turns, eventually coming to the Mating Cave, and then the gates to the grotto. The rowboat was still there, and Niamh climbed down into it. "Pass me the oars." Arhianna did as she was told and then lowered herself down into the boat.

Niamh rowed them out of the grotto and through the tricky maze of rocks, whispering to herself. Her timing was perfect, navigating the little boat like a fish through the currents as if she had done it a thousand times. Once past the breakers, Arhianna loosened her grip on the sides of the boat and sighed. "You could have been a sea captain."

"I love the sea." Niamh gave her a faint smile.

Arhianna looked back at the grotto, dark and treacherous as the mouth of a dragon, its dangerous spires of rock teeth jabbing out of the shore's jaw as the sea churned around them. "You said you were found in the grotto. Perhaps you have selkie blood. Do you think one of them might have left you there?"

Niamh shook her head. "I'm half-Sídhe, not selkie, can't you tell?"

Now that Niamh had mentioned it, Arhianna had always thought there was something otherworldly about her eyes, and her hair was so fine it seemed to glow. And though it was said the Sídhe of this land were no friends of Finbheara, she could not help but feel anxious. "I suppose that makes more sense. Have you ever met a Sídhe?"

"A few. But none I trust. I imagine one of the warriors here fathered me, and my Sídhe mother abandoned me. Maybe she didn't want a half-breed. Or thought I was a gift. I'll never know. Lucky for me, Scáthach's fond of half-breeds. I'm sure she hoped I'd have strong powers of prophecy or enchantment, but my gifts lay in healing. Not as exciting, but needed far more often. Especially here."

"Oh, yes," Arhianna agreed, her suspicions soothed. She used Niamh's salves and tonics on a daily basis. She remembered well the day they first met. The broth and poultices Niamh had prepared to curb her bleeding from childbirth had been the only kindnesses she received the day she had arrived at the fortress. "I was so weak when I arrived. I might have died without your help."

"I don't think so. It would have taken longer for you to recover, that's all. Childbirth's not to be your end in this life."

41

Childbirth. Strange. It seems no more than a dream now. Arhianna tried to picture her daughter's tiny face and found she could not. "She'll be three moons now. I wonder if I'll recognize her."

Niamh gave her a concerned look. "I was afraid of this. I think Uathach is hoping you'll see her and decide not to come back."

It was relentless, Uathach's venom. "Gods, why does that woman hate me so much? Even after I saved her from Ingvar's filthy men!"

"She hated you before, because her mother made exceptions for you, and she couldn't figure out why. She'll hate you even more now that she knows you're a Firebrand, because if you stay, you'll threaten her position."

"What position?"

"As the next mistress of Dun Scáthach."

"But I don't want to become Mistress of Dun Scáthach!"

"You asked why she hates you. I'm telling you."

In truth, Arhianna could think of no reason why she should stay after they secured the fortress. Uathach would do nothing but torment her, and she would never get the training she had come for. "Maybe I should leave, then. With Scáthach gone, I've no reason to stay." She looked out to sea to the now visible outline of Selkie Island. "I'll do as she wishes. I'll fetch my daughter and leave."

Niamh stopped rowing. "And go where?"

"I'll take her to the Sisterhood, down in Gwynedd."

"Gods, Ronin! Are you truly that foolish? You'll never make it that far. Sídhe spies still watch the fortress. I can feel them. They'll follow you, and the moment you fall asleep, they'll take your child!" Her words billowed out of her mouth in angry gusts, dissipating into the chilly sea air. "You should know Scáthach made me swear to protect you. She doesn't want you to leave. She and the rest of the clan will be back soon, and you'll get the training you seek. You must have faith."

Faith was something Arhianna had lost long ago, but Niamh's words gave her an idea. "Why don't you come with me? We can take turns sleeping and watching the baby. You can escort me to Gwynedd, and you'd be back at Dun Scáthach before the warriors return. We can find a ship down in Alt Clud. You said Scáthach made you swear to protect me. So, protect me."

42

The worry on Niamh's face had only increased. "That's not what she had in mind, but if you insist on going, I suppose I'll have no choice."

"Uathach would certainly not object. And the two of them can easily defend the fortress until the warriors get back. And, you're part Sídhe! You'll know if any are about, won't you?"

"I'll think on it."

Arhianna felt a deep calming in her chest and stomach. *Everything's going to be fine. There's nothing to fear.*

Arhianna and Niamh reached the island and pulled the boat up on shore. The thousands of tiny pebbles forming the beach made a soothing sound as they pulled the boat inland. They walked along the beach a bit, Niamh scanning the shore, brow wrinkled.

"What's wrong?"

Niamh shook her head. "Strange. They usually come down to greet us. At least a few of them."

Arhianna did not know much about selkies but assumed they might behave more like wild animals than people, at times, and that this was nothing to worry about.

They crested a ridge and took a rocky path through hedgerows of brush and stunted trees, blown bare from the wind. Arhianna spied a small village with several dome-shaped structures made of driftwood. "Is that where they live?" She smiled at the creativity of the construction and looked at Niamh, but Niamh was not smiling. "What's wrong?"

Niamh ignored her question and rushed downhill toward the strange huts.

"Niamh!" Arhianna ran after her. "What's wrong?" But what was wrong became obvious as she looked around. "Oh, gods. There's no one here." She felt a sickening heat flash from her stomach up through her chest and neck to her face. "Is this the only village?"

"It is."

No. This isn't happening. Everything's fine. She's fine. They went into the huts and discovered broken pottery and overturned baskets. Arhianna felt her knees weaken. Her hands shook as she picked up a broken shard. "They've been attacked." She sank to the ground. "I let them bring her here, and now, she's..."

"Stop." Niamh gripped her shoulder. "It's only a few broken pots. It's been especially cold. Much colder than normal. Perhaps they moved south a bit...somewhere with more shelter..."

Arhianna noticed Niamh's attempt to hide the worry in her voice, and it sent her into a frenzy. She sunk her fingers into the walls of the hut, clawing at the pieces of wood and tearing them apart. She heard Niamh yelling at her to stop, but she did not stop. When the hut was nothing but a pile of driftwood, she set it ablaze, crying into the sky with so much rage that it seemed to her two pillars of black smoke billowed into the air—one from the fire, and one from her throat. When she could yell no longer, she fell to the ground and hit the dirt until Niamh came and grabbed her. "Stop it! This won't help!"

Arhianna stopped and stared into the grey ribbons of smoke, sea and sky, cursing herself. *She's gone or dead—and it's my fault. I'm such a fool!* She turned to Niamh. "Scáthach lied to me. She was never safe here. I should never have let her out of my arms. Never!" She felt hope draining from her, like blood from a mortal wound, flowing into the dirt.

Niamh gripped her by the shoulders. "I'll help you find out what happened here, but first we must secure the fortress. Without that, we can do nothing, do you understand?"

Arhianna felt nothing now. The idea that her daughter was lost to her left her empty and without fear. *Let them come.*

They did not speak on the return voyage back to the grotto. It seemed everything Arhianna heard was far in the distance; the oars seemed to belong to another boat, and even the cries of the gulls appeared to be miles off. She noticed Niamh often glancing at something behind her with worry in her eyes. She turned around, expecting to see a storm brewing on the horizon, but both sea and sky looked calm.

"What do you see?"

Niamh averted her eyes, as if she had been caught watching someone bathe. "They've grown," she croaked and cleared her throat. "Your wings."

Arhianna felt encouraged. "Good, because I intend to use them." She recalled well what Niamh had told her: *Hungry to experience the*

44

world again, they will offer you knowledge, or they might share ancient spells and curses. Sometimes, however, a Shadowmaster demands a service from them in return for freeing them. "I'm going to the Underworld to bring back as many souls as I can to search for my daughter. Should they find her dead or harmed, I'll demand they torment those responsible until they beg for death."

Niamh nodded. "As is your right. But first, the fortress."

Arhianna pictured Ingvar and felt her wings stiffen. "Yes."

Niamh and Arhianna reached the grotto and secured the boat. They climbed the narrow rocky tunnel to the rusted iron gate past the Mating Cave and ventured into the labyrinth of passageways. Niamh threw her a rope. "Tie that to your belt, and keep your hands stretched in front of you. We can't risk a torch. They could have men prowling around in the passages."

Though far easier than scaling the side of the fortress mount, the climb to the top proved steep and strenuous. Niamh saw as well as a cat in the dark, calling out warnings when she encountered low-hanging rocks.

Once the steep pitch in the corridor evened out, Niamh halted. Arhianna felt a breeze.

"Give us a bit of light, now, would you?"

Arhianna conjured up a single flame and looked around. "Where are we?"

Niamh turned around and smiled. "You can't see it?"

"See what?" Arhianna scoured the surface of the passageway yet saw nothing but the same rocky birth canal they had been walking within for an hour.

"This." Niamh turned to her left and seemed to walk directly into the wall and disappear.

Shocked, Arhianna put her hands out in front of her and walked into the wall where she had seen Niamh go. To her surprise, she passed beneath an arch and found herself standing next to her at the foot of a small spiral staircase.

"There's one on the other side of the ring as well, hidden in the same way. These are the only two ways to get to the top of the wall, unless you climb up from inside the ring. You take this one. I'll take the other and meet you at the top. Kill anyone you find." She disappeared before Arhianna could ask any questions.

Arhianna crept up the stairs like a cat, dagger drawn. She felt her way through several turns up the staircase, until a faint hint of moonlight whispered to her that she had nearly reached the top. She climbed the last few turns with caution, poking her head out at the top, like a mouse scanning the sky for hawks before coming out of her burrow. She looked left and right, listening until she felt it was safe to stand up. The wall was wide enough for two to walk abreast, provided good cover from the chest down, and had well-placed notches for archers along both sides. The sea churned and glittered in the moonlight below. She scanned the perimeter of the wall until she spied Niamh's silhouette rise on the opposite side and beckon to her.

She crept along the wall to join her, observing the activity down in the fortress as she went. A few men guarded the bridge, and a few more stood at the gates leading into the tunnels, but the rest seemed unconcerned and unprepared for an attack. Some stumbled around the combat ring, charging at one another with practice weapons they had helped themselves to. She spied one urinating against the wall directly below her. Loud voices and laughter spilled out of the hall. "They've clearly found our ale," she whispered with disgust.

"Good." Niamh sneered. "May they drink every last drop, the swine. They'll fall like culled wheat when we attack."

"Are we going to attack from here?"

"As soon as Uathach gives the signal." Niamh squinted at the men below, her mouth moving as she counted their number. "Twenty outside, at least," she said. "I don't know how many are in the hall, but it doesn't hold more than forty."

"So, there could be sixty men down there."

"Perhaps. But they're on our ground now. We'll make quick work of it."

Arhianna felt surprised by Niamh's assessment of the odds. "I'm not so sure."

Niamh turned away from the scene below and looked at her. "You're a Firebrand, Gawyr's a giant, and Uathach's the fiercest warrior alive, save her mother. It's true I'm not the warrior I used to be with a sword or spear, but I never miss with a bow. These bastards don't stand a chance."

46

Arhianna still felt unconvinced. She had only once attacked more than three or four men at a time—that had been long ago in Gloucester, when thieves attacked Amlawth and the men who had been escorting her back to Mynyth Aur from Dumnonia. She looked at the distance with dismay. "I need to be closer. The closer the better."

Niamh raised her brows. "You can't attack them from here?"

Arhianna felt a shudder of shame, which quickly turned to anger toward Scáthach, who had promised to train her and never did. "I can, but the closer I am, the more control I have. And the more powerful the blaze."

Niamh nodded. "Then get closer. You could go up through the cold cellar beneath the kitchen. I'll be up here to cover you."

Arhianna knew the cold cellar well. She had often helped Niamh pull out the loose flagstone in the kitchen floor that covered it. She loathed going down there, always cursing as she descended the shaky ladder into the dank darkness below, scraping her shins and knees against the sharp edges of protruding rock. For all its unpleasantness, however, the small cavern served them well as a cellar, keeping their stores of fish, meat and root vegetables cold. She had never noticed, or even wondered, about whether one could get in or out of it any other way than from above, for she had always been in a hurry to fetch whatever it was Niamh had requested by the faint, wobbly light of a candle that did not stretch far beyond what was right in front of her.

"Come. I'll show you." Niamh slipped along the fortress wall and back down the stairs. She led Arhianna through the corridor to a place where another tunnel forked off in a different direction until the smell of smoked meat filled the air.

"We're here," Niamh announced.

Arhianna summoned a small flame and looked around. Indeed, they were standing in the cold cellar, surrounded by winter stores. Niamh motioned toward the meat. "We should eat something." She sawed off a piece of salted venison with her dagger and handed it to Arhianna, then took one for herself. She motioned up the length of the ladder to the stone slab above. "Some of them might be in the hall when dawn breaks. Be careful when you push the stone up."

"I'll be fine," Arhianna whispered between chews. She had not realized how hungry she was.

47

"And mind the bridge, will you? And my apothecary?"

"I'll do what I can, but men on fire run, and they'll likely run into the hall looking for water."

"Not if I shoot them dead before they get there."

"Then we both know what we need to do, don't we?"

"Yes." Niamh gripped her by the shoulders and looked her in the eyes. "And I swear to you, when this is done, I'll help you find your daughter. I have a few friends among the Sídhe of this land. We'll find her."

Arhianna's heart fluttered with hope. "Thank you." She reached out and embraced her, daring to believe she might at last have found someone she could trust.

CHAPTER SEVEN
Stranger in the Dark

Arhianna wandered the corridors near the cellar, not daring to sleep lest she miss the call to attack. It was not long before she felt something brush by her in the darkness. "Niamh? Is that you?" she whispered, hands flaming. She waited, watching the light of the flames dance on the rocky surface of the corridor.

A voice came from the darkness beyond, but it was not Niamh's—it was deep and low, like the coldest, slowest part of a river. "All the men who wronged you are here, my lady—right above your head, in all their foulness, awaiting your justice."

She backed away from the voice, heart pounding, hands poised to defend herself. The air around her changed. Instead of smoked meat, she smelled cool mountain air, fresh and full of pine and petrichor. The scent transported her to a time before all the pain and fear; a time before the hate. She remembered exploring the Sacred Grove with Taliesin and her brother, and with each breath, fell into a deeper state of relaxed happiness.

"Scáthach didn't send your child to be raised by the selkies, did she?" asked the calm voice. Its owner stepped out of the shadows and into her light. He stood as tall and slim as a birch sapling with hair as silver-white as its bark, regarding her with wide, limpid eyes. She could not decide whether they seemed cruel or kind. *Daoine Sídhe*, she concluded, holding his gaze with courage.

"Scáthach is no fool," he continued. "She knows power when she sees it. Ask yourself, my lady, why would she agree to take a woman with child to Dun Scáthach? Do you truly believe it was because she thought you would make a great warrior?"

Arhianna's anger mounted. "Finbheara sent you, didn't he?"

The strange man smiled, revealing a white streak of teeth. "He would like to think so, but I don't serve him."

"Why are you here, then?"

He stepped closer, moving as if he might take her hand to dance with her. "For you."

She backed away. "Why?"

"To bring you a gift." He spread his graceful hands apart, again attempting to close the space between the two of them.

She felt fascinated by the pearlescent quality of his face, now so close she could study its perfection in detail. The smell of the forest again wafted toward her, strong and pure, and she nearly wept from the memories that came in its wake. She fought the impulse to bury her face in his chest and fill her lungs with his scent.

"What have you brought me?" she asked, desperately hoping he would say, 'your daughter.'

He raised his hands in the direction of the ring above them. "The revenge that will make you whole again."

Arhianna tried to conceal her disappointment. "I see. You've brought me Earl Ingvar? Is that your gift? You would've done better to lead me to him and leave my friends in peace. He and his men are defiling this fortress with their presence. It'll take moons to rid it of their foulness."

"Friends, is it?" Maelwys raised a brow. "Well, I can toss the Saxons into the sea in a moment, if you wish. They mean nothing to me. Truth be told, I find them repugnant." He shook his head. "It pains me to think I've offended you, my lady—that wasn't my intention. I felt certain you'd relish the opportunity to send Ingvar to hell. Would you not?" He paused and looked at her, waiting for a response, but she gave none. He shook his head and chuckled. "My, my...imagine his face when he discovers he's completely powerless against you! He certainly won't be expecting your fire—nor will his men. I'm certain when they see you, they'll all assume they're about to enjoy another thrilling night of holding you down and—"

"Hold your tongue!" she barked in a sharp whisper. Shame and rage shot up through her stomach and out her wings like a bolt of lightning. She clenched her fists to keep flames from bursting out of her fingertips. "What is your name, gift-bringer?" she managed to ask through gritted teeth.

His voice softened. "Forgive me, my lady. I am Lord Maelwys of the Summer Country." He inclined his head. "At your service."

"Well, Lord Maelwys, you're right," she admitted. "I do hunger for his pain. Thank you for your gift. I promise you I won't fail to make the most of it." She ventured closer to him, angry enough now to resist the spell of his scent. "But I'm not fool enough to think a mage offers a gift without asking for something in return."

The left corner of Maelwys' mouth hooked itself into a half-smile. "True, I had hoped you would recommend me to Uthyr Pendragon and ask for his favor on my behalf."

"The Pendragon?" Arhianna stepped back, feeling surprised. "Why would he listen to me?"

"You know his queen quite well, I understand."

Arhianna's thoughts trailed back to the moons she had spent with Igerna and her family down in Dumnonia. "We were close when we were younger, but I haven't seen her in years. Much has changed."

"It certainly has, my dear lady. It certainly has." Maelwys looked at her with an intensity that seemed to say many things at once, but none she felt certain of. She backed away another step, feeling as if she were standing naked in front of this strange man. He motioned toward the small passage that led into the tunnels. "Please, might we sit and talk a while? I assure you, many hours lay between dark and dawn. I'll not deny you your moment." He stood rooted in the earth, eyes pinned to her, until she spoke.

"I suppose," she murmured.

Arhianna followed him out of the small cavern that served as the cold cellar to the small passageway she had not known about before, ducking her head to fit through. When she stood up, it was no longer the tunnel they stood in, but a forest clearing; the pine and dark earth she had been smelling now surrounded them. The moon and stars shone above their heads, as if the cave ceiling had been removed to reveal the glory of the heavens. Before she could accuse him of deceiving her, he held up his hands and spoke. "I hope you don't mind—I took the liberty of creating a better place for us to talk. I don't much care for caves. But rest assured, this is no more real than a dream. Or, more precisely, *as* real." He waved his hands, and the forest disappeared. They stood in the tunnel where she had expected they would emerge, with the passage to the cold cellar behind her. "So. Tell me. Would you prefer to speak here?"

Though wary, Arhianna felt thrilled by Maelwys' ability to command illusions. She thought of Niamh's comment that his power would wane within the fortress walls, yet that did not appear to be so. *He must be Fae, or part Fae, at least—even the druids cannot command such visions.* She weighed the risk and then shook her head, resolving to make an ally of this powerful being if she could. "No. Bring it back."

Maelwys smiled fully this time, wide and thrilling, as he restored the illusion and pulled it in around them like a fantastic, cosmic cloak. He conjured up a pair of stumps with a small fire between them. "Shall we?" He offered his arm, led her to a stump and sat down after she did. "Let me explain why I seek the Pendragon's favor. I assume you wish to know?"

"I do."

Maelwys nodded. "My father's land in the Summer Country was stolen long ago by a vile adder of a man who killed both him and my mother, as well as any loyal to them. I escaped and sought refuge with my father's druid, who took me in and protected me. Only my elder sister was not there at the time of the attack; she had sailed for Ynys Wydryn, feeling called to become a priestess of Arianrhod. Over the years—and there have been many, since that time, though my face does not tell of them—I visited my sister in Affalon, first to tell her of the terrible things that had befallen our family, and later, after I finished my studies, to try and make a home for myself there. But it was not to be." Maelwys' face twisted into a sneer. "She is as selfish as the wretch who stole our family's land. She would keep it all for herself."

Arhianna felt the hand of fate close its long, cold fingers around her and tighten its grip. "Forgive me—is your sister the Lady Nimue?"

"She is, alas." He did not wait for her to say anything further. "And she will never let me live in Affalon. So, I must seek land elsewhere. Finbheara offered me a place in Knockma in return for bringing him your child, but his lands are in danger, as are my sister's. I have seen it in the pools and flames, as have others who know these arts—the White Dragon shall return, and his gods shall prevail over ours, until they all fall beneath the church of Rome." Maelwys paused and raised a long white finger. "But—before they do, a great king shall unite these lands, granting hope and peace to a few blessed generations. I wish to serve him and enjoy that peace while it lasts."

Arhianna's thoughts had been reeling since Maelwys had mentioned her daughter, the terrible wreckage on the isle of the selkies still fresh in her mind. *Could he be responsible? Might he have her in his clutches?*

"And what of your promise to take my child to Finbheara? Do you not fear him?"

Maelwys shrugged. "I'll say I searched but couldn't find the child, for that is the truth. Instead, I've found you."

Arhianna bristled, her thoughts curdling with suspicion.

"Don't worry," Maelwys said with a chuckle. "I'll make no attempt to return you to Knockma against your will. But, for your child's sake, why don't you come with me to speak with him and Queen Oonagh? You have no reason to fear them anymore—not now—" He glanced up over Arhianna's head and continued in a low voice, "—now that you have the Dark Queen's favor."

Arhianna tensed her wings, again impressed by the man's abilities. "You can see them?"

"Oh, I can. Quite glorious, they are." He leaned in closer. "Do you have *any idea* what you can do with them?"

Arhianna thought back to the short conversation she had had with Niamh. "I can fly to the Underworld."

"Yeeeeess," Maelwys cooed, the sound cascading over Arhianna's skin like a caress. "In short, if you use them well, you can have anything you desire from this world." His limpid eyes widened and glittered, sparks flashing within their depths. "But who shall teach you how, I wonder?" He sat back and turned his palms out. "Scáthach has abandoned you. And, who knows? Perhaps it's she who is responsible for the disappearance of your babe. It's well-known that children aren't allowed within Dun Scáthach until they are of training age. Where did Scáthach tell you she sent your babe? Did she tell you she sent her to the selkies?"

Arhianna's stomach clenched. She felt a twist of truth in his words but dared not admit it to him.

Maelwys shrugged. "If she did, she lied to you. I went there in search of your child—before I learned you could help me, of course—and I swear to you, there were none but selkie babes on that isle when I searched it. And now, there are no selkies at all. They've all fled. That was my fault, I fear—I can be quite frightening when I want to be." He winked. "If you don't believe me, go and see for yourself. That isle shelters nothing but seabirds now. If you want to know what I think, I'd say your enemies lie within this fortress. But that's for you to decide."

Arhianna already knew the truth. She did not reveal her thoughts, turning her questions on him instead. "How did you know where to find me?"

"I found your old village. Some of your former clanswomen told me where to find you."

Arhianna found this hard to believe. "They just told you where I was?"

"I can also be quite persuasive." He looked at her in a way that set her heart racing. "Charming, even." His voice sent a shiver down her spine. "Lady Ragna was not pleased with their openness, if that is any comfort to you."

"Some," Arhianna admitted, struggling to rein in her rapidly changing emotions.

"I told her I meant no harm and that I was willing to prove it."

"And?"

"Lady Ragna is no fool. She could see I was a man of great power. I don't say this to boast. It's simply true."

Arhianna said nothing, waiting for him to continue.

"In return for the knowledge her women gave me, Ragna asked me to swear to do three things for her, and all three I have sworn by my blood to do."

"And, what did you swear?"

"That I would bring no harm to you or your child, that I would bring the men who wronged you and your clanswomen to justice, and that I would ask you to return to her so that she might come to know her grandchild." He paused to gaze at the stars a moment, and then looked back at her. "So, you see, I've nearly fulfilled my three oaths. I've done neither you nor your child any harm, nor shall I; I've delivered her message, though I suspect it will do her no good; and I've brought you a gift—that of allowing you, yourself, to deliver the justice I swore to ensure. Know this, however—should you fail, my oath demands that I finish this last deed."

Arhianna felt her wings twitch. "I won't fail."

"Good." Maelwys gave her a nod of confidence. "Oh! I almost forgot—your friend, the bard, Taliesin, is in Eire, apprenticing under the great druid, Amergin. Finish off those Saxon bastards tomorrow, and I'll take you to him. And, if you wish, I can teach you how to use those terribly wonderful wings you have."

Arhianna's heart leapt at the sound of Taliesin's name but promptly withered from the fear that this strange man had come to trick her into sailing to Knockma. "And all I must do in return is go to the Pendragon on your behalf? You must understand, I find this hard to believe." She stared at him, searching his face for clues—anything that might reveal his intentions, but found nothing. "If you've lied to me, I swear I'll kill you. Do you understand? If it's the last thing I do, I'll kill you."

Maelwys chuckled, his laugh tumbling toward her like a spring brook down a green hill. "I tell no lies, because I do not fear the truth. I have no need of lies to get what I desire."

Arhianna still did not trust him. "And if I agree, what if I should fail to secure you the land and favor you seek from Uthyr Pendragon?"

Maelwys cocked his chin and narrowed his eyes on her. "Oh, you won't fail. Just as you won't fail tomorrow. Or, today, rather…I believe the dawn has broken at last." With a flourish of his hand the forest disappeared, as did he, leaving Arhianna alone in the stone corridor.

CHAPTER EIGHT
An Eye for an Eye

Arhianna hurried back into the cold cellar and up the ladder until she felt the stone slab that led into the kitchen. She pushed it up and peeked out. The first hints of dawn angled through the archway that led into the combat ring, so she slid the slab to the side as silently as she could. She crept toward the archway for a better look, poking her head out of the hall to survey the combat ring. It was littered with lumps of sleeping men clad in leather and fur. She slipped back into the darkness of the apothecary at the rear of the kitchen and peeked out the narrow window providing a view of the bridge and a way for an archer to shoot at invaders. A few men were posted there, but they also seemed to be sleeping. She ventured back toward the combat ring and watched the men from the shadows, waiting.

She did not have to wait for long. Moments later, Uathach's blood-curling battle cry shattered the morning air like a hammer on glass, startling the lumps in the ring to their feet. Arhianna's chest flooded with adrenalin as she strode into the combat ring. Flames surged from her hands like poised dragon heads, her fingers crooked, like vicious fangs toward her enemies, while Niamh rained arrows down upon them from above. Gawyr came bounding across the bridge, swiping the two guards off the edge of the cliff as if they were children, with Uathach running behind him with the speed of a wildcat, her spear tip thirsting for blood.

Screams of agony and the smell of burning fur and flesh poisoned the sky, sending billows of black smoke into the air. Arhianna fanned her invisible wings, causing the flames to erupt into volcanic fury, engulfing every man in her wake. She scanned them all for Ingvar's cruel features, ravenous for her revenge, until, at last, she spied him bursting from Scáthach's chamber. She burned a path toward him, like a ship cutting a wake through a violent sea. Men turned away as she passed, shielding their eyes and face from the heat and flames she threw in all directions. But just before she reached him, she felt a jolt of searing pain. A dagger had hit her in the left shoulder, knocking her back a few paces. She pulled it out and seared the wound shut. When she looked back up, Ingvar was gone. She swirled around, searching for Ingvar's face, engulfing any man in her path in a blast of flames.

"Where are you, you filthy bastard!" Arhianna yelled in Saxon. She scanned the chaos around her in desperation, searching for Ingvar's face. The thought of him escaping a second time drove a bolt of panic through her stomach. *No. Not again!* She scanned the ring frantically until she spied him scaling the wall to the top. Niamh had not noticed.

"Niamh!" she screamed, running in her direction, but Ingvar had already climbed over the lip of the wall.

Niamh soon saw what was happening. She ran to one of the staircases and disappeared. Ingvar went in after her, and Arhianna lost sight of them both.

Uathach yelled at her. "What are you doing? Finish off these bastards!"

Not many were left. Perhaps twenty. They had killed twice that many. The adrenalin in Arhianna's blood was now enough to simultaneously engulf the remaining warriors in flames. Gawyr and Uathach made quick work of them, driving spears through all their hearts as they floundered around the ring, screaming. Yet Ingvar was not among them.

The ring held at least fifty dead men, charred and smoking. The smell of death fouled the air and choked them.

"Where the hell are the selkies I sent you for?" Uathach demanded, breathless.

"Gone," Niamh stated flatly. "No idea where they went. There were none on the island."

Arhianna thought she might have glimpsed a look of concern in Uathach's eyes, but her coldness quickly returned. "They've probably gone south." She gestured to the bodies. "Take their heads." She pulled a long-handled axe from the wall, threw it to Arhianna, then turned to Gawyr. "Toss what's left of them into the sea. I'm going to help Niamh."

"I'm going with you—" Arhianna protested.

"No. Stay here with Gawyr. I'll deal with that bastard."

"No! He's mine to kill!" Arhianna could not abide the idea of Ingvar dying at anyone's hands but her own. She felt a jolt of anger so powerful, flames lurched from her hands. Luckily, they were by her sides.

Uathach stared at her, and this time, by some miracle, she did soften. "Fine. I'll bring him here, and you can do whatever you like with him."

"No—" Arhianna blurted. "The mage is somewhere in there, too—I saw him last night."

"What?" Uathach's eyes resumed their malice.

"He found me in the tunnels before the attack—said he brought Ingvar and his men here for me, as a gift."

"And you believed him?" both Uathach and Gawyr asked at once.

"He wants me to speak to the Pendragon for him."

"What else?"

"You said his powers would weaken within the fortress, but if what I saw last night was weak, you're no match for him."

"Bloody hell!" Uathach cried. "You didn't think to tell me this sooner?"

Arhianna stood there, mouth open. *When could I have told her?* "The battle's only just finished! Let me come with you—I can help."

Uathach grabbed her by her tunic. "I don't have time to argue with you, Ronin! You don't know these tunnels. You'll be nothing but a hindrance to me and end up getting us all killed! Stay here, and do as I command, or I'll knock your fucking teeth out!" Uathach gave her a shove, snatched several daggers from the wall and tucked them, one at a time, into a series of leather straps on her leggings, boots and tunic. "Deal with the bodies and watch the bridge." She ran for the gate, unlocked it, and disappeared into the blackness.

Gawyr sighed and took the axe from Arhianna's hands. "I'll do that." He chopped the heads off the dead as easily as a cook lopping off the tops of carrots, and Arhianna piled them up for Uathach to add to her grisly wall. Then, Gawyr carried their headless bodies to the edge of the cliffs by the bridge and tossed them down into the sea below, until all that remained of the battle was a pyramid of ghastly heads and several black pools of blood in the ring.

Gawyr washed his hands and fetched himself some ale, as if he had spent the morning chopping logs rather than heads. After drinking most of its contents, he held his drinking horn out to Arhianna. "Drink. It'll calm you."

58

"I can't."

"Drink! You're as tense as a bowstring."

Arhianna took the horn with both hands, managed a few swallows and handed it back.

"Better?"

Arhianna shrugged.

"Good. Now help me finish this foul job."

Together they washed the blood off the blades they had collected from the dead and hung them on the wall.

"These are well-made," Arhianna observed.

Gawyr gave her a nod. "I've seen worse."

Arhianna stared at the blackness beyond the gate to the tunnels, her anxiety mounting.

Gawyr looked down at her, brow furrowed. "Don't worry. Uathach will find them."

Arhianna wanted to believe him but could not shake her fear. *Niamh's my only friend. And what if Uathach kills Ingvar? Or worse, he escapes?* The possibilities felt like cords cinching ever more tightly around her neck.

After a few minutes, Gawyr narrowed his eyes on her. "What's this mage want you to ask the Pendragon for?"

"He wants me to get his father's land back for him. And his title, I suppose."

"What title? And where might this land be?"

"He claims his father was a king—but I've never heard of a king named Baeddan, have you?"

"No. But I'm not from the south."

"I'm not either." Arhianna said, almost to herself. *I'm not from anywhere, anymore.*

"And the land?"

"It lies across the sea from Caer Leon, near Ynys Wydryn, from what I understand."

Gawyr nodded, glancing back at the dark gate, as if the mage might be listening from behind its bars. "I don't care what he promised you, my lady—you should stay away from him. Now, come with me. Help me keep an eye on the bridge."

After the violent chaos of the morning, she felt as if she were drowning in the quiet world around them. Occasionally, the bridge let out an ominous creak. Besides that, no sounds filled the air but the cry of seabirds and the distant sound of the surf churning against the rocks far below. Hours passed without incident, until the sky began to redden in the west. "That's it," she announced. "I'm going in. I can't wait here anymore."

She ignored Gawyr's protests, ran across the ring and pulled open the dark gate, still unlocked from that morning. She stood there at the edge of the blackness, barely breathing, listening—but nothing met her ears.

Gawyr had followed her. "My lady, please don't go in there. I'm too big to follow you into the passages on this side. Niamh and Uathach can take care of themselves."

"You don't know that. What if you're wrong? What if they're down there somewhere, injured?" She said nothing more and plunged into the darkness, moving deeper and deeper into the heart of the mountain until his protests faded behind her.

Arhianna relied on the ground's pitch to tell her which direction she moved in, feeling along the sides of the rough passageway with her fingertips. She sensed crossroads where tunnels intersected, for the breeze and the sounds and smells riding upon it changed. At each place, she listened, hoping to hear something that might lead her in the right direction. *Morrigan, lead me to my enemy.* Her wings stiffened and guided her through the inky black labyrinth of passageways, as if they were the handles of a plow and she its blade.

Down she moved, deeper into the mountain, hands in front of her, searching in the dark for low-hanging ledges or sharp outcroppings until the air changed, bringing with it that painfully beautiful scent again. Her wings relaxed.

"Maelwys?"

"Arhianna," a voice whispered over her left shoulder. A cascade of chills tumbled over her skin.

"Where's Niamh?"

"She's safe. As is the other one. I imagine they're back in the fortress, by now."

His was not the only voice she heard—there was another, cursing in the passageway, coming toward her in the corridor.

"It's just you and him, now," he said in a low tone. "Now's your moment."

She felt him move away. In his wake, the dank, mineral-tasting cavern air rushed in around her. She stood alone in the corridor, heart racing, fingers itching with hatred, the thrill of imminent revenge coursing through her blood. When she heard him but a few feet away, she filled the corridor with flames. Ingvar's eyes flew open in surprise, and then filled with terror as the flames attacked his hair and clothes. He stumbled backward in the corridor, wailing like a stuck pig, slapping at the flames in vain. The sound of his cries echoing through the corridors fueled Arhianna's excitement. She let him scramble on, enjoying the sight of him stumbling and crawling along the ground, just as he had forced her clan sisters to do so many times.

"What did you think would happen?" She rekindled the flames he had managed to slap out. "That you would simply take this fortress and we would suffer you to defile it?"

Ingvar struggled to his feet and turned around, dagger in hand, squinting at her through the smoky corridor. "Come and fight me, you loathsome witch!"

She could tell he did not recognize her. "Have you forgotten me? What a shame."

She spied the glint of a blade in his hand. "Come closer, then," he challenged through gritted teeth.

She ventured closer, just out of his reach. He stared at her, his breath labored with pain, but still did not know her.

"I can see your eyes no longer serve you. No need to keep them." With the speed of a hawk, she slashed a dagger across his left eye. His hands flew to his face, dropping the dagger he had been gripping. Over his deafening curses, she cried, "I am Arhianna, queen of Jørren, and you shall die by my hands!"

"Kill me, then," he cried. "Come! Kill me!"

She kicked him to his knees. "Crawl."

He shook his head and would not move.

"Crawl!"

"Rot in hell!"

"Ronin!" Arhianna heard a voice yell. She whirled around to see Uathach standing behind her.

"I told you to stay in the fortress!"

61

Ingvar began to laugh. "Looks like your mother has come to scold you. Best obey her." His laughing echoed off the walls of the corridor, stoking Arhianna's rage.

"And I told *you*, he's *mine* to kill!"

Arhianna kicked Ingvar so hard in the face he fell over. He lay limp in the corridor.

"Do it then. Finish him."

"No." Arhianna had only begun to unleash the burden of her revenge. "Death would be a mercy to him now. I want him chained in the ring, suffering from his burns, until he dies."

"Well, I'm not dragging him all the way back up this mountain."

"Then I'll do it myself."

"You're a fool. Just be done with it."

"No!"

"I'll help her," a voice said. Arhianna turned around to see Niamh in the corridor.

Uathach threw her hands up. "Fine. Tie his hands and feet."

The three women walked single file, dragging Ingvar by his bound feet, whimpering from pain, until they reached the gate that led into the combat ring. The stars greeted them as they emerged.

Gawyr stood on the other side of the gate, axe in hand. "Great Dagda, it's about time! I've nearly gone mad up here!"

The three women tugged their prize into the ring. Arhianna reached down and touched Ingvar's neck. His heart still beat. "Gawyr, chain this bastard to the wall."

Gawyr looked at Uathach, who nodded in agreement. He picked up the prisoner and threw him over his shoulder. "Gods!" Gawyr grimaced. "He stinks!" He carried him to a section of the wall with several pairs of shackles attached to it and propped him up beneath them.

Arhianna shackled Ingvar's wrists and ankles and cut his clothes off him. Sheets of burned flesh peeled off with them.

Gawyr let out a low grumble. "The bastard's done for! I say we throw him off the bridge and be done with him."

Arhianna shot him an icy look. "Leave him where he is."

She followed Uathach and Niamh to the hall, put some bread in her pocket, filled her drinking horn with ale, and grabbed a low stool. She was about to leave when Uathach stopped her. "If he's not dead in three days, you're going to kill him. I don't want him stinking up the ring. Agreed?"

"Fine." Arhianna went back to where Ingvar lay shackled and settled herself across from him.

Gawyr was still there. He raised his eyebrows. "Now what?"

"Now, I'm going to watch him suffer and die." She took a drink, never taking her eyes off Ingvar's tortured body.

"Looks like he's already dead."

"I don't think so." Arhianna targeted an oozing patch of Ingvar's flesh with a blast of flames. He cried out, curdling the night air with his agony.

Gawyr sighed and walked away, shaking his head.

Arhianna remained on her stool, watching Ingvar shake from pain and exposure. He cursed her and spit in her direction, but she did nothing but stare at him. *He hopes he'll make me angry enough to kill him. But I won't.* For the first few hours of the night, she tolerated his vitriol, because it satisfied her to watch his hatred for her grow. When she tired of it, she sent flames to lick his skin each time he insulted her, driving him to howl into the night. At last, he stopped, and fell limp from exhaustion.

The sun rose. Arhianna felt surprised to see his eyes flutter open. She smiled at him. She perceived unhurled curses building up in his eyes and mouth, but he swallowed them unspoken. She ate and drank in front of him that morning, watching him lick his cracked lips and rasp through his dry throat, choking on his hatred for her.

Once the sun disappeared on the second night and the cold came, he began to fray.

"Kill me!" he demanded, at first. Soon after, he begged for it. "Please! Please...kill me. I deserve to die. Kill me!"

She said nothing. The hours of the night passed without incident, except for his moaning and rasping, and she slept a bit. When dawn broke the next morning, so did he. His face no longer held any fight or hatred—only desperation. He wept openly in front of her and prayed to Woden for a chance to die with honor.

Arhianna laughed. "You'll be nowhere near Valhalla. You'll die here, in a pool of your own piss and vomit, which is more than you deserve."

He hardly moved or spoke that day, fading in and out of consciousness.

The third morning, Uathach came to her.

"Not yet," Arhianna said.

"We agreed on three days."

"So we did. Today is the third, and he'll suffer through all of it. When night falls, I'll kill him."

Ingvar whimpered, and Arhianna knew it was from relief, not dread.

"Or maybe I won't."

"What do you mean?"

"Maybe I'll free him."

"Free him? Are you mad? Just kill him and be done with it."

"He won't get far. But maybe I'll let him try."

The groan that came from Ingvar's throat thrilled her. "Maybe I'll let you run away—like the women in Ragna's village—and when I catch you, I'll make you suffer the way they did. I don't have a dozen men here to rape you, but I suppose I could figure something out that would give you some idea of how they must have felt." She took the butt-end of a spear and shoved it between his buttocks. He wailed, and she spit on him.

"I want him out of this fortress by nightfall," Uathach said. "I don't care how you do it. Just get rid of him. This has gone far enough."

Arhianna sat back down on her stool. "I'll honor our agreement."

The hours dragged by. Arhianna passed the time sharpening her daggers. When the hour grew late, Niamh approached. "How do you feel?"

Arhianna felt glad of her friend by her side. "Better."

"What will you do with him now?"

"I should kill him, but I don't want to end his suffering. I want him to go on as I have, remembering what happened to him every night, cringing at the memory of it like a beaten dog. I want him to limp through life, like you and I, damaged."

64

"I limp. This is true. But I wasn't damaged as you were." She felt Niamh's hand on her shoulder. "I understand why you want him to suffer. And when I think of what he and his men did to you, I want him to suffer as well—but if you let him live, and he recovers from this ordeal, you know he would seek you out with such vengeance you would forever remain a slave to the thought of it. You must kill him."

Arhianna nodded.

Niamh squeezed Arhianna's shoulder and then walked away.

Ingvar looked up at her, a flash of triumph in his eyes.

"I suppose I must kill you, then. That was the agreement." Arhianna took out her dagger and stood over him. He closed his eyes and relaxed. She leaned down and whispered in his ear. "You fool! Do you think I'd let you die? No. I'm going to set you free! But you'll never rape another woman again." Before Ingvar could cry out in protest, Arhianna's blade had done its work. Blood gushed from the wound as she unshackled him from the wall. His arms fell to the ground like birds shot from the sky. He fell over on his side, rasping a silent scream into the dirt.

Arhianna reached down and grabbed his chin, directing his face toward the weapons on the wall. "If you can get to the bridge before I can grab that bow and arrow from the wall and shoot you, you'll be free to toss yourself from the cliffs. Otherwise, I've got a dozen spear shafts for you."

Ingvar, in what could only be a surge of adrenalin, got to his feet and ran for the bridge. Niamh came running from the hall. "What are you doing?" she cried. "Are you mad?"

"Leave him be!" Arhianna cried. She lowered her bow as Niamh ran to block him from the bridge. Then, in a flash of movement no one expected, Ingvar changed direction and charged Niamh like a bull. Arhianna's arrow shot him just as he collided with Niamh, but it was too late. She stumbled backward, and the two of them disappeared over the edge of the cliff.

Arhianna denied her eyes what they had seen. *No. This hasn't happened. This hasn't happened! Oh, dear gods, what have I done!* She ran to the edge of the cliff, along with Uathach and Gawyr, just in time to see splashes in the water below.

All the satisfaction she had felt over the past three days drained out of her and flowed over the cliff, drawing her to the edge; coaxing her to follow its path and surrender to its gravity. *There is no pain here*, the breeze whispered. *Fall and be free of it at last.*

It was Uathach who broke the spell, her voice trembling. "You stupid, selfish, half-witted fool! You're a curse! A curse on us! Leave and never return!" She glared at Arhianna, her hands gripping her staff so tightly her knuckles were white. "It should have been *you* that bastard dragged over the cliff!" Uathach smashed her staff into Arhianna's chest, sending her stumbling into the stone wall. "Leave this place and never return!" She spit in her face and walked away.

Gawyr came to her side and put his hand on her shoulder. "I'm sorry." He looked at her with the same disappointed expression her father had worn when she had worried him. "Go home to your people." He took her hand and put a pouch of coin into it.

Arhianna wiped the spit off her cheek with the back of her hand, her mind still struggling to grasp the tragedy that had occurred, and walked across the bridge.

CHAPTER NINE
Summons

Arhianna made her way down the dark tunnels winding through the mountain, stopping only when she reached the Great Chamber. She took Arianrhod's feather off Scáthach's tomb, chiding herself for leaving it as an offering. *My prayers have never been answered by you or your daughters. It's been Morrigan, and only Morrigan, who's been there for me.* She tucked the feather in her tunic and turned to go, but young Connla's ring caught her eye. In a moment of anger, she slipped the ring off the carved hand of Dun Scáthach's most precious son and put it on her finger.

She went and stood in the corner of Morrigan's eye, peering down into the churning waters of the Bay of Skulls, until the weight of her anguish caused her to crumple to the ground and sob. *Oh gods. What have I done? What have I done? I'm so sorry, Niamh.* She could not rid her mind of the terrible scene. Its poison leaked into her blood and filled her with so much regret she could not bring herself to move for hours.

You've wept enough, child. Get up. Arhianna's wings stiffened so fiercely she let out a yelp of surprise. Again, she heard her Mistress' voice. **What's done is done. Get up. Your place is with me, now.**

Arhianna did as she commanded, allowing her wings to guide her through the mountain as they had done before. They urged her to turn into corridors she did not remember, moving ever downward. After an hour of descending, her wings relaxed in front of the mouth of a dark cavern. She tried to illuminate it with the flames from her fingers, but the darkness seemed to swallow the light, pulling it into its black gaping maw. She detected faint sounds coming out of it. *Voices? Or perhaps wind or sea.* She eyed the darkness with growing suspicion, trying in vain to see something within its depths. "What's in there? Where am I?"

On the edge of the world, Child.

Chills rippled along Arhianna's skin as if it were water. Her wings nudged her toward the darkness, causing her to flash back to the day she and her mother stood atop the wall at Caer Gwythno, looking out over an angry sea with the Saxons closing in. She felt the same way, now, frozen with fear. *You're a woman now,* she chided herself. *A servant of Morrigan! How dare you quiver like a child? This time, you jump!* She summoned her courage.

"One…two…thr—"

Arhianna became part of the darkness, split into countless tiny pieces—like glass shattering, or seawater sprayed against the rocks. She felt as if she had been plunged into deep water, except she could not hear or feel anything at all. Her eyes were open, but she saw nothing but blackness. She tried to cry out, but she could not breathe.

Then, just as quickly as she had been dismantled, she felt herself being knitted back together, stitch by stitch, until her aborted cry came forth, distorted and strange, and filled the space around her. As if reborn by the sound of her own voice, her other senses came alive. She spied faint sunlight coming into the cavern and heard a voice.

Come into the light.

Eager to leave the darkness, she stretched her wings and vaulted toward the light, out of the cave and into a dream-like sky. She took in the pastoral scene below, awash in a strange golden light. A figure that could only be Morrigan stood atop the highest hill, feet and spear rooted in the ground, a battered shield against her thigh, and her enormous black wings tucked between her shoulder blades. An impressive herd of red and white cattle roamed the valley below, each fine animal well within her watchful gaze.

Arhianna sailed to the ground in front of her and fell to her knees. Her wings remained awkwardly outstretched, for though she had grown accustomed to feeling them behind her, she had never used them to fly before. "Mistress."

"Rise, Daughter of Lucia."

Arhianna rose and beheld her patroness. Her eyes blazed like two tiny suns within the dark wild storm of her hair, which was streaked with lime. Her skin was painted with woad, and she had smeared wide red stripes of what seemed to be blood across her high cheekbones. Her body looked as if it had been carved of cream-coloured stone and polished to impossible smoothness except for the many scars she bore.

"You've been followed." She pointed her spear down toward the cave.

Alarmed, Arhianna looked behind her, knowing in her bones who it must have been. "I'm sure it was the mage, Maelwys. He works for Finbheara."

Morrigan nodded. "I know of him. He is a rogue halfling, apprenticed by Myrddin Wyllt. I would warn you not to make an enemy of him."

Myrthin? A knot formed in Arhianna's stomach as she recalled how Myrthin had betrayed her and Taliesin. *I was right not to trust him.*

"Don't be afraid. He wouldn't dare harm you while you're with me."

Arhianna shook her head. "I don't fear him. My fears lie elsewhere." She looked at the ground, heavy with thoughts of her missing daughter, and summoned the courage to ask what she longed to know. "Please, Mistress—is my baby alive?"

Morrigan gave one nod of her head. "She lives."

Relief washed over Arhianna, and she let out the breath she had been holding. "Where is she?"

"I cannot see where she is. None from this world can. Cerridwen has concealed her."

Cerridwen? Arhianna knew of only one Cerridwen—a priestess of the Isle with a talent for sorcery unequaled in the history of the Sisterhood. In her father's time, she had stolen the Sacred Cauldron from the Sisterhood and used it to resurrect the dead, seeking to command an immortal army more terrible and deadly than any that had ever threatened their shores. Unfortunately, her attempt at glory succeeded only in creating half-dead savages who roamed the hills in search of blood, bringing pain and terror to Arhianna's clan and the clans they called friends. Cerridwen reached too high and failed, the story went, bringing nothing but suffering to her people.

As an ever-eavesdropping young girl, Arhianna had learned, to her horror, that this same Cerridwen was sister to her grandmother. At first, she had recoiled at the knowledge she was related to such an evil woman, but, over the years, she began to take perverse pride in it. Though what Cerridwen did had caused terrible consequences, such achievements in sorcery were unheard of. Not only had she succeeded in bringing men back from the dead, but she managed to obtain all the sacred relics and capture the grove, as well. If it had not been for the divine intervention of Arawn, she would have succeeded. In other words, in the world of men, she was considered invincible.

"Cerridwen of the Isle?" Arhianna asked, wanting to be certain. Morrigan did not blink. "The same. Although she is far more than that. She is Consort to Arawn and Queen of the Underworld."

Arhianna wondered, with growing dread, why Cerridwen would conceal her daughter. She knew her clan had done much to thwart Cerridwen's efforts in her mortal life, especially her father, and feared this might be an act of retribution. "Why would she do such a thing?"

"Her reasons are her own," Morrigan said. "You must pray to her for answers."

Arhianna did not give up. "Please—I must find her. Is there nothing you can do to help me? I'll do anything you ask."

Morrigan regarded her a moment. "You may look into my shield, if you wish. It may reveal something to you."

"Yes, please!"

"So be it." Morrigan reached for her shield, suspended it in the air, and then spun it. "Don't fight the pull."

Arhianna kept her eyes on the spinning shield, allowing herself to be drawn toward its center until she felt herself being pulled through it. After a dark moment of void like the one she had experienced coming through the black cave, though nowhere near as frightening, she found herself on top of a hill overlooking a bloody battle in full force. Heavy rain fell from angry clouds, pelting the exhausted warriors below. Blood and rain streamed down the creases of their fierce faces as they slipped in the mud, struggling to see through the deluge as they lunged at one another with sword and spear.

Flying high in the gusting wind, Uthyr's red dragon flashed its fiery tongue from his banners, but those banners were disturbingly few. *He's losing.*

Arhianna could do nothing but watch as the Saxon army closed in with their axes, tightening their ranks around Uthyr's men. One by one, the last of the dragon banners fell, trampled by enemy feet into the mud. Arhianna did not have the stomach to watch the enemy finish off her kinsmen and loot their dead bodies for spoils. *Is this to be Uthyr's fate? To die trampled in the mud?*

70

Thunder rumbled through the air, as if the sky were answering her questions. It grew stronger behind her, and she turned to see it was not thunder at all, but riders, bursting from the tree line. War chariots came blazing from the opposite direction, led by a warrior with a battle cry that curdled the blood.

Like a flash flood, the two companies overcame the battlefield, attacking with fluid, unified force. They soon turned the tide of the fight, their green and gold banners surging over the field like waves upon the seashore.

As the enemy ranks thinned, Arhianna spied the Pendragon in the center of the field. He emerged from the muddy chaos, sword poised with lethal grace as he carved a sharp, silver path out of what surely would have been his last battle.

Arhianna had lost sight of the chariot driver but heard his distinctive war cry and jerked her head toward it. She spied the driver charging around the perimeter of the battle, Uthyr's banner in one fist and the green and gold in the other, forcing the enemy where he willed. The sky darkened as he rode, as if he had summoned nightfall. Arhianna looked up.

Ravens.

Thousands filled the sky, sailing toward the battleground from all directions. Once overhead, they joined together, circling the battle below and blacking out the sun.

The driver reined in his horses and removed his helmet, releasing a cascade of dark hair and distinctively female features.

A woman! Arhianna watched with increased interest as she raised her hands to the sky, tipped her head back and bellowed into the swirling flock. Like a volley of arrows, the ravens dove down from the sky, driving beak and talon into the faces of the enemy. Within minutes, what men were left fled the field in terror. Green riders picked them off with bow and arrow until none were left.

The woman leapt from her chariot and ran toward the Pendragon, who dismounted and threw off his helmet just in time to take her up in his arms and kiss her.

Who can she be? Arhianna sailed down the hill on her shadow-wings for a closer look. Men attended to their wounded kinsmen. As always on the battlefield, joy and misery bled together in a stomach-churning, grisly scene. It was only then that she saw the faces of the green and gold army clearly—skin pale and luminous, with wide limpid eyes, high cheekbones and ears curved like tree-leaves.

Uthyr, fighting alongside the Sídhe? No. It can't be. Arhianna thought of the churches Uthyr had built since marrying Igerna, and how faithfully he was said to consult Archbishop Dubricius on all matters, both large and small. *He's become nearly as pious as his brother, Emrys—he would never accept such allies.* And yet, he clearly had. *She must have seduced him. Who is this Sídhe-queen who's captured Uthyr's heart?* She floated through the throngs of warriors like a ghost, drifting toward the Pendragon and the Sídhe-queen until she was close enough to behold their faces.

Chills rippled through her as she realized the man was not Uthyr, though he had similar features. She looked closely at the dark-haired woman, studying her anew. Her heart leapt at the green and amber flecks dancing in her violet eyes. *Morrigan! Oh, gods, my beautiful daughter!*

The maiden looked up at her and smiled, her face beaming through time and space. *I see you, Mother. All is well. Rejoice with us! We have won at last!*

Shock threw Arhianna out of the vision and back onto the hill. She stumbled backward from the force and fell to the ground, skin clammy with sweat. She could not move.

"Rest a moment. Give your body time to adjust."

She could do nothing but stare at the sky and think about what she had seen. After a time, she could move her fingers and toes, and then her limbs. She sat up.

"What did you see?"

Arhianna felt helpless. "She's to be taken by the Sídhe, no matter what I do."

"You saw her future, as have I. You are wrong to lament."

"How can you say that? All hope is lost!"

Morrigan's expression grew so fierce, and her voice so thunderous, Arhianna cowered, unable to look at her. "Your daughter shall become a powerful druidess and unite a great people. How can you see such a grand destiny as hope lost? You think ever small, Arhianna of the Oaks—ever only of yourself, and I have grown weary of your self-pity! I demand you prove yourself worthy of my gift, or I shall cast you aside!"

Arhianna instinctively felt her wings stiffen with obedience. She spoke up, voice trembling. "Please forgive me. I wish to serve you, Mistress—any way I can. What would you have me do?"

Morrigan continued. "I am raising an army and wish to have the fiercest warrior ever born to our people—the great Cú Chulainn of Ulster—to oversee its training. You will fly to the Underworld and secure his release."

Arhianna felt confused. She had assumed Morrigan would make her prove herself in the fighting ring. She had not the slightest idea how to attempt what the goddess had asked of her. "The Underworld, Mistress?"

"Have you not heard of the great Cú Chulainn? You must know he died long ago."

"I have, Mistress, of course, but surely, such a warrior must be in the Summerlands."

"He is not."

Arhianna did not understand. Cú Chulainn's victories were legendary. "But why?"

"That is not for you to know. Do you accept?"

Arhianna felt fearful but managed to summon her voice. "I accept, Mistress. But how am I to pass into the Underworld?"

Morrigan reached a hand into the sky. A raven descended and perched on her hand. "She shall show you. Be swift, and don't look back. Thanks to your friend, the mage, the Rangers of Connacht will have learned you're here by now. They'll send hunters." Morrigan released the raven, who soared toward the entrance of the cave.

Arhianna wasted no time asking who the Rangers of Connacht or their ominous-sounding hunters were. She bowed her head in obedient farewell, spread her wings and sailed into the twilight after the raven, who plunged into the dark opening of the cave. Arhianna summoned flames from her hands, navigating by their light to follow her escort's flashing black wings. Within moments, she heard shrieks and hisses echoing off the stone passage around her.

She struggled to keep the raven within view and her limbs from being battered and scraped along the sharp corridor walls. Soon, sounds of scuttling and clicking joined the sound of shrieking. She risked a quick look behind her and nearly slammed her head into a low-hanging ledge. She swooped down in time to hit it with her right wing instead. The pain shot through her shoulder and into her chest as she fell to the ground.

The scuttling sounds closed in on her from all sides. Something latched on to her leg, with either teeth or talons, and she screamed. She yanked her dagger from its sheath and stabbed at her assailant until it let go, shrieking and tumbling behind her in the darkness. She took to the air again, letting loose a terrible battle cry as she cast a ring of fire behind her, hoping it would keep her enemies at bay.

The raven had waited for her and now cawed so loudly the sound hurt her ears. She flew off down a much narrower corridor. Unable to spread her wings within its confines, Arhianna gave chase on foot, until, at last, she burst from the cave into a cold twilight.

Panting, she surveyed her surroundings, dread slowly replacing her relief. The stars did not twinkle; they were dull and dim, as if merely painted on the sky, or struggling to shine through a shroud. No insects chirped. No breeze rustled the leaves on the trees. The air smelled of nothing.

Yet as unnerving as the silence was, the sound that broke it was worse—ominous shrieks emanating from the cave. She scrambled up the rocky slope in front of her, momentarily forgetting she had wings. Just as she reached the top, she bumped into something and stumbled backward, landing on her back. Out of nowhere came two white hounds. They pounced on her chest, barking and snarling, their red eyes pinned on her neck. She raised her hands to engulf them in flames, but a stern voice cried, "Off!"

The hounds jumped off her and ran toward the voice. After a few moments of silence, the silhouette of a large horse and rider towered over her, blocking out the sky. The rider dismounted and helped her to her feet. "Dear Gods—Arhianna? Is that you?"

Arhianna's heart raced. *I know that voice.* Though he was twice as large as he had been in life, she knew who stood before her.

"Father!"

She jumped up and clutched him tightly. His body felt as hard and cold as stone, but she did not care. For the first time in years, she wept for joy.

CHAPTER TEN
The Underworld

Arhianna's father released her and stepped away. "You shouldn't be here, *cariad*—it's not your time." Seemingly curious, his horse turned its head and eyed her. She felt a surge of recognition and smiled. "Gethen!" A warmth filled her chest as she reached up and stroked the side of his impressive head hovering some three feet above her. He looked young and strong again, his muscles rippling beneath a coat as purple-black as the midnight sky on winter solstice. He leaned down and nuzzled her.

"He's happy to see you, as I am, but why have you come?" Whenever her father spoke, his every word reverberated in her ears, as if they were within a cavern or grotto. She tried to make out his features within his dark cowl, but the grey light of the shrouded moon only revealed the slightest contours of his jaw.

"I'm here to do a service for Morrigan. I cannot leave until it's done. What are you doing here? And how did you get so big?"

He remained silent a moment. "I see you wear her wings. Hide them, and do as I say." He reached out to her. His hand was enormous, every bone beneath his flesh visible. She tried not to gasp and ceased her attempts to peer within his cowl. She could not bear to think of beholding his face in such a way. "Father, what's happened to you?"

"I'll tell you, but now is not the time."

Arhianna kept her eyes on his hand, willing herself to grip its coldness, and allowed him to help her into the vast black leather seat of his saddle. He swung himself up and settled behind her while questions dizzied her mind.

The hounds stood on either side of Gethen's giant form, every muscle tense beneath their sleek white coats, their crimson unblinking eyes pinned on her.

Her father urged Gethen forward toward a twisted mass of trees growing so tightly together she could not see any feasible way through. Yet, in they went. As they moved through the forest, the trees dissipated, as if made of nothing but smoke and shadow. Arhianna looked behind them in surprise, watching the forest swirl and billow in their wake and then reform.

After a time, they emerged from the forest and came to the edge of a lake so vast she could not see the other side. She had smelled it long before it came into view—a strange stagnant smell, and one that overwhelmed her with regret and sorrow. The lake stretched for miles toward the foothills of an imposing chain of sharp mountains. The greenish-grey light of the crippled moon shone off the surface of the water, its reflection still and undisturbed.

The Lake of the Dead. Arhianna stared at its placid waters as they rode along its shores, wondering how many souls languished within its depths. Large white stones lined the lakebed like cobblestones, forming a road of sorts. *What would happen if we were to take such a road down to the bottom of the lake?* Her wings, which she had folded tightly against her back, began to twitch. The stone closest to her moved. *Or did it?* The surface of the lake stirred, as if by a slight breeze, but she felt no breeze. She felt her father stiffen at the sight. He gave a fierce yell and kicked Gethen into a full gallop, the sudden speed throwing Arhianna backward against his chest. She gripped the saddle with both hands and held on with all the strength she could demand of her thighs while Gethen thundered away from the lake and back into the darkness of the forest, splintering trees into shards of shadow as he went.

After a time, they came to a meadow that looked deceptively like the one she had played in as a child. A lone hill rose out of it in the distance, and atop it stood a large roundhouse. Blue smoke curled from its center into the sky, now full of dazzling stars. The moon seemed to have been polished, for it now shone bright and clear upon the land.

Her father encouraged Gethen toward the hill, cutting straight across the meadow until the land began to slope upward. A path spiraled the great mount, and as they circled, she surveyed the wild, shifting landscape below. Forests, lakes, rivers and mountains shifted in and out of view, fading and moving in strange ways beneath them, like ships sailing a vast sea. Clouds added to the disorienting scene, obscuring and then revealing the world below.

She knew they had reached the top when she spied the roundhouse she had spotted from below. Its heavy oak doors stood wide open, fierce dragons carved upon them. The warm glow of firelight beckoned from within. Her father dismounted and offered her his frightening hand. She took it, allowed him to help her dismount, and followed him inside.

She stopped just past the threshold, mystified by the familiar scene that greeted her. In the hearth, her mother's battered cauldron hung over a fire that blazed with more shades of red, orange and blue than she had ever seen flames contain. Next to the hearth sat the basket filled with toys Maur had carved for her and Gareth when they were children. Her mother's fine weavings hung from every wall and beam, their colors as vibrant as the day she had tied their final knots. No detail was missing from her childhood home. The only thing new was that her father's throne, which had normally stood within the mountain fortress, now sat directly across from the entrance on the far side of the roundhouse.

"We're home," she whispered.

She watched her father move toward his throne and sit down. The hounds followed and lay at his feet. "It's not home, but it comforts me."

She took up the stool she had sat upon as a child, now large enough for an adult, and set it down across from him, eager for answers. She knew he had traveled to the Underworld before, as a young man, and had heard the story many times. He had sworn himself to Arawn's service in return for the death lord's help defeating Cerridwen's cauldron-born. Arawn had done so, intervening on behalf of the clans in the Battle of the Grove, and punishing their enemies. Now, it seemed, he was honoring his side of the agreement.

"You will find me much changed. Don't be afraid." He reached up and removed his cowl, revealing a face she knew, but had not seen before. Though she had been preparing herself for it, it took all her willpower not to cry out. His face was as translucent as his hands, his skull and teeth visible within it. Only his blue eyes brought her comfort, for they alone had remained the same. Bards often sang of the eyes being the windows to the soul. Perhaps it was true, for her father's eyes regarded her now with as much love and kindness as they ever had, melting away the cold horror in her breast.

She stared at his imposing figure and took a deep breath. "Father, have you just come to visit Arawn once more, or, are you..." She paused, summoning the words. "—here to stay?"

77

He gave her a kind and ghastly smile. "I am here to stay, Daughter. My time on Earth is over."

Arhianna thought of her mother and brother, and the grief they must have suffered. *And I wasn't there for them.* "When, Father? How long has it been?"

"Time does not work the same way here as it does in the world of men. I must rely on you to tell me how long it has been since we last beheld one another."

Arhianna thought back to the day she had last seen him, standing at the gate to their village, his hand raised in farewell as she and Jørren rode toward the terrible fates that awaiting them. She had thought of that morning a thousand times, wishing in vain she could go back to that moment and make a different choice.

"It's been but a handful of years, Father." *Though it feels like a lifetime.* "Please, tell me what happened."

He folded his white hands and leaned forward a bit. "I was deeply ill, Arhianna, crippled by constant pain. I became a burden to your mother and our people, and could no longer rule Mynyth Aur. I didn't mean to leave the world without telling you. I sent men to every kingdom in the north with orders to find you and bring you home, but none succeeded. I could wait no longer. I called to Lord Arawn, and he came for me. Now, I rule the Underworld in his name. He has left his kingdom in my hands, as he once did with Lord Pwyll of Dyfed. Where he's gone, and why, I don't know. He didn't tell me, and I didn't ask. He isn't one to be questioned."

Arhianna looked at the ground to hide her tears. *Oh, poor mother. I'm sorry I wasn't there for you.*

"Your mother grieved deeply, but she has healed. She knows I won't enter the Summerlands without her. When her time comes, I'll be there to greet her. In the meantime, I shall remain here."

Arhianna looked around in confusion. "But this isn't Arawn's fortress...what is this place? *There are no skeleton guards, or a giant brazier of light—no black stone corridors, or terrible bridge across a chasm.* The story of her father's journey to the Underworld had been her favorite as a child, and she had made him tell it dozens of times, insisting he did not leave out any details.

Her father chuckled, the sound both eerie and happy. "You know I loathe cold, dark places. And Arawn's fortress is woefully so. I couldn't abide there. I built my own fortress from of the most

78

beloved memories I have of the places that were once home to me." He rose up and walked to the large doors they had passed through and caressed the carved dragons with pride. "These are the doors of the hall I grew up in." He turned and motioned toward the sturdy oak pillars that held the hall up. "The pillars are the ones Maur and I made for the motherhouse from the oak trees we cut down together." He looked out the open doors and pointed. "Down the hill lies our village stable, its gates always open to let Gethen come and go as he wishes."

But it's not real, Arhianna thought. *It's conjured. And none of your loved ones are here with you.* "But Father, you must be lonely. Mother will understand. Go to the Summerlands. There you can be with your loved ones who have passed on. There's nothing for you here."

He shook his terrible head. "No. I will wait. At least I'm useful here. And I have Gethen." He smiled a gruesome smile. "It's a lonely post, but one I've grown accustomed to. Arawn has left his hounds in my care, and, though they're fearsome to behold, I must admit I'm beginning to enjoy their company. They trust me as well as if I'd raised them from pups, and they obey my every command."

"Do they bring the dead to you?" She looked at the hounds, taking care not to look directly into their red eyes. They were far more fearsome than she had ever imagined.

"With their help, Gethen and I hunt the souls of the dead wandering in Glyn Cuch, the forest we passed through. We deliver them to their fate—be it the Summerlands or the Lake of the Dead. That is what I struggle with the most."

"Sending souls into the Lake of the Dead?"

"It is not I, or even Arawn, who sends a soul to the Lake of the Dead. It's the weight of a soul that determines its fate. Those who are too heavy sink into its depths. Those who are not, walk upon its waters, as easily as if the lake were frozen solid, and cross into the Summerlands. Not I, or Arawn, or any other power in the world, can determine the weight of someone's soul. They alone are responsible for that."

"I don't understand. No one is judged?"

"No. They are simply souls moving toward the place they feel they belong. As in life."

He stood up and motioned toward his table. "Are you hungry?"

"Yes, terribly."

"The dead don't sleep, but we do eat and drink, in our own way—for the memories."

She sat down with him at his table, and he conjured up her favorite breakfast—a basket of crisp autumn apples and a platter of barley cakes, dripping with butter and wildflower honey. "One of the privileges I enjoy."

"Oh!" Arhianna crammed a cake into her mouth and sunk her teeth into it with a moan of relief. She had not eaten anything since the bit of salted pork in the cold cellar of Dun Scáthach. Two cakes and two apples later, she sighed and sucked the butter and honey from her fingers.

"Now, tell me how and why you're here." He leaned toward her, his gaze chilling and intent.

Her hunger satisfied, she turned her mind back to her quest. "I've come to find the great warrior, Cú Chulainn, and take him to Morrigan."

Her father eyed her wings. "This is why she gifted you wings?"

"I don't know if it's the reason why—but she asked me to bring him to her."

"And I suppose you don't intend to refuse her."

"No. But how do I find him?"

"Like you find anyone else—you search for him." He gestured out the large doors, still standing open, toward the vast expanse of the lake. "I expect it won't be easy."

"No." Arhianna felt a chill of trepidation. "I don't expect it will." She got up from the table and walked outside for another look at the world below. The clouds had thinned a bit, allowing her to make out a bit more of the terrain. She spied the dark mass of Glyn Cuch fading in and out of view, mist snaking through its treetops. Beyond it lay the vast Lake of the Dead, stretching as far as she could see beneath the dour watch of the crone-faced mountains.

Her father came and stood beside her, his dark cloak rising on the strange breeze like the dreaded sail of an enemy ship.

"How many souls lie in those waters, Father? Do you know?"

"The skulls of countless millions, king and slave alike, roam its depths, telling tongueless tales of torment to one another. Sometimes, I force myself to stand on those joyless banks and listen." He shook his head, squinting at the horizon. "I never thought I'd find anything more disturbing than the piles of corpses I encountered in the caves when I was your age, but I was wrong."

Chills cascaded down her shoulders.

He turned and touched one of her wings as if it were an injured limb. "I've felt your suffering, *cariad*. Yours, and your mother's. It's the reason my own soul is too heavy to pass into the Summerlands. The truth is, even if I wanted to enter them now, I suspect I could not."

"Oh, Father! Don't say that!"

"Don't fret for me. Perhaps with your mother by my side, and knowing you've found happiness, I could." He reached down, took her hands within his cold grip, and looked at her. "Hear me, Arhianna. If you continue down your path of vengeance, your soul will grow heavier still. You must lighten it. I could not bear to see you suffer such a fate as those who lie within that lake."

Arhianna felt a surge of injustice. *Now, after all my suffering, I'm to be denied even the joy of the Summerlands?* "But none of it was my fault!" she cried. "I didn't ask to be kidnapped, or used by a mage for his selfish plans, or beaten and raped by a dozen men, or—" She could not get the last words out. She could only think them. *Have my daughter stolen from my arms.* She spread her wings, wanting to fly away from him and his terrible warning, but her father reached out and gripped them with strength far beyond her own.

He pulled her close and held her. "No, it isn't fair, *cariad*. You deserved none of it."

Her rage turned to tears, and she wept.

"I rule this realm with as much strength and compassion as I can, for there are more tragic deaths than noble ones. It pains me to take a child from his mother, or a mother from her child, but too often I must. The only comfort is the promise of the Summerlands, where all is healed and forgiven—but they cannot be reached until we have healed and forgiven ourselves."

"And what if I can't?" she whispered, fear rising into her throat. "Father, certain things scar the soul and can never be forgotten. I can never forget." She gritted her teeth in frustration.

"I know it's hard, *cariad*, I know." He stroked her head, as he had when she was little. "But you must try."

"I cut my hair," she whispered, remembering how much he had loved her curls.

"Perhaps you'll see things more clearly, then."

"Perhaps." She smiled. It comforted her to see he still had his sense of humor, even in this dark, uncertain place.

"Oh, child. I've missed you. We are too quick to wound one another and love not nearly enough." He sighed, and the long grass around them seemed to rustle. "Not nearly enough."

CHAPTER ELEVEN
The Search for Cú Chulainn

Arhianna slept in a pile of furs surrounded by the safety of her father's hall. She awoke to find it empty, so went outside in search of him. He stood exactly where she had last seen him, staring at the horizon, his white hounds sitting at his heels.

She went to his side and gazed again at the lake, feeling defeated. She had hoped with some sleep she would feel better about what Morrigan had asked her to do, but she still had no idea how to start. *Find one soul, within a lake that holds thousands? It will take years!* "Father, what do I do? The lake is vast."

Her father smiled. This time, his garish grin did not stop her heart, like it had the first time. She focused on his eyes to avoid studying the bones beneath his pallid skin as he pointed to her wings. "Did she not teach you how to use those?"

Arhianna shrugged. "I assumed they were for flying."

"I can't imagine what else they would be for."

She thought of flying out over the lake and shuddered, remembering the countless skulls beneath its waters.

Her father put a hand on her shoulder. "Do you remember fishing the river at home?"

"Yes. Of course. I loved it." Arhianna wondered if he might be suggesting she somehow fish Cú Chulainn out of the lake and felt confused.

"You were far better at it than your brother."

She smiled. "He always got so angry whenever I out-fished him."

"Yet you did, nearly every time. What was your secret?"

Pleasant memories came to her of standing in the river with her dress hiked up, squishing her toes in the cold mud; of watching the sunlight dance off the river's bouncing current as she threw out her line, over and over, humming in harmony with the river's rush.

"What was your secret, *cariad*?" her father repeated, breaking the spell.

She swallowed hard as she realized what he was suggesting. "The right bait."

He gave her a nod. "The right bait. What else?"

"Thinking like a fish."

"What else?"

"Patience." She recalled how, whenever challenged, she would plant herself in the riverbed like a tree, hardly moving, until she out-fished her brother. Sometimes she stood there until dark. "Or stubbornness," she added.

He smiled again, but it faded quickly. He reached for her hand. "What Morrigan has asked you to do is dangerous, Arhianna. Every soul within that lake, and there are millions, is desperate for a chance to return to the world of the living. Some hunger for revenge, some seek to atone for their sins, others desire nothing but physical pleasure." He looked at her wings. "You, and those like you, are the only way they can return to the living. If they manage to tempt you, or pull you into the lake, you'll have two choices—to do their will or suffer their fate."

Arhianna felt insulted. *He thinks I'm still a child…still the same impetuous girl I used to be.* "I'll be fine," she said, after a moment. "They won't tempt me."

"Remember that, *cariad.* I couldn't bear to lose you."

"I'll be fine, Father." But she did not set out for the lake that day.

How many days and nights Arhianna spent on the hill with her father in the comfort of the hall crafted from his memories, she did not know. She came to understand what he had said when she had first arrived—the passing of time was not the same in that strange place. The weather and the changing of sun to moon seemed to happen only when she felt they should, reflecting her moods and thoughts, as if the world surrounding her were a kind of mirror. The sky had been dark and cloudy for days and showed no signs of clearing. She had no plan for finding Cú Chulainn. All she knew about him was that he was the most celebrated warrior of Eire—the only man to ever have matched the formidable Scáthach in battle— yet, for all his worldly glory, he now dwelled among the forlorn and heavy-hearted.

The songs she remembered told only of his triumphs and victories, not of his sorrow or failures. *What caused him to sink into the lake? How long has he been there?* These were the questions she pondered as the hours passed, or seemed to pass. And so, day after day, she sat on her father's hill, staring at the lake, feeling at a loss, until, at last, her father came and sat beside her. He gazed off toward the dark bank of clouds stretching across the horizon. "Quite troublesome weather we've been having. Doesn't seem like it'll ever clear up."

Arhianna sighed. "I don't know how to do this, Father. I don't know where to start."

"At one end of the lake, perhaps."

"And then what? Fly its length calling his name?"

"You could try that, I suppose."

She grew irritated. "You're no help at all! Do you truly know nothing about Shadowwings?"

"All I know is they are gifted by Morrigan and tolerated by Arawn, who allows those who bear them the privilege of retrieving souls from the lake."

"Yes, but how do they get them out?"

"They lift them out. If they can manage to grab the one hand they wish to grab, that is." He took her chin in his transparent hand and turned her face toward him. "And there is always more than one hand, Arhianna. There are thousands; thousands clamoring for a chance to escape. They watch the sky for the Winged Ones the way a spider watches her web. When one flies low enough for them to latch onto, they strike. Many of the Winged Ones have drowned in these waters or gotten torn to pieces in the frenzy."

The calmness her father displayed unnerved her. "How can you let me do this?"

He shook his head. "It's not my choice to make. It's yours."

Arhianna stared at him, speechless.

"I can only pray that should you fail and die in that lake, your soul will rise to the surface, light enough to enter the Summerlands. For that to happen, you must unburden yourself of anger and sorrow."

Arhianna swallowed hard, knowing such a thing was impossible. *So, I simply cannot fail.* She stared at the leagues of grey water stretching toward the horizon and felt her blood run cold. "I'm scared, Father."

He put his enormous arm around her and squeezed her. "Only a fool wouldn't be. But I have faith in you, daughter. I know you can do this."

Again, she rifled through possibility after possibility in her mind, seeking an idea or plan that would give her hope, but came up with nothing reassuring. *There's no way to prepare for this. I must simply try.*

Her father stood up and offered her his hand. She took it, and he pulled her to her feet. "I'm sorry you have to do this alone, but I cannot interfere with the fates of the souls who dwell in the lake, nor help those who come for them. I can, however, protect you from everything else." He unsheathed his sword. "*Drynwyn* belongs to our people, and I can think of no one worthier to wield it than you. Use it in your quest and return it to the world. Its power serves no one here."

Arhianna's heart pounded as she gripped the hilt and watched the sword flame to life. *This is it. Truly. The sword my father carried into the caves; the one coveted by Cerridwen and taken into the Underworld by Arawn after the Battle of the Grove.* "Arawn will permit this?"

"Arawn has given it to me, to do with as I see fit. I wish for you to have it." He removed the scabbard from his waist and buckled it around hers. Somehow, it shrank to fit her hips.

"Thank you." She sheathed her clan's legendary sword, and an immediate sense of well-being and confidence came over her. *Dyrnwyn* felt like a guardian at her side.

Her father smiled, looking her up and down. Then he turned toward the stable, cupped his hands around his mouth, and whistled. Gethen burst from the stable doors and galloped up the hill, shades of purple and midnight blue dancing along the ripples of his muscles beneath his black coat. "Gethen knows the Underworld. He'll take you to the edge of the lake with the least—" Her father paused. "—*visitors*," he finally decided.

"Visitors?"

"There are always those who trail behind the big fish, follow armies, or dwell on the fringes of large cities, looking for opportunities. The Lake of the Dead is no different. Should you choose to deal with any of them, know the price and whether or not you can afford it." He looked down at one of his white hounds. "I'm sending her with you. None will dare lead you astray with her by your side. She can't help you once you fly over the lake, but she'll protect you everywhere else."

Her father kissed her forehead and pulled her close. "You have everything I can give. The rest is up to you."

She felt better than she had since arriving. "Thank you, Father. For everything."

"I'll be watching, *cariad*."

Arhianna pulled away and smiled at him, now able to look at his face wholly without fear. "I'll make you proud, Father."

She mounted Gethen and rode down the sloping path toward the deep gloom of the Underworld, casting a final look back before it curved around the hill. Her father raised a hand in farewell, exactly the way he had when she had left Mynyth Aur with Jørren, all those moons ago.

CHAPTER TWELVE
The Lake of the Dead

The world faded rapidly from day to night as Arhianna spiraled down the hill on Gethen's back to the edge of Glyn Cuch. What faint light the muted sky provided disappeared as they entered its strange acres, leaving only the luminescent white coat of her father's lone hound to follow. Gethen shadowed her closely, like a mantle of night around an evening star, until that strange smell of regret signaled they were near the lake.

The hound led them out of the trees to a stretch of shore that provided an unobscured view of the lake. Gethen snuffled and shook his mane, as if to signal they had arrived—or that he did not like it. Arhianna remained astride for some time, clutching thick handfuls of his dark, wiry mane for comfort as she studied the ominously smooth lake in front of them. A fog rolled along its quiet surface, making it impossible to see what lay beneath. She watched the sky for "Winged Ones"—others like herself—hoping to discover how they retrieved souls from its depths, but the sky was as obscured as the lake by the shifting fog.

She climbed off Gethen's back and approached the water. The white hound stayed by her side. She had been near the edge but a moment when the hound began to growl, baring her fangs and crouching to attack. Arhianna backed away a few steps just as a body lurched out of the water and lunged for her ankles with both hands. Gethen reared back, whinnying in distress, but the hound charged in. She latched onto the attacker's wrist and yanked an entire arm from its body. It screamed and hissed, thrashing wildly as it slithered back into the water on its belly like an eel.

Arhianna screamed and ran for the woods, so frightened she could not think. She forgot about her wings, her sword, her Firebrand—she knew nothing but fear.

Arhianna forced Gethen and the hound to wander the woods for hours while she pondered returning to her father. *Morrigan didn't tell me fetching Cú Chulainn would be this dangerous. And she didn't tell me anything at all about this lake!* The more she thought about it, the angrier she became. *She's just using me, like all the rest.* "Damn you, Morrigan!" she cried out.

"I'd not insult the Goddess of War if I were you, child," a woman's voice said. "Harsh punishment has been swiftly delivered for far less."

Arhianna's head snapped in the direction she had heard the voice come from. "Show yourself." She unsheathed *Dyrnwyn* and ventured deeper into the forest, its flames lighting her way. The hound stayed at her heels, red eyes blazing.

"I've been watching you, mumbling to yourself, blaming Morrigan for your fear, thinking of running back to your father like a wee bairn...such a shame to see a woman blessed with so much power acting like such a coward. And after everything you've been through! You killed that wolf with such fierceness! Gave birth alone! Trained with the strongest warriors! Where's it all gone, child?"

At this, Arhianna lost all sense of caution and clambered toward the voice, struggling against tree limbs and fumbling over large roots. Branches snagged against all her limbs, as if the trees were reaching out to hold her back. *How can this be?* For her father, the trees had burst apart in his wake, as if formed of nothing but coal dust, but they were real enough for her.

"Where are you?" she cried in frustration, yanking her sleeve free of a thorny branch. "Show yourself!"

"I'm right here," a voice said behind her.

Arhianna turned around and saw an old woman in the clearing where she had left Gethen. She stood by his side, stroking his coat with admiration. "Fine steed, lass. Fine steed."

Arhianna went back to the clearing, never taking her eyes off the old woman. "I know you, Crone—" she realized with a shock. "You came to me in Gloucester—you warned me I was being hunted."

The woman nodded. "I did. I was deeply grieved to hear the hunter found his quarry, and about what you suffered at his hands."

Arhianna felt a jolt of rage at the memory, now further embittered by Niamh's death. The pain of losing her friend eclipsed any satisfaction she had milked from the torture she had made Ingvar endure. But she shared nothing of this with the crone. "Who are you?"

The old woman laughed. "To the world, I am Queen of the Underworld, Keeper of the Cauldron, Consort to Arawn." With the declaration of each title, her face changed, like the phases of the moon. The crags and lines smoothed out and took on a youthful glow, then fleshed into a woman in her prime, then once again withered and furrowed back into folds of wisdom.

Arhianna could not believe her luck. *Cerridwen!* "Where's my daughter?" she blurted, voice trembling. She suddenly felt terrified Cerridwen would disappear before telling her, or, worse, refuse to. She kept her eyes pinned on her, refusing to blink, ready to grab her at the slightest sign of flight.

"She is where she is meant to be, as are you. When she comes of age, her whereabouts shall be revealed to you. Until then, I will continue to keep her hidden."

Arhianna's disappointment curdled into anger. "Why? What do you care what happens to her? She's no one to you! Why are you doing this? Is this revenge for what my father did? Was it you who made Arawn call him here to this horrible place?"

Cerridwen's eyes widened into a menacing glare. "You're a fool. I can make Arawn do nothing. And you know nothing of what that child means to me or anyone else. You're selfish and ambitious, Daughter of Lucia—grown arrogant from the gifts of your bloodline and brittle from your suffering, as I was when I walked the earth. You would do well to hear my counsel and change your ways. I have come to help you. Will you accept? Decide now, and quickly. I'll not offer it again."

Arhianna stood mute in the clearing, fighting back tears as she considered her predicament. She had no solid plan for finding Cú Chulainn, and after what had happened at the edge of the lake, she knew she would indeed be a fool not to accept Cerridwen's offer. "Yes," she nodded. "I will accept your help. Thank you."

Cerridwen smiled a toothless smile. Arhianna watched in amazement as teeth grew from her gums and her cheeks filled out. The loose flesh on her neck and forearms receded, becoming taut once more, and her crow's feet disappeared. Within moments, the crone was gone, transformed into young woman her own age. "I need a body more suited for such work," she explained. "Come with me."

Arhianna followed her away from the lake. They traveled for quite some time, Cerridwen dispelling trees into clouds of smoke with her hands, as her father had done, clearing a path through the tangled black forest. At last, they emerged on the other side, the forest once again standing between them and the lake.

"Where are we going?" Arhianna inquired.

"To Arawn's fortress." Cerridwen mounted Gethen. "Climb up, child. We've a long way to go."

Arhianna climbed astride Gethen behind her, noting how small she was. The moment she settled into the saddle, Gethen took off at a gallop. The hound bayed with delight and charged ahead, forging the way, again, like a white beacon.

Arhianna watched the strange countryside roll and twist, shifting into shapes and shadows as Gethen furrowed a path through the darkness toward the ominous clutch of the mountains on the far side of the lake. Her heart pounded in anticipation of entering the fortress so often described by her father in the gory bedtime tales he had told her and Gareth. Next to his tale of the white dragon, it was her favorite—how he had first met the great and terrible Arawn, Lord of the Underworld.

Gethen charged through the valley into the ever-rising foothills with a tireless gallop, his mane dancing back and forth as his hooves hurled up chunks of strange silver turf behind them. The hound disappeared and reappeared often. At times, Arhianna spied her on the crest of a hill far in the distance, whole body tense, ears pricked for the sound of Gethen's hooves and nose poised for scent. Once satisfied they were still following her, she blazed ahead once more.

They came to a dark, narrow slit in the mountains where the path grew steep and rocky. Gethen remained undaunted, climbing at an even pace on sure hooves. The hound stayed close, now, waiting for them at the crest of each ridge until they caught up to her. After several switchbacks, the pass widened into a rocky plateau and revealed the fortress, held fast within the rocky knuckles of the mountain's grasp. An alarmingly narrow bridge without any visible rails or supports led to its open gates. Nothing but blackness beckoned from within. *The bridge,* Arhianna marveled.

Cerridwen dismounted and stroked Gethen's neck. "He'll wait for us here."

The hound was clearly eager to return to her master's hall. She bounded across the bridge and waited for them on the other side. Cerridwen strode out onto the bridge without hesitation. Arhianna followed close behind her, fascinated by the vast expanse of space on either side. An ocean of air lay beneath them, inhabited by nothing but strands of mist and strange, mournful sounds.

Once across, Cerridwen took down a torch from the wall. "Make use of your gift, child."

Arhianna set the torch alight, and Cerridwen plunged into the dark maw of the fortress, the white hound by her side.

Inside, the terrifying tales of her childhood came to life. The skeletons of warriors flanked both sides of the long high passageway, spears in hand. Tiny points of light burned within their eye sockets and ribcages. They bowed toward Cerridwen as she passed, the gruesome sound of stretching vertebrae echoing down the hall. A thrill filled Arhianna's chest. "Who were they?"

"The warriors I resurrected with the Cauldron during my mortal life. After Arawn ended the battle in the grove, he ushered them all into the Underworld. Some were able to pass into the Summerlands. Some were not. I appealed to Arawn, on their behalf, for I felt responsible for them. He granted me permission to bring them here, to serve as my warriors. They are free to return to the lake and attempt to pass into the Summerlands whenever they wish, but until they can actually do so, they enjoy this privilege."

Arhianna felt confused. "My father said he had no power over who sunk into the lake and who didn't."

"He doesn't," Cerridwen confirmed. "Nor do I, or even Arawn. But that's not what we've done. We're simply granting them permission to stay here until they manage to unburden themselves."

Unburden. There was that word again. Arhianna felt a twinge of irritation at how simply her father and Cerridwen referred to the idea—as if one could simply set their grief down, like a heavy sack of grain or a bucket of water. "It's not that simple."

"No, child. It's not easy at all, is it?"

Arhianna regarded the warriors once more, wondering what bonds of shame and horror hung coiled about their souls. *What's keeping them here?* Pondering this gave her an idea. "What do you know of Cú Chulainn? Why is he not singing in the halls of the Summerlands with his people? From what I understand, he was a hero without rival while he lived."

Cerridwen turned her palms up. "One can guess, but he is the only one who truly knows. You will have to ask him that question yourself."

They emerged from the long passage and entered the vast vaulting hall of her father's stories. Arawn's enormous throne loomed directly across from them, on a dais some ten feet in the air.

"Come and look," Cerridwen commanded, walking to the edge of a brazier that occupied the center of the hall. It stood on three large feet, the shape of dragon talons, and was so large its rim came up to Arhianna's waist. She stood at its edge and looked in, taking great care not to touch it or lean against it.

A wave of Cerridwen's hand revealed a miniature scene of the Lake of the Dead surrounded by the dark forest of Glyn Cuch and the sharp crags of the Crone Mountains. On the far side of the brazier, Arhianna spied her father's hill and hall surrounded by slow-moving, wispy clouds.

Cerridwen motioned toward the lake. "Keep your eyes on the lake, and watch for the Winged Ones. Study how they rescue the chosen. Some succeed, some fail. Those doomed to the lake will do everything in their power to prevent the Chosen from being rescued. They are always watching. Always waiting."

"What happens to those who fail?"

"If they manage to drag you under, you'll be held captive by the worst of them until you agree to carry them back to the world of the living. But you must not. Were you to do so, you would bring horrible suffering into the world."

Arhianna shook her head. "I won't do it."

"That's easy for you to say now. You haven't seen the horrors that live beneath those waters. What you saw by the lakeside is nothing."

Arhianna did not want to think about what she had seen at the lakeside. *I simply cannot fail.*

Arhianna peered closely yet saw nothing fly over the lake but an occasional raven. "Where are the Winged Ones? I don't see them."

"They will come." Cerridwen stepped away from the edge and began walking away.

Arhianna turned around. "Wait—where are you going?"

"I have many things I must attend to."

"You're leaving me? I thought you were going to help me!"

Cerridwen laughed. "I have! You have a safe vision of the lake and all the soldiers of the Underworld at your disposal—what more do you want? I can't fetch him for you!"

Arhianna felt at a loss. "But—how will I find him? How will he know I'm coming for him, or even what I look like?"

"I'm afraid that's up to you, child." Cerridwen called out a command, and a clicking sound came out of the darkness. A skeleton warrior emerged from the hall.

"Should you need anything, he is yours to command."

Arhianna stared at the macabre warrior, her skin crawling. But she was wise enough not to show it. "Thank you, Lady Cerridwen. I'm grateful for your help."

"Should you wish to sleep or eat, there are rooms that way." She pointed across the hall toward a dark archway. Arhianna swiftly decided she was neither tired nor hungry.

Cerridwen turned away, walked out of the throne room and disappeared, leaving Arhianna alone with her strange new servant. *Now what?* He had no skin and no organs. There were only three signs of life within him—two bluish lights within his eye sockets, and a white, iridescent ball of light within his ribcage, mottled with greyish bruise-like areas. "Do you have a name?"

The skeleton opened his jaw and pointed to the empty space.

"Ah. You cannot speak."

He shook his head.

"I understand."

She did not know what else to say, so turned back to the scene contained within the brazier, watching for any sign of the Winged Ones. Many times, she thought she caught sight of one, but it always turned out to be a raven.

Then, before she saw it herself, the skeleton warrior's sharp finger pointed toward a pair of wings approaching from the opposite side of the brazier. Arhianna moved around for a closer look and saw the body of a man beneath the wings. *At last!* "Thank you," she whispered to her mute companion. She watched as the man circled the lake, his giant wings casting wide long shadows across the water below. She noticed the longer she stared at a particular place or thing, the larger it became. She now had a closer view of the part of the lake she had been focusing on. The shadows of the man's wings soon attracted attention. The water began to agitate. Hands came rising out of the lake, reaching toward the man flying above them. He flew closer, skimming so close to the surface that Arhianna feared for him.

A few times, a hand shot out of the water and nearly grabbed his foot or wrist.

After a while, he vaulted back out of reach and circled the lake again, until he came once more to the place where he had nearly been caught.

"He knows the one he's looking for is there," Arhianna mumbled. She turned to the skeleton. "Doesn't he?"

The skeleton nodded.

"How?"

The skeleton shrugged and turned up his bony hands.

You must use the right bait, her father had said. *But what good is bait if you have no line or pole? Or know where to fish?* That gave her an idea. *I could ask my new servant to search the lake for Cú Chulainn.*

"Could you get a message to the one I'm looking for?"

Instead of answering, the skeleton's finger shot out in alarm toward the lake. Arhianna turned in time to see the winged man struggling over the water. There were at least four pairs of hands attached to his limbs, all pulling him down toward the water.

Arhianna gasped. "No!" She gripped the lip of the brazier, leaning over the edge to get as close to the scene as she dared. The man flapped his wings frantically, struggling to pull away from the surface of the lake, but he could not break free.

"He's not going to make it." She realized, turning with horror toward her companion, who shook his skull. She forced herself to watch as the man finally succumbed to the grasping hands and sank into the lake. His wings were the last things to disappear beneath the water.

Arhianna's heart thumped at the memory of the corpse lurching out of the lake and nearly grabbing her ankles. She could easily have suffered the same fate, not so long ago. She stepped away from the brazier and paced the hall. The skeleton warrior stayed where he was, awaiting her orders, she suspected. She began to ask questions.

"Can you enter the lake and return?"

The skeleton nodded.

"Can you bring the dead back with you?"

The skeleton shook his skull.

Well, it was worth a try. "Can the dead leave the lake without the help of a Winged One?"

Once again, the skeleton shook his skull.

"Do you know who Cú Chulainn is? Do you think you could find him?"

The skeleton nodded.

"Yet you cannot speak," Arhianna whispered to herself. *So you cannot deliver a message for me.* She paced a while longer, this time around the brazier, round and round, all the time watching the surface of the lake. At times, Winged Ones appeared, and, true to Cerridwen's statement, some succeeded in their task, and some did not.

She thought of writing a message. *But can Cú Chulainn even read? And, even if I had parchment and ink, once under the water, the paper would fall apart, and the ink will run.*

Around and around the brazier she wandered, over and over. Again, she spied a Winged One and stopped to watch. This time, to her joy, the Winged One succeeded, diving with the speed and force of a falcon. She snatched her charge and rose back into the sky with such precision, Arhianna gasped. As she vaulted skyward, it seemed to Arhianna that her wings were expanding; growing larger and more powerful, as if they were adapting to the task of carrying two. Down below in the lake, the hands lashed about, like a school of strange fish in the throes of a feeding frenzy. She watched the lake a while longer, realizing without the skills she had just witnessed, she would fail. *If it can be done, I can do it, but I must practice.*

She looked at her ghastly companion. "Come with me. If I fail, I order you to enter the lake and pull me out—even if you must summon all your brothers from the hall."

He nodded in acquiescence.

She turned away from the brazier and made her way toward the main gates. The white hound that had been resting at the foot of Arawn's throne leapt up and followed her, as did her silent, skeletal companion, his bony feet clicking behind them.

Arhianna felt a wave of relief when she spied Gethen on the other side of the chasm that separated the fortress from the rest of the Underworld. She smiled and kept her eyes on him as she crossed the bridge. He nuzzled her cheek in greeting once she reached the other side. "Oh, you beautiful beast," she cooed, stroking his neck. "We must go back to the lake, my friend. I've work to do." She climbed astride and motioned for her new friend to do likewise.

They set off down the rocky trail, winding back down through the foothills and into the black tangle of Glyn Cuch, until the trees grew so thick that they could scarcely pick their way through. Arhianna dismounted, drew *Dyrnwyn* and slashed madly at limbs and branches, sending them spinning in shards of splintered shadow in all directions. The violent exertion forced the fear from her stomach, leaving no place for it to burrow in and weaken her. She carved her way to the lake. Once again on its shores, she turned to the skeleton warrior. "You will come for me if I should fall?"

He nodded.

"You will not rest until you find me? No matter how long it takes?"

He shook his skull.

She gathered her courage and reached out her hand and forearm to acknowledge their pact. He grasped her arm with surprising strength, pressing his finger bones deep into her flesh. "Thank you." She let go of him, and he of her.

As if Gethen and the white hound knew what she was about to do, they ventured closer. She glanced their way and back to the skeleton warrior. "Take them back to the fortress. I'll fly back at sunset. If there is no sign of me by the time night falls, come and find me."

The skeleton nodded, bowed and backed away, leading Gethen and the hound back into the forest.

Once they had disappeared, Arhianna turned to face the cold, grey expanse of the lake. Her heart thumped as she secured her weapons, wondering how useful they would be to her on her quest. *They can't kill the dead, but they could sever heads and limbs—that would at least slow them down, wouldn't it?*

A cold breeze snaked its way around her clothes, like an intruder running his hands along the edges of doors and windows, looking for a way in. "I'll not suffer you to be my enemy," she murmured to the wind. "You will serve me, instead." She stretched and flapped her dark wings, testing their strength, pushing this way and that until she rose into the air.

The surface of the lake stirred. Smooth-lined wakes began streaming in her direction. Fear stoked her efforts, and she flapped her wings harder, vaulting herself above the trees where the air currents were stronger. She soon learned each feather could tell her something unique about the angle and direction of the breeze, whispering to her in a language not of sound, but of touch; of a thousand tiny trembles triggered by the changes in the air around her.

For hours, she flew in circles, experimenting with her altitude and speed. Any unexpected burst of wind sent her heart racing and wings flapping until she learned how to correct her course.

She remained in the air the entire day, committed to the level of practice she had grown accustomed to at Dun Scáthach. No one went to bed without pain singing from every muscle. *Tonight shall be no different,* she told herself. *Nor tomorrow night, nor the next.*

When the sun began to set, she flew back toward the ghastly peaks of the Crone Mountains and into their shadowy clutch. She felt relieved to see Gethen grazing on the grassy plateau before flying across the chasm and into the dark mouth of Arawn's fortress. She tucked her wings in tightly and sailed through the corridor lined with skeletal guardians and burst into the main hall. The white hound jumped up from the foot of Arawn's throne and barked furiously as Arhianna threw her feet forward and pulled back with her wings to reverse her forward momentum. She succeeded in finding the ground without breaking any bones, but there would be bruises.

The hound bounded toward her. She closed her wings around her to protect her face and body, but once close enough to bite, the hound ceased barking.

"It's me," Arhianna confirmed from behind the shelter of her wings.

She then heard the clicking of bone feet on the floor and opened her wings to see a skeleton warrior walking toward her. At first, she was not sure it was the same warrior as before, but when he got close enough, she recognized the shape of the crack along his forehead and his surprisingly straight upper teeth. The skeleton warrior held out a hand to help her to her feet and motioned toward the dark hall Cerridwen had pointed out earlier.

She felt tired enough, now, that she no longer cared what might roam those chambers. The warrior walked beneath the archway, leading her down a long corridor clearly carved directly into the mountain. Whatever remained of Arhianna's anxiety vanished when she caught a whiff of something hearty in the air.

The corridor culminated in a cavern that reminded her of the Great Chamber of Dun Scáthach. This one, too, opened out to the world below and beyond. A fire, now low to its coals, licked around the bottom of a black pot hanging over it, the source of the delicious smell. In the corner lay a bed with a pile of furs large enough for an entire family to sleep in.

Arhianna did not know what purpose this chamber normally served, but she doubted it was to house a guest. She looked at the skeleton warrior, her initial hesitation having turned to genuine affection. "You did this for me, didn't you?"

He nodded.

"Thank you. I'll fly back to the lake at sunrise. Again, if I'm not back by sunset, come for me."

He nodded, bowed, and left her.

At dawn, or what seemed to resemble it, Arhianna summoned the courage to fly out of the cavern, over the vast chasm below, and down to the lake. She hoped she might meet others like herself and ask their advice. She had seen a few the day before, but they had either been wholly engaged in their endeavors or had ignored her attempts to catch her attention. She did not know which.

You don't need their advice, she counseled herself. *Just do this and get out of here.* She could feel the slow depressive ache of the Underworld seeping into her spirit and feared what an extended stay in such a place might do to her.

It went against every instinct she had to fly out over the water, and she soon learned why. The moment she did, the weight of a thousand eyes lanced toward her, as if they had grappling hooks attached to them. It took far more effort to stay aloft. That, along with the feelings of regret invoked by the smell of the water below, made her intended task of surveying the entire lake seem impossible.

I'm not strong enough for this yet!

As if sensing her weakness, the pull of the eyes within the lake strengthened, drawing her closer to the surface. She fought to regain the distance.

Damn you, Morrigan! I can't do this!

Again, the pull of the eyes strengthened, heightening Arhianna's panic. She pumped her wings, aiming for the sanctuary of Glyn Cuch. The moment she found herself above its trees, she shot some thirty feet into the air, so strong had the pull been upon her.

The lightness of her being felt liberating, and she let out a sigh of relief as the pain of her straining muscles released. For a while, she relished the joy of flying, sailing with ease upon the wind. But soon, the call of the lake returned. She eyed it with renewed determination. She channeled her fear into will, filling her wings with its power, and flew back out over the lake. She felt prepared for the pull when it came and remained resolute. "You'll not have me!" she yelled down at the reaching hands.

She resolved to fly the full perimeter of the lake before the sun set, to strengthen her wings. *That, at least, I shall do today.* She let no whisper of doubt enter her mind and flew with purpose, glancing down at the lake only long enough to ensure she had not flown too close to the surface. She had to occasionally fly over the forest to rest, but she did not allow herself to land until she had flown the entire shoreline and returned to the place she had started from.

She flew back to the fortress at sunset, resolved to resume her labors the following morning.

Her skeleton servant was waiting at the opening of the cavern for her. She smiled at the sight of him, surprised by her growing affection for him.

"I circled the lake today," she announced with pride.

He could do nothing but nod, of course. He motioned to the fire, where food awaited her once more.

"Thank you."

He bowed and left.

Arhianna sailed out from the fortress, on ever-strengthening wings, to circle the lake until she could do it in half the time without seeking relief over the forest. Then, she worked on crossing the lake's numerous bays. She started with the smallest ones, perhaps a few miles wide, then attempted the larger, until there was nothing left to do but cross its entire length. It took her three days to muster the courage to attempt it, but, when she did, she succeeded.

With renewed confidence, she practiced diving down close enough to the water to snatch a leaf or twig, or anything she could spy bobbing upon the surface. She knew these were simple, light objects, nowhere near the weight of a body, but to come that close to the surface without being caught was a feat she had to master. She grew accustomed to being grabbed at and learned how to dive and dart, increasing her agility in flight. She became confident enough to risk diving into the water and flying back out. Sometimes a soul would grasp her as she flew out, but she always kept her sword ready to slice herself free.

Every night, her skeleton warrior stood waiting in her cavern chamber, with a fire made and food prepared. Over the passing days, she grew accustomed to the macabre. Death and decay lost their cold grip on her heart until she no longer feared the dark, clammy corridors of the fortress, the scores of skeletal warriors that roamed them, or the cries that rose up from the misty chasms of the Crone Mountains.

One night, when she arrived back from the lake, she felt surprised to be greeted not by her skeleton warrior, but by Cerridwen.

"You're making progress, I see."

"I've grown much stronger," Arhianna replied.

Cerridwen nodded. "You've managed to rescue a good many leaves and twigs from the lake, but the dead don't care about them. When you try to rescue Cú Chulainn, things shall be different."

Arhianna felt deflated. "I know that!"

"And, once you decide you are ready, how shall he know where to meet you?"

Arhianna had a plan for this. It had come to her the day after she had realized her skeleton warrior could enter the lake. She reached under her tunic and removed a chain from around her neck. Connla's spectacular ring hung at the end of it, its gems glittering in the firelight as it swayed back and forth. "This is Cú Chulainn's ring. He gave it to Scáthach when their son Connla was born. He bid she give it to Connla when he grew to manhood so that he would know him by it. When I'm ready, I'll send my warrior into the lake with it. Cú Chulainn is sure to follow him."

Cerridwen smiled. "Aren't you clever? How did you come by this prize?"

Cerridwen's approval filled Arhianna with confidence, making it easier to admit her theft. "I stole it from Connla's tomb at Dun Scáthach."

Cerridwen raised her brows. "It's almost as if you knew you would be sent to find him."

Of course, there was no way Arhianna could have predicted such a thing, but she had to admit, her theft had proven providential. "I didn't. I stole it out of anger."

Cerridwen took the ring and inspected it. "Such a crime will bring the wrath of Scáthach upon you. Not something you want. Now you have twice as many reasons to rescue Cú Chulainn, for only his intervention shall curb her anger. You cannot return to the living without him."

Arhianna knew the truth when she heard it. "I won't fail."

"See that you don't."

Cerridwen handed the ring back just as Arhianna's skeleton warrior entered the chamber carrying her supper. She smiled at the sight of him. "Please—tell me his name. I've grown very fond of him."

Cerridwen raised her brows. "Have you?"

"I have."

"I suspect he is quite fond of you as well. You are related."

Arhianna felt a jolt of fear. "We are?"

"Yes. His name is Gareth."

My brother? Arhianna felt sick and nearly fell to her knees.

Cerridwen raised a hand. "Not your brother, child. His namesake. Your father's cousin, from long ago.

Arhianna let out a huff of relief. "Oh, thank the gods."

Cerridwen motioned Gareth forward. "He was one of the men who suffered at my hands. I suspect he does not even know your father rules in Arawn's place."

"Why is that?"

"Because your father refused Arawn's offer to live here in the fortress. A foolish choice, if you ask me."

Arhianna had no desire to hear why Cerridwen thought her father had been foolish. Instead, she turned her attention toward

Gareth. "I'm Bran's daughter. He named my brother after you. Did you know that?"

Though there was naught but a skeleton left of him, it seemed to Arhianna that Gareth seemed moved by the news. He hung her supper over the fire and ventured closer, looking at her as if for the first time.

Inspired, Arhianna hung the chain with Cú Chulainn's ring around his neck. "Lord Gareth, I need you to go to the lake and seek out Cú Chulainn. Lead him to the shallows on the side of the lake closest to my father's hill and wait there for me."

Gareth grasped the ring within his bony grip and bowed his head.

As awkward as it seemed to do so, Arhianna could not suppress the desire to give him an embrace. She felt him tentatively reach around her and return it. She smiled. In that moment, she knew they would not fail. "Tomorrow, my friend, you and I will rescue Cú Chulainn," she whispered. She gave Cerridwen a look of resolve.

Arhianna called for Gareth the moment dawn broke the next morning. She soon heard the clicking sound of his feet and the thud of his spear shaft upon the stones. He appeared in the cavern and bowed his head.

"Good morning, Gareth. I shall carry you to the lake today. Do you consent?"

He raised his head slowly, moving tentatively in her direction. He did not seem to know what to do next.

Arhianna had thought for some time on the best way to carry him and motioned for him to climb upon her back. "Grip my shoulders and wrap your legs around me."

Gareth hesitated, but at her insistence, eventually did as she asked.

His bony form felt like a cage upon her back, as if she were a merchant taking birds to market. Once she felt his arms and legs grasp her firmly enough—again, at her insistence—she spread her wings and soared out over the chasm. Soon they were flying over Glyn Cuch. Arhianna aimed for the shallows near her father's hill, where she had seen the most successful rescues take place, and

103

landed on the widest expanse of shoreline running alongside them. She felt Gareth's grip release and turned to face him, breathless from the flight. It dawned on her that perhaps he might fear going into the lake. "Are you willing to do this for me?" she asked, ashamed she had never considered how he might feel about it.

He nodded and bowed his head in reply.

She unsheathed *Dyrnwyn,* and it flamed to life. "Take this with you. I've no idea if it will help within those waters, but it's the sword of my father's clan—your clan." She held it out to him. "Take it—for courage, if nothing else."

Gareth did not hesitate. He took up the sword and swung it a few times, with a strength and swiftness that caused Arhianna to gasp. Up until then, she had assumed he and the others like him to be capable of nothing but what a skeleton could manage. That was clearly not the case. He commanded the weapon with as much force and skill as any of the warriors at Dun Scáthach.

"Good luck," she said, feeling more confident than ever about her plan.

He nodded, turned, and walked into the shallows.

She watched him until his skull and the flaming tip of *Dyrnwyn* both disappeared beneath the surface.

Now, there was nothing for her to do but wait. She flew up into the shelter of a tree, where nothing could lurch out of the water and snatch at her, and settled in. She had no idea how long it would take Gareth to succeed—or if he would succeed at all. She could only wait and hope.

Two days passed, and Gareth still had not returned. The food Arhianna had brought was nearly gone, and the smell of regret coming off the lake had begun to drive her mad. Visions of giving up her daughter, of Jørren's murder, of Ragna's face when she had left her, and of Niamh tumbling over the cliffs at Dun Scáthach tormented her, night and day, like biting insects, never giving her a moment's rest.

Where is he? What's happened? she thought for the thousandth time, staring at the placid surface of the lake. *Perhaps I've sent him to a fate worse than the one he was already suffering.*

She climbed down from the tree and paced the shore. *Perhaps he needs help.* After an hour of deliberating, she flew back to Arawn's fortress and addressed the legion of warriors in the halls. "One of your kinsmen is lost in the lake. He was helping me with a task for Morrigan. Who will help me retrieve him?"

Every bony foot clicked forward, and Arhianna felt a dark chilling thrill at the sight and sound of it. At her request, they marched out of the hall and across the bridge. Arhianna took to the sky and flew above them like a dark, feathered general, circling at times. Their white skulls gleamed like a string of pearls below her, twisting through the dark landscape to the lake, where, one by one, without hesitation, they disappeared beneath the water.

Arhianna soared out over the lake, her confidence renewed. She flew close to the surface, peering down into its depths for any sign of *Dyrnwyn's* blue flames, calling out Gareth's name. Hands reached for her, eyes pulled at her, but she did not give up. Occasionally, a hand managed to snatch a feather or two from her wings, sending pinches of pain through her body. She allowed it only to fuel her will.

Around the lake she went, time after time, until the flash of a blue flame caught her eye. *There he is!* Like a tern, she hovered above the spot where she had seen the flash.

The dead began to gather, like sharks smelling blood in the water. She pumped her wings and rose higher, her eyes pinned on the flash of the blue flames below. She waited until some of her warriors caught up to her. "Surround whoever holds that sword!" she cried. "Let no one touch me!"

Once she could see the circle of skulls form around the flames, she summoned her courage. She pointed her head toward the flames and tucked her arms and wings tightly against her body. Like an arrow shot from a bow, she entered the water with such force she soon encountered the source of the flames—it was indeed *Dyrnwyn,* but to her dismay, it was not Gareth who wielded it, but another—a warrior who reminded her of the Saxon brutes employed by Ingvar. Perhaps more shocking, she found she could breathe. Baffled, she looked up. Indeed, she saw the surface of the lake above her head, but it seemed like a strange version of the sky, nothing more. She regarded the man before her with contempt. "What have you done with the man who wielded that sword?"

The brute laughed. "Man? I'd not call that creature a man. He was a mere servant of Arawn! A sack of bones!"

Arhianna's rage doubled in on itself. She grabbed her dagger. "Where is he?"

The warrior laughed again. "Woman, I'm dead already, don't you know that? Your threats mean nothing."

Arhianna did not hesitate and slashed the dagger across his throat and then stabbed him in the heart, merely because it gave her pleasure to do so. By this time, corpses from the lake had nearly overcome her warriors. She knew what would happen if she did not escape.

She released a burst of flames all around her, yet it held them back but a moment. The warrior laughed. "They do my bidding, foolish woman. As will you. You serve me now."

The corpses closed in from all sides. She fought beside her warriors, fending them off as best she could, sending blue flames in enormous arcs all around her.

"What a wildcat you are! You fight as if you were trained by Scáthach herself!" He chuckled, the sound strange and distorted in the air. She did fight well, but it was not a fight she could win, and she knew it. She had learned that much at Dun Scáthach. Just when she felt she could not manage to coax one more blast of fire from her hands, the corpses began to turn away from her. The rest of the warriors she had sent to the lake appeared behind her attackers. She felt relieved to see Gareth marching in front of them, the ring still hanging about his neck. Hope filled her chest. She knew she had been given her moment and did not waste it.

With a powerful surge of her wings, she thrust herself up toward the surface of the lake and into the sky above, but, unfortunately, not without a passenger. She looked down to see the warrior who had stolen her father's sword hanging from her leg. His slit throat gaped open, but no blood flowed from it. She attempted to shake him loose; to pry his hands away, but his grip was firm. She did not have the strength to struggle with him there, over the lake, so flew with all the strength as she could muster, aiming for Glyn Cuch.

Once the pull of the lake released her, she positioned herself over a muddy piece of shoreline and then, with all her strength, clubbed her stowaway square in the forehead with the butt of her dagger. He let go and fell a good twenty feet to the ground below.

106

The squishy slap of his body against the mud brought a smile to her face. She hovered over him, just out of reach, sneering. "How would you like to fight the true owner of that sword?" She thought of her father and wished he were there. "Why don't you challenge him? I dare you!"

The warrior laughed as he sat up. "I fear no man, living or dead! I am Cú Chulainn, Hound of Ulster!" He stood up and grinned at her. He swiped the air with *Dyrnwyn*. "Now, be a good lass and come back down. I don't want to hurt you."

The irony was more than Arhianna could bear. *Mistress, no. How can this be the man you seek to lead your army?* She shook her head in disbelief and landed in front of him. "Did you know the man you stole my sword from had your ring?" She pointed to Gareth, now standing on the shore along with the warriors from the fortress, awaiting her orders. "The one you gave Scáthach to give to your son when he came of age? Or did you not notice it hanging about his neck? It's not as if he's wearing anything else!" She scoffed, irritated by how long she had suffered by the side of that dismal lake as a result of his ignorance. "Though I suppose if you didn't notice it on the finger of your own son, I was foolish to expect you would notice it this time."

Her blow hit its mark, and the moment it did, she wished she could take it back. Cú Chulainn's face transformed from that of a self-satisfied brute to looking like a man who had just been stabbed in the heart. He stared at the ring but said nothing. Then he dropped the sword on the sand, turned, and began walking back down into the lake.

Arhianna panicked. "Wait!"

The water was up to his waist before he turned around and looked at her. "You're right. I didn't notice. Not this time, and not the last. I murdered my own son, born of the greatest love of my life. And for that, I deserve to rot here for eternity." He continued descending until his head disappeared beneath the water.

"No!" Arhianna splashed in after him and grabbed him by the hair, yanking him back up. In a sudden rage, he turned around, picked her up and threw her back onto the shore. She hit the ground hard but scrambled to her feet. "Bring him back!" she cried to Gareth and his skeletal brothers-in-arms. Thanks to her training at Dun Scáthach, she was never unprepared. She tossed Gareth a coil of rope she had been carrying around her shoulder. "Bind him and bring him to me."

Like a swarm of spiders, the army of the Underworld descended upon Cú Chulainn, bound him, and dragged him back to shore. He struggled against his bonds like a wild animal caught in a snare, lurching and twisting as if possessed by a horde of demons. Gareth returned to her side, removed the chain with the ring on it from around his neck, and bowed. "Thank you," she said. "For this, and for saving my life. I couldn't have done this without you." She put her arms around his frame, imagining him as he might have looked in life. "There are loved ones waiting for you in the Summerlands. Do you remember? Think of them. Think of them and remember."

Gareth looked out across the water. Gradually, the light upon him changed, as if the sun had broken through a small sliver of sky and shone upon him alone.

"You should go to them, don't you think?" She motioned toward the beckoning light.

Gareth took a tentative step upon the water and did not sink. Arhianna felt elated as he then took a few more, his eyes fixed upon the horizon.

"Yes, go to them, Gareth. They're waiting for you!"

Arhianna took flight and accompanied him on his journey across the lake. She watched, with waxing joy, as nerves and veins grew like vines around his skeleton, then muscles formed, then flesh, hair and features, until he was once more a man in his prime.

On the opposite shore, the sky seemed to split apart, revealing green fields awash in the golden light of a summer morning. Arhianna had become so accustomed to the grey listlessness of the Underworld that she had to avert her eyes from the dazzling brightness of color contained within that small sliver of paradise.

"Go!" she called down to him. "Run, Gareth!"

He looked up at her, grinning and smiling, and then ran the rest of the way across the lake into the gap, where figures were indeed waiting for him. The moment he stepped inside, it snapped shut, leaving no trace of its happiness behind.

Encouraged, Arhianna flew back to the shore to collect her prize. He sat motionless on the shore, no fight left in him, his gaze fixed on the horizon. He, too, had glimpsed the Summerlands. She said nothing and sat beside him, doing perhaps what he was—

memorizing every glorious detail of what she had seen. When she felt the moment was right, she spoke. "Let us leave this place," she said to him. "The world has need of you." She took her dagger, cut his bonds, and held out the chain with his ring on it. He said nothing but took it and put it around his neck. "Morrigan has chosen you, so count yourself fortunate."

He scoffed. "And why is that?" he said, the words soft and distant, as if spoken to himself.

"Because whether its redemption or punishment you crave, she can surely deliver it."

Cú Chulainn stood up, pulled the strands of rope from his wide chest and arms, and flung them aside. "I am coming with you for one reason, and it's not for redemption or punishment. Do not presume to know me, woman."

Arhianna, though it was difficult for her, kept her mouth shut. She dared not anger him—not now that she was so close to accomplishing her task. Instead, she bit her tongue, picked up *Dyrnwyn* from the sand, and led the great Cú Chulainn to her father's hill.

The moment Arhianna escorted Cú Chulainn into her father's hall, he knelt and bent his head, no sign of his previous bravado. Arhianna did the same—for the being enthroned at the end of the hall seemed not her father, in that moment, but rather fully the acting servant of Arawn, God of the Underworld. He now looked every bit the part— formidable, awe-inspiring, frightening, and cold as ice. The folds of his cloak draped over the edge of his dais like a sheet of blood, spreading out onto the floor around him. His two ruby-eyed hounds, now reunited, sat erect on their haunches at his feet, as still as if they were carved of white marble.

"Son of Deichtine, you have been chosen by Morrigan to serve the living. I give you my blessing to return and urge you to seek a life worthy of the Summerlands."

Cú Chulainn kept his head down. "Thank you, Great Arawn."

Arhianna dared to glance up at her father. His eyes met hers. "You've done well, Daughter of Lucia. Depart with my blessing. Seek a life worthy of the Summerlands."

Arhianna knew in her heart this would be the last time she would see her father before that day came. "Thank you, Great Arawn," were the words she spoke with her voice, but *I love you, Father,* were those she said to him with her eyes.

"My hounds shall show you the way back." With a nod, they were dismissed.

The hounds accompanied them from the hall, and Gethen stood just outside the gates waiting. Arhianna smiled and climbed astride, but Cú Chulainn simply stared at her, his brow furrowed.

"Well?" she asked, after a moment. "Are you coming or not?"

He pursed his lips. "We're not going to fly out of here?"

He looked so disappointed, Arhianna almost giggled. "I wouldn't mind, but in case you haven't noticed, you don't have wings."

He rolled his eyes. "Don't mock me, woman. You're not strong enough to carry us both?"

Arhianna cocked an eyebrow. "You expect me to carry you?" She felt as if she were taking care of a child who wanted to be chased and swung about.

"Of course! Could there be anything more exciting than seeing the world through a hawk's eyes?"

In truth, Arhianna felt there was not. Despite the dark dreary landscape of the Underworld and her fear of the lake and what lay within it, she had never taken more pleasure in the honing of a skill than she had at mastering her wings. "No. There isn't. But I'm not carrying you anywhere. And stop calling me woman!"

He ignored her comment. "I thought you Winged Ones were supposed to snatch us from the lake and fly us out of here!" He sighed. "You really won't do it?"

"No, I really won't. Get on the horse."

He sighed and climbed up behind her. He leaned forward and spoke in her ear. "If you're not strong enough, why don't you just say so?"

Again, Arhianna bit her tongue but kicked Gethen in the flanks hard enough to send her companion flailing for a handhold. Unfortunately, it ended up being her thigh. He quickly found a place on the saddle to grab instead, and she pretended not to notice.

The hounds led the way down the hill and back toward the road that led past the lake, through the dark tangle of Glyn Cuch, and into the rocky foothills of the Crone Mountains. Just as the sky was turning from grey to darkness, they ran down a slope that ended in front of a cave opening shrouded in mist. There, they stood at its entrance and barked.

"We must be here," Cú Chulainn deduced.

"I believe we are," Arhianna agreed.

Cú Chulainn dismounted and offered a hand to assist her. She acknowledged him but dismounted without his help. She gave Gethen a farewell embrace and kissed him on the muzzle. "Take care of Father," she whispered up at him. He looked at her and shook his mane. "I know you will." She gave him a final pat on the rump, and Gethen trotted off into the twilight. The hounds, however, remained in front of the cave, as if given strict orders to ensure the two of them passed out of the Underworld before they returned home to their master.

Arhianna turned to Cú Chulainn. "Shall we?"

"I suppose it will be a long journey? One that might be made quite a bit shorter if we were flying?"

"I'm not carrying you." She plunged into the darkness of the cave. "Wait! I'm no cat—I can't see in the dark. We need a torch!"

She answered by unsheathing *Dyrnwyn*. "We have one. Or did you forget?"

"I won that sword in combat. It belongs to me by right."

"You won nothing. It belongs to my clan. It was my father's before me, and now it's mine. And, in case you've forgotten, you left it behind." Because he was walking behind her and could not see her face, she indulged in a proud smile.

"I suppose I'd best let you have it your way, woman."

That's it. She whirled around. "I told you stop calling me woman! I have a name, and you will use it!"

Cú Chulainn held up both hands in surrender. "Fine. Why don't you tell me what it is?"

Arhianna felt embarrassed. "Arhianna." It was the first time in moons she had introduced herself by her given name. She had been Ronin for so long, it felt strange to do so.

All the rancor left his expression. "Arhianna. Beautiful name for a beautiful wo—"

Her glare withered his compliment on the vine, and she turned back around, moving deeper into the labyrinth of Oweynagat. "You

111

must have a real name as well. Cú Chulainn, Hound of Ulster—that can't be what your mother named you."

"No." He paused. "She named me Sétanta."

Arhianna smiled to herself. She much preferred this to his war moniker. "May I call you Sétanta?"

"That depends." He chuckled. "May I call you woman?"

She let out a grunt. "Gods. Never mind."

Somehow, there was only ever one passage to follow within the cave, and it eventually led Arhianna and Cú Chulainn to the pasture with the grassy hill where she had first encountered Morrigan. She was there, once more, watching over her prized cattle. Arhianna smiled, thrilled to have succeeded at her task and eager to deliver Cú Chulainn to her mistress. "There she is," Arhianna announced.

"There she is indeed." Cú Chulainn's eyes were round with admiration, feasting on the sight of Morrigan's physical perfection.

Arhianna could not help but shake her head. She turned to chide him but nearly gasped at how changed he was; he was no longer the corpse she had pulled from the lake. He had grown young and strong again; restored to the state she assumed he had been in before he had died. *Does he know? How does he feel?* She decided it would be better for everyone if he remained ignorant of his good looks. His arrogance was by far his worst quality.

"Don't judge me, wo—Arhianna."

"Warhianna, is it now?" She felt so relieved to be free of the heaviness of the Underworld, she ignored his near-miss and enjoyed a good laugh. "I don't fault you. She's a glorious sight. If I were a man, I'm sure I'd feel no less passion than you."

He pinned his eyes on her. "Would you not, then?" he murmured under his breath. Her comment had clearly stoked the fire in his loins, and she refrained from commenting. "Come," she said, leading the way to where Morrigan stood.

Morrigan watched as they climbed the hill and greeted them with a smile. "You've done well, Daughter of Lucia." She turned her eyes on Cú Chulainn. "Welcome to the Borderlands, Son of Deichtine. I hope you have chosen to accept my offer."

"I wouldn't be here if I hadn't. It's an honor. I shall forever be in your debt, Great Morrigan. May I serve you well, for as long as you will have me."

His speech pleased Morrigan. "I'm certain you will. Follow me—we must prepare. There is a great war ahead."

Taliesin

CHAPTER THIRTEEN
Homecoming

Taliesin stood atop Uthyr's fortress wall, gazing out over the town of Caer Leon. The smell of bread and cookfires signaled the start of the day. For him, however, it was but the continuation of another long night. Again, he had dreamt of the Red Dragon. He felt a thrill as the vision of her eyes and words erupted into his mind once more.

"Taliesin?"

Startled, he turned toward the deep voice interrupting his thoughts. Amergin, Archdruid of the Ulaid, stood gazing up at him from the bottom of the stairs.

"At last! Did you find her?"

Taliesin had waited weeks for Amergin to return from his search for Nimue, all the while fearing she had either betrayed him once more or been the victim of treachery.

Amergin nodded. "I did. She is safe, in Affalon."

Taliesin let out a sigh of relief and rubbed the worry from his brow as he descended the stairs. "Why did she leave us like that? I've been worried for weeks."

"She was kidnapped from the ship by Myrthin and Maelwys."

Maelwys? Taliesin shook his head. "No. That's impossible." He gripped the handle of *Straif* and unsheathed it. "I stabbed him with this very dagger."

Amergin raised his brows. "You may well have, but I am telling you he lives. Myrthin deserves the credit for healing him, I'm certain. There are few with such power. He is one of them."

Taliesin felt his heart turn to ice. "He and Nimue." His mind raced. "Perhaps she healed him and this tale of her kidnapping is a lie." The words tasted like poison as he said them.

Amergin's expression turned to stone. "She also has such power, but only on Affalon. Not as Lady Viviaine. She could not have managed such a feat."

Taliesin led Amergin to Igerna's garden, where they could talk privately. Amergin sat down on the boulder beneath the crab apple tree, leaving Taliesin to take the wooden bench Igerna favored. "Where are they, then? My enemies who refuse to die?"

Amergin shrugged. "I know nothing of Maelwys except that he lives. I imagine he has returned to Finbheara or is still searching for

114

your daughter. Myrthin, however, has been dealt with. Nimue has imprisoned him in Affalon and begs your forgiveness."

Taliesin felt impressed, yet wary. "How has she done that?"

Amergin smiled. "Her power in Affalon is supreme. I've no doubt she's managed it. Though, to be fair, Myrthin knows he's no match for her there. He must not have thought he was in any danger. Or else he's a willing captive. He's loved her from the moment they first met. Quite a love affair, that one..."

Taliesin raised a hand. "I don't want to hear it."

And he did not. The thought of his rival making love to Nimue turned his stomach. He resolved to feel content she had made her way home, so he changed the subject. "Maelwys must be found and dealt with. Does your offer to take me as an apprentice still stand?"

Amergin raised his brows. "You would leave Caer Leon?"

Taliesin nodded. "I'd rather not, but if I must, then I shall."

Amergin put a hand on Taliesin's shoulder. "I shall teach you all I know, but you must come to Eire. Now that Nimue is back in Affalon and Myrthin is no longer a threat, my place is there."

Taliesin turned and looked toward the window of the chamber his daughter slept in. *Do I dare leave her, now? And what of Igerna? She'll have to carry the burden of this secret alone. Yet I dare not waste this invitation.* He resigned himself to Amergin's terms. "Then I must go with you to Eire." He glanced once more at his daughter's window. "But I ask we go by way of Gwythno. I have something I must tell my father."

"As you wish."

Heavy-hearted, Taliesin told Igerna his news. She looked at him with such desperation he nearly relented.

"What do you mean, you're leaving? For how long?"

To make matters worse, Morgen lay in her lap, staring up at him in apparent disbelief, her grey-violet eyes so knowing he feared she might start speaking to him, though she was but a few moons old. He reached down and stroked her head, aching to hold her, but fearing he would change his mind if he did. "I'm sorry, but I must go," he croaked. "And I don't know for how long. As long as it takes for me to learn what I must."

Igerna looked at the floor.

"Please, my queen, try to understand—I must become as powerful as our adversaries, or Morgen will never be safe from the Sídhe. Besides, if their spies are still about, they'll be watching two people closely, and I'm one of them. We know Arhianna can't lead them to her, because she doesn't know where she is, but what if they're watching me?" He shot a suspicious glance toward the window and fireplace and lowered his voice. "Can you imagine? One morning, you'll reach for her, and she won't be in the cradle." He tilted his head with yet another horrible thought. "And what's to stop them from taking Arthur as well? We cannot risk such a tragedy."

Igerna met his gaze again, her face drained of color. "Go, then. Learn all you can, as quickly as you can. If something should happen, I'll send word."

He nodded. "I am sorry, my queen. I truly am. But I swear to you, I won't let you down." He glanced at Arthur, asleep in the cradle, and then bent down to kiss his daughter's tiny fist. "Any of you."

Morgen's eyes were pinned on him as he backed away. His heart cringed as he turned and left.

"What do you mean, you're leaving?" Uthyr scowled, his brow furrowing ever deeper the longer Taliesin took to answer. "Half the chieftains in my land insist on druid counsel, yet my wife insists no druid, save you, shall ever set foot in my hall. What am I to do?"

Taliesin turned his palms up in surrender. "This is why I must go. I am but a bard. I haven't completed the deeper studies a druid must undergo. To that end, I'm going to Eire to study with a man who may very well be the most powerful druid alive."

Uthyr raised his brows. "Who?"

"Me," a deep voice said.

Uthyr and Taliesin both jumped at the unexpected interruption and turned to see Amergin standing at the entrance to the hall.

Taliesin collected his wits and motioned toward his future teacher. "Uthyr Pendragon, may I present Amergin of the Ulaid."

Uthyr stood up, taking the measure of Amergin with his eyes. "I hear you wish to take my bard from my hall. Can you not train him here? I'll provide you with anything you need." He held up a hand. "No—make that more than you need."

Amergin shook his head. "You are very generous, Pendragon, but I'm afraid I must return to my order."

Uthyr let out a sigh of exasperation and paced the hall, hands on his hips. "That leaves me with no one but Dubricius, I suppose."

Taliesin had already made peace with this. There were worse men Uthyr could consult than Dubricius, but there was no doubt as to what that counsel would be. He was, after all, an archbishop, and the church's agenda was clear—to turn all hearts away from the old gods of their land toward Christ.

Uthyr sighed. "How long will you be gone?"

Amergin answered on Taliesin's behalf. "Such training is rigorous and would normally take the better part of a young man's life, but Taliesin already knows much—far more than any bard I know. I imagine it will not take him long to gain the knowledge he seeks. I give you my word he shall return to you with far more to offer your kingdom."

Uthyr pinned a tired eye on Taliesin. "Go, then," he muttered. "Learn quickly, and return as soon as you can."

"Thank you, Pendragon." Taliesin bowed his head in respect, smiling to himself at the near identical farewells both he and his queen had given. For all their trials, they were still a mighty couple, united in purpose.

Taliesin left the hall wondering what the price of his absence would be. *What is to become of you, Great Mother, if men like Dubricius succeed in capturing the souls of our people? They worship only one aspect of you, in the mother of Christ; embrace only one of your faces. What of the others? And what's to become of the rest of our beloved gods? Cernunnos and his May Queen, and our Oak and Holly King? What of Arawn in his Underworld, and Arianrhod up in the glory of Caer Sidi? What shall become of them, when our people cease to sing their songs?*

Taliesin shuddered and resolved he would indeed learn as much as he could, as quickly as he could.

Taliesin and Amergin set sail on a trading ship bound for Gwythno the following morning. The winds were kind, enabling them to dock by mid-afternoon. They disembarked into a bustling crowd and wound their way through the seaside market up toward the fortress. They had not been walking long before Taliesin spied a familiar silhouette coming from the opposite direction. *Irwyn, you salty old Saxon!* He smiled and waved.

Irwyn recognized him as well and quickened his pace, grinning as the gap closed between them. He threw his large arms around him. "Taliesin! Your father did not tell me you were coming!"

"He doesn't know," Taliesin confessed. "We left in rather a hurry."

"I see." Irwyn looked over at Amergin, and Taliesin introduced him simply as 'a friend' and then asked about his brother. "I'm looking for Arvel. Do you know where he is?"

Irwyn laughed. "You mean the lad who is going to run the shipyards when I die?"

Taliesin felt relieved. "He's doing well, then?"

Irwyn smiled and shook his head. "He has learned how to build a ship faster than anyone I have ever taught. He knows the sea like no one else."

Taliesin chuckled. *Of course, he does.* "Where can I find him? I have news."

Irwyn pointed toward the grotto that lay on the other side of the fortress. "The day is nearly done. He has gone to swim, as always. He will be back when the sun goes down. I'll bring him to the hall when he returns. I want to hear of your travels."

Taliesin gave him a weak smile at the prospect. He had no desire to speak of his misfortunate travels. Though he had succeeded in finding Arhianna, he had failed to reunite with her. He had betrayed the Pendragon by convincing Queen Igerna to protect he and Arhianna's infant daughter by passing her off as twin sister to her newborn son, Arthur. And, he had brought about the death of his mother by asking her to deliver the infant to Caer Leon. And yet, he

118

nodded to Irwyn. "I'll tell my father. We'll look forward to seeing you this evening."

Taliesin and Amergin reached the fortress and discovered news of their arrival had preceded them. The gates stood open, and Taliesin's father, Elffin, lord of Gwythno, waited just inside. He stood with his feet wide apart, grinning, his arms crossed over a thickening belly. He thrust them out and came forward to enfold Taliesin in a warm embrace. "I thought it'd be years before I saw you again. What brings you back so soon?" Elffin glanced at Amergin. "And who's your companion?"

"Father, this is Amergin of the Ulaid."

"From Eire, then?" He reached out to clasp Amergin's extended arm.

"That I am, Lord Elffin."

"We're famished," Taliesin interrupted, eager for some privacy.

"Forgive me. Of course you are." Elffin clapped Taliesin on the back and put an arm around his shoulders, heading for the hall. "I'll call for food and ale straightaway."

"Thank you, but Amergin is quite tired." Taliesin glanced back at his companion. "We must prepare a bed for him and send supper up."

"My apologies, Lord Elffin." Amergin shot Taliesin a grateful look. "Though I'm certain a good night's rest will restore me. I will be sorry to miss the pleasures of your hall tonight."

"Well, as my son has chosen to surprise me, there's no time to prepare much, I'm afraid. Not that I'm complaining, of course." Elffin summoned a servant and charged him with seeing to Amergin's needs.

"I wish you a good night, then." Amergin inclined his head toward Elffin and followed the servant down the corridor.

Taliesin felt relieved. What he had to say could only be said in private. "Father, could I speak to you alone?"

Elffin raised his brows. "Of course. I've some good wine we can drink. Keep it for myself. Selfish, I know, but an old man with no wife has few pleasures in life."

Taliesin swallowed down the lump in his throat. "I could do with some wine."

Elffin pulled him close. "What's wrong, son? I've missed you. Wish you'd just stay here, but I don't dare ask you to. Always end up disappointed."

Taliesin mustered a smile. It felt good to be held, even briefly, by someone who loved him. He fought the urge to weep and put his hand around his father's waist. He chuckled. "You're eating well, at least."

"As I said, son...few pleasures."

Elffin's chamber was sparse by Gwythno standards. A lone chair sat by the hearth. As promised, a jug of wine stood within arm's reach. Taliesin could not help but picture his father there, in that simple room, drinking alone every night.

"You can sit on that." Elffin motioned toward a nearby wooden chest. "Your young body can take it."

Taliesin pulled the chest next to his father's chair, sat down, and took a cup of wine from his outstretched hand. He took a long draught and sighed. "You're right. This is good. I daresay it's better than the wine the Pendragon serves."

Elffin chuckled. "Uthyr Pendragon is a warrior at heart. I imagine he likes to stay sharp. Wine like this'll make you soft." He patted his belly.

Taliesin smiled but felt it wither on his face under the weight of what he had to say. "Father, I have to tell you something, and I fear it's going to break your heart, but I'm hoping my other news might soften the blow a bit."

Elffin's expression darkened. He leaned forward, eyes closed, took a deep breath, let it out, and then opened his eyes again. "Go on."

"Mother is..." Taliesin paused, unable to bear the weight of the words. He held his breath a moment, fighting the rising tide of sorrow swelling up in his chest, but it was no use. The moment he tried to say the word *gone*, he broke down into sobs, like a child of three, hunching forward into his hands.

"In the Summerlands?" His father finished for him.

Taliesin could only nod. He felt his father's hand squeeze his shoulder. Neither of them said anything for some time. Only the logs dared break the silence, crackling beneath the flames in the hearth.

"How?"

For moons, Taliesin had pondered what he was going to say to his father. Though he ached to, he could not tell him about Morgen. "She died at sea."

To Taliesin's relief, his father did not ask any further questions. He simply sat in silence, staring into the fire, and Taliesin let him. After a long spell of stillness, Elffin refilled their cups and raised his, addressing the heavens. "To my beloved Ula, the most beautiful creature I have ever known, and the only woman I have ever loved."

Taliesin raised his cup, drank, and then, after what he felt was an appropriate period of silence, reached over and gripped his father's hand. "There's more, Father."

Elffin expelled a heavy sigh. "Gods, that's not enough?"

Taliesin looked his father in the eye. "You have another son. A true son, of your blood, borne of Ula."

The creases in Elffin's brow deepened. His mouth fell open to speak, but no words came forth. At last, he croaked, "What?"

"Arvel, Father. Arvel is your son. That's why I brought him here." He held up a hand. "And before you say anything, you need to know how sorry I am—Mother made me swear not to tell you, just as she made everyone swear—but before she died, I convinced her to see how wrong it was of her. She wanted you to know. She wanted your forgiveness."

Elffin pulled his hand back, turned away and stared blankly at the wall. "How long have you known?"

"Only a few moons, Father."

Elffin put his face in his hands and crumpled forward on his elbows.

Taliesin put his arm around his father's shoulders, praying Arvel and Irwyn would not arrive until his father had had time to process this shocking news.

Elffin's muffled question rose up, his face still buried in his hands. "Why didn't she tell me?"

Taliesin shook his head. "She feared you'd try to turn him into a lord. Thought it was better for him to grow up with her people. But,

121

in the end, she knew she'd made a mistake. I told her you'd forgive her."

Elffin stood up and paced. "I can't believe this."

Taliesin's heart ached for his father. "I couldn't either. I was so angry after she told me, I couldn't speak to her for a week."

Elffin sat back down and put his forehead back into his hands. "I need some time to myself, if you don't mind."

Taliesin realized he had made a terrible mistake inviting Irwyn and Arvel to the hall that night, but it was too late now. "I'm sorry, Father, but Irwyn and Arvel are coming to sup with us tonight. Shall I tell them you're unwell?"

Elffin threw his hands up in an uncustomary show of emotion. "How am I supposed to speak to him, now?" His brows flew up. "Gods—does he know I'm his father?"

Taliesin shook his head. "No, he doesn't know any more than you do. Or, than you did know, until now. How and when—and if— you tell him, is up to you."

"Me, tell him?" Elffin sat back down. "Gods. I don't know how to deal with this—what the hell do I say?"

Taliesin shook his head. "I don't know." He thought of his daughter, and how, someday, he very likely would face the same situation. *What will I say to her? How will I say it?* Then came a far worse thought. *Maybe I'll never say it. Maybe I'll never have the chance...*

The two of them sat immersed in their thoughts until at last, Elffin broke the silence. "Could we tell him together? You're better with words than I am."

Taliesin reached over and patted his father's knee. "Of course, Father."

Elffin nodded, resigned, reached for his cup of wine and drained it.

By the time Irwyn and Arvel arrived in his father's hall, it felt as if a year had passed.

"Come in." Elffin beckoned to them, eyeing Arvel with an unblinking gaze. Taliesin noticed, in that moment, his father realizing the truth of the news he had brought him. *Perhaps, somehow, a part of him knew all along.*

The newcomers joined them at the table close to the hearth, now ablaze with a hot bed of coals built up beneath its flames. Servants were quick to offer the ale and large bowls of mussels swimming in broth Elffin was famous for serving in his hall, along with baskets heaping with hot bread. The evening stretched out much the way most evenings in Elffin's hall did—with stories and laughter.

When nothing was left of the meal but crumbs and large piles of black shells, they stretched out in front of the hearth with the hounds. Elffin looked over at Taliesin and raised his brows slightly.

It's time. Taliesin felt his throat close in defiance of the heavy news he had to give his brother, who was scratching one of the hounds behind the ears and grinning. He did not want to see his brother's joy turn to ashes, but it had to be done. So, he did what he always did when he felt at a loss for words—he took up his harp.

Melodies came to aid him, lifting him like a gentle ocean swell, until he felt courageous enough to sing his selkie mother's story. His voice resonated with his fierce love for her, and though it trembled with deep sorrow, his voice did not falter. When the last note rang out in the hall, every face was wet with tears.

Taliesin reached over, gripped his brother's shoulder, and motioned toward Elffin. "Her last wish was for you to know Lord Elffin is your father."

Arvel stared at Elffin, much the way Elffin had stared at him when he first entered the hall. No one spoke, but Taliesin sensed the Great Mother at work on their hearts. In time, all would heal.

Taliesin walked down to the docks with his father the next morning. He had arranged for him and Amergin to board a ship headed for Ynys Manau. From there, they could easily find passage to Eire. Amergin was already there, staring out to sea with a longing gaze as if his lover were beckoning to him from across the waves. Taliesin walked up and stood beside him until he glanced over and asked, "Ready?"

"I am. That's our ship." He pointed to the vessel at the far end of the dock.

Amergin gave him a nod, said his farewells and left Taliesin to do the same. Taliesin regarded his father and brother side by side, noticing the subtle similarities in their faces. *I've done it, Mother. They know. Everything's going to be fine, now.* He smiled, fully believing it, his heart hopeful. Though the pain of losing her still hung in the air between them all, it hurt less now. He embraced his father. "I don't know when I'll be back, but I'll send word when I can."

"Please do, son." Elffin embraced him. "You're always in my thoughts."

Arvel stepped in and threw his arms around him the moment Elffin stepped away.

Taliesin smiled. "Farewell, brother."

Arvel squeezed him tightly, like a child. "Farewell."

Taliesin waited until he let go, then picked up his harp and crane bag and boarded the ship. His heart thumped with anticipation as he stepped onto the deck, much as it had when he had first ventured out to sea in his tiny boat, at the age of five, to answer the call of the Sacred Oak. That was the first time he had felt what he called the "larger powers" at work, guiding him towards his destiny. He felt them again, now, looming all around him in the wind and the water, present in his every breath and thought. *We did the right thing, Mother,* he thought, gazing into the waves. *Arvel might be more like Father than you think.*

The voyage was uneventful in terms of weather, but inside his mind, Taliesin's thoughts were stormy enough to capsize the most seaworthy of vessels. *Now, what? How long will it take for me to learn what I must learn? And what kind of man will I be once I learn it? Will I become like Myrthin?* He could not simply forget the endless warnings Islwyn had given him, over the years, about binding magic and its consequences. *And yet, Amergin is a good man. Isn't he?* He glanced over at him, wondering how much he did not know about the druid. All he knew for certain was that Amergin thought of Finbheara as an enemy and threat to his people. They had that in common, and that was enough.

For now.

CHAPTER FOURTEEN
Eire

"We're here." Amergin motioned toward a small harbor, where curragh boats bobbed together, like a string of beads, within the green cleavage of two rain-swollen hills. Seabirds circled the nearby fish market, their darting calls piercing the muted sunlight of the murky afternoon as they dove for cast-off morsels.

The ship docked, and Amergin led the way through the market to a village where he secured lodging for the night. He spoke to the innkeeper for some time and then followed him to the stables to see about some horses. Taliesin waited inside, warming himself by the hearth in the common hall. He spied a dish of cream and a hunk of bread near the window, and an iron horseshoe nailed above the door. There were but two other patrons. Their wind-burned faces hung wearily over cups of ale gripped in rough hands. One glanced over at him, raised his chin and gave him a smile a few teeth short of a row. "Nice harp you have there, lad! Let's have us a song, eh?"

The other man turned around to see who his companion was speaking to. His eyes lit up. "Oh, aye! Right fine, that is! Come, have a cup and play us something—the sea was unkind to us this morning, the stingy wench! Need a bit of cheering up." He stood up, fetched a third cup, filled it and pushed it to the edge of the table.

Taliesin saw no harm in a bit of music. "Thank you." He joined them at the table, raised his cup to them and slaked his thirst. "Now, then. Something cheerful." He unslung his harp and set it on his knee like a beloved child. He thought through the scores of songs he knew until he made his choice and smiled.

Notes trilled forth like a thousand birds on a summer morning. The men sang along, grinning like love-struck boys, bouncing their knees and tapping out rhythms on the table. Soon the ale was gone, and one of the men ran to find the innkeeper.

It was not the innkeeper, but Amergin, who appeared in the doorway moments later. He glanced toward the window, walked over and inspected the dish of cream. There were but crumbs where the hunk of bread had been. "Come," he said to Taliesin. "We must go."

The men at the table protested, but Amergin ignored them.

Taliesin apologized for their early departure, bid the men farewell, and followed Amergin outside to the stables.

Amergin shook his head. "We cannot stay here now. We must find protection, and quickly, before nightfall." He sighed. "I should have told you to keep your harp hidden."

Taliesin turned his palms up. "Why? I don't understand."

"The offering by the window when we arrived was gone. The Sídhe must have heard your music and come to listen. Now they know you're here. Whether they're loyal to Ulster or Connacht, we cannot know, but if the latter, it's only a matter of time before news of your arrival reaches Knockma. We must leave." Amergin mounted his steed, glancing briefly in all directions before speaking. "And we must ride hard, I'm afraid. My hall is some distance from here. We won't make it before sundown, but if the road is kind, we'll arrive soon after."

The air felt heavy as the day's light ripened in the west, thickening like a pudding as it cooled. Taliesin and Amergin had not spoken since leaving the inn.

"How much further?" Taliesin asked, breaking their silence.

"Not long now."

Taliesin did not mention the dark figures he had seen out of the corner of his eye moving along the fringe of the woods. He knew Amergin had seen them too.

"The horses are tired, but they can still run," Taliesin suggested in a low voice, eyeing the tree line. He reached down and stroked the side of his mare's neck in reassurance.

Amergin glanced toward the woods and nodded. "Don't stop, no matter what happens." He kicked his horse in the flanks. Taliesin and his mare gave chase.

The further the sun sank, the larger and more defined the shadows at the tree line became. Taliesin reached down and gripped the hilt of *Straif*, ensuring it still hung by his side, as his mare struggled to keep up with Amergin's stallion.

Over the next half-hour the woods retreated, like dark leafy waves pulled back into the sea. The road then cut through a loamy-

126

smelling meadow of waist-high grass, affording a wide but dim view of the land around them. Amergin pointed to the silhouette of a hillfort in the distance. "There she is."

Taliesin squinted at the stone walls and roof of what appeared to be an enormous roundhouse within them. He felt surprised. He had imagined Amergin's home would be a small hut in the woods, like Islwyn's. Nothing in Amergin's clothing, manner or possessions revealed him to be a man of means. *Perhaps he serves a chieftain, and the fort belongs to him.*

His thoughts were cut short when his mare reared up and squealed in distress, tossing him off her back and into the grass. He rolled away just in time to avoid being crushed by her frantic prancing. She bucked as if she were being stung by a wasp, pawing at the ground and sky, and then, despite her fatigue, took off at a full gallop into what remained of the dying sun.

Taliesin looked around in the trampled grass, searching for what had startled her, but the grass was thick and the light too dim.

Amergin struggled to stay astride his mount, as he, too, had become frantic. "Run for the gates!"

Taliesin did not question his command. He unsheathed *Straif* and took off toward the hillfort. The grass moved and rustled around him as he raced toward the hill, until, at last, he saw what had disturbed the peace of the meadow—black adders. They swarmed out of the grass across his path, twisting and slithering over one another, cutting him off from his destination. He cried out and stopped in his tracks.

Amergin began chanting something out across the land, in a language Taliesin did not understand. His voice seemed to sink into the earth and rise through every long strand of grass around them, filling the twilight around them.

Taliesin charged forward, slashing at the snakes with *Straif*. They reacted as if he held a blazing torch instead of a sword, slithering away and retreating into the cover of the tall grass. Taliesin seized his opportunity and doubled his pace. He raced up the hill and did not stop until the path rose out of the grass and began traversing the hillside. He could now see the gates of the hillfort clearly. Encouraged, he looked back to see how Amergin was faring. It was good he did. Amergin was thundering toward him at a full gallop. Taliesin leapt to the side of the path just in time.

"Get on!" Amergin bellowed, reining in his horse. Taliesin jumped up behind him, and they rode for the gates now standing open to receive their lord and guest.

Taliesin glanced back at the woods and spied a shadow lurking at the edge of the tree line. Though he could not make out its eyes, he knew, in the marrow of his bones, it was glaring at him.

Taliesin and Amergin's dramatic arrival sent the hillfort into a scramble of activity. A white-haired man in a fine robe approached, surrounded by several younger men and a few boys wearing plain woolen ones.

Amergin dismounted. "Bar the gates!" he commanded. No one questioned him. All ran together to the gates and pushed them closed. When they went to pick up a large wooden brace, Amergin shook his head. "No, the iron bar." Expressions furrowed into deeper concern, but the men ran into a nearby forge and emerged a few moments later, carrying a long iron bar. Together they lifted it up and slid it into place.

Amergin put his hands upon the bar and began to chant something. The commotion attracted several others, who, upon seeing Amergin and their kinsmen so engaged, ran to join them at the gates and chant along.

The white-haired man held a leather bag out to Taliesin. "Here. Help me cast salt beneath the walls, lad—seems the Dark Sídhe are afoot. You go that way and I'll go this way."

Taliesin snatched the bag and did as the old man told him. He quickly memorized the chant the men were singing and joined in as he worked his way around the hillfort, casting handfuls of salt at the base of the wall as he went until he met up with the old man on the opposite side. The old man took back the bag of salt and eyed Taliesin up and down with a squinting glare before walking back to join the others.

When the work was done, the men gathered in front of the large roundhouse, casting hesitant glances at one another.

Amergin raised his hands. "I'm sorry for the harsh welcome, brothers. We were followed by Sídhe with bad intent." He pulled back the skins covering the roundhouse door, ushered Taliesin in, then followed. The old man came in after him, and then all the men and boys wearing plain robes.

The ceiling of the roundhouse was high and thickly thatched. Lanterns hung around the perimeter of the hall. The smell of onions wafted from a large cauldron hanging over a firepit made of well-stacked slate. Ogham sticks and musical instruments leaned against the walls behind several low benches, underneath which cups and bowls were stacked. There was another doorframe on the opposite side of the roundhouse, crowned with a tree branch from which several bells were tied with woolen string. Skins hung down from the frame. Taliesin eyed it with curiosity. *Where does that lead?*

The white-haired man approached with a pitcher. "You've been sorely missed, Ollam Amergin. Sorely missed, indeed. We were beginning to fear you'd never come back."

Amergin held out his drinking horn. "I'm sorry it took me so long, but it could not be helped." He motioned to Taliesin. "I've brought a new apprentice. This is Master Taliesin. It's clear to me he was born to wear the crimson feathers. I wager he may already have a golden branch's worth of words within his tongue. Taliesin, this is Ollam Feidhlim."

Ollam Feidhlim's brows raised. "New apprentice, eh?" He glanced at Taliesin, let out a grunt, and sat down. "Just what we need."

"Come, now, Feidhlim." Amergin checked him with a cautionary look.

Ollam Feidhlim ignored Taliesin and threw a gnarled old hand toward the others. "I daresay I've done well with them while you've been gone, but you bring a knowledge and presence to the order I can't replace."

"As do we all, my friend."

Feidhlim managed a half-smile. "Well, you'd best tell us what's happened. I'm old and must eat and go to bed if I'm to be of use to anyone tomorrow. And if I should be hanging a horseshoe over my bed tonight, I'd rather know now, so I can fetch one from the forge."

Amergin nodded. "Not a bad idea, I'm afraid."

129

"Weren't the friendly sort, then."

"No. Not that I've ever met any who were particularly friendly."

"Nor I," Feidhlim agreed. "What do they want this time?"

"Something we've taken great pains to hide and have no intention of revealing."

Feidhlim groaned. "Well, whatever it is, tell me you haven't brought it here."

"No. We haven't brought it here."

Feidhlim pulled at his chin, looking Taliesin up and down as if he were measuring him for a coffin. "Your young apprentice here has something to do with it, doesn't he?"

Amergin motioned for Feidhlim to lower his voice. "We can speak of this later. Privately." He motioned toward the steaming cauldron. "Why don't we eat?"

Feidhlim shrugged and backed off, but it was clear, from the set of his brow, that it was temporary.

Amergin took advantage of the reprieve and stepped forward, taking the bowl of stew offered by one of the druids-in-training, along with a hunk of bread. After sharing the meal and a few stories with the members of the order, he stood up. "Good night to you all. Thank you for your help. I'm certain we won't be bothered tonight. Get some sleep."

It was a clear signal it was time for the others to retreat to their quarters. They stood up in silence and filed out of the roundhouse.

Once the initiates were gone, Amergin walked over to the mysterious second doorway and pulled the skins back. "Let us speak now."

Ollam Feidhlim was quick to accept the invitation. He took down a lantern with one hand, picked up a pitcher of ale with the other, and ducked beneath the furs. Taliesin followed, eager to see what lay beyond the door. He was not disappointed. He found himself standing in a long rectangular room flanked on both sides by meticulously organized shelves. One side held an extensive apothecary of pots and jars of all sizes, and the other an ample collection of scrolls, parchments and ogham sticks. The far end of the room culminated in another hearth, where Ollam Feidhlim went to build them another fire.

Although Taliesin felt tempted to linger and study the shelves, he resisted and followed Amergin to the end of the room. There, it widened enough to accommodate a bed on one side of the hearth and a desk and stool on the other, positioned beneath a small window with a view of a grand oak. The tip of a full moon could be glimpsed rising from behind the hills in the distance. In front of the hearth were a half-dozen cushions with a low table between them, now employed for Feidhlim's pitcher of ale.

Taliesin found the exotic furnishings refreshing after the sparseness of the main hall. He studied the carpets with interest, captivated by their complex patterns.

"From the land of the pharaohs," Amergin said, noting his interest. "Hand-tied, knot by knot. There are countless hours of work beneath your feet."

Taliesin bent down and ran his hand over one of them, losing himself in its spectacular design and bright array of colors.

Amergin sat down on one of the cushions, crossing his legs beneath him as easily as if he were a young child.

Ollam Feidhlim lowered himself down onto one of the cushions as well, but with nowhere near the same nimbleness. He groaned as he tucked his legs and feet into place, let out a sigh, and then looked at them with raised brows.

Amergin motioned toward Taliesin. "Taliesin has knowledge of something Oonagh and Finbheara want. Should they succeed in finding it, it could enable them and their people to leave the hills and take these lands back in the name of the Tuatha de Danaan. I've no doubt they would force the same fate upon us that my people once forced upon them."

Ollam Feidhlim's eyebrows curled in dismay. "But how? Surely this cannot be done."

"I don't know if it will come to that, but we must continue to take measures against the Sídhe here in the hillfort and advise the initiates to be on their guard, especially while sleeping and bathing. None should venture outside the hillfort after dark—be sure the sheep and cattle are brought in well before sunset." Amergin turned his gaze toward Taliesin, eyes flashing in the firelight. "And you must learn quickly."

Conversation then turned to all that had happened over the moons Amergin had been gone, until the fire had retreated into a pulsing bed of orange coals, surrendering the room to the cool light of the now fully risen moon.

Amergin stood up and motioned to the bed. "Get some rest, Taliesin. I'll join Feidhlim in his hut. It will be like old times, when we were young initiates, eh, Feidhlim?"

"No." Taliesin shook his head. "I won't hear of it. If you'll just grant me one of your furs, I'd much prefer to rest beneath that fine tree." He pointed to the oak outside the window.

Amergin eyed him. "So be it." He pulled a bearskin from the bed and handed it to him. "Take this one. It's been blessed at least a thousand times. Keep it and your wits about you." He then pointed at *Straif*, still hanging by Taliesin's side. "And that within reach."

CHAPTER FIFTEEN
The Order

The next morning arrived as a dreary grey whisper, and Taliesin cursed its intrusion. He had slept only a few fitful hours, his mind reeling with worries and plans. Those few hours had not done him much good, for they had been fraught with terrible dreams of Arhianna calling his name from the surrounding forest. Yet, no matter what he did, he could not find her.

He groaned, rubbed his eyes, and pushed himself up into a seated position. The air smelled fresh and bracing, full of clean nothing, the way only cold morning air can. It was still dark, just a hint of the coming dawn behind the hills, but the men of the order were already up. Some were placing offerings on altars. Others sat in prayer or meditation beneath the trees in the yard. No one spoke to one another. Taliesin followed their example and began to pray.

When dawn broke, the order retired to the hall for the morning meal. Taliesin spied Amergin sitting on the far side of the hall. He looked up from his bowl and beckoned.

Taliesin took an apple and joined him. "Good morning."

"Good morning." Amergin motioned toward a nearby stool. "How was your first night's sleep?"

"Restless, but I haven't enjoyed a restful night in some time."

Amergin nodded. "I'm familiar with the problem. The only thing that seems to work for me is training until I can scarcely raise my limbs."

"I'd welcome the feeling."

"Good. Because you must hone your fighting skills. There's a war coming. You favor a bow, is that right?"

Taliesin shrugged. "I favor a harp, to tell you the truth, but if I must choose a weapon, I do favor a bow. At least it has strings."

Amergin chuckled. "Well, a harp's good for many things, but it doesn't help much on the battlefield."

Taliesin raised his brows. "You'd be surprised."

Amergin raised a hand. "You're right, of course—I meant in actual combat."

Taliesin gave him a nod.

"And a bow is only good at a certain range," Amergin continued. "It's useless in close combat. For that, you need dagger and sword. That's where I imagine you could use more training."

Taliesin's hand strayed to *Straif*. "I could. When do we start?"

"Now. Come with me." Amergin stood up, led him outside and pointed to a fair-haired man in the yard engaged in sword exercises with four men of the order. He was not any taller than the rest but somehow managed to keep them all at bay.

"That's Master Oisin of Clan Baíscne, Fianna warrior and the son of none other than the great Fionn Mac Cumhail himself."

Taliesin felt impressed. Tales of Fionn Mac Cumhail and his legendary Fianna warriors had been brought across the sea to the shores of Brython on many a bards' lips.

"Master Oisin—!" Amergin called.

The man turned. He wiped the sweat from his brow with his forearm, motioned for the others to continue training, and jogged across the yard to where Taliesin and Amergin stood waiting. "Good morning, Ollam Amergin."

Taliesin surveyed the many scars marring Oisin's wide chest and shoulders, singing their silent songs of war, and wondered how many battles the man had seen.

"Oisin," Amergin gripped Taliesin's shoulder. "This is Taliesin, my newest apprentice. He needs to improve his fighting skills. Teach him as much as you can in a moon. You can leave the training of the others to whomever you deem fit."

Oisin glanced at Taliesin. "You know how to handle a sword?"

Taliesin had put in his time on the practice field, just as all the men of Mynyth Aur had, but knew he was nowhere near the warrior Gareth or Bran was. "I'll let you be the judge of that."

Oisin chuckled. "I can see from your fingers you play the harp more than you swing a sword."

"True." Taliesin examined his callouses. "A man's hands tell no lies."

Oisin nodded. "Well, music brings more joy than war." He put a hand over his heart. "I much prefer poems to bloodshed, myself, but, alas, blood is what has too often been demanded of me. It seems the clans of Eire tire of poetry too easily, for we are ever at war."

"And a fine job you do at them both," Amergin added, backing away. "I'll leave you to it."

Taliesin had trained a good deal in his youth when all Gareth wanted to do was train, but that had been years ago. His muscles had fallen out of practice, and they let him know it over the next few days. He felt glad of his bed every night, falling asleep quickly and waking with soreness in every muscle. His one advantage was that his reflexes were quite quick, occasionally affording him a victory.

"Seems you're a better swordsman than you let on," Oisin said after Taliesin won his first match. "I'll not go easy on you anymore."

And he did not. Taliesin did not manage to win another match for weeks. Oisin had the stamina of a wolf and the patience of a spider, waiting for the perfect moment to strike. Day after day, Taliesin inevitably tired first, until, at last, he would falter, and Oisin would strike the would-be death blow. But Taliesin refused to be discouraged. He knew strength would come with time. He had demanded performance from his fingers and voice for years. Now, they obeyed and delivered whatever he asked of them with a smooth, effortless grace. He expected no less of his arms and legs, now that they were being put to task. *One day, they shall comply.*

He embraced his new daily routine, thriving within its structure. Every morning, he and Oisin trained from dawn until the mid-day meal. After that, he retired with Amergin to walk the woods until dark. His studies with Amergin required a different kind of discipline—one of equally intense focus, but inward rather than outward. At first, transitioning between the two proved difficult, and Amergin noticed.

"You must learn how to take the fire stoked by one training and use it to serve the other. What you do with a sword or a spear, you must learn to do with your magic, for it, too, can be aimed and thrust at your enemies." He leveled his gaze on Taliesin. "You must learn how to coax the elements into doing your will." Amergin looked toward the sky and raised his hands, murmuring under his breath. Clouds began to collect above them, ripening into dense purple billows. The wind picked up, bringing with it the smell of rain. His

135

fingers grew tense and crooked, moving in and out as if he were palpating the sky. Then, like a spider weaves a web, his fingers drew thin, white hot strands of lightning from the clouds and hooked them to the top of a nearby tree. The blast split the tree down its center with a horrendous crack, sending sparks and wood flying in all directions.

When the smoke cleared, Amergin looked back at Taliesin. "Once you can do that, you'll have no need of crude weapons anymore."

Taliesin felt convinced he knew more of elemental magic than Amergin supposed. The next morning, after his training with Oisin, he returned to the blasted tree. He laid his hands on its trunk. He could feel the weakened, crippled life within it, struggling to repair itself. He channeled the vital energy built up in his body from his morning training into the trunk, directing it down into the tree's roots and up into its limbs, until he became weak and light-headed.

Within a week of his visits, Taliesin could feel the tree had recovered to a point where it would survive. Pleased with himself, he gave its trunk a farewell pat and turned to make his way back to Amergin's fortress. To his surprise, he found Amergin standing a few feet away, watching him.

"Well done," he said. "A bit slow, but with time, you'll improve." A squirrel bounded between them and scurried up the trunk of the tree. Amergin's fingers shot out toward it like a viper as it ran across a tree limb, and it fell to the ground.

"He doesn't have a week," Amergin said. "See if you can save him."

Though a squirrel was but a small thing most men did not value, Taliesin felt horrified. He bent down, picked up its limp body, and cupped it in his hands. He could feel no breath or heartbeat. He shook his head. "I can't. He's dead."

Amergin's face remained hard as stone. "Try harder."

Taliesin held the squirrel close to his chest, but it was no use. He could not coax fire from a flame that had gone out. "It's no use. I can't do it."

136

"Not the way you're attempting to," Amergin agreed. "This is what lies at the heart of dark magic—twisting the natural world and imposing your will upon it." Amergin took the squirrel and held it. It stirred and twitched. He laid it upon the ground. A moment later it leapt to life and scrambled up a nearby tree. "It can be done, but—"

"—there's a cost." Taliesin interrupted, watching the squirrel disappear into the canopy.

"There is. Taking and calling back life is the darkest, most dangerous kind of magic, but there are others."

"Like the lightning."

"Not the lightning, so much, but rather what I did with it to the tree."

Taliesin looked at the blasted tree. "So, any magic that harms others, or enslaves them to your will."

"Indeed."

Taliesin nodded, thinking of the cruelty committed by Hraban's seer in the Sacred Grove when he was a young boy. He shuddered. "Evil magic."

Amergin paused a moment before answering. "The fault lies not with the magic but with the practitioner. What I did to the sky and the tree will have consequences, just as anything I do—or even choose not to do—has consequences—but was it evil? I don't know. Was blasting the tree with lightning worse than taking an axe and chopping it down?"

Taliesin shrugged. "I suppose not."

"And is slaughtering animals evil?"

Taliesin did not eat much meat but did not fault those who did. "Not if we give thanks to the animal, honor its sacrifice and take care not to endanger the herd."

Amergin raised his brows. "So then, sacrificing a young maiden to Cernunnos is not evil, provided we honor her?"

Taliesin recoiled with the sudden fear that perhaps Amergin and his order did indeed engage in human sacrifice. "That's different."

Amergin's face gave him no clues. "Dark magic is a weapon, Taliesin, far more powerful than the sword. It can corrupt the noblest of hearts and tempt even the humblest, most vigilant of practitioners. Do not engage it lightly."

The moon waxed full. As she waned, Taliesin's progress doubled. Spell and sword began hitting their mark twice as much as they had in the first few moons. Yet, just when he felt he was truly beginning to make progress, Amergin came out to the training yard and put an end to it. "You're done with those. Put them down," he said, motioning toward Taliesin's weapons.

Taliesin, huffing from the morning's exercises, sheathed his sword and threw his shield to the ground. Once he had caught his breath, he glanced back and forth between Amergin and Oisin. "What now? Spear? Staves?"

"Neither," Amergin said. "Come with me."

Oisin looked surprised but shrugged and said nothing.

Taliesin followed Amergin across the yard. He felt dismayed to see several of the men in the order stop what they were doing and follow them. They gathered around, enclosing Amergin and Taliesin in a circle, whispering to one another and staring at him.

Great Mother. What sort of test is this? He noticed Ollam Feidhlim walking over, as well, a smirk perched in the corner of his mouth. "Bit soon for that, don't you think, Ollam Amergin?"

Amergin shot a glance his way but ignored his question. "Now, Taliesin—imagine you are holding your sword and strike at me."

Taliesin's heart sank, for it was clear by the faces around him what typically happened to an initiate when they reached this phase of their training. *I'm about to be made a complete fool of.* Still, he had endured far worse. He resigned himself to it and wrapped his fists around the imagined hilt of his practice sword, picturing the blade coming out of it.

The initiates whispered and smiled. Taliesin shut them from his mind and swung. It felt as if he had swatted a birch sapling at Amergin, and even he could not help but chuckle at his weak attempt.

Amergin swatted Taliesin's flaccid energy away and thrust his palms toward him. Taliesin felt a firm blow of force and stumbled backward, even though Amergin's hands never touched him. He landed with a thud. The satisfied chuckles of onlooking initiates folded in around him. Oisin bent over and offered him a hand. "Not

138

bad. At least you made something happen. No worries. Nobody gets it the first time, brother."

Taliesin grinned and stood up, smacking the dust from his tunic. He no longer cared what the initiates thought, or how foolish he might look, for he now believed without a doubt that he had made the right decision coming to study with Amergin. Nothing could dampen his mood.

"Again," he said to Amergin with a grin. "Show me how."

Three more moons passed, and with each, Taliesin became more skilled at what the order called shadow combat. He still could not best Amergin, nor did he expect to, for some time—or perhaps ever—but he started winning occasional matches against his fellow initiates.

He had some experience doing such exercises with Islwyn, but Islwyn had taught him only how to work with already moving forces, such as fire, flowing water, or a strong breeze. Collecting silent energy and focusing it to your will proved a far greater challenge. Many nights Taliesin went to the hall with a headache so terrible he thought his skull might burst from the pressure.

Evenings were spent with fellow brothers of the order calling up dozens of songs, poems and histories. In this, he shone. He easily surpassed even the most accomplished bards among them. Yet, there remained much for him to learn in terms of material. He memorized all he could, adding dozens of new ballads, poems and stories to his repertoire.

With his heightened shadow skills, he became more adept at navigating the dream world. He took to practicing new songs and ballads in his dreams, which greatly increased his ability to commit them to memory.

The most thrilling aspect of his new technique was that as he sang or told the story in the dreamtime, it came to life around him in stunning, vibrant detail—bloody battles waged across field and moor, testing the mettle of the most courageous; voyages pitching and lurching on merciless seas, sparing none but a tenacious few; cautionary tales of mortal men who dared challenge the will of the gods—he saw the sweat upon every brow, smelled every horrid scent on the battlefield, heard every lover's euphoric or heartbreaking cry. With practice, he found he could enter the story and engage the characters in conversation. Over time, he came to know them as friends.

His experiences in the dreamtime became so potent, in fact, that his memories became a fabric woven equally of both realms, each as real as the other.

The repeated telling of the stories he chose to foster fell upon the terra of his mind like a thick blanket of autumn leaves: greening, reddening, withering, and falling onto the dark soil of his soul a thousand times, where they slept until he called them forth once more. His voice plumbed each story's every nuance, flowing like dark honey over every inch of it, slow, sweet, and deep. His fingers grew deft and precise in the pursuit of its deepest wisdom, coaxing the most elusive hint of the divine from the crudest of strings or pipes.

He and Amergin continued to spend the afternoons alone, with Amergin supervising his progress on manipulating the life force of plants and animals.

"Have any of the others learned what you're teaching me?" Taliesin inquired, one day, after bringing a rabbit back to life.

Amergin shook his head. "Some wish to learn, but I inherently distrust those who covet such power." He stopped and turned to face Taliesin. "With that in mind, I feel it is time to ask you to swear an oath. Bringing animals back from the dead is one thing. Calling our fellow brothers and sisters back is quite another."

This did not surprise Taliesin. Such knowledge surely required sacrifices and oaths.

"Follow me." Amergin took a different path than he normally did. After walking an hour or so, they came to a circle of stones standing within a grove of oak trees. The circle held a firepit and an altar formed of a large angular boulder with a long flat stone laid across it. A stream had been coaxed to flow around the edges of the grove and then allowed to continue its path on the other side. Firewood had been chopped and stacked high on the south side of the circle, along with a good amount of kindling. Before entering, Amergin honored the Guardians and whispered praises to Arawn and the Great Mother. Taliesin did the same. Once inside, Amergin fetched a handful of wood and kindling. It was quite a cold afternoon, and Taliesin suspected it would rain before evening fell. He helped Amergin build the fire and they crouched next to its warmth.

After a moment, Amergin let out a tired sigh and looked at Taliesin. "I have my own reasons for agreeing to teach you these arts. Selfish reasons."

A hint of betrayal darkened the edges of Taliesin's mind, creeping into his thoughts like a slow-moving storm. *Of course, he does. What was I thinking? That he would teach me such secrets and ask nothing in return? I shouldn't be surprised.* "Oh?"

"The oath I've brought you here to swear is that if ever I should let such power overwhelm me and abuse it, you will use the arts I teach you to bind me, as Nimue has bound Myrthin. In return, I shall swear to do the same for you. We must hold one another accountable."

Taliesin considered the situation. "You must speak plain, if I am to swear such an oath. What do you consider abuse?"

"Murder. Enslavement. Torture—these are the obvious transgressions."

"And the not so obvious ones?"

"Bringing back the dead. That, perhaps, is the most tempting of all."

Taliesin shook his head. "But you did that just the other afternoon."

"With an animal, I did," he agreed with a nod, "but animals share a collective soul. When brought back to life, they don't go mad, or long for blood—they simply go on as they did before. What I'm speaking of is calling a man or woman's unique soul back from the Underworld or the Summerlands after Arawn has claimed it—often against their will as well as his."

Taliesin intimately knew the terrible consequences of such a practice. He, in his former life as Gwion Bach, had sacrificed himself to destroy the dark vessel Cerridwen had employed to such an end. He had learned of this lifetime in Caer Sidi, where he would surely have gone mad if not for Arianrhod's mercy.

"I would never do such a thing," he stated with complete conviction.

141

Amergin continued, "Madness and a thirst for blood are but a few of the terrible afflictions that can befall men and women called back from death. Not all of them suffer such things, especially if the practitioner is skilled, which is what makes the temptation so fierce, but the risk is too great. I know this, firsthand, unfortunately."

Taliesin narrowed his eyes on his teacher. "What did you do?"

Amergin raised his brows. "I brought someone back, of course—someone I felt certain I could not live without." He paused and looked at the sky until a bittersweet smile pursed his lips. "We are all fools in love, Taliesin. All of us."

This was something Taliesin agreed with. "Love delivers its own kind of madness."

"It certainly does." After a stretch of silence, Amergin continued. "I was young. Foolish. The woman I brought back was Queen Maeve. Fiercest queen to ever rule Connacht. You know her now by the name of Oonagh, wife of Finbheara, Queen of the Daoine Sídhe."

Taliesin felt as if the dawn had just broken. "That's why Nimue sent for you." He quickly calculated how old Amergin must be to have loved Queen Maeve. "I suppose another temptation of dark magic is to live beyond one's years."

Amergin did not deny it. "It is. Though the price is not nearly as high as bringing back the dead."

"You're as old as the Sídhe, then?"

"Older, perhaps." The trees rustled as Amergin looked at them, their leaves fluttering as his eyes passed over their boughs. "I'm to blame for their imprisonment. It was my song that sent them into the hills; my song that sent my one true love, changed and mad, into them as well. Only there could my dear Maeve find peace. True to her nature, she became queen of that land as well, but remembered nothing of her life in this world. Or of our love."

Taliesin weighed this new knowledge on the scales of his mind, knowing the risk he was about to take. *Perhaps I'm a fool, Great Mother, but I don't believe I shall succumb to it.* "Myrthin has knowledge of such magic, as, I suppose, does Maelwys."

"They do. As well as some of the seers among the Saxons."

With such enemies, Taliesin knew he would need all the knowledge Amergin would deign to give him. "I shall swear this oath to you, then."

Amergin looked pleased. "Come, then," he said, motioning toward the stone altar. "Let us make this blood pact."

Summer Country

CHAPTER SIXTEEN
A Visit to Dumnonia

Igerna descended the stairs as quickly as she dared in the half-light of dawn. Her heart still beat like a rabbit, so angry had she gotten with the maid. *How could she have let this happen?* The maid had wailed her apologies, but Igerna had granted her no sympathy and sent her off, rushing from her quarters like a spooked doe.

They can't have gotten far. Besides, the fortress gates are locked. They've probably wandered to the kitchen, or the scullery. Yes—that's where they'll be—no one's taken them. Calm yourself.

Igerna continued silently placating her fears as she rushed to the kitchen. And indeed, there, by the hearth, sleeping soundly between Uthyr's hunting hounds, lay Morgen and Arthur, hands clasped.

Igerna let out the breath she had not realized she had been holding. She sat down on the stool the scullery maid used to scrub pots and regarded her children a moment, marveling at how they had, once more, managed to get past the nursemaid and wander all through the fortress without anyone seeing or hearing them. *Oh, Morgen...clever as a fox.* The girl had always been so, continually surprising everyone with her intelligence. She had been in the world but three moons when she had spoken her first word. Igerna had felt so shocked she had shaken Uthyr awake to tell him.

"Morgen said *mama*, Uthyr—clear as day."

Uthyr had rolled over to look at Morgen nursing at her breast. "Is that not customary for a child of three moons?"

She had laughed. "Not at all—and what's more, I swear she knows the meaning of the word. She looked up at me and touched my cheek when she said it. I'm telling you, husband, this child is special."

"Well, my love, if you say she did, I believe you." He had leaned over and kissed Morgen's head as if it were a sacred thing, delighting in her behavior, but that had soon changed.

It dismayed Uthyr that of his two children, Morgen was the first to speak, the first to eat solid food, the first to walk—the first to achieve every milestone. Igerna had been quick to remind him both Arthur and Morgen were exceptional, and female children often outdid their male counterparts in the early stages of life. This placated him for a while, but Morgen had continued to outshine her brother.

Now, with each passing moon, Uthyr grew ever more anxious about Morgen's uncanny knowledge of things, as had many of the servants.

As babes, Morgen had babbled incessantly to Arthur in the cradle they shared, until he began to respond. Igerna had to admit, it had felt a bit unnerving, the way their voices ebbed and flowed in ways too advanced for their age. It seemed they spoke a language only they understood. Yet, as strange as the conversations they had with one another were, they were not nearly as disturbing as the ones Morgen seemed to be having with other beings—beings no one else could see. The nursemaid had come to Igerna once swearing Morgen had been talking with spirits in the nursery.

"And not just talking, my queen—but laughing!" She had crossed herself. "Laughing, as if Pan himself had told her a dirty joke!"

Igerna had scolded her and told her she had best get down to the church and pray for the Lord to bless *her*, for only the truly deceived could ever believe something as pure and innocent as a babe's laughter could be the result of the devil.

The nursemaid had been repentant, apologizing to the point of irritation, until Igerna had forgiven her—but once the dimwit began whispering of it to the other servants, Igerna lost no time turning her out.

Igerna had gone back to nursing both babes herself after that. She did not want them drinking the milk of a superstitious cow with ridiculous ideas about the devil in her head. She knew, then, she would have to be far more careful with those she chose to bring into the household. She was quick to dismiss any who showed even the slightest sign they found her children strange or afflicted. *May the good Lord and the Great Mother protect them.*

As if she had heard Igerna's thoughts, Morgen opened her eyes and turned to look at her. Her little brows rose up in concern. She carefully disentangled herself from her brother and the hounds and padded over, silent as a cat. "Don't be sad, Mama," she whispered. "Arthur's safe—he's here with me."

Igerna forbid the tears from welling in her eyes, but she could not stop them.

Morgen's face ignited with alarm. "Don't cry!" She shook her head, brow furrowed. "I'm sorry, Mama—please don't cry. Arthur had a bad dream, and he likes the hounds, so I brought him here. I promise, I won't do it again. Don't be sad." She clutched her mother, her little arms tense.

Igerna shook her head, at last, willing the tears away. "Everything's fine, my love. Everything's fine."

"Do you promise?"

"I promise."

Morgen took her mother's hands and held them. "Don't worry. Arthur protects me, and I protect him. Grandmother says we shall always be together."

Igerna felt confused. Her mother had not visited Caer Leon in nearly two years. "You must have a very good memory, *cariad*— Mamm-wynn hasn't come to visit in a long time." *Far too long*, she thought. She had been considering taking the children to Dumnonia and spending the summer there. Uthyr was rarely home, and it was he, after all, who had first made the suggestion. He knew how lonely she grew while he was away.

Morgen shook her head. "No, not Mamm-wynn—our other grandmother. She talks to me at night when I'm supposed to be sleeping."

Igerna's heartbeat quickened. "She does, does she? What does she say?"

Morgen nodded. "Sometimes she lets me look into her big pot like that one—" Morgen pointed to the cauldron hanging over the kitchen hearth. "She makes pictures and stories in it for me!" Morgen's eyes lit up with delight, but quickly dimmed again. "I wish Arthur could see her, but he can't. It makes me sad. She tells the best stories. Better than anyone."

"Is that so?" Igerna forced herself to smile but, inwardly, felt dismayed. She thought of Arhianna and Taliesin, as she did several times a day, desperately wishing at least one of them were there in Caer Leon for her to turn to. *Oh, my dear friends—I fear I shall not be able to protect our daughter much longer—Uthyr looks at her as if he no longer knows her, and no child but Arthur wishes to play with her.* She gazed at Morgen's pearl of a face and stroked her cheek. *I won't be able to shield her from all the prying eyes and fearful wretches in this terrible*

146

world much longer…not alone. I need help. And if you cannot come to my aid, I must seek it elsewhere.

As Morgen told her all about her 'other' grandmother, Igerna scoured her mind for someone she could trust who might understand Morgen's abilities. There were wisewomen and midwives who lived near Caer Leon at the edge of the woods or along the river, but as wife of the Pendragon, she had to be cautious. If she were to be seen consulting those women, tongues would wag, and news of her visits to the heathens would reach the priests. They would certainly tell Uthyr. Then she would be asked to explain herself—something she had no desire to do. The burden of the secret she carried was heavy enough. She could not bear the thought of adding more lies to its weight.

Then, like a blessing, her childhood nursemaid, Derwa, came to mind. She remembered that, on more than one occasion, Derwa and her mother had snuck out into the hills to secretly worship among the tors. It had been Derwa who had taught her mother the Old Ways, and Derwa who had taught her grandmother before that. Some said the woman was nearly a hundred years old. Growing up, Igerna had often scoffed at her advice, as silly young women are wont to do, but now, she craved it. She mumbled a prayer, hoping the old woman had not lost her health or her wits.

Later that morning, she pulled out a piece of vellum and wrote to her mother, announcing she and the children would come for a visit in the spring.

She felt much better as she sealed it.

It's something, at least.

Morgen could hardly contain her excitement upon hearing the news that she, Arthur, Morgause and her mother would be spending the summer with their grandparents.

"When do we leave?"

"In ten days or so."

"When the moon is full?"

Morgen noticed her mother's expression change and wondered what she had said to make her look worried.

147

"Yes, *cariad*. When the moon is full."

She and Arthur rattled off relentless questions across the breakfast table, hungry to know everything about the journey they were about to take.

"What does Dum-monia look like?"

"Is it by the sea? Can we go fishing?"

"Do Mamm-wynn and Sira-wynn have hounds?"

"Do they have giants there?"

Morgause rolled her eyes from across the table. "Of course, there are no giants, there! Or selkies or dwarves or trolls or Sídhefolk, or anything else from Rhosyn's silly old tales. What do you think? That Mamm-wynn and Sira-wynn live in the Hollow Hills?"

Igerna gave her a stern look. "That's enough, Morgause. There are many creatures in the world, both seen and unseen. Only fools imagine they know them all."

Morgause rolled her eyes again, then looked down at her porridge and scowled.

Morgen reached over and pinched her sister. "Watch yourself when you speak of the fair folk!"

Morgause yelped and yanked her arm away.

"Morgen!"

"What?"

Their mother sighed and stood up—a signal they were about to be dismissed. "Enough. Morgause, why don't you take Morgen and Arthur to see the lambs?"

The lambs! Morgen had nearly forgotten. They had been born a few days ago and the shepherd had promised to let her and Arthur play with them. *Come back after three sleeps,* he had told them. Last night had been the third. She looked over at Arthur with wide eyes. "Hurry up!"

Arthur shoved the rest of his bannock into his mouth and scrambled down from the bench, cheeks bulging. As they ran from the hall, Morgen heard her mother cry, "Obey Morgause and don't vex the shepherd—and where are your shoes, Morgen? You're not to go out without shoes!"

Morgen grimaced and marched back to fetch her shoes, cramming them on with a huff. She pursed her lips to keep any complaints from escaping until her mother let her leave. As soon as she stepped outside, she kicked them off again and shoved them in her pockets. She and Arthur spent the better part of the morning chasing the lambs around the yard while Morgause sat nearby, watching, arms crossed. When they tired of that, they begged a few of the old women to give them some of the feed from their aprons to toss to the geese and chickens. Once Arthur heard the blacksmith's hammer clanging, however, he dumped his feed out on the ground and ran off.

"Arthur!" Morgause cried. She grabbed Morgen's hand and ran after him.

The forge fascinated Arthur. If he could, he would stay and watch the blacksmith all day. Morgen preferred to play with animals but knew how much he loved to watch the sparks fly and the metal turn orange.

"I want to go back inside," Morgause complained. "I'm tired of running after you two. Besides," she paused and looked up at the clouds, "it's going to rain."

"No, it won't," Morgen assured her after a quick sniff and glance at the sky. "Not for a few hours. Go inside if you like. I'll stay with Arthur." She climbed atop a barrel and he climbed up after her.

Morgause shook her head. "Oh, no. You'd like that wouldn't you? Mother would kill me."

"Then I suppose you must stay with us," Morgen reasoned. "Sit and watch. Watch him make the metal move—it's magic."

Morgause scoffed. "It's not magic. It's just fire."

The blacksmith looked up from his work. "Oh, I'd say it takes a bit o' magic." He looked at Morgen and winked, then gave Arthur a nod. "You back again, then, Master Arthur?"

Arthur nodded. "I want to be a blacksmith, like you."

"You do, eh?"

"Yes, I do."

"Why's that?"

"I want to be strong and use fire magic!"

Morgause giggled and shook her head.

Arthur frowned at her.

"Don't mind her," Morgen whispered to him. "You'll be a dragon, one day, like father—stronger than the blacksmith. You'll keep Mother safe—and all these people, too."

149

Arthur smiled and exclaimed, "Father's not a dragon!"

Morgause looked over from the stool she had found to sit on. "What nonsense are you two talking about now?"

Morgen ignored her and turned back to Arthur. "His spirit is. And so is yours."

Arthur wrinkled his brow and screwed up his mouth. "His what?"

"The part of you that never dies—the part that can fly. You can't see it, but you can feel it." She smacked her chest. "Right here!"

"So, I'm a dragon inside?" He looked down at his chest and poked it.

"You are."

"And so is Father?"

"He is. Why do you think they call him the Pendragon?"

This seemed to placate her brother. He nodded to himself a few times, staring at the sparks flying from the blacksmith's hammer. Then he turned and looked at her. "What are you?"

Morgen shook her head. "I don't know. Sometimes I dream of being a seal, swimming in the sea, sometimes I'm a bird, flying in the clouds, sometimes I'm a cat, walking along the fortress walls, and sometimes—" She stopped, her throat choking. She had dreamt the night before of racing through the woods after a deer and sinking her teeth into its neck. She could still taste the blood, even now. She shuddered. Perhaps sleeping with the hounds had caused the dream. *Yes, it must have been the hound's dream—not mine.*

"What?" Arthur looked at her with wide eyes. "Sometimes, what?"

"Nothing."

"So, you're a seal, a bird or a cat?" Arthur sighed and patted her hand. "I'm sorry. None of those are very strong. But don't worry. I'll protect you."

Morgen thought again of the deer's neck between her teeth. "Oh, I don't need protecting. But thank you." She kissed him on the cheek.

Every night Morgen looked out the window, glad of each new sliver of moonlight in the sky, until, at long last, the moon shone full and round.

She awoke the next morning feeling as if she had a frantic bird in her ribcage, fluttering to get out. Buzzing with excitement, she skipped to her mother's chamber, clambered up on her bed and gently shook her. "Wake up, Mother!"

Her mother mumbled for her to go back to sleep, but she could not. Neither could Arthur, who was awake by the time she got back to their chamber. Together they dressed themselves and readied the last of their things. Morgen ignored her shoes, however. *Those can wait.*

Their nursemaid must have heard them because she came and ushered them to the kitchen, where servants were fetching water and lighting the cooking fires. "Let your mother sleep and don't make trouble. Rhosyn'll give you breakfast."

Morgen and Arthur ate quickly and ran outside to watch the stable boys ready the horses for their journey.

At last, Morgen spied their mother and Morgause striding across the courtyard to the stables. She turned to Arthur. "It's time to go!"

Morgen watched her mother mount her favorite horse and settle into the saddle. "Come, Morgen!" she called. "You'll ride with me. Arthur, you ride with Father Dubricius."

Morgen felt dismayed. She looked across the yard to see not only Father Dubricius, but several of her father's warriors making their way to the stables. She stifled a moan. "They're coming with us?"

"Of course, *cariad*—they're going to make sure we get there safely."

Morgen tried not to show her disappointment. She thought it would be only the four of them traveling together. Her mother was not the same when father's men were around. She did not joke or smile or laugh as she normally did, and Morgen did not like it. *At least I get to ride with her.* She took comfort in that.

When the gates opened, at last, and the horses moved forward, her heart began to race. She clutched the reins, twisting them between her fingers, and glanced over at Arthur. He beamed back at her with a wide smile.

151

They rode through the gates, down through the early morning bustle of the village, then out onto the road that followed the river.

Morgen could scarcely contain her joy—she wanted to both laugh and cry as she watched the world unfold around her in a glorious parade of trees, clouds, swaying grass and running water. She felt as if she had been kept in a pen like one of the farm animals, and had just been let loose. Though Mother let them play outside, they had never left the hillfort. There were only a few trees within it, and she and Arthur had climbed every inch of them scores of times. But here, along the road, tall legions of trees beckoned to her with unexplored limbs, their leaves whispering things to her in the breeze.

And then, of course, there was the river herself. Her wide currents spun a silver-green magic that seemed to hang upon Morgen's eyelashes, twinkling in the morning light. With wide eyes, Morgen watched the people working along her banks: fishermen pulling up their weirs from the peat-brown water, mumbling curses when they found nothing in them, women hunched over river rocks, scrubbing clothes and wringing them out, and children struggling to carry buckets of water to the nearby huts.

"The river will lead us to the sea," her mother told her. "Then we'll take a big boat to the other side. From there, it won't be long to where Mamm-wynn and Sira-wynn live."

Morgen nearly bounced in the saddle. She clapped her hands and called over to Arthur, "We're going on a boat!"

Arthur's eyes popped. He punched his fists in the air, threw back his head and launched a wild howl from his chest. "We'll see selkies! And porpoises!" He turned and tried to look up at Father Dubricius. "Father! Come on! What's wrong with your horse? Can't it go any faster?"

Morgen giggled while her mother scolded her brother. She felt certain she had never been happier.

They reached the sea sooner than Morgen thought they would. She found it strange for it to be so close, yet her mother had never taken them to the seashore before. *Why does Mother never take us anywhere?*

Why must we stay inside those dark walls? Father's never there anyway. The thought of going back made her shudder.

"Morgen, look!" Arthur cried.

Morgen turned her gaze to where her brother pointed. It led her eyes to a long boat with oars and a tall mast, creaking against the ropes of a wide dock. Her heart soared as they dismounted. Arthur ran over and grabbed her hand, leaving Father Dubricius to fuss with one of the crew about leaving his belongings on his horse, explaining he would not be sailing.

Good, Morgen thought. Her mother was forever telling her to keep quiet and behave whenever Father Dubricius was around. She felt he would surely spoil their fun if he were to come along.

A large man jumped from the ship and walked their way. Morgen recognized him as their mother's cousin. He had been to their hall many times. He raised a hand in greeting.

Their mother smiled. "Oh, Cynyr, thank you for coming."

Cynyr glanced down at Morgen and Arthur, and then at Morgause, who had since joined them. "This way, please. We can leave as soon as you wish."

Her mother smiled. "I see no reason to delay. The children are eager."

"Understood. Cai is about the same age as your twins. He drives me mad asking when I'll next take him out on the sea." He smiled, led them down to the dock and helped them board the ship.

Arthur immediately settled into a place where he could hang his arms over the side. Morgen found a spot beside him and together they peered into the water below. The shifting blue, green and yellow patterns made by sunbeams mingling with the water beckoned to Morgen. She longed to touch them.

After staring at the water awhile, Arthur sighed. "No selkies."

"Oh, don't worry, we'll see them." Morgen looked up and pointed at the blue-green expanse stretching out before them. "I know we will."

"Do you think so?"

Morgen nodded. "I do."

Arthur's brow relaxed.

Soon, they were sailing away from the dock. Morgen turned toward the prow, closed her eyes, and breathed as much of the sea breeze as she could fit into her lungs. She felt strange, as if she had been there in that moment before. She enjoyed it for as long as it lasted, let her breath out and opened her eyes, just in time to catch a seal's large brown eyes staring at her before it disappeared beneath the waves. Her heart sang with joy.

Igerna felt her chest loosen as soon as the dock faded from view. Now, for a time, at least, she could feel free of the pressures of Caer Leon. There, she had to act like a queen at all times, and with everyone. She looked forward to going home, where she could simply be daughter and mother. Her heart gladdened with the prospect of this respite. She had not seen her brothers and sisters for far too long. She thought of her youngest brother, Llyg, and wondered if she would even recognize him. *He'll be seventeen this summer—sure to look more like a man than a boy. Or has he seen seventeen summers already?*

The hours passed peacefully, the wind and water mercifully compliant, as if in favor of her plans. She took to daydreaming, letting the sounds and rhythms of the waves against the boat lull her into a half-sleep.

"Mother?"

Igerna snapped out of her reverie and turned to see Arthur standing before her. He looked as wild and frightened as a hare beneath a hawk's shadow. She felt her happiness fade in an instant. "What's the matter?"

"Something's wrong with Morgen," he whispered.

Igerna looked to see Morgen still hanging over the side of the boat, staring into the water, as still as stone. "Maybe she feels ill—the sea does that to people sometimes."

Arthur shook his head. "No. Something's wrong."

She squeezed his shoulder. "Very well. I'll go and see." Igerna made her way toward the prow. "Morgen?"

Morgen did not answer. She did not even turn her head. Igerna put her hand on her daughter's back. "Are you unwell, *cariad*?"

Still, Morgen did not answer.

Igerna gently moved her daughter's hair aside and knew the moment she saw her unblinking eyes that her daughter was in a trance, likely having a vision. It would be unwise to wake her from it.

Calmly, Igerna pulled Morgen's cowl up around her face, hopeful the crew had not noticed. There was already too much talk around the village about the strange things the Pendragon's daughter saw. She did not want these men going back home and spreading the dangerous gossip any further.

She nestled in close and slipped an arm around Morgen's waist to keep her safe, and then beckoned to Arthur, who came and sat beside her. "All is well," she whispered. "Nothing to worry about. Morgen's just having a dream while her eyes are open. Sometimes that happens. When she wakes, she can tell us what she saw. But for now, we must leave her be. Do you understand?"

Arthur nodded, worry draining from his face.

And so, they sat, all the while Igerna wondering what her strange, beautiful daughter might be seeing within the waves. *What stories are being spun for you, sweet child? Do you see the past or the future? And who is this grandmother you speak to? Is she Fae? Can she be trusted?*

At last, Morgen stirred. Igerna could feel the change and turned to look at Morgen's face. The girl blinked.

"Ah, my love," Igerna cooed. "What did you see down there?"

Morgen stared at her with her wide eyes, the color of the sea shot through with blooming heather. "Oh, Mother!" Morgen fell against her and clutched her waist.

"Don't cry, my love. Don't cry. What's the matter?" Igerna held her close, eyes darting left and right to determine who might be watching, but the crew was occupied with their duties.

"I'm just sad. I saw something sad."

"What did you see?"

Morgen shook her head and remained silent.

Igerna did not pry. "Keep it to yourself for now, then. You can tell me about it later, if you wish."

Not long after, Cynyr pointed out a small village along the coast. "That'll be the town of North Hill."

Igerna smiled. She had made arrangements for her father's men to meet her and the children there and escort them to Exeter. "Look there, children—we'll be at Sira-wynn's house soon."

Morgen, Arthur, and Morgause sat up like three march hares, craning their necks to get a better view as the ship maneuvered its way into the small harbor.

Igerna scanned the docks, searching for men carrying her father's banner, but there were none waiting to greet them.

"Do you not see them?" Cynyr asked.

"I don't." Igerna grew anxious. She knew Cynyr would refuse to let her out of his charge unless her father's men were there. The idea of having to return to Caer Leon made her heart sink, not to mention how disappointed the children would be. "They'll be here. Give them some time."

"As you wish."

By the time the crew moored the boat, Igerna's faith was rewarded; doubly so, because it was her own brother who appeared on the dock, waving in greeting.

Igerna's heart took flight. "There! It's my brother, Cynwal!"

Cynyr squinted and looked to where she pointed. "Good. Looks as though he's brought quite a company with him." Cynyr turned and ordered the crew to begin unloading their goods and belongings and then helped Igerna and her children disembark.

Igerna watched her brother dismount a fine black stallion and come striding down the dock to greet them. "Sister!" He took her in his arms and kissed her on the cheek.

She squeezed him tightly. "Oh, Cynwal, how I've missed you!"

"And I you, sister. We all have." He nodded toward Cynyr. "And if it isn't our favorite cousin! This is a welcome surprise. How go things up in Gwynedd?"

"Well, thank you." Cynyr smiled and embraced him. "Come up and visit any time."

"We all should," Igerna said. "Arthur, at least. He and Cai should get to know one another."

"They should," Cynyr said, ruffling Arthur's hair. "They've got a similar zeal for adventure."

"Then it's settled. I'll be sure to send at least Arthur your way sometime soon." Igerna smiled. "Thank you for your service, cousin—I must beg one last thing of you before you go."

"Of course."

"I understand you're returning to Caer Mincip. This letter is for my husband. Would you see that he gets it?"

"With pleasure." Cynyr tucked it into his tunic. "I'll give it to him myself."

"Thank you." Igerna turned to her children. "Bid farewell to Lord Cynyr."

They did so and then were lifted onto small ponies. "The first of Sira-wynn's gifts." Cynwal winked at Igerna.

Arthur's eyes widened. "Our own ponies?"

"Yes, and that's not all. Sira-wynn has missed his grandchildren."

"Let's go!" Arthur kicked his little heels into his pony's flanks and rode ahead.

"Arthur!"

But Arthur did not listen. He rode to the head of the company beside the riders bearing Amlawth's banners.

Cynwal smiled at her. "Seems he knows his place. No reason to tarry, I suppose. Shall we?"

Igerna nodded and followed her brother. Morgen, too, seemed at one with her pony, already maneuvering it as if she had ridden the beast for moons. Only Morgause struggled.

Cynwal smiled. "The twins are but five years old and already such fine riders—you must have raised them on horseback."

Igerna shook her head. "No. They simply understand the beasts. Dogs, as well."

"Indeed. Maybe I'll get them to help our shepherd. He's forever losing sheep on the bluffs."

"They'd just wander off with them, I'm afraid. It's a constant task for their maid to keep them within sight."

Cynwal chuckled. "Reminds me of us when we were young. Poor old Derwa! We ran her ragged, bless her."

Igerna braced herself. "I trust she's still alive and well?"

"And how. She'll outlive us all, the stubborn old crone." Cynwal laughed and then gave a shout. "Walk on!"

157

Igerna gave silent thanks for Derwa's health as the company departed, snaking its way through the small harbor and surrounding village, up into the rolling hills and then out onto the windy bluffs of the Dumnonian countryside. The gusts caused tears to stream from the corners of Igerna's eyes, blowing the cobwebs off a thousand childhood memories. Her mind wandered through countless afternoons spent with her siblings stashing nuts and stones in the boles of trees, running after butterflies along the flower-decked flanks of the hills, and hiding behind craggy stone outcroppings to jump out and scare each other. Then, at the end of the day, they would lie exhausted on their backs in the grass, watching huge ribbons of sunset-reddened clouds stretch out over their heads in a slow, smooth procession, pulling the robe of night across the sky.

"Still windy, as ever," Cynwal commented, "but it'll let up as we get inland a bit."

Igerna shrugged. "I don't mind. It makes me feel alive."

The children sang song after song to pass the time. Morgen sang with a voice that had the maturity of a woman. Though it was certainly the voice of a young girl, she never sang off key, nor with any trepidation, trilling through complex sequences of sounds that sent chills across the skin like smooth pebbles across the surface of a lake. Igerna had soon run out of songs to teach her and insisted Uthyr find a bard to teach her to play the harp. *Oh, Taliesin. You should be the one to teach her. You would be so proud. Please, return to us soon.*

CHAPTER SEVENTEEN
Summer Country

As always, Igerna felt a thrill at the first glimmer of her father's castle, its unique silhouette beckoning from across the green, rocky hills. *Home.* She smiled. "See that, children?"

"I do!" Morgen said immediately.

Arthur's eyes lit up a moment later. "Sira-wynn's castle!" he yelled.

"Shhh, yes. That's it. I'm sure they can see us coming now."

Arthur waved enthusiastically. "Sira-wynn! Mamm-wynn! We're coming!"

Igerna did not bother to hush him again.

Morgen raised her brows. "Can we ride ahead?"

"Yes! Let's go!" Arthur chimed.

Igerna shook her head. "No, children. We'll be there soon enough. It's rude to arrive too quickly. We must give everyone time to prepare. Now that they've seen us, the stable boys will be getting ready to take the horses, the cook will tell her women to finish the food for the feast..."

Arthur closed his eyes and clutched his belly. "Oh, I can't wait for the feast. I'm starving!"

"How can you be hungry again?" Morgen asked with a scowl.

"Well, I'm a dragon, and you're a bird, remember? Dragons must eat all the time. Birds can just eat a berry or a nut the whole day. What do you think we'll have at the feast, Mother?"

Arthur's comparison was apt. Morgen ate nothing more than fruit, nuts, bread, milk and cheese. She refused to eat any meat. Uthyr had insisted upon it, once, saying she looked sickly and needed the blood. Morgen had immediately thrown it up and fallen ill for two days. She had been allowed to eat as she wished since then.

"Fish stew and mussels, for certain, roasted hens with turnips and onions, perhaps some venison or boar..."

Arthur's brow wrinkled. "But what about Morgen?"

Igerna smiled at Arthur's concern for his sister. "Oh, there'll be lots of delicious cheeses, hot bread, cream, nuts and berries..."

Arthur moaned. "Oh! Let's hurry!"

"Soon."

In truth, it was not long before Igerna spied her father riding out to greet them. Or, at least, she thought it was him, for the rider was tall and lanky, but as he neared, she realized the rider was far too young to be her father. She squinted and looked more carefully. "Llyg!" she cried with a smile, raising her hand high.

Llyg grinned and maneuvered his horse alongside her.

"Brother!" Igerna exclaimed. Llyg's golden curls had turned a bit darker, and his face and body had lost their plumpness. "You're a man, now! How dare you grow up without telling me?"

Llyg chuckled. "It had to be done, I'm afraid." He eyed the children. "And speaking of growing up, last I saw these two they still fit in a cradle."

"I'm Arthur, son of Uthyr Pendragon," Arthur said with surprising volume and clarity, looking Llyg in the eye. "I'm pleased to meet you, my lord."

Llyg's eyes widened. "Pleased to meet you, Arthur, son of Uthyr. I'm Llyg, son of Amlawth Wledig, youngest brother to your mother. I welcome you to Dumnonia."

Arthur gave him a nod of respect. "Well-met, Llyg, son of Amlawth Wledig."

Igerna felt both shocked and proud of her son's sudden change in tone and manner.

Llyg said to her in a low tone, "Seems I'm not the only child who's grown to manhood."

Arthur motioned to Morgen. "This is my sister, Lady Morgen."

Morgen bowed her dark little head in Llyg's direction. "Pleased to meet you, Uncle Llyg."

Llyg gave her a smile. "Not as pleased as I am to meet you, Lady Morgen. I hear you both enjoy being out of doors. Is that true?"

"Oh, yes," Morgen confided, after glancing briefly at her mother.

"We've a good many places to discover, then. Now that you've both got ponies, I can show you all of Dumnonia."

The violet in Morgen's eyes seemed to light up from within. "Oh, that would be grand, Uncle. So grand. There's nothing we would love more."

"Settled, then. Let's get to the feast, find our beds, and we'll go riding tomorrow."

Both Arthur and Morgen became children once more, letting out whoops of excitement.

Igerna felt anxious but refused to deny her children the thrill of roaming the moors. Nothing could have kept her off them at their age.

The next day, and every day after that, the children explored from the time the morning meal finished until the evening one began. They went out with whomever would take them—sometimes Llyg, sometimes Cynwal—and returned mud-stained and rosy-cheeked, their hair blown wild from the wind.

Igerna lost no time in seeking out the company of Derwa, now so old she rarely left her room except to walk the moors for a spell each morning and evening, no matter the weather.

"You need to be careful, Derwa. You could fall and break a bone. Or be struck by lightning," Igerna cautioned.

"True, my hips and ankles can't hold me up like they used to," she confided. "But this can!" She brandished a crooked walking stick and smiled a now nearly toothless grin. "And lightning favors the tall. I'm as short as the boulders you and your brother used to say I looked like."

Igerna felt embarrassed and began to stutter an apology.

Derwa laughed. "You were just children, then. And besides, you were right. More so every day. I think if I were to sit my old behind on that hill, all who passed would take me for a tor." She shrugged and raised her furry brows. "Maybe I'll do it one morning. Sit up there with nothing on and grab the young lads as they walk by, eh? That'd scare the barley out 'o 'em!" She cackled for a long while, eyes crinkling with delight. Once she recovered, she pinned a look on Igerna. "So, now, out with it, lass. What's on your mind?"

There was no fooling Derwa, and Igerna had learned long ago not to bother trying. She got straight to it. "It's Morgen. She has the gifts."

"That's clear," Derwa pursed her old lips. "And you're afraid for her."

"I am." Igerna shook her head. "I don't want to shame her or scare her, but the people of Caer Leon have already noticed. There's talk. I don't know what to do."

Derwa nodded. "It'll only get worse. Or better, depending on how you look at it."

"I must help her."

"Help her do what?"

"I don't know."

Derwa chuckled. "That's not a good start. Tell me first what you want for her."

"Love," Igerna began.

"Is she not loved?"

"She is—by me, by Arthur, by her father, though he worries more than I do about how others see her…"

"Is that so? It sounds to me like you're very worried indeed. What else, then?"

"Happiness. To be accepted by her people. A good husband." Igerna sighed. "What a foolish question! I want for her what all mothers want for their children!"

Derwa shook her head. "You want for her what brings *you* happiness," she said, poking Igerna's chest with a bony finger. "I can assure you, a big castle and a husband lording over her is not what's goin' to make that lass happy. And if you try to force her to walk that path, it'll end in tears. This, I can promise you."

Igerna knew the truth when she heard it. "Then what do I do?"

Derwa looked up at the clouds a moment, as if the answer were hiding somewhere inside their silver-grey folds. "I know someone who may have some advice. Are you up for a bit of a journey?"

"To where?"

"Ynys Wydryn. Just a few days from here."

"Why? To visit the sisters?"

It was believed, among the Christians, that Joseph of Arimathea had journeyed to Briton to spread the word of God and built a small church atop Ynys Wydryn, for it was the tallest hill around for miles. They said that to mark the end of his long journey from the Holy Land, he planted his walking stick into the hill's fertile ground, which later sprouted and grew into a hawthorne tree that had flowered twice a year ever since. The church eventually became home to a small order of sisters, who cared for the apple orchard and kept bees, selling the fruit and honey to sustain themselves.

Derwa shrugged. "We can say that, if people ask. But there is another who lives there, and has, for far longer than the sisters. I know how to find her. Someone who can help your daughter."

"Who?"

Derwa leaned closer and covered her mouth. "The Lady of the Lake," she whispered. "But, of course, we don't say that," she added with a wink. "We'll say we're going to see Holy Joe's thorne tree, or something of that sort. That's good enough for anyone."

"Arthur will refuse to be left behind," Igerna said.

"Who said he couldn't come?"

"And my father will insist on sending men with us."

"Bah!" Derwa threw a hand in the air. "Fine. Pick a few who hate going to church. We'll find them an inn to drink at. They'll be no trouble."

Igerna nodded. "I can manage that."

"I know you can, clever girl—you were always smarter than your brothers."

Igerna shook her head. "Not smarter. More cunning. I'm not proud of it."

"Why?" Derwa scowled. "The fox doesn't have the brawn of the bear, yet she must still eat, mustn't she?"

Igerna changed the subject. "I'll make the arrangements."

Derwa took her hand and patted it, then turned back toward the castle, poking her walking stick into the hide of the hill as she went.

"Another adventure?" Morgen's eyes widened. "When do we leave?"

"Tomorrow," her mother replied.

"Who's coming?"

"Arthur, Derwa, you and I, and a few of Sira-wynn's men."

"And we're going to see Joseph Arima-nea's magic tree?"

"We are. It grows on an island."

"So, we must take another boat, then!"

"Yes, I suppose we must."

163

Morgen felt thrilled. Being out of doors every day had taken away what she called her 'dark feelings,' and her bad dreams had stopped. Now, she was about to go on another journey to see a magic tree with all her favorite people in the world. She dared to think she might love Old Derwa as much as her own Mamm-wynn. "I'll pack my things," she said, and scuttled off to the room she, Morgause and her mother shared, heart pattering.

The journey took them two days, but Morgen would have been happier if it had taken them far longer. She loved being on the road, moving through the world and seeing things she had never seen before. On the afternoon of the second day, she spied the tall hill her mother had described. "Look!" she cried, pointing. "There's the tor!"

"Indeed," Derwa confirmed with one of her winks. "We'll be there soon."

Arthur squinted. "What do you think lives up there? Giants?"

Derwa clucked her tongue. "Oh, no. Not on that hill. But I know of such a hill. A fearsome giant, named Ysbaddaden Ben Cawr, lives atop it, in a fortress that can be seen for miles around. Has a beautiful daughter, Olwen, about your age. Poor lass."

Arthur frowned. "Why? What happened to her?"

"Oh, her father won't let her leave his fortress. Says she's too beautiful and that someone will steal her from him."

Morgen narrowed her eyes on Derwa. "How do you know he said this? Have you been to Ysbaddaden's castle?"

"Clever girl," Derwa said with finger wag. "No, but I've heard stories from the giant's servants. He's so terrible, none of his servants last more than a week. Kills most of 'em. The lucky ones he simply throws down the hill. They bring the stories with 'em. They say wee Olwen has skin that shines like a pearl, fresh from the sea, and hair dark as yours," Derwa looked at Morgen, "so long it nearly sweeps the floor. Her father won't let her near a knife or scissors, lest she try to unlock her door."

"He locks her up?" Morgen asked, horrified.

"Oh, yes."

"Why?" Arthur demanded.

164

"Oh, I'm sure he thinks he's protecting her."

"But that's cruel!" Morgen protested. She imagined being locked up in her rooms at Caer Leon and felt panic tighten around her throat.

Arthur set his jaw. "Morgen's right. I'm going to save her."

Derwa raised her brows. "Are you now, young Arthur?"

"I am. When I'm grown. I'll rescue her and let her go wherever she pleases."

"Well," Derwa said with a smile. "You sound like you'll make the right kind of husband."

Arthur made a face and stuck out his tongue. "I said I'd *rescue* her, not marry her!"

Derwa chuckled.

They reached the marshes soon after Derwa finished her story and paid a man with a skiff to row them over to the shores of the island. Morgen imagined it was indeed the hill where the fearsome giant Ysbaddaden lived, and that she would be the one to rescue Olwen. She thought of this and grew wistful.

The boatman brought them to a tidy dock and helped them out of the skiff. Her mother told him when to return for them and then offered her hands to her children. "Come along."

They began climbing the trail toward the nunnery. It wound around the grand tor in green coils, each revolution offering up a finer view of the misty lands below.

Arthur kept running ahead, eager to reach the top.

"I'm holding the lad back," Derwa commented. "Why don't you take him on up, my lady. Morgen will keep me company. We'll be along in a bit."

"I'll race you, Mother!" Arthur said, running ahead.

Morgen reached out to take the old woman's hand. "Yes, go with Arthur, Mother. I'll walk with Lady Derwa. We'll meet you there."

Derwa smiled and squeezed her hand.

As soon as her mother was far enough away, Morgen whispered, "Can I take off my shoes?"

Derwa shrugged. "Don't see why not."

Gleeful, Morgen yanked off her shoes, tied the laces together and hung them over her shoulder. She clutched the grass with her toes, feeling the softness of the earth beneath her feet, and let out a long sigh.

Derwa tousled her hair. "Let's go, then, shall we?"

The mist had begun to rise from the waters below, and soon Morgen could no longer see the path ahead.

"Why do people call this place Ynys Wydryn?" she asked. "It's not made from glass." She had been disappointed when she had realized the isle was made of solid green earth, and not anything even remotely resembling glass, as its name implied.

Derwa looked down and squinted at her. "Some say that from far away, when the tor is surrounded by mist, like it is now, it looks as if it's made of glass. Others say it's because there's another world surrounding the tor, and, when you see the people inside it, it's as if you're looking at them through ice or glass. What do you think of that?"

"Oh, I want to see them," Morgen thought aloud, staring hopefully into the mist with round eyes.

"Perhaps we will," Derwa said, her tone cheerful. "We could wander through the apple grove a bit."

"We can?"

"Why not?"

Morgen felt a thrill. She had been longing to run into the trees for as long as they had been walking. "Can we eat one of the apples? Will the sisters mind if we take one?"

"Look how many there are. I don't see how taking a few could hurt, do you? Just the same, though, we'll give them some silver when we get to the top."

Morgen let out a squeal and ran into the trees, leaving Derwa to pick her way through the flatter areas of the hillside. She went from one tree to the next, determined to find the two most beautiful apples in the grove for them to eat. Then, just when she was about to choose the first, she saw something shimmer. She turned and spied a tree with a trunk as dark and blue as the night sky, and apples as luminous as the moon. "Lady Derwa!" she cried.

Derwa's voice sounded far away. "Yes, child?"

"You must see this!"

The tree was so spellbinding, it took all of Morgen's willpower to turn away and go back for Derwa. "That must be it! That must be Joseph's tree!" She gamboled like a fawn, darting through the tree trunks to where she was. "This way! You won't believe it. Wait until you see how beautiful it is!" She held Derwa's hand firmly, leading her toward the place she had seen the tree. To her deep relief, she found it again. "*That's* the tree I want to pick our apples from. Do you think they'll mind?"

"Take as many as you like," a new voice said behind them. "That tree belongs to me, not the sisters."

Derwa and Morgen both let out a yelp of surprise and turned around.

A few feet away stood a woman with hair as silver as the apples they coveted, dressed in a robe that Morgen thought looked as if it were spun from clouds at sunset. She widened her eyes, attempting to drink in as much of the splendor before her as she could. "The hawthorne you seek is on the other side of the island."

Derwa got to her knees and bowed her head to the ground.

She must be an angel! Morgen thought after seeing Derwa kneel. She fell to her knees as well but found she could not bear to take her eyes away from the woman to bow her head. "Are you an angel?" she managed to croak, trembling.

The woman's laugh trilled like a brook. "No, child. I am Lady Nimue. Please, rise."

Derwa struggled back to her feet. "We've come to pay our respects to you, Lady Nimue."

"Then I say welcome to you, with all my heart." Nimue smiled at Morgen and caressed her cheek. "Visitors come so rarely now. There aren't many who know the way into Affalon anymore. You're lucky Derwa has shown you." She winked at Morgen before turning around, plucking an apple from the silver tree, and handing it to Derwa. "For your devotion."

For a moment, Morgen thought she might have been left out, but Nimue turned toward her and said, "You may choose your own."

Morgen felt Nimue's eyes studying her as she approached the tree. She felt as if she could hear what she was thinking. She hesitated, glancing over at Derwa for approval. Derwa waved a hand at her. "Go on, lass! She'll not ask again."

Morgen hesitated. "Could I pick one for my brother and mother, too?"

"You may."

Morgen looked at the apples in turn. She knew by looking at them which ones would taste the best. After scanning the boughs, she made her choices and held one to her nose. "I know this smell," she whispered, swooning from the scent. "I've smelled it before."

Nimue smiled, staring at Morgen a moment and then stretched out her hand. "I wish to show you something. Come with me."

Morgen took Nimue's hand, heart racing. Her fingers felt as soft and cool as flower petals after a rain. Morgen reached over and took Derwa's hand as well. "We must stay together."

"Yes, of course, we must," Nimue agreed. "I don't think you'll need that walking stick for the rest of the journey, though, my dear Derwa. Why don't you leave it here?"

Morgen almost protested on her old friend's behalf, but Derwa smiled and leaned her stick up against the shimmering apple trunk. She took a few tentative steps. "Hee-heeeeee!" she cried out, grinning as widely as her puckered old mouth would allow. "Oh, thank you, my lady. Thank you. Even if it's just for the afternoon, what a gift."

"You can walk?" Morgen said.

"No pain at all, my dear. Oh, bless you, Lady Nimue. Bless you a thousand times."

Derwa had no problem keeping up with the two of them now, her steps as sure as a goat on a mountainside as they made their way along the ridgeline, back down, and up to the top of yet another hill. A large hawthorne reigned over the peak, in glorious full bloom. "Saint Joseph's tree!" Morgen exclaimed.

Nimue laughed. "It was only his walking stick until I blessed it. But, to be fair, you may certainly call it his tree if you wish. After all, he did carry it all the way here. And because of him, I was able to travel to that dry and yellow land he came from." Nimue shook her head. "I've never seen so much sun, or skin so dark, or heard language so beautiful and strange."

Morgen reached out and touched Joseph's tree. "You can travel through trees?"

"Oh yes. Trees such as these have a special magic. Holy magic. Their roots connect the world together beneath the earth."

Morgen often dreamt of trees. "Trees talk to me, sometimes."

"Do they?" Nimue looked at her again with that strange look. "I've only known one other person who could speak to trees the way I do. He could travel between them as well. It's not an easy thing to do. Has that ever happened to you?"

"No, but I wish it would!" Morgen's mind raced. "Can you really do that?"

"Oh, yes." Nimue glanced down at her. "You should try someday, when you're older."

"Why do I have to wait?"

"I suppose you don't. But what would you do if you couldn't get back?"

"I didn't think of that…"

"Perhaps we could try together. Would you like that?"

Morgen again looked at Derwa for approval, but this time, Derwa's expression was decidedly not encouraging. "One day, when I'm older, as you said," Morgen ventured, "but not today." She secretly swore to herself she would make that day come, one way or another.

"As you wish," Nimue replied. "Do other things speak to you, besides people?"

Morgen nodded. "Horses, ravens, cats, hounds. They don't talk like we do, but when they look at me, or if they let me touch them, I know how they feel." She paused a moment. "Lady Nimue—" She wanted to ask Nimue a question, but then hesitated. *Mother told me never to tell anyone.*

"What is it, dear?" Derwa prompted. "You can trust Lady Nimue."

Morgen decided to risk it. "Lady Nimue, can you see the green light around Lady Derwa? I see light around you, too. Like moonlight, or the silver of fish swimming in the sun."

"I can indeed. Everyone's light is a little different, isn't it?"

Morgen felt thrilled. *At last, someone who can see it, too!* "They are! And animals have it too! And plants and trees!"

"They do, you're right. Even if others cannot see the light, it's there. You're truly fortunate."

169

"She's got the gift," Derwa confirmed, patting Morgen on the head. "Her mother's line is strong."

"Or her father's." Nimue smiled. "Morgen, can your brother see any of the things you do?"

Morgen shook her head. "I don't think so. Sometimes he says he can, but I'm not sure. I think it makes him feel bad when he can't."

Nimue nodded. "Perhaps if you keep showing him, one day he will. People like your brother need people like us to help them see where the magic is." She stopped, knelt in front of Morgen, and looked her in the eyes. "But you must know this, Morgen—there are many people who don't want to see it at all. And you mustn't try to make them. You'll know who they are when you meet them."

Morgen already knew the truth of this. "Mother says they're afraid."

Nimue nodded. "They are. Some are very afraid. Others think we're lying, or that we're trying to make fools of them. Worst of all are the ones who think we mean them harm."

"But that's not true." Morgen felt tears well up in her eyes thinking of how the cook's children always ran away whenever they saw her coming. They had been friends once, until she had shown them how she could light a candle without a match and make water swirl in a rain barrel without touching it. She knew better, but she had felt convinced they would be pleased. They were not. And they had never spoken to her again.

"No, it isn't, dear child. But that is what they think, and there's no use trying to make them think differently." She stroked Morgen's cheek. "But I shall always listen to you, if you ever need a friend. And, when you're older, if you wish to learn more about what you can do, you may come and live with me. For now, though, play your music, ride your pony, play with the hounds—but you must do as Lady Derwa and your mother say—do not let anyone see your magic. You must do things the way others do them. If the trees or animals speak to you, or if you see things in your dreams that come true, tell only Derwa or your mother. Do not tell anyone else. Not even your brother."

Morgen gasped. "Oh no, Lady Nimue. I can't keep secrets from Arthur. We tell each other everything."

170

Nimue squeezed her hands. "He may understand, now, child, but there will come a time when he may not. When lads come of age, things change."

Morgen shook her head. "I don't believe you." The thought of Arthur turning away from her caused all the happiness in her heart to drain away. "You don't know my brother. Arthur shall always understand me. Always."

Nimue smiled and squeezed her hand. "I hope so, Morgen. I hope so. But if it should ever not be so, and you need a friend, return to Affalon and call on me. You will always be welcome here."

171

The Young Stag

CHAPTER EIGHTEEN
Alliances

Uthyr shifted uncomfortably in his chair, his old war wounds twinging like dark harbingers. All along the eastern shores were tales of Saxon skirmishes, from Gododdin all the way down to Anderitum. Hanging over it all, like stubborn storm clouds were reports that Octa yet lived. Uthyr's men in Gaul said he had amassed an army the likes of which Brython had never seen. Uthyr was wise enough to know that rumors grew like tumors, feeding off each teller's fear and imagination, but there was one thing he dared not question any longer.

"Uthyr?"

He looked over to see Igerna standing in the archway of his hall. She came and sat across from him, concern rippling her brow. "What's wrong, husband?"

He knew it was selfish of him to burden her with such matters, but sometimes he needed to confide in someone who would simply listen, rather than attempt to further their own agenda. He reached for her hand and kissed it. "What I feared has come to pass. We must accept that Octa's alive, or that there's a warlord who's taken his name and convinced every bloody Saxon on Earth that he is. In the end, it's all the same to us. Whoever he is, he'll be sailing across the sea with war on his mind, as young and fierce as Emrys and I when we sailed from Armorica to avenge our own father." He rubbed his temples, trying to ward off a headache.

Igerna sighed and looked at the floor. "Dear God, Uthyr, will this never end? Are we to be at war for the rest of our lives?"

Uthyr shrugged. "I don't know, love. I pray every night it will end, but I don't see any end in sight."

"So, what are you going to do?"

"My men say we need more spies—Saxon-speaking spies who can judge the mettle of an army and bring back every stinking detail about Octa—or his imposter—and the men he commands." He clenched his fists, remembering the day he had publicly executed the prisoner whom he believed was Octa. "That bastard will meet his death by my hands, yet—I swear it before God." He glanced heavenward to show he was in earnest.

"Do your men have any idea where he'll attack first?"

Uthyr sighed. "They do. That's the problem. All we have are ideas. We argued about it all damn day. Lot of Gododdin says Octa knows the north best and that many are still loyal to him there. He thinks he'll sail up the Humber, attack Caer Ebrauc and work his way south along the coast, where he can fatten his ranks from the settlements of his people and take refuge in their forts. But my gut tells me differently. I believe he'll attack from Kent. The Saxons are strongest there. That's enough of a reason alone, but I think there's a more personal reason than that. Octa's as arrogant and proud as his father—if he truly is Octa, that is—and surely harbors the blackest of hate toward me. I think he'll try to take Caer Lundein, the place I was made a fool of by executing his brother, thinking it was him. If he succeeds, it'll be as if he's risen from the dead to mock me. He'll be a hero to his people and could become as powerful as his father."

"So, you'll send your forces to Caer Lundein?"

Uthyr sighed. "Some—but not all. Octa's not the only one we need to watch. A chieftain named Aelle has conquered the shore south of us. He's a fierce and ambitious bastard with three young sons as hungry for power as he is. It's only a matter of time before they become troubling to us as well."

Uthyr had known of Aelle's threat for a while and had entrusted Camulos with defending Caer Gwinntguic. The man had held not only its borders against the Saxons, but the borders of the neighboring lands of Rhegin and the settlement of Caer Mincip as well—but he would not be able to hold it much longer, if Aelle chose to attack.

"It sounds like you need more men."

Uthyr nodded. "We need more men." He let out a defeated huff, thinking of how the council had debated for hours and managed to come up with nothing that had inspired any enthusiasm. "We've no choice but to prepare for both possibilities. I asked Lot to call upon his bannermen in the north, as we need all the men we have here to stay in the south. I must refuse his request for support."

It had bothered Uthyr to disappoint Lot, for it seemed all the fire of youth and bloodlust for battle had burned out of all his bannermen's hearts save one—Lot of Gododdin.

His wife looked at him sideways. "And how does he feel about your decision?"

173

"I'm certain he isn't pleased with it, but I know that if any kingdom can survive against impossible odds, it's Gododdin."

Igerna furrowed her brow. "We daren't send him home empty-handed, do we? He traveled further than any of the others to sit on your council."

"I know, I know. I feel the same, but we can't spare the men—not with Aelle in the south and the threat of an attack from Kent."

"Then supplies, perhaps? Food? Weapons? That we can spare. The harvest was kind—the best in five years. I can arrange for wagons of grain, and commission some swords from Mynyth Aur."

At a time like this, Uthyr did not want to part with any resources, but he valued his northern allies. He nodded. "Yes. That we can do, at least. I'll meet with him tomorrow."

Uthyr strode toward his hall the next morning, eager to speak with Lot. A solution had come to him in the night. He felt surprised he had not thought of it before. *Lot is but two and twenty and unmarried. I can send him home not only with grain and supplies for his troops, but with a wife and a large dowry as well.*

He came upon the young warrior pacing in front of the large hearth. "Lot! I'm sorry we didn't have time to speak alone before yesterday's council. Thank you for making the long journey."

"It was an honor, Pendragon. Especially with the colder weather coming on. Bit of a respite before the Cailleach digs her icy nails into us."

Uthyr felt surprised by Lot's jovial manner. He was typically quite saturnine. Though young, he had the manner of an older man accustomed to leading, and he had proven himself on the battlefield many times. His father, Edor, had been a loyal bannerman, never wavering in his support, and it seemed to Uthyr his son was as trustworthy. Despite constant challenges, including the sudden death of his father, Lot had managed to hold the northern kingdom of Gododdin firmly in his grip—not an easy task for any man, let alone one so young.

Both Igerna and Morgause will be thrilled with the match, he assured himself. *How could they not? Lot could do no better, and neither could*

174

Morgause—God knows Gorlois could not have found her such a husband.
Besides, as much as Uthyr knew any woman's mind, Lot was
considered quite handsome. He smiled at the man and gripped his
shoulder. "Come with me, I've something to discuss with you."

He led Lot down a hallway to a smaller chamber with a warm
fire in the hearth, where Dubricius awaited them. The archbishop
stood up to greet them, inclining his head toward each of them in
turn. "Pendragon. King Lot."

Lot bowed his head. "Your grace."

They sat down. Uthyr reached for a pitcher of ale and poured
them a round. "So," he said, serving the archbishop first and then
pushing a cup toward Lot. "Tell me more about what the people are
saying in the north about Octa. Now that we're alone, you can speak
freely."

Lot raised his dark brows. "But I have spoken freely—it's exactly
as I said in the council—the people say he lives. The news is
spreading like a plague. Everyone believes it, and things have been
the worse for it. Saxon attacks on my lands have doubled. This is why
I've implored you to send support."

Uthyr let out a tired sigh. "You don't think he's mad enough to
invade during the winter, do you?"

"It wouldn't be considered wise, but you never know."

Uthyr raised his brows. "No, you never do, do you?"

Lot leaned forward. "Pendragon, they say Octa commands an
army of some four thousand men. How many do you have at your
command?"

"Five hundred here in Caer Leon, but we have that many in the
other settlements as well, and I can call upon my bannermen for the
rest."

Lot nodded. "Perhaps Camulos is right and they'll attack in the
south—especially if they move in winter. I pray that he is, for
Gododdin's sake. In any case, you can count on us. You've but to give
the word as to where and when. I'll return home and ready my men."

Now, more than ever, after his display of humility and
willingness to follow the will of the council, Uthyr felt convinced he
had made the right decision.

"Lot, I've something else I'd like to discuss with you." He
stopped to refill everyone's cup. "I wish to unite our families.

Morgause is a woman, now, and in need of a husband. I can think of no man better suited for her than you."

Lot seemed stunned. He remained silent a moment, his eyes darting between Uthyr and Dubricius. "Truly, Pendragon?"

"Yes, you've seen her before, I know, when she was just a girl. But I assure you, she's become quite a beautiful woman with a keen mind and wit to match. And, of course, a generous dowry."

Lot was quick to accept. "Pendragon, I can't find the words to tell you how honored I am to be entrusted with so great a treasure."

Uthyr felt a wave of pride and relief. "I'm so glad. You'll be happy, I'm sure of it. She's as strong and shrewd as Gorlois." He felt his chest grow heavy with guilt and glanced at Dubricius. "Bless the man's soul."

Though it was but a tiny gesture, Uthyr noticed Lot raise his brows in surprise. Uthyr knew why. None but those who had spent the past few years with him were accustomed to hearing him speak of the Lord or his blessings. That had been his brother's habit, not his. He had changed much since the archbishop had come to Caer Leon.

"When do you picture this wedding taking place?" the archbishop asked. "And where?"

Uthyr had not thought through anything past the offer of Morgause's hand. *Where, indeed? We'll be preoccupied with moving to Caer Lundein—and then I'll need Lot in battle. It could be years before we defeat Octa. And what if I die in battle? Then what? Who will lead the armies? Arthur is but thirteen, so it must be Lot.*

"Now," Uthyr blurted. "I'd like you to be married now."

Lot's brows shot up. "That's sudden—but, as you wish, Pendragon. I would be happy to have the warmth of a beautiful wife to ward off the lonely chill come winter."

"It's done, then." Uthyr raised his cup and toasted the new couple, then reached across the table and clasped Lot's arm to seal the arrangement. He turned to Dubricius. "Prepare the church, Archbishop."

"It will be my honor, Pendragon."

Uthyr then stood up and went to talk to his wife. *Forgive me, Igerna.*

176

Igerna's eyes popped open in a flash of rage. "You did *what*?"

Uthyr tried to explain. "Lot's a trusted bannerman—he's young, respected, tried in battle—"

Igerna threw up a hand. "Stop! We spoke of giving him grain and weapons, Uthyr—not my daughter! How dare you give her away without consulting me?" She came so close he could feel her breath on his neck. "As if what you did to her father wasn't enough." She stormed out of her chamber, leaving a chill in her wake.

Oh, God help me. Uthyr knew it would be folly to run after her in such a state. She would be angry for a good spell. Instead, he went to the church to speak to Dubricius, whom he could always count on for sound advice. *Gods, I've spent more time beneath a church roof in the past few years than I have in my entire life before it.* He glanced upward. *Suppose you're pleased, eh, Emrys?* He smiled but then winced, as he always did whenever he thought of his brother's murder. *Poison! What a coward.* The idea that Octa yet lived and had escaped justice was more than he could bear. *One day soon, you wretch, I'll rip you to pieces with my bare hands for what you did to him—and the fool you made of me!*

Dubricius turned around at the sound of Uthyr's footsteps. "Greetings, Pendragon."

Uthyr sighed. "I fear I've upset my wife."

Dubricius raised his brows. "Not in favor of the marriage, is she?"

"Not exactly."

Dubricius nodded. "Understandable. The queen and her daughter are quite close. She will feel her absence sharply."

Uthyr wished he could start the day over and do things properly, but there was nothing to be done for it. "I've given my word, so it must happen."

"Yes, it must. And soon, as you've pointed out. Perhaps send for the queen's mother? Her visits always seem to raise her daughter's spirits, and likewise. She would want to be present at the wedding of her granddaughter in any case, I'm certain. As would Lord Amlawth."

Uthyr slumped down on the nearest pew and put his face in his hands. "Oh, Dubricius. I'm weary of trying to please everyone."

"Best not to try, then. You've only God to answer to, in the end."
Uthyr moaned. "That's no consolation, I'm afraid."

Dubricius walked over and sat down beside him. "What would you have me do, Pendragon? You've but to ask."

Uthyr shook his head. "Nothing to be done, I'm afraid. My only hope is that Morgause will be happier about the match than my wife is. I'm no expert on women—clearly—but I've seen how she looks at Lot when she thinks no one is watching. She fancies him."

Dubricius smiled. "Well, perhaps therein lies your redemption. Why don't you go and ask her? Best she learns of her betrothal from you. News like this travels like wildfire."

"You're right. I'll go and speak to her."

Morgause appeared in the doorway of the hall, waiting to be invited in. "You wanted to speak with me, Father?"

"Come in, daughter." Uthyr smiled to put her at ease, though in truth, he felt he was likely the more nervous of the two of them. "Please, sit down."

Morgause came over slowly, hands folded in front of her. She perched herself stiffly on the edge of the chair across from him.

Dear God, did Igerna already speak to her? Uthyr stifled the impulse to groan and reached for the pitcher of ale on the table next to him.

"Oh, let me, Father." Morgause jumped up and filled his cup. His stomach churned at her eagerness. *What the hell's wrong with me? I can lead armies against some of the most notorious enemies Brython has ever known, but I balk at talking to a young girl?* His irritation at the situation brought on a wave of anger. "You're to be married," he spat out.

He regretted his boorish delivery the moment it left his lips, but at least the deed was done.

Morgause's eyebrows flew up in surprise. *"Married?"*

"Yes. To Lot of Gododdin. He is one of my most trusted bannerman, and—"

"Oh! Father!" Morgause jumped up, her hands flying to her mouth. Her eyes could not have lit up more if he had presented her with a chest of jewels. "Lot? He's the most desired lord in all of Brython!" She looked up at the ceiling, eyes dancing, as if she were watching the actual wedding ceremony play out upon its stone surface. She jumped from the chair and paced, holding her stomach. "I can't believe it." She shook her head, smiling from ear to ear. "*Lot of Gododdin*, Father?" She took a deep breath and sat back down. "When did he ask for my hand? When's the wedding to be? And where? Isn't he bound for Gododdin soon? Am I to wait for him to return?"

The list of justifications, placations, explanations and praises for Lot he had rehearsed fell unspoken out of his gaping mouth. This, of all things, he had not expected. "We wish for you to wed soon, so you may go with him to Gododdin," he stammered.

"How soon? Oh, but Father, it cannot be for a week at least—I must have a fine dress, and we must plan for the feast ...Oh, I must speak with Mother!"

Uthyr felt so relieved he would have promised Morgause the moon itself if he could have. "Of course! You'll have the finest dress in all Brython and all the jewels your mother's been saving for you. Don't worry about a thing. It'll be the finest wedding Caer Leon has ever seen. I promise you."

Morgause forgot propriety and threw her arms around him, giggling and squealing. "Oh, I can't believe it. I'm the luckiest maid in the world!" She ran towards the door and then stopped in her tracks and turned around. "Oh! By your leave, Father..."

Uthyr smiled and waved her on. "Yes, lass—go. You and your mother have much to plan."

She grinned and ran out of the hall, leaving Uthyr shaking his head, dumbfounded. *I'll never understand women.*

CHAPTER NINETEEN
A Plea for Morgen

Igerna felt her ears and cheeks redden with anger. They felt so hot, she would not have been surprised to see steam rising from them into the cold September air. *Everything has been going so well, and now this?*

Lately, she had felt happier than she had felt in some time. The wedding of Morgause to Lot, though rushed, had been splendid. It had been only three moons since the marriage, and Morgause had already sent word she suspected she was with child. On top of this wonderful news, Uthyr, too, seemed to be improving, both in health and spirit. He had made love to her that morning with such eagerness, anyone listening outside their bed chamber would have thought they were newlyweds. Afterward, at his suggestion, they had gone riding together, talking and laughing as if all the Saxons in Brython had packed up their boats and sailed home. They had stopped a moment ago at the river to let the horses drink. There, without warning, he had ruined it all.

"So that's why you've been courting me all day like a randy lad on Beltane, is it?" she demanded. "No, Uthyr. I'll not have it. You will *not* betroth Morgen to Urien of Rheged! How can you abide the thought of that old man sweating and grunting over her? He's surely rough under the furs, that one—I'll never forget the way he looked at me when I first met him. His eyes devour every pretty maid in the hall like a wolf hungry for lamb. Have mercy, Uthyr—for God's sake, Urien is older than you! Morgen is not for such a man and you know it! And why Morgen? Not that I would have allowed it, but why did you not try and betroth Morgause to Urien? She's a woman, at least, and far more disposed to marriage."

"You know the answer to that."

"Perhaps. But I want to hear you say it."

"Igerna—please."

"Say it!"

He sighed. "Because Morgause is the daughter of Gorlois, and Morgen is my one true daughter. Urien deserves the stronger alliance."

Igerna felt the irony sharply—the lie meant to protect the girl was the reason for what might become the source of her misery. Hearing mention of Gorlois caused her to think back on him, and her

180

first wedding night. How frightened and lonely she had felt in that windy castle surrounded by the sea! Caer Ligualid, Urien's fortress, was ten times more terrible than Tintagel, and ten times further away, in lands ever under threat from both Pict and Saxon. Even the Romans, who had conquered most of the world, had given up holding their ground that far north.

She had been older at the time of her marriage to Gorlois. In truth, Igerna believed Morgen to be the strongest person she had ever known but refused to allow this to be her fate. She would do anything necessary to avoid it. *Besides, if Arhianna or Taliesin ever return, they'd never forgive me for allowing it.*

Uthyr took her hand and held it between his warm, giant palms. "My love, please listen—I can't leave you unprotected. Urien's a good man. Yes, he's old and a bit ill-mannered, but he's well-respected, wealthy, and he commands a great army. It will be either him or Lot who will become the next Pendragon if I should meet an untimely death, and then all of you would be provided for and well-protected. For now, I'm speaking of betrothal only—the wedding can wait a few years."

Igerna pulled her hand away. "Absolutely not. She'd be better off with the sisters on Ynys Wydryn."

Uthyr snorted. "A nun? My one true daughter? You must be joking. No, Igerna. She doesn't have the temperament, and you know it. Besides, she must have children."

Igerna felt a fury rising in her breast. "She is not a brood mare for you to sell to the highest bidder!" She held back several other things she wanted to say, for she was wise enough to know this was not the way she would accomplish her goal, but she could not remain in her husband's presence. She jumped on her horse, kicked him in the flanks and galloped back toward Caer Leon, feeling used and betrayed.

That night, when Uthyr came to bed, Igerna changed her tactics and nestled herself in the crook of his arm. "I'm sorry, husband—please forgive my harshness this morning. I know you're only trying to protect us. I know. Just promise me one thing, my love..."

181

The fire in Uthyr's eyes died down and his brow softened, and she felt encouraged. *I shall win this battle, at least.* He pulled her close and kissed her forehead. "What would you have me do?"

"Make no promises for now. Say nothing to Urien. Let us consult the archbishop and ask his advice."

She felt reasonably certain the archbishop would side with her in this matter, but she could not know for sure. Either way, it would buy her daughter some time.

Uthyr remained silent so long she feared he would refuse her. She closed her eyes and prayed to both Mary and the Great Mother for mercy.

At last, Uthyr spoke. "Very well. We'll consult Dubricius."

Though she still felt angry with him, Igerna kissed him with as much passion as she could muster. "Thank you, husband."

Igerna left the fortress early the next morning to ensure she would be the first to speak with the archbishop about Morgen. She took a few of her handmaids with her so that her outing would look like just another trip to market. She often went into the village with her maids.

She felt pleased to see the doors of the church standing open and candles flickering within. She entered and spied the archbishop near the altar, head bent in prayer. She crossed herself before walking softly to the pew closest to the statue of Mary. She knelt in front of it, using the time to pray for her daughter. *Mary, Mother of God, holy face of the Great Mother, have mercy on my daughter. Shield her from the selfish desires of men. Grant her sanctuary on Ynys Wydryn, where you, in your many forms, may teach her your mysterious ways.*

"My queen?"

Igerna jumped, for she had not heard Dubricius approach. She hastened to her feet, smiled and bent her head. "Archbishop."

He smiled in return. "I'm glad to see you here. The early morning is my favorite time to pray. It feels like the sins of the entire world are washed away when dawn breaks."

Igerna glanced at the clean early light outside the church doors and nodded. "I like hearing nothing but birdsong on the air."

He smiled. "That too."

"I've come to speak to you about my daughter," Igerna ventured.

"Oh?" The archbishop raised his eyebrows. "Morgause or Morgen?"

"Morgen. I'd like to send her to the nuns at the abbey on Ynys Wydryn. You know how clever she is—and what a talent she shows for healing and music. I believe she would flourish at the abbey. The nuns could teach her so much."

The archbishop cocked his head and raised a brow at her. "And what does the Pendragon think of this?"

Igerna sighed. "I'm afraid he feels differently. Uthyr wants to marry her to Urien of Rheged." She did not attempt to hide her distress. "What kind of life would she have up there, at the edge of oblivion? That man is old enough to be her grandfather!"

Dubricius paused a moment. "So, do you wish for her to become a nun to avoid such a life, or because you believe she has been called by God?"

Igerna took her time choosing her next words. "I wish for her to have the chance to determine that for herself. And I feel certain living among the sisters would give her that chance." She ventured closer, lowering her voice. "She can speak to spirits and knows by touching a plant whether it will harm or heal. Such gifts surely come from God, do they not? Where better for her to learn how to serve the Lord than among the sisters?"

The look on the archbishop's face told Igerna her words had fallen on fertile soil. She waited a moment, letting them take root.

"And what does your daughter want, my queen?"

That the archbishop had even bothered to consider what her daughter wanted encouraged Igerna further. "She would tell you she wants to live in the forest and create medicine for the village. Such a life we could never allow, but perhaps she could do such things among the sisters. What do you think? I know they have a grand apothecary, several beehives, and many gardens and orchards that need tending—I'm certain Morgen would be happy there. You know how she loves to be outdoors. She can scarcely abide coming inside for the night. And, in the end, if the life of a nun is not for her, think of what a much better wife she will make—pious and hard-working, with skills that are sure to benefit her future husband's household."

183

The archbishop nodded slowly. "Have you made these entreaties to your husband?"

Igerna looked at the ground. "He would only agree to seek your advice on the matter." She looked up and met his gaze again. "Please, Archbishop—you know Morgen better than anyone, save Arthur and me. Marriage is not for her. Please help her."

The archbishop took her hand. "I shall pray for her, and for Uthyr to hear you; however, in my experience, it is most often a man's wife who can best open her husband's eyes and soften his heart. Spend some time in prayer, and entreat him again."

Igerna nodded and mustered a smile. "I will. Thank you, Archbishop."

Uthyr felt the hitch in his hip sharply as he plodded down the corridor to the main hall where Dubricius awaited him. As usual, the archbishop sat close to the fire, his graceful hands poised with palms toward the heat, gazing at the dancing flames with a slight smile.

"Thank you for coming, Archbishop."

Dubricius turned to face him. "Always a pleasure, my king. How can I be of service?"

"Bit of advice, if you don't mind." Uthyr groaned as he sat down and reached for a pitcher of ale. He glanced toward Dubricius' cup, still full on the table. "Would you prefer wine, Archbishop?"

"No, no. Just enjoying the fire. That's all."

"Are you certain?"

"Quite certain, thank you."

Uthyr nodded, filled his cup and took a long draught. Then he let out a sigh and stared at the fire a moment. "It's about Morgen."

"Yes?"

Uthyr leaned in closer and lowered his voice. "I need to find my daughters good husbands while I still can. Morgause is safely married to Lot, and I've no doubt it was the best match I could possibly have made. What's more, she's over the moon about it. Morgen, however, is another story. Igerna wants to send her to Ynys Wydryn for a few years. Says she's too young to marry. She refuses to accept that Morgen's a woman, now. She still thinks of her as a little girl."

Dubricius smiled. "Such is the way with mothers. Their children remain ever so in their eyes, even when they're grown with children of their own."

"I know I should wait a few years or seek a younger husband for Morgen, but I can't wait." Uthyr shook his head. "I'm dying, Archbishop. Igerna doesn't know it, but I do."

Dubricius furrowed his brow. "Why do you think you're dying, my king?"

Uthyr did not tell Dubricius about the blood he had begun to cough up. "I just know."

"And what of Morgen? Have you spoken to her about your plans?"

Uthyr shook his head. "I haven't. But I will. I think she'll love the north. She's strong. Much stronger than Igerna thinks she is. I think Urien is just the man for her. He's encountered strange powers up there in his lands over the years, and none ever seem to disturb him. He won't be frightened by her strangeness."

"What do you mean, her strangeness?"

Uthyr shrugged his shoulders and sighed. "She hates wearing shoes, won't wear any of the fine dresses or jewels I bring her, won't bother with her hair beyond the simplest of styles."

"That's perhaps uncommon for a young woman, but I'd not call it strangeness."

Uthyr paused and lowered his voice to a whisper. "She sees spirits wandering about the grounds, swears the animals speak to her, spends her afternoons plucking flowers and mushrooms from the woods to make horrid-smelling poultices and ointments for me..."

"And, do they work?"

"They do," Uthyr confessed. "Better than any my physician can concoct. But that's just it—she's but a maiden of thirteen summers, with no training in the healing arts. How is it that she knows these things?"

"Have you asked her?"

Uthyr cocked his head back and forth. "She says she can see what a plant is good for by the 'light around it,' but what the hell does that mean?"

185

Dubricius chuckled. "It means just that. You should feel blessed to have such a child."

Uthyr sighed. "I do. Please, don't misunderstand me—I love my daughter—believe me, I do—but I fear for her. People fear such power in a woman. They already avert their eyes and make the sign of the cross when she looks at them. I say, if Urien will have her, and he's said as much, we could do no better for her."

The archbishop folded his hands in his lap. "Marriage is not the only answer, Pendragon. The holy sisters are revered by all. Surely, the villagers would have nothing to fear if Morgen were to join them. What's more, Igerna says Morgen wishes to go to Ynys Wydryn. Why not let her? To allow a daughter to live in service to the Lord is one of the most honorable sacrifices a father can make. There, she can put her healing power to good use, and all will swear it comes from God. Who would dare suggest anything else?"

Uthyr sat in silence a while. "And she would be protected."

"She would, indeed. I would do all I could to ensure this. And she would be close to Caer Leon and her mother's family in Dumnonia."

Uthyr had thought long on the prospect, wanting to please Igerna and his daughter, but he had needed to be certain of Dubricius' support. Without it, he feared even the sisters might reject Morgen. "You will speak to them about her gifts? They must know everything before I will agree to send her there. I cannot risk having her cast out by the sisters."

"I shall escort your daughter myself, if you wish, and ensure the sisters understand her blessings. I give you my word she will come to no harm there."

Uthyr nodded. "Then it seems there is no reason for me to deny my wife's request."

"Good." Dubricius smiled. "Let her spend a few years there, among the sisters. Who knows? Perhaps she'll discover a way to cure you of your illness."

"Perhaps, Archbishop." Uthyr glanced at the elaborate cross standing upon the altar. God had not answered his prayers on this account. His aches and pains had only worsened over the years. *Very well, Lord. I shall grant you my only daughter. Just let me live until my son is old enough to take my place.*

186

"I'm going to live with the sisters?" Morgen asked, heart soaring. *At last, the day has come!* She had been praying for it ever since she had first visited Ynys Wydryn all those years ago. "When?"

"Soon, my darling," her mother replied. "They'll teach you about the word of God, and…" She stopped short and looked down to hide the tears that had welled up in her eyes.

Morgen smiled and took her mother's hands in hers. "Please don't cry, Mother. I'll not be gone forever. It's as it should be."

Her mother looked up, brow furrowed. "Is it?"

"It is." Morgen nodded. "And I'm so grateful."

"You are?"

"I am, Mother. Do you think I want to go marry an old man? Or any man, for that matter?" She grimaced. "I'd rather die."

"Don't say that." Her mother shook her head. "One day, you'll know love."

"I already know love, Mother—a love far greater than that."

Her mother chuckled and stroked her cheek. "You're still young, *cariad*. When you meet the right man, things will change."

Morgen shook her head. "I don't want them to change."

"Wanting won't stop it."

Morgen took a deep breath and resigned herself to dealing with whatever sort of madness might come upon her when the time came. She had watched it turn her sister into an idiot over that simpleton, Lot, and vowed she would never allow herself to succumb to such an illness. Now, with God and the Mother's grace, she felt determined she never would.

"If the sisters mistreat you in any way, you must send word to me immediately."

"They won't."

Her mother nodded and gathered her into her arms. "I'll miss you so much. So will Arthur."

"It will be best for Arthur. Best for both of us." Morgen paused, thinking of Arthur's strong attachment to her. "You and father should consider sending him away, as well. Somewhere he can become a man."

"What do you mean?"

"Somewhere he can train for battle, surrounded by men."

"He is training for battle, surrounded by men!"

"But they serve Father. They treat him like a little lord, and you know it. He knows it, too. He wants to go someplace where no one knows he's the son of Uthyr Pendragon. Or cares, at least."

"He said this?"

"You should speak with him."

Her mother turned toward the fire. "I'm to lose both my children, then," she murmured, as if addressing the flames. "How is this fair?"

"You always say life isn't fair."

Her mother nodded. "I know."

"What isn't fair?" a voice asked from behind them. Morgen turned to see her brother standing in the archway of the hall. "Life," she said, glancing at him.

He nodded, poured himself some ale, and joined them by the fire. His hair and tunic were soaked with sweat. Morgen gave him a look to let him know she had breached the subject with their mother. "Who were you training with?" she asked, providing him an opportunity.

"Camulos." He took a long drink. "But not in earnest. He's going easy on me. I know it."

"Well, you are only thirteen," their mother reasoned.

At this, Arthur's amber eyes flashed. "Have you told him to?"

"No," she protested, but Morgen saw a look in her eyes that spoke to the contrary.

Arthur pressed on. "Mother, if the Saxons push this far west, do you think they'll care whether I'm thirteen or twenty?" He shook his head. "No, they'll disembowel me just the same. Best I know how to fight, and I won't learn like this."

"I'm sorry. Perhaps we can find you someone else to train with?"

"No. Not here." He paused a moment. "I want to train with Cynyr's men up in Gwynedd. They say Cai is unbeatable on the battlefield. I can train with him."

Morgen saw hope rise in Arthur's eyes when their mother did not answer right away, which meant she was considering his request.

Igerna sighed. "There's more to life than learning how to cut men open, Arthur. I've worked for years to find you the best tutors in Brython. Am I now to ask them to go with you to Gwynedd? And for Cynyr to house and feed them?"

Arthur opened his mouth to protest, but Morgen raised two fingers and slowly shook her head. Though it seemed he might explode from it, he swallowed the words he had been about to speak and finished his ale instead. Once he resurfaced from behind the brim of his cup, his features had smoothed.

"Of course not, Mother." He knew the meaning of Morgen's signal. The seed had been planted. That was enough for now. They had long worked in tandem to steer their parents toward their aims, and rarely had their efforts fallen short of success. He felt certain he would be under Lord Cynyr's roof training with Cai before the summer ended.

CHAPTER TWENTY
Taliesin's Return

Taliesin.

Taliesin woke with a start. He sat up and looked around the fortress yard from beneath the Oak, listening. He heard no voices, saw no candles or lanterns, and smelled no woodsmoke. The stars seemed the only ones awake. He wrapped his cloak about him and whistled to Vala. She flew down, from somewhere in the limbs above, and perched on his outstretched arm. Each time she came to him, Taliesin felt grateful he had taken Amergin's advice to train a bird.

Over the past year, he had considered various birds as a companion. At first, an owl or raven felt like the obvious choice, but once he saw Vala, he immediately knew she was the one for him. He had seen her in a dive, and she had taken his breath away. He recognized her quickly as a *peregrinus*, to quote the Romans, by far the fastest of all falcons. Her grace and her huge, round eyes had drawn him in. He had courted her for weeks, tracking her, bringing offerings of small prey, and mimicking her call to perfection. To his delight, she eventually succumbed to his charms.

Her small size made her much easier to handle and manage than a hawk. She would be considered small even among her own species, weighing a mere pound and a half, which suited him well. He had taken to always wearing a thick padding of leather on his shoulder, so she could perch there if she wished. Vala had become a near constant companion and an invaluable ally for shifting. He could not imagine life without her now.

Taliesin climbed the steps at the wall. A chilly breeze met him at the top. He adjusted his body heat while he surveyed the countryside. The meadow below looked like a lake. A thick even mist lay across it, concealing the long grass except for a few stalks reaching out here and there. It spread to the edges of the forest, where it broke up and swirled in between the trees, disappearing into pools of blue-black darkness. He watched the land until the sky began whispering of dawn. Then, at the edge of the forest, he saw a raven flap its wings.

Taliesin.

He descended the wall and woke the guard sleeping by the small door beside the gates.

"Hmmmf? What is it?"

"I must venture out."

The guard, eyes squinting and groggy from sleep, sat up and rubbed his eyes. "Ollam Taliesin?" He glanced at Vala. "Going hunting?"

"Hurry, please."

"Right away." The brother on guard scrambled up, rubbing his eyes, then helped Taliesin remove the crossbar and unlock the door. He bowed his head as Taliesin exited. Such gestures had been hard-earned over the past ten years. The men of the Order were a tough, strict lot, none of whom had been happy about Amergin taking an outsider as an apprentice. Gradually, however, with constant effort, he had earned their respect. There were now only a few he could not best in shadow combat, and none who could match him in story or song. His cloak boasted his triumphs with an elaborate trim of crimson feathers. Each represented a poem, story or song he had mastered or a match he had won. No one now dared say he had not earned his place among them.

Follow me closely, Taliesin thought to Vala. She launched off his shoulder into the air as he descended the hill. He ignored the path and cut across the meadow to the edge of the trees where he had seen the raven. Mist unfurled in front of him, swirling away in waves of silver-blue as he ran. Soon his legs and feet were soaked from the dew clinging to the long grass. He reached the forest's edge and steadied himself against a tree while catching his breath.

The raven's croak came again, this time from above. He looked up to see a glossy black eye staring down at him. The raven ruffled her wings and hopped closer. She turned her eye down at him again and then flew to the next tree.

Taliesin followed her through the forest until the trees began thinning out, and the distance the raven flew between one and the next became longer. She did not stop until they arrived at a large hawthorne growing above the entrance to a cave. She perched on one of its low-hanging branches and croaked, hopping back and forth across the limb, turning occasionally to aim an eye in his direction.

Taliesin glanced up, happy to see Vala circling, and called her down. He held out his arm, and she landed on it. He rewarded her with a bit of meat, wary of what might await them inside. He took out *Straif,* murmured a protective spell, and moved into the dark opening.

The passage curved to the left and sloped downward, extending further from there, reminding him of the time he, Uthyr and Bran had followed the scales of the white dragon, Níðhöggr, deep into the earth, on Arawn's orders.

He invoked Owl Sight and ventured into the darkness, seeking his summoner. He had earned the privilege spending countless nights wandering the forest, tracking the owls. He learned to imitate their calls as well and brought them gifts of food, until, at last, the blessing of Owl Sight had come. His affinity for birds had only grown since then. They had become his preferred companions for shifting, though dogs had always proven good allies as well.

Taliesin.

He turned toward the sound of his summoner's voice and caught sight of flames flickering in the distance. He followed their light down a passage that led to a limestone cave, some sixteen feet high, illuminated by several torches. A dark warrioress gripping a shield and long spear stood at its center, her feet planted in a wide stance. Black wings arched behind her, casting ghastly shadows on the glistening cavern walls within the dancing torchlight. He knew her at once.

"Greetings, Great Morrigan." He dropped to one knee and waited for her to speak.

"Rise, son of Cerridwen. I bring tidings of war. You are needed elsewhere." She held her shield out in front of her like a serving tray. It remained suspended, as if she had set it on the surface of a lake instead of into the air. "Look and see."

Taliesin did as she commanded. The nearer he got, the faster the shield spun, causing the intricate designs on it to appear three-dimensional: its carved warriors ran in circles, spear points flashing, while the horses on the outer rim seemed to gallop over endless hills, never reaching their destination. After a moment, the images changed and stopped repeating.

A forest grew up out of the shield's burnished surface, and a clash of stags came leaping toward him, dodging between tree trunks. Beyond the forest, the clouds parted to reveal the peak of a mountain he recognized at once—Dinas Emrys, lair of the Red Dragon.

The stags charged up the mountain's rocky slope, bounding with purpose to the summit. There, they locked horns in a relentless fight for high ground. Dust and turf flew in the wake of furious hooves and horns as the stronger bucks sent the weaker skidding and tumbling down the slope. The fight raged on until a rumble of thunder shook the mountain so violently, the narrow split in its side burst wide open, sending shards of rock avalanching in all directions.

White adders slithered out from between the stones and attacked the stags, sending all but one into a frenzy; he alone held his ground, stamping at the serpents with angry hooves and withstanding their wicked strikes until all were trampled to death.

He stood victorious upon the summit, but peace was short-lived. Smoke began billowing forth from the split in the mountain as if there were a great inferno boiling up from within. Taliesin watched, with unblinking rapture, as the magnificent red head and claws of the mountain's most fantastic denizen emerged, her enormous wings unfurling like two red sails from the mast of a great ship. Crushed between her jaws was the neck of Níðhöggr, the white dragon of their enemies. She gripped the side of the mountain and launched herself into the sky, dragging the beast, coil by coil, out of her lair.

The images melted back into the shield, and soon only the galloping horses and spear-wielding warriors ran along its surface once more.

Morrigan reached out and gripped her shield, stopping the elaborate illusions with one swift motion. "The Young Stag must be made ready, and you have learned enough to counsel him. Return to Caer Leon." She pointed toward a black opening behind her. "Take that passage." The flames within Morrigan's eyes flared as if they had been hit by a blast of strong wind.

"Yes, Great Morrigan. Thank you."

Taliesin did not like the idea of leaving without a farewell to Amergin, but there were other ways to accomplish that. They were both skilled shadow-walkers and often consulted one another in their sleep.

Taliesin felt the heat of Morrigan's terrible eyes as he moved toward the dark maw at the far end of her strange throne room and entered its darkness. He made his way through the dank corridor, which led him through a series of caverns until pale sunlight beckoned from ahead. The passage began to narrow, until he had to get down and crawl. Vala went ahead of him, eager to exit the earth and return to her preferred element.

He crawled from the cave and blinked, willing his eyes to adjust. When they did, he found himself at the base of a hillside beneath a late afternoon sky, its clouds infused with heavy golden light. He spied Vala perched in a nearby tree. The passage promptly collapsed, earth and grass folding in around the opening until it disappeared.

He took a deep breath, grateful for the fresh air. *Apple blossoms.* He chuckled and nearly wept with happiness.

Trembling with nostalgia, he climbed the hill and crossed a green meadow to the silver-trunked apple grove he knew would be there. He embraced the nearest tree and pressed his cheek against its bark, swaying from the ache of memories filling his chest. He stood there, suspended in a dream, until a woman's whisper broke the spell.

"Welcome home, my love."

Taliesin turned toward the sound of Nimue's voice. His heart sang at the sight of her splendor, now shining from her eyes as brightly as the Midsummer sun. There, in her rightful place, she was again his first love, free from the dark shroud of disappointment and sorrow that had veiled her beauty when she walked the world as Viviaine.

He pulled her to him with a sigh. She softened in his embrace and melted against his body, despite his muddy clothes. In the span of his next breath, he forgave all her treachery, remembering only the perfect moons they had spent together in that grove, suspended in love's immaculate dream.

"Have you forgiven me?" she whispered.

He squeezed her tighter. "I have, my love. Now, we must work together, you and I." Taliesin pulled away and cupped her face in his hands. "Swear, before Arianrhod, you'll never conceal anything from me again."

She smiled up at him. "Upon my life, I swear it."

194

He unsheathed *Straif.* "Swear it with blood."

Nimue hesitated a moment, then nodded and took the dagger. She dropped it and let out a cry of pain as if he had handed her the end of a hot poker, backing away from him with a whimper, clutching her hand.

"What is it?" Taliesin ran to her side and inspected her hand. A dark bruise marred her palm. He knew such a mark could mean only one thing. "You have Sídhe blood?"

Nimue's mouth fell open. She looked at him sideways, brow furrowed. "You didn't know?"

Taliesin felt like a fool. "I knew only that Arianrhod had blessed you," he stammered. "You never told me of your bloodline—only that King Baeddan was your father."

Nimue stared at him a moment, brow furrowed, as if unable to believe how blind he had been. "Come with me."

She led him down the hillside to the shelter of the Willow and beckoned for him to sit beside her. Taliesin's heart beat faster, recalling the passionate nights they had spent within the shelter of its green veils. He felt enflamed by her nearness, the smell of her inciting a thousand intimate memories, flooding his gut with longing. He fought the desire to clutch her to him. Instead, he took her bruised hand in hers and kissed it, breathing in the scent of her skin.

"Long ago," she began, "there were rituals at Beltane between the Sídhefolk of my father's land and its chieftains. I imagine they still go on, hidden from the eyes of the church. Some of the children born of these rituals were kept by the Sídhe, and some were given to the chieftains who fathered them. Through these exchanges, peace was kept." She sighed. "I didn't know the woman I'd called 'Mother' my entire life was not truly my mother until I my twelfth summer. That's when I began showing signs of my Sídhe blood. She chose to tell me the truth, saying I deserved to know, but swore me to secrecy. She fell ill not long after that. After she died, I confronted my father and asked him how I could find my true mother, but he refused to tell me. By then, it had become clear my brother Maelwys was a halfling as well, so I told him what I'd discovered. He went to our father in a rage, demanding to know where our mother could be found. Again, our father refused to tell us. Either that, or perhaps he didn't know."

Taliesin bristled at the mention of Maelwys. He put a hand on her shoulder and locked eyes with her. "You saw me kill him, did you not?" He gripped *Straif* and held it up. "You saw me drive this dagger into his heart?"

Nimue recoiled from the blade and croaked, "I did."

"Yet Amergin insists he lives. Is that true?"

She nodded. "It is."

Taliesin shook his head. "How? When you, a priestess of Arianrhod, can scarcely bear the sight of this blade?"

"I imagine Myrthin must have healed him. He has that power."

"As do you." Taliesin put the dagger down and grabbed her hands. "Please, Nimue...if you know where your brother is, you must tell me."

Nimue's face twisted from shock to anger. "Back to Finbheara, I'd wager, now that I've forbid him entry to Affalon and imprisoned Myrthin for you." She yanked her hands away and stormed off, leaving strands of willow leaves flying in her wake.

Taliesin ran his fingers through his hair and let out a sigh. *Now, what have I done?* He jumped to his feet and rushed after her, but she moved as swiftly as a deer. He found her standing at the edge of the lake with her arms crossed, staring out over the water. "I didn't mean to anger you. I would understand if you healed him—he is your brother, after all."

Nimue shook her head. "He *was* my brother, once, long ago. Now, he's a stranger," she murmured under her breath. "An enemy, even. He's become someone else...as I have." She turned to face him. "And you have."

Taliesin marveled at the reflection of the setting sun on the blue curves of her eyes. They looked like two crescent moons on the rise.

"I know why you've come back," she confided. "I've seen the signs. The Pendragon's days are numbered. You've come to advise Arthur, haven't you?"

Taliesin nodded. "I have."

"He shall be blessed for it."

"I pray I'm ready for such a role."

Nimue gave him a look of confidence. "I'm certain you are. You'll be a strong sage counselor to him, and to your daughter, as well."

Taliesin felt a strange flutter in his chest. "What do you mean?"

"Morgen is her name, is it not? She lives here on the isle now. Did you not know?"

A jolt of shock struck Taliesin like lightning. It soon turned into a cold feeling of betrayal that trickled like icy water through his limbs. There was no use denying it. *She knows.* "What do you mean she lives here? What have you done?"

"What do you mean, what have *I* done?" Nimue backed away with a wounded look. "I've done nothing! Igerna sent her to live with the sisters in the abbey."

"Who told you she's my daughter?"

Nimue shook her head and looked at him as if he were a boy of five summers. "No one had to tell me, my love. She has your smile and your gifts. I knew she was your daughter the moment I saw her. I'm curious—does the Pendragon know she's not his? Or is Igerna keeping that from him?"

How can this be? Taliesin feared asking his next question but asked it just the same. "How long has she been here?"

"A few moons. Why do you fret so? She's well looked after. And happy, thanks to Queen Igerna. If not for her, the poor lass would be married to that old boar, Urien of Rheged!"

The thought shot Taliesin through with dread. "Uthyr was going to marry her to Urien?"

"He was."

Taliesin let out a sigh, sat down on a fallen log and stared out over the lake. He caught the smell of evening primrose on the air and noticed the sound of crickets rising from the nearby thickets. He felt a wave of calm descend. "Has she found Affalon yet?"

Nimue smiled and sat next to him, taking his hand in hers. "Oh, yes."

"So, you've spoken to her?"

"Many times." Nimue's eyes then strayed behind Taliesin's shoulders and her expression changed. "Perhaps you'd like to?"

He turned around to see what had caught her attention and beheld a young woman. She had long dark tresses and wore a roughly-woven robe of undyed wool. She looked at him with wide eyes the color of lichen and heather.

"Welcome back, Morgen," Nimue said softly. "This is my most beloved friend, Master Taliesin."

CHAPTER TWENTY-ONE
Reunion

Morgen felt her heart flutter like a startled dove as Master Taliesin stood up and smiled at her. His gaze fell soft and kind upon her face, never shifting or wavering as he approached. "Hello, Lady Morgen."

Master Taliesin looked the way Morgen imagined Jesus might have looked when he walked the Earth. She ached to ask him about the dragons that slept in the belly of Dinas Emrys and what it had been like inside the Sídhe kingdom of Knockma. *And how did he escape the Saxons after being captured? And is it true his mother was a selkie?* She burned to hear him tell of all of it, but knew it was rude to assault someone you had just met with questions. Instead, she said, "I've been so eager to meet you, Master Taliesin. Lady Nimue told me you're the greatest bard in all the world, and there's nothing I love more than music."

His smile widened, crinkling the corners of his eyes. His cheeks and brow seemed to glow from inside, as if he had swallowed the sun. "Is that so?"

Morgen felt strongly drawn to him, the way she felt drawn to the forest and the sea. She noticed the tip of a harp peeking out of the pack slung across his back. "Would you play something for us? I'm supposed to be in prayer right now, but music is a form of prayer, don't you think? I feel closer to God when I sing."

He nodded. "I do, as well."

Morgen frowned. "I so wish I had my harp with me. I had to leave it at home." She could not help but sigh. She loved playing her harp, but she had not been permitted to take it with her when she left Caer Leon. "I had to leave all my possessions behind when I came to live with the sisters. Even my clothes. Now, I wear only this." She looked down at her simple wool dress and held out its edges. "But I like it better than my robes at home."

Taliesin raised his brows. "You do?"

"No hooks or ribbons to fuss with, and I've no need of a maid to help me dress. I can do it myself, now. And the sisters don't make me wear shoes." She suddenly felt she had spoken of herself too much. "Shall we sing? I don't wish to neglect God."

Taliesin smiled again. "Let's not keep him waiting, then." He set his harp on his lap and began to play. She fell into a trance watching his strong, masterful fingers glide over the strings.

Morgen did not know the words to the first song Taliesin sang, yet it seemed like her soul had heard the melody a thousand times. A rush of rapture came over her when he reached the chorus, as if every drop of her blood had a voice and had joined in. When the song ended, she begged for more. His music had unleashed a thirst in her that could not be sated. "Oh, don't stop. Please, play on…"

The hours wove on through the afternoon, one song leading to another, until dusk fell. Taliesin took his cue from the sky and sent the final note of his last song sailing over the lake toward the setting sun, as graceful as a swan in flight.

Morgen felt her spirit strain against the limits of her flesh, threatening to rise out of her body and soar with that note toward heaven. She covered her face with her hands and convulsed into sobs. She felt Nimue touch her shoulder and stroke her hair. When the emotion had ebbed, she wiped her eyes and looked over at Taliesin. "You're an angel, aren't you?"

Taliesin raised his brows and chuckled. "No, dear maiden. Not an angel."

Morgen nodded. "Yes, you are. God sings to the world through you." She felt as if she might start weeping again, so stood up. "I must go, now. I have evening chores to do. The sisters will scold me. But I'll come again tomorrow."

She bid them farewell and left, shaking as she made her way through the apple orchard to the thorne tree. She gripped its trunk and closed her eyes, willing herself to return to the humble daub-and-wattle huts of the sisters. She concentrated on her breath flowing in and out until she could smell the bread baking on their cookfires. She opened her eyes and ran back to the largest hut where they cooked and gathered together. All the women turned to look at her as she entered. Some scowled, others smiled and shook their heads.

"Where've you been?" the abbess asked. "Sister Brigid had to bake the bread tonight."

Morgen bowed her head. "At prayer, Abbess. Please forgive me. I could not bear to leave."

The abbess frowned at her. "There is a time to pray and a time to work, Sister Morgen. Please don't forget your duties again."

"I won't. Thank you." Morgen felt glad her status as the Pendragon's daughter had gained her no special treatment from the abbess. From the moment she had arrived, the sisters had been kind, yet firm, with her. She slept in a simple cot in one of the huts with five other women and was expected to work just as hard as the rest of them—harder, in fact, as she was young, and many of them had grown frail with age. She regretted burdening Sister Brigid with her chores, but nothing could dampen her spirits.

Morgen rose with the sun, still filled with the joy of the day before, and busied herself in the apothecary. She had such a shrewd talent for identifying and harvesting herbs that the abbess had given her the sole responsibility of keeping it stocked. Since she had taken over this duty, no one had suffered any pain or illness for long. What the abbess did not know, was that she harvested every herb in the apothecary exclusively from Affalon.

She began singing one of Taliesin's songs as she worked, refilling the jars and baskets with the herbs she had harvested the day before.

Sister Brigid gave her a poke and raised a brow at her. "What song are you singing?"

"Oh, I don't know the name."

"I do," she murmured. "And it's not to be sung here."

Morgen felt stunned. "Why not?"

"It praises the Great Mother. Here we sing only songs that praise our Lord God."

Morgen felt confused. She thought back on what Nimue had said to her about the Great Mother. *"Mary is but one face of the Great Mother, but many followers of the Roman church do not see this. Perhaps men feel closer to the great mystery when they have a man to worship."*

"But we praise Mary as the holy mother of God. Couldn't the song be about her?"

"It isn't, child."

201

Morgen felt a rush of injustice prickle her skin. "I feel it could be, and that is the spirit in which I sing it. Therefore, it is holy and right."

Sister Brigid shook her head. "I fear you don't belong here, Lady Morgen. The sooner Dubricius comes back for you, the better." She walked away, muttering a prayer.

Sister Brigid's words stung, but Morgen ignored them. She went back to humming Taliesin's song as she finished her work, determined to let nothing ruin its beauty for her.

The pull of Taliesin's presence in Affalon made it harder and harder for Morgen to make it back to the abbey on time, until, some days later, the inevitable happened. Morgen's stomach sank as she spied the abbess' stout silhouette in the dying sun waiting for her at the edge of the apple orchard.

Before she could utter an apology, the abbess raised a hand and spoke. "I'm sorry, Sister Morgen, but you're not to wander the forest to engage in your devotions any longer. You'll pray here, where we can watch over you."

Morgen felt like a rabbit trapped in a snare, her heart racing at the thought of being kept from Nimue and Taliesin. "But that is where I speak to God," she protested. "That is where I feel his presence."

The abbess shook her head. "He is here, as well. He is everywhere. You will pray here, with us."

Morgen, though only thirteen, knew well when to leave off. This was a battle she knew she would not win through argument. Though the words felt like broken glass as she spoke them, she complied. "As you wish, Abbess. You know best." She bowed her head to hide the defiance in her eyes and quietly knitted a plan to return to Affalon — for good.

Taliesin's thighs burned as he led Nimue up a grassy hillside. He chose a spot near the top of the tor with a wide view of the marshlands below. They settled into the soft grass to watch the sunset and wait for Vala to return from her day's adventures.

He soon spied Vala's keen form knifing through the ripening clouds. She landed a few feet away with a thrush in her beak. She dined nearby as he and Nimue watched the last of the sun's glow melt into the horizon.

Taliesin felt a deep calm descend over him as the sky cooled and the stars came out. He was beginning to feel he could trust Nimue again, and the relief of it felt like cold water to a man parched with thirst. He knew, now, that she could have easily delivered Morgen to Knockma many times over, but had instead chosen to protect and mentor her. However, one matter yet troubled him. "Tell me, my love, what has become of Myrthin Wyllt? Amergin told me you imprisoned him."

Nimue did not answer right away, causing Taliesin's wariness to rise. He counseled himself not to jump to conclusions and patiently waited for her to reply. At last, she spoke.

"It's true I've imprisoned his body here in Affalon, but his spirit cannot be contained." She looked up at the heavens. "I imagine he roams the kingdom of Caer Sidi. Or perhaps he's off exploring realms beyond it. It's not like him to remain in one place for very long."

Taliesin thought of the knowledge and power Myrthin was sure to be gaining and did not feel comforted. "Where is his body? In the crystal cave?"

"It is. And there it will stay, for as long as I desire."

Taliesin thought of how she had once kept his body in that cave and shuddered. "What's keeping him from escaping, as I did?"

Nimue turned toward him, brow furrowed. "I placed your body in the cave to protect it, my love—not to imprison it."

Taliesin nearly challenged her but thought better of it, reminding himself that thirteen years had passed. *What she did, she did out of desperate love for me.* He reached for her hand and kissed it. "Let's forget the past," he said, voice low and soft.

She nestled close to him. "Some of it, perhaps."

They spent the rest of the evening on the hillside, Taliesin weaving a healing spell around the two of them that salved the wounds they had given one another. When the moon rose, he led her by the hand, back to the shelter of the Willow and its lush bed of grasses, and lay down with her. One taste of her mouth drove what remained of his hesitation away. He made love to her that night as if he had never left Affalon and nothing had ever come between them.

Once their passion was spent, he lay beside her, feeling at peace for the first time in many moons. He longed to remain in Affalon's idyllic throes, close to her and his daughter, but he could not ignore the oath he had made to Morrigan.

Two more nights, he bargained with himself. *Then, I'll journey to Caer Leon.*

CHAPTER TWENTY-TWO
Arthur

Taliesin woke to the tantalizing smell of Affalon's silver apples on the breeze. Hunger drove him out from beneath the Willow toward the stream that led uphill to the orchard. The sun had not yet risen, but there was enough light for him to spy Vala circling overhead, hunting for her own breakfast. He crested the hill and there, where the stream tumbled down to flow into the lake, stood Morgen, a basket of herbs at her feet.

"Lady Morgen! It's a bit early to be harvesting herbs."

"I came to speak to you, but I must be back before sunrise."

Taliesin grew concerned. "What is it, child?"

She took a breath. "You're the one, Master Taliesin."

"The one?" Taliesin felt a surge of both excitement and dread at what she might be referring to. *Does she know I'm her father?*

"The one I've been praying for to help my brother. You said you're a dear friend to both my mother and my father, so they must trust you."

"I believe they do."

"Good. You must convince them to let you take Arthur away."

Taliesin felt surprised by Morgen's boldness. She had been soft-spoken and almost timid the day before. "Take him where?"

"To my mother's cousin, Lord Cynyr, up near Dinas Emrys, where he can train the way he needs to. Mother dotes on him. He wants to get away from her."

"That sounds harsh."

"It isn't." Her expression darkened. "He needs to become the best warrior he can be, and soon."

"Why is that?" Taliesin asked, even though he agreed with her.

"My father is sick, and nothing in the apothecary will cure him. Every time he comes home from battle, his light is weaker. It used to burn bright, like hot metal pulled from the forge. Now, it's like metal cooling, or coals dying down." She choked on the last words.

Taliesin felt proud his daughter had inherited so many of his gifts. "You can see his light?"

She nodded. "I see everyone's. Nimue's is silvery blue, like starlight." She looked around his head. "Yours is bright and golden, like a late summer afternoon."

205

He badly wanted to tell her, in that moment, that he was her father—not Uthyr—but he refrained and turned the conversation back toward Arthur. "I'll soon be leaving for Caer Leon. Long ago, I promised your mother I would teach your brother all I knew when he came of age."

Morgen did not look satisfied. "But you must do *more* than tutor him, Master Taliesin—please, take him to train with Lord Cynyr—it's what he wants. And he's right."

"If that's what he wishes, I'll consider it."

Morgen's face relaxed, and she pressed no further. "Thank you."

"And what of your wishes, Lady Morgen? Are you happy here?"

"I was, as long as I could come here to pray, but now, the abbess has told me I must pray within the church." She shook her head. "But God isn't there. At least, I don't feel him there. Not like I feel him here." She thought a moment. "Or feel her." She looked around her, as if hearing a voice on the wind. "Lady Nimue has been teaching me about the Great Mother." She looked Taliesin in the eyes. "I love God, but I like Nimue's teaching better than what the sisters teach."

"Why is that?"

Morgen shrugged. "Because I don't feel as if there's something wrong with me when I'm with her—or that she's afraid of me, or what I can do."

Taliesin nodded and smiled at her. "That's as it should be." He longed to take her in his arms but embraced her with his words instead. "There's nothing wrong with you, Lady Morgen. Nothing at all. Never forget that."

"That's what Mother says, but she seems most frightened of all. She's always telling me not to show anyone what I can do."

"And what else can you do? Besides see the light surrounding things?"

"Lots of things. I know what animals are feeling. I can make fire dance by looking at it. I can touch a plant and know if it's good or bad for you. And I can ride and swim faster than anyone my age in Caer Leon—boy or girl."

"And you can certainly sing beautifully," Taliesin added. Morgen had the purest voice he had heard in years. It was untrained, but breathtaking.

Morgen blushed. "Thank you, but these things make the sisters wary. It's why they want me to stay in the abbey with them." The creases in her brow deepened. "But I just can't, Master Taliesin — could you? If you knew this place were here? Could you stay away?"

"No," Taliesin said definitively. "I couldn't."

"And neither can I. But if I don't return, the abbess will send word to the archbishop. Then Father will surely send for me and marry me off." She shuddered and lowered her voice. "But I've thought of a way to make them think I've returned to Caer Leon, so that I can live here with Nimue."

Taliesin frowned. "How will you manage that?"

"Well, it must be true, of course. Simply take me with you. Besides, if you agree to escort Arthur to Lord Cynyr, I want to spend time with him before you leave. After that, I'll return to Ynys Wydryn."

"But not to live with the sisters," Taliesin concluded.

"No. Not to live with the sisters."

Taliesin nodded. "And what if your mother writes to you, and discovers you're no longer at the abbey?"

Morgen's eyebrows flew up. "Oh, I've no intention of hiding anything from my mother! She knows of Lady Nimue."

"She does?" Taliesin felt surprised. "How?"

"My mother's nursemaid brought us here to meet Lady Nimue long ago — Mother, Arthur, and me. Arthur and I were only five. It's my father who must never find out."

Taliesin's concern thickened. "And you don't fear he will?"

"No." Morgen's face grew somber. "As I said, his light is fading. I fear he won't see another summer. And, even if he does, he's never home. Sometimes I can't remember what his face looks like. When I try to picture it, his features are dark and unclear, as if I'm seeing his reflection in a lake." She glanced up at the rising sun, and the muscles in her face tensed. "I must go, now, before the sisters wake."

Taliesin nodded. "Very well, Lady Morgen. I had planned to leave tomorrow. Shall I come to the abbey to fetch you?"

"Yes." Morgen's face lost all traces of worry. "I'll be ready."

"I'll be there after the morning meal," Taliesin promised.

"Thank you, Master Taliesin—thank you so much!" She gave him a parting smile before plunging into the trees, prancing barefoot through their trunks with the agility of a young fawn.

"I'm taking Morgen with me to Caer Leon tomorrow," Taliesin announced to Nimue. He watched her eyes change from blue to grey, like the sea beneath a brewing storm.

"Why? I thought she was happy here."

"She is. She means to return to you."

Nimue's countenance brightened a bit. "And what of you, my love? Do you mean to return to me?"

He managed a bittersweet smile and kissed her. "Someday. But, for now, I must return to Caer Leon. Igerna and Uthyr have protected and cared for my daughter all these years, and now it's time for me to return their kindness. When Uthyr dies—" Taliesin sighed at the thought. He was fond of Uthyr and knew the heartache his death would cause Igerna. "—it will fall upon Arthur to look after his family and unite all the clans of Brython. He must be ready."

As promised, Taliesin collected Morgen from the abbey the following morning. He secured passage for the two of them across the channel to the mouth of the river Usk. From there, they continued on foot along the busy river road.

"How long before we reach Caer Leon?" Morgen asked. "I seem to remember it took us some time to reach the river from my father's fortress. Will we be there by nightfall?"

"Oh, I think we shall." Taliesin uncovered his harp and slung it across his back. It gleamed in the sun like a fish lure and he hoped it would serve in much the same way. Instead of attracting hungry fish, however, he meant for it to grab the eyes of travelers upon the road who might have room in their wagon and felt eager for a song. If that did not work, there was always Vala. One could not help but slow down and look at her.

208

They had been walking no more than ten minutes before someone called out, "Right lovely harp! You need a ride?"

Taliesin winked at Morgen and waved to the driver of a large wagon filled with hay. "I'd be pleased to play it for you if you've room for us."

"I'd be grateful for some music. I've a long ride ahead of me. Where're you headed?"

"Caer Leon."

"You're in luck, then!" the man grinned, flashing them a smile short of a few teeth. "That's where I'm going. Climb in!"

"Thank you!" Morgen cried, shooting Taliesin a grin. She clambered into the wagon with the agility of a cat, leaving him to follow. Taliesin unslung his harp and laid it across his lap. He launched right into song, and soon, to his delight, Morgen joined in. If the driver knew the song, he, too, sang out, and the afternoon breezed by in a haze of joy and laughter.

Toward evening, Taliesin noticed subtle changes in the air and knew they were drawing close. Large settlements had a distinctive odor.

Morgen soon pointed out the silhouette of Uthyr's immense hillfort on the horizon. "There it is, Master Taliesin! Oh, I can't wait to see Arthur!"

They reached the busy outskirts of Caer Leon as the last of the sun's light danced upon the surface of the river.

"This'll do," Taliesin announced to the farmer. The amount of activity upon the road had slowed them to a walking pace anyway. They bid the farmer farewell and continued on foot toward Uthyr's impressive fortress.

I'm a stranger here now, Taliesin thought, observing the looks on the faces of the villagers as they passed.

The city had grown much in the past decade. Dozens of new structures had risen, both within and around the hillfort mount, like new crops poking out between the folds of its green furrows. Even the church seemed to have grown, as if, like a tree, its girth had slowly increased over the years. "I scarcely recognize this place," he marveled aloud.

"When were you last here?" Morgen asked.

"It's been many years. You and your brother were still suckling at your mother's breast."

"Long ago, then." Morgen smiled. "By keeping the Saxons at bay, my father has made all this possible."

Taliesin nodded, proud of his old friend. "He's done Brython a great service."

Morgen raised her brows. "You were taken by the Saxons when you were my age, weren't you?"

"I was." He thought back to the horrible day of the attack and recoiled from the feeling of helplessness it always brought on. It suddenly occurred to him that Morgen might not be any more exceptional than her mother had been at her age. Arhianna had displayed such strength and power when they had been taken. *So fierce.*

"How did you escape?"

Taliesin had expected the question and told the story as only a bard could tell it. By the time he had finished the tale, Morgen's face was flushed with excitement. They were also at the gates of the Pendragon's fortress.

A guard approached and squinted at him. "Name yourself and your business."

"Master Taliesin to see Queen Igerna. I've escorted her daughter, the Lady Morgen, from the abbey at Ynys Wydryn."

Morgen took off her hood so the guard could see her face. The guard said nothing but opened the gates, never taking his eyes off her. Taliesin noticed the way he looked at her, wondering if it were fear or lust causing him to stare. *Likely both,* he thought with a pang of anxiety. Women who inspired such emotions were often abused—by both sexes. He shuddered to think of his daughter so treated. In that sense, he most certainly did not want her to become like her unfortunate mother.

Once inside, an older woman who looked to run the household quickly recognized Morgen. "Lady Morgen! You're back so soon!"

Morgen smiled. "I've come for a visit. Will you tell my mother I've come home and that Master Taliesin is with me? We'll go to the main hall."

"Right away, my lady." The woman went running with the news, but there was no need, because Igerna had already noticed their arrival. She came rushing to greet them.

Taliesin smiled when he saw her face. *Igerna*. Though she had aged, she remained as radiant as the day he had last seen her. Her blue eyes shone from beneath the braided tower of her white-gold hair, piled high on her head, wearing what Taliesin considered a woman's most desirable accessory—a bright and genuine smile. He noticed she had put on a little weight, which only added to her beauty. She had ever been slight of build with a wren-like quality. Now, her breasts and hips had bloomed.

"Taliesin!" she cried, eyes dancing. "Oh, dear God! At last!" She embraced him. "And Morgen!" She clutched her to her chest. "What's happened, *cariad*?" she whispered in her ear, glancing quickly around to see who might be watching. "Have the sisters mistreated you?"

Morgen shook her head. "No, Mother. No, not at all. Master Taliesin came to Ynys Wydryn and said he was on his way here. I wanted to come with him."

Taliesin noticed a crowd gathering and gave Igerna a look. "Shall we go inside?"

Igerna glanced around and nodded. "Yes, inside...we'll talk in the hall." She ushered them through the nearest doorway, down a few corridors to the kitchen, where she barked a few orders, and then into the main hall. It was empty save a young man stacking wood beside the large hearth. "Stoke the fire, please," she told him. "Then you may go."

Igerna eyed them both, back and forth, until the boy was out of earshot, and then spoke. "Arthur's out hunting. He should be here soon. He'll be thrilled to see you, Morgen. I hate to say it, but he hasn't been the same since you left."

Taliesin did not like the sound of that. He could not help but remember how close the two babes had been in their infancy—ever entwined in their crib, crying whenever they were separated—as if they were two halves of the same child. As king, Arthur would need to be wholly independent from his sister. There would be many relationships that would take precedence—his advisors, his war council, and, of course, his wife.

"I've been well-treated. There's no need for anyone to worry."

"So, nothing's happened?"

Morgen smiled. "I wouldn't say that, exactly…I've been spending time with Lady Nimue. She's taught me quite a bit about medicine." She untied a leather pouch from her belt. "This is for Father when he returns. Steep a walnut-size measure in boiling water and make a tea of it."

The lines in Igerna's forehead deepened as she took the pouch and put it in her lap. "I'm not sure when he'll return, my love. He's gone to lead our men against Octa." She looked over at Taliesin. "The Saxons have taken Caer Lundein."

Taliesin did not exactly feel surprised by the news, but it was worrisome. "When?"

"A few moons ago."

Taliesin wondered whether he should ride on to find Uthyr but dared not abandon Igerna so soon after returning. "Who did he leave behind to defend Caer Leon?"

"Arthur, at my insistence. He was nearly killed the last time Uthyr took him into battle—came home with wounds I never thought would heal." She shuddered. "Morgen nursed him, day and night. I fear if it weren't for her, we would have lost him." She clutched at her chest. "He's much better at managing the fortress. No one seems to understand good rulers can inspire men to fight for them. They don't need to ride out for every battle there is."

Taliesin did not comment. What she said was true, however, he knew men did not respect leaders who did not fight alongside them. He spied a large table not far from the hearth with carved wooden figures on it, much like enormous chess pieces. He walked over for a closer look. A map of Brython had been painted over the entire surface of the table, and the pieces were placed over various areas on the map. He marveled at the colors and detail. Mountain ranges and rivers were well-marked, seeming to rise and flow from the surface of the table. "Whoever painted this did a remarkable job."

"He did, didn't he?" Igerna agreed, coming to join him at the edge of the table.

Morgen came over as well. She reached out and caressed the fortress of Caer Leon gently with her fingertips. "Arthur painted it for my father. To help him plan his battle strategy."

Taliesin felt surprised. "Arthur painted this?" He stared at the details with new appreciation, incredulous of the boy's talent.

"He did," Morgen stated proudly. "He could be a painter. Or a bard, like you. He can sing better than any of the bards who play for us, and he recites poems with such richness it takes your breath away."

Taliesin picked up a candle and walked around the perimeter of the table, studying the intricate details along the shorelines of Brython up to Hadrian's wall and into the great wild forests, lochs and mountains of the north.

"But his father would never allow it," Igerna murmured. Taliesin could hear defeat and disappointment in her voice. "He's to become a warrior, like him." Her tone became clipped and sour. "I so wish I could have borne him another son—one more suited to his...aspirations." She sighed. "Morgen's right. Arthur is—"

"Is what?" a voice asked.

The three of them whirled around to see a tall youth standing in the archway of the hall, cheeks flushed and thick hair wind-blown, a pair of red grouse hanging limp by his side.

Arthur. Taliesin felt stunned by how much the young man looked like Uthyr, yet Igerna had clearly left her mark as well—his cheekbones were high and pronounced and his features smoother and more aquiline than his father's, all set in a graceful balance that sang his mother's praises.

It took only a moment for Arthur to notice Morgen. "*Sister?* Is that you?" He ventured closer to confirm he had indeed seen her.

"Hello, brother." She emerged from behind the table. "I've come for a visit."

Arthur's mouth exploded into a wide grin as she rushed into his open arms. Taliesin saw their light double in brightness when they embraced. Morgen pulled away and motioned in his direction. "This is Master Taliesin. The greatest bard who ever lived."

Taliesin chuckled and shook his head. "Please, you'll ruin my chances of ever impressing anyone." He stepped forward and took Arthur's offered arm. "I'm honored to meet you, Lord Arthur."

"The pleasure is mine, Master Taliesin. Morgen doesn't grant compliments often. I look forward to hearing you play." He looked over at Morgen. "We can all sing together tonight. I've a few new stories I've picked up as well."

Igerna frowned. "From where?"

Arthur shrugged. "Here and there."

She moaned. "Oh, Arthur. Please tell me you haven't been at the tavern again."

Arthur turned his palms up. "How else are we to know what's really happening? Certainly not by staying up here on this hill. Besides, I like drinking with the villagers."

Taliesin could see the words Igerna wanted to say swimming in her mouth, but she kept her lips closed.

Arthur seized his opportunity and held up the grouse. "I'm going to deliver these to the cook." He bid Taliesin a polite farewell, winked at his sister and ducked out of the hall.

Taliesin watched Arthur disappear into the darkness. *Great mother, can such an artful, jovial youth truly be destined to become Brython's next warlord?*

CHAPTER TWENTY-THREE
A Turn of Events

Rain came in the night, pelting roof, leaf and stone without mercy until morning. The cool, damp smell of wet fields mingled with cookfires wafted in through Taliesin's window, waking him from a surprisingly restful night of sleep. He did not normally sleep well indoors. He went to the window and peered out into the glistening world, breathing its green freshness deep into his lungs. Heavy rain clouds rumbled in the distance, threatening more of the same throughout the day. He felt grateful he and Morgen had arrived in Caer Leon the day before. Traveling today would have been a slow and muddy business, and there were sure to be far less wagons on the roads.

Out of curiosity, he picked up the looking glass that lay on the table and laughed at the volume of hair and beard he had grown. *I do look the Wildman!* As there was wash water, soap, and a comb in his chamber, he took advantage of them and tamed his appearance before heading to the main hall.

He heard voices as he approached, so stopped short of entering, not wanting to interrupt.

"The sisters have forbidden me to spend my days in the woods," he heard Morgen say, "but I can't bear to be kept a prisoner in that abbey. I must be free to go to Affalon and see Lady Nimue. She's taught me so much, Mother. I belong there, with her."

Taliesin felt a pang. He, too, felt that way about Nimue, despite all that had happened. He did not want to eavesdrop, so took advantage of Morgen's pause and walked loudly into the hall. "Good morning, my queen. Good morning, Lady Morgen."

The women turned toward him and smiled. "Well, you're looking fine!" Igerna exclaimed. "I hardly recognized you yesterday. But I know this handsome fellow."

Taliesin felt himself blush, knowing the amenities left in his room had been arranged by her. "Thank you."

Morgen, too, looked pleased. "You look very fine, Master Taliesin."

"Come and have some breakfast with us." Igerna motioned to a place clearly set for him at the table near the fire. "The bread's still hot."

215

That sounded welcome indeed, and Taliesin felt his belly growl in approval. "I hope I'm not disturbing. It sounded as if you were discussing something important."

"We were," Morgen confirmed. "I was telling Mother how I cannot stay at the abbey with the sisters, and that I want to live with Lady Nimue."

Igerna let out a long sigh and looked at her daughter and Taliesin in turn. "And what am I supposed to tell Uthyr? Or the archbishop?"

Morgen shrugged. "You're assuming they'll ask. If they do, tell them the truth—that I'm happy on Ynys Wydryn."

Igerna looked pained. "Oh, Morgen. That may be true, but it's not the truth."

Morgen let out a sigh of exasperation. "They won't pursue it. You're the only one who has ever written to me, and Taliesin told the sisters I won't be returning, so they won't ask about me. In truth, they were glad to be rid of me—they won't give me a second thought."

Igerna closed her eyes a moment and took a breath. After a slow shake of her head, she opened them and said, "Go back then, but I'll not deceive your father. I'll tell him the truth if he asks."

"Uthyr has met Lady Nimue," offered Taliesin. "He met her long ago, with me."

Morgen's eyebrows flew up. "He has?"

"I convinced her to let him into Affalon, once, long ago. I feel that may be part of the reason he allowed Morgen to go to the abbey in the first place. He won't protest if he knows she's there."

"You assume too much, Taliesin," Igerna interjected with a furrowed brow, "but I'll accept the blame for it, if the day comes."

"You'll not regret it, Mother," Morgen said through a grateful smile. She grabbed her mother's hands and kissed them. "Thank you so much."

After three weeks in Caer Leon, learning all that had happened during his long absence and getting to know young Arthur better, Taliesin escorted Morgen back to Ynys Wydryn and saw her safely into Nimue's hands. He left Affalon knowing his daughter would not

216

only be happy and well-cared for, but also that she would learn much. She was at a crucial age. The moment she got her blood, her power would wax, and he took heart in knowing she could be with no better counsel through that transformative time. This peace of mind allowed him to return to Caer Leon wholly intent on Arthur's training.

After spending a few nights in the hillfort, he sought out the hut in the woods he had lived in before. He felt glad to see no one had claimed it. It had fallen into disrepair, but with new thatch and a bit of work, he could make it his home again. He told Igerna to give him a few days and then send Arthur to him there.

It was nearly a fortnight before Taliesin spied someone bouncing along the rough trail that skirted the woods in a horse-drawn cart full of goods. It was late afternoon, so he assumed it was a farmer, on his way home from market, taking a shortcut off the main road. As the cart approached, however, he saw it was Arthur who held the reins. The lad raised his left hand. "Good afternoon, Master Taliesin!"

Taliesin had noticed Arthur favored his left hand the night he met him, watching him play his harp. *A good sign.* The youth was musically gifted, like his sister. *Or perhaps because of her.* With training, he could certainly become an accomplished bard, but that was not the future Taliesin had been tasked to prepare him for. *Yet,* he reasoned, *a mastery of music lends grace and power to anyone. Surely, it's to be prized in a king as well.*

"Hello, Arthur. Are you planning to live here with me?"

Arthur's eyes widened. "Could I?"

"Not much room, I'm afraid. What's in the cart?"

"Oh," Arthur said, a tone of disappointment in his voice, "this is for you, from my mother."

Arthur dismounted, threw the cover off the cart, and began pointing out baskets, sacks and barrels to Taliesin, announcing what they were. "Flour, salt, blankets, mead, honey…Some jars and bowls for your apothecary, broom, extra flint, axe—freshly-sharpened, and a cooking pot."

Taliesin smiled, surveying the goods with satisfaction. "Very generous of her. I must find a way to show your mother my appreciation."

"She expects nothing. She's so happy you've returned." Arthur looked at the simple hut with a wistful gaze. "I envy you, living out here in the woods, with no one to bother you. And I envy Morgen." He shook his head. "I wish I could have gone with her to Affalon."

Taliesin nodded. "Your paths lead in different directions now, but they'll cross again. I promise you that."

Arthur unhitched the horse to let her graze, and started to unload the cart, but Taliesin stopped him. "Leave that, for now," he said, handing him a basket. "Come, I need to gather mushrooms and herbs while the light's still good. Let's take a walk."

Arthur covered the wagon back up and followed him into the woods. Taliesin soon found specimens of what he was searching for and threw a few into Arthur's basket. "Pick any of those you find."

They walked along, heads bent to the ground, scanning the edges of the creek bed and the base of tree trunks until Arthur broke the silence.

"Do you know how famous you are in the village, Master Taliesin? Everyone's heard of you. You're as famous as my father."

Taliesin's ego tugged at him, asking to hear what the people said, but he ignored it.

"Mother said you went to Eire to study with Amergin the Bard. Is it true he's hundreds of years old?"

Taliesin shrugged. "The only way to know that for certain would be if I, myself, were hundreds of years old."

"People say he is. And that he still looks like a man of thirty summers."

"That, at least, is true. And I do know he can pass in and out of the Hollow Hills."

"Land of the Daoine Sídhe," Arthur murmured. Then, as if suddenly realizing it was a possibility, he stopped and asked, "Did he show you how to get in? Have you ever been inside?"

"I have."

Arthur stopped in his tracks. "Truly?"

"Yes, truly. More than once, actually."

Arthur shook his head, eyes wide in disbelief. "Why didn't you stay?"

"It's not the paradise you assume it is. Besides, I had work to do. Promises to keep." Taliesin motioned toward the fortress in the distance. "I swore to your mother I'd return to counsel you. But I'm afraid we won't have as much time as I had hoped for."

"Why?" Arthur frowned. "Are you leaving again?"

"No. Your father's illness. I fear he doesn't have many years left."

"Ah." Arthur sighed. "I fear you're right."

Taliesin felt surprised by Arthur's cool acceptance of his father's imminent death, but considered he probably had known about it for some time, thanks to Morgen. "Your sister has many gifts. She's in the right place now to learn how to use them all."

Arthur deftly gathered a patch of mushrooms he had discovered. "I'm glad for her. Glad she's found someone who can teach her something she doesn't already know."

Taliesin felt compelled to appeal to Arthur on behalf of Morgen, unsure of how aware he was of the danger she was sure to face in the near future. "You must protect her, you know. Many will call her a witch."

Arthur's face twisted, like a crazed Pict about to charge the battlefield. "I'll kill anyone who tries to harm her!"

Taliesin felt glad to see how strong Arthur's protective instinct toward his sister was, but counseled clemency. "Killing people isn't the answer, but you must watch over her—and your mother, as well." He paused and looked through a gap in the trees toward Uthyr's hillfort. "When Arawn comes for your father, the wolves will gather."

"I know," Arthur murmured in a weary tone. "Lot and Urien will fight for his title. There's already talk of it." He shook his head. "But Lot's a greedy bastard, and Urien thinks every battle can be fought and won the same way."

Taliesin felt a pang of shame. *Urien. One more person I owe a debt to. He'll likely die before I can fulfill my promise to him.* He turned his thoughts back toward Arthur. "Your mother told me you've attended every one of your father's council meetings since you were eight summers old. Is that true?"

"Longer, to tell you the truth. Before my father invited me—or, rather, ordered me—to attend, Morgen and I would hide in the hall behind the tapestries and listen."

219

Taliesin thought of the many dry council meetings he had struggled through and felt shocked any child would feel compelled to listen to them. "And did you understand what was being discussed?"

"Not all of it, at first. But we understood how each man felt toward the others. We could hear it in their voices. We knew who our father's true allies were." Arthur paused. "I believe I still do."

Taliesin felt impressed. "Who would you say they are?"

Arthur cocked his head and thought a moment, swinging his basket idly on his middle finger. "Camulos can be depended on. He's watched over Caer Leon for as long as I can remember. I also think he may be in love with my mother. Aelhaearn is loyal, as well. My father put him in command of the troops up in Viroconium. Then there's Cynyr, my mother's cousin, who holds lands in both Dyfed and Gwynedd, and my grandfather, Amlawth, who commands a good force of men throughout Dumnonia. They're both steadfast. Urien and Lot are loyal to my father, but I'm no fool—I know that doesn't mean they'll support me when the time comes. Especially not Lot. My father nearly handed him the title when he gave him Morgause's hand."

Arthur's grasp of the situation was both apt and shrewd, and Taliesin felt encouraged by the young man's acumen for politics. "Yes. He's sure to challenge you. As will Urien."

"I know. And, thanks to my mother, they both have more battle experience than I. However, things have changed. My father has just returned and learned of Lot's failure to recapture Caer Mincip. He's making plans to take it back himself. Hence my delay in coming to see you." Arthur looked down at the basket of mushrooms in his hand. "It's only thanks to Morgen's medicine that he's able to, though. He looked like a corpse when he returned—I scarcely recognized him."

Taliesin felt glad to hear of Uthyr's return but worried by the report of his health. He had clung to the hope that his death remained a few years off. "How bad is it?"

Arthur sighed. "As you said, his time will come soon. And I need more battle experience."

"Battle experience isn't everything," Taliesin countered, taking his mother's side. "Perhaps more valued in a king are skills of strategy and diplomacy that help keep men in their beds, surrounded by their families. Especially with the type of warriors we're facing now. You say you've only seen a few battles, but you've surely seen enough to know the Saxons are brutal on the field, many with twice the girth and ferocity of our simple farmers and fishermen. We can't hope to win with a campaign of brute strength."

"We can't," Arthur agreed, "but do you know what our farmers and fishermen know? And our shepherds and hunters? They know our woods, our fields, our rivers and mountains—and they know them as intimately as they know their own wives. This is our advantage." He nodded with utter confidence. "We can win."

Taliesin smiled at the passionate tone in Arthur's voice and the amber flash in his topaz eyes. It struck him, in that moment, how strong the lad's physical presence was—as if the sun were shining upon him even though he stood in shadow.

Arthur did not seem to notice Taliesin studying him. He bent down with his dagger and deftly harvested a clump of mugwort, tossing it in Taliesin's basket. "I want to ride to Caer Mincip alongside my father," he added, bending down to harvest another handful. "I swear, sometimes I think he would prefer Lot take his place as Pendragon. And my mother doesn't help. She fears I won't come back. She doesn't understand how important it is for me to be seen on the battlefield." He stood up, threw the second clump in the basket, and raised a dirt-stained finger. "I'm no Camulos, but I'm twice the warrior my father is right now. Did you know he could scarcely dismount his horse? His bannermen shouldn't see him like this."

Taliesin attempted to see things from Uthyr's point of view. "The people need to see him at the head of our armies, ill or not. It shows his devotion."

Arthur shook his head. "It shows his weakness. Everyone will see he won't last the winter, and then, as you say, the wolves will gather." Arthur stopped and shook his head. "I don't trust Lot."

Taliesin regarded Arthur a moment, considering all he had said. "I believe you're right, Arthur. You should be seen by your father's side. I'm eager to see him. Why don't we go and speak to him together?"

Arthur stared a moment. "Truly?"

"Yes."

"When?"

Taliesin shrugged. "Now. I see no reason to delay, do you?

Arthur smiled. "Not at all."

Together they unloaded the wagon and rode it back to Caer Leon, arriving just after sunset.

"Taliesin?" Uthyr's face flashed through a quick storm of emotions as Taliesin and Arthur entered the main hall. "Good God—it's true!"

Taliesin inclined his head. "It is, Pendragon."

Uthyr rushed over and smothered Taliesin in a bear hug so fierce it felt as if it might break his ribs. Taliesin felt glad at the display of strength, for it contradicted the ashen color of his skin and gauntness of his face.

"I thought you'd never come back."

Taliesin smiled, his heart flooding with happiness at seeing Uthyr again, regardless of his poor health.

"Have you come back for good, then?"

"I have," Taliesin confirmed.

"Good. You're just the sort of man Arthur needs as an advisor. He's got your sort of gifts."

Taliesin felt Arthur bristle at his father's remark.

Arthur motioned toward the map he had painted. "What's the situation at Caer Mincip, Father? Lot had enough men. Why did he fail?"

Uthyr joined Arthur at the map. "Urien and Ceredig refused to follow his orders, the sour old bastards, that's why—and while they bicker, Saxon ships slide onto our shores by the dozens." Uthyr shook his head, anger twisting the lines in his face, until it erupted like thunder. He slammed his fist down on the map, sending wooden pieces rolling and clattering to the floor. "Damn their pride!" The outburst triggered a fit of coughing which he muffled with a blood-stained cloth. Once it subsided, he crushed the cloth in his fist and sat down in a huff. "Their stubbornness will be the death of us all!" Arthur poured his father some ale and handed it to him. He took a long drink and let out a sigh of aching defeat.

Arthur shrugged. "Lot failed to inspire their trust. He may be your choice for Pendragon, Father, but the northern kings will never follow a man they don't trust. I fear they took it as an insult."

Taliesin stared at the northern lands on the map, noting their leaders in turn. "The north does breed stubborn like nowhere else."

Uthyr's face slackened. "Then God help us. We can't keep fighting each other and expect to drive off the Saxons. And my time is coming to an end." He opened his fist, revealing the bloody cloth. "I've held our clans together for as long as I can. Someone else needs to unite our clans. I thought that man would be Lot."

"It isn't," Arthur stated plainly, "but I can, Father."

Uthyr raised his brows. "Believe me, son, there's nothing that would please me more than for that to be true, but you and I both know I'll die before you're ready."

"I am ready."

Uthyr chuckled. "You're only thirteen, Arthur—you've seen but a handful of battles. And I'm sorry, but if Urien and Ceredig won't follow Lot, they certainly won't follow you."

Taliesin cringed at Uthyr's dismissal of his son, but Arthur seemed unaffected, at least on the surface.

"Five battles, all victories, and I believe they will." Arthur's topaz eyes did not blink. "Give me a chance. I won't let you down."

Uthyr held his son's gaze a long time before responding. "Give you a chance to do what?"

"To show them I can lead."

"You do have a head for strategy, that I'll give you," Uthyr conceded with a nod. "You see things even I don't."

"I do." Arthur remained still, his eyes trained on his father.

Uthyr glanced at Taliesin and then back at his son. "Fine. Our bannermen will be here in a week. If you're so certain you can win them over, present me with a battle plan."

Taliesin felt thrown by Uthyr's sudden change of attitude toward his son's abilities, yet Arthur remained constant.

"I'm honored, Father. I won't let you down."

A parade of lords, commanders and kings trailed into Caer Leon over the next few days, many with tales of Saxon skirmishes along the road. Strongholds in the east were waning, and travel between them grew riskier by the moon.

Taliesin went to the hall quite early on the morning of the council to find several chairs arranged in a circle around Arthur's impressive table. Several new wooden pieces painted with the banners of every clan present had been placed upon it in various configurations. Curious, Taliesin leaned over the map to study it again. In addition to the wooden markers, many details had been added marking out high ridges, forests and river crossings. The fact that Arthur had accomplished such fine work in less than a week impressed him. *But these men aren't looking for an artist,* he reminded himself.

Taliesin lost himself in the map as well as the placement of the various troops, considering every detail of Arthur's battle plan until the sound of heavy boots broke his concentration. Urien had been the last commander to arrive in Caer Leon, but he was the first to enter the hall.

"Master Taliesin," he roared. "If memory serves, I believe you still owe me a year of songs!"

Taliesin smiled and bowed his head. "I do, King Urien. And now, with ten more years of experience and training, they shall be the finest songs ever composed in the history of all Brython."

Urien shook his head and chuckled, then smacked Taliesin on the shoulder. "Nice try, you sly bastard—we both know you're never going to make good on your promise. But I forgive you."

Taliesin felt the comment sharply. "I fear you're right. But you never know—fate may send me north yet."

Urien stood behind the nearest chair. "I hope so. You're always welcome in my hall."

Taliesin saw sincerity in Urien's eyes. "Thank you, King Urien."

Arthur arrived next, and Taliesin felt dismayed to see that Urien glanced over at him with no more regard than a servant come to stoke the fire.

"Welcome to council, King Urien."

Urien inclined his head toward Arthur. "Thank you, Arthur. We've much to discuss with your father."

224

"There is indeed much to discuss," Arthur agreed.

Uthyr entered the hall next, followed by the rest of his commanders and bannermen. He stood beside Arthur as the men gathered around the table and then raised his hands. "Please, brothers, take a seat."

Servants immediately served ale to the assembly, resulting in a chorus of approving grunts and exhales.

Taliesin took note of every man present. Most concerning to him was Lot of Gododdin, who sat to the left of Uthyr, on nearly equal footing with Arthur. Lot's flippant remarks and posturing over the next hour revealed he considered himself equal, if not superior, to the Pendragon's own son. *Is this the result of Morgause? Or has he been a wolf in sheep's clothing all along? Great Mother forbid Uthyr's created Arthur's worst enemy with that alliance.*

Loyalty and support were assured, however, from Amlawth of Dumnonia, the queen's father, and her brother, Cynwal. Also, from Cynyr "Fork-Beard" Ceinfarfog, the queen's cousin from Dyfed, and his son, Cai. Taliesin studied the latter two well, for he remembered it was to Lord Cynyr that Morgen had said Arthur wished to be sent to for training. *If his son's fighting skills are equal to his fitness, Arthur would do well to train with them.* Cai loomed beside his father as massive and silent as a mountain. He was dark-haired with a thick beard, like his father. His frame scarcely moved during the council, nor did his lips. Unless asked a direct question, he seemed content to let his father do the talking. *Or else he's been advised to keep his mouth shut.* Taliesin hoped it revealed only that Cai was a man of restraint; a quality greatly prized, but rare, among young, strong men.

To the right of Cynwal, sat Gereint Llyngesoc, husband to the queen's younger sister and his son, Cadwy. Gereint commanded a substantial fleet, and Taliesin made a point of learning exactly how substantial. *We'll need ships, perhaps more than anything else; with Irish raiding from the west and Saxons crowding in from the east. Armorican shores may quickly become our only refuge.*

There were several other men around the table, however, whom Taliesin did not recognize. *Much has changed while I've been gone.* Throughout the council, he made sure to learn their identities. Most verbal and affable of the group were Bedrawt, who now ruled Glywysing, one of the landholds east of Caer Leon, and his son,

225

Bedwyr, who, like Cai, had a stature that would be an asset on the field. *And in the beds of women,* Taliesin thought, for the young man was everything most women found irresistible—strong-jawed with a full head of curls, broad-chested, muscular, and of a good height. *An Adonis, the Greeks would say.*

Perhaps the most unpleasant man among them was Cadwallon "Long Hand" Lawhir of Gwynedd. Throughout the entire council, he looked as if he had just drunk sour milk. The dry thin line of his mouth opened only to criticize whoever was speaking or to dismiss whatever suggestions came forth, stating it was the 'bloody Irish' they should be fighting. He had apparently led many successful campaigns, to just that purpose. It seemed quite clear to Taliesin he had no plans to spare even one warrior to fight the Saxons until the Irish were driven off his shores.

Many agreed with Long Hand about the Irish problem, most prominently Cynyr, the queen's cousin. He made it clear, however, that his loyalty lay with Uthyr. "I shall send my men wherever you deem they're needed most, Pendragon."

To that end, Uthyr had wisely summoned Illtud Farthog of Armorica, the queen's nephew by her elder sister, Rheinwylydd. Known to be scholarly and soft-spoken, he was nevertheless rumored to be quite capable on the battlefield. Taliesin listened to him with interest, appreciating his even-handed responses, no matter how heated the discussion became. *The more men like him on the council, the better.*

In addition to Arthur, Gereint, Cadwy and Illtud, Taliesin learned there was yet another of Arthur's cousins among the council—Caradoc "Strongarm" Freichfras, of Gwent, son of yet another sister to the queen.

Yes, Amlawth married his daughters well, mused Taliesin with a renewed appreciation for the elder's foresight. He had seen to it that each of his daughters married a man of ample status and power all over Brython. His reach now stretched from across the sea in Armorica all the way into the northern forests of Caledonia. On top of this, each of his daughters had given birth to at least one strong son, as well as plenty of fierce daughters, who Taliesin had no doubt would grow up to be as formidable as their mothers. *Arthur and his cousins shall rule Brython.* He studied each of the young men. *Uthyr and Igerna should have had more children.* With so many powerful cousins and uncles, as well as Urien and Lot to contend with, Arthur would have to prove himself worthy of the title "Pendragon" beyond the shadow of a doubt.

The council wore on, growing more heated as the ale addled thoughts and tempers wore thin. Even Taliesin struggled to keep his mood from growing heavy and irritable. Then, as if to punctuate the vast difference between father and son, Uthyr stood up with an authority that reached out from where he stood and seemed to grip the shoulder of every man in the hall at the same time. All bickering ceased and every head turned. Sitting beside him, Arthur looked more like a child than ever.

The son is still a far cry from his father, Taliesin noted with gnawing anxiety. This thought caused a sinking feeling in his gut. *Is Arthur the Young Stag foretold of?* he wondered, feeling terrible. *Perhaps he shall be, one day, but not now. Perhaps another is meant to rule first.* The doubt made him faintly sick.

"My lords and kings," Uthyr began, his voice steady and resonant, any sign of his ailment gone. "We find ourselves in grim times. Our supplies and patience have grown meager. I understand in times like these, it's natural for a king to be less generous—to hold his purse strings tighter, to stockpile his goods, horde his crops, and keep his warriors close—after all, what's more important than his own wife and children? His own clan, livestock and lands?" Uthyr paused, and whispers of assent filled the room. He motioned toward Cadwallon. "Indeed, Lord Cadwallon, I understand—how could I ask you to send your men east while the Irish pillage your shores?" He turned his palms up. "Or you, Urien, to send your men south, when the Saxon threat creeps ever closer to your gates? Not to mention the bloody Pict raids."

Every eye rested on Uthyr as he paused, brows raised at his audience, before he dealt his blow. "Yet, for the sakes of all our wives and children, I must ask you all to do just that."

Cadwallon and Urien looked away, but Uthyr's expression remained calm. "Things are worse than they've ever been. We face the threat of Aelle in the south, Octa in the east, the Irish in the west, and those crazy sky-smeared bastards in the north. We have only so

227

many hands that can grip a spear, many too old or too young to do so with any skill, and we're surrounded by enemies."

"Tell us something we don't know," Taliesin heard Urien murmur to himself.

Uthyr's ears were sharp. He turned and pinned his eyes on Urien. "Speak your mind, friend."

Urien shook his head. "With respect, Pendragon, this has been the state of things since Rome left us to the dogs. It's only a matter of time before the Saxons grind our bones into the dust. A warrior's death awaits us all. But my men want to be near their families when it comes for them."

"As do mine," Cadwallon said, nodding in Urien's direction. This ignited a fresh argument around the table that grew more and more heated until Uthyr slammed his fist down on the table. Like a hammer on a bell, it shocked every man into silence.

"This is why we're losing our lands!" he bellowed. "This!" He thrust his enormous hands at the table. "Fighting amongst ourselves!" Flames flickered from his eyes, leaping out at them. "You know what happens when you allow the enemy to divide your men, do you not? So why are we doing the work for them?" He glared at each of them in turn. "No man sitting at this table possesses enough warriors, hillforts, weapons or crops to defeat his enemies alone—not for long, at least. You all know it. Urien speaks the truth—if we continue in this way, we have but a few years left." He lanced his gaze at Cadwallon. "You may have enough men to defeat the Irish today, Lord Cadwallon—but what about tomorrow? Or next year? Ten years from now? And what of your crops? Blessed this season, perhaps, but what about next year's harvest?" Uthyr shook his head. "If we are to survive, we must think of ourselves as *one* clan, or we'll perish. Looking at the numbers leaves no doubt of this!"

Whether it was Uthyr's logic or his passion that held the men's attention, Taliesin did not know, but whatever it was, it worked.

"What do you suggest we do, Pendragon?" Urien conceded, his expression weary.

Uthyr, his battle won, sat down. "Fortify our hillforts, keep our women, children and elders behind their walls, and pledge all our crops, warriors and weapons to a common cause. It's true that some of you will have to hold out against your enemies while your men

228

fight battles elsewhere—but the threat to your lands will be addressed in accordance to need. I give you my solemn word. Right now, I believe, the most important thing is for us to destroy Octa—or whoever's stolen his namesake." He stabbed at Caer Mincip with his index finger, as if he were smashing an insect. "We crush him, and the other chieftains will scatter."

Cadwallon turned a palm up. "And after our men fight this battle? Then what?"

Arthur stood up. Taliesin glanced around the table at the confused expressions at this surprising turn of events and cringed. Uthyr had just begun to win these men over. If Arthur said anything foolish, he could easily endanger their support. *And what thirteen-year-old boy doesn't say something foolish at least ten times a day?*

Arthur regarded the council a moment, perhaps contemplating the gravity of the situation, and then looked over at his father. "May I speak, Pendragon?"

Uthyr had no choice. He could not shame or embarrass his son. "Of course."

Arthur proceeded. "It's no secret that Octa and his men call my father the 'Half-Dead King.'" This caused a ripple of surprise on the faces around the table, Uthyr's included. "He and his men think they've won already. They seized an easy victory at Caer Mincip, and now, they're raiding every village for miles around, working their way west."

Taliesin felt relieved. Arthur had a clear, confident voice, as resonant as his father's.

"How do you know this?" challenged Urien.

"I know this, because I've spent nearly every evening of the past year down in the village tavern, listening to all the news that passes through it. I know, because I've met men who are good at finding out such things, and I've paid them to keep me well-informed. I know, because I've seen the Saxon raids myself."

Uthyr's shock was perhaps not apparent to every man in the room, but it was clear to Taliesin.

"I've learned to speak their tongue," Arthur added. "Not well enough to pass for one of them, but well enough to understand what they're saying to one another."

The hall now nearly crackled with silence as each man regarded young Arthur. *It's more surprise than respect,* thought Taliesin, *but it's progress.* He chided himself for his hasty dismissal of the boy.

Arthur seemed emboldened by the silence and seized the opportunity to launch into the battle plans he had so painstakingly spent the past week laboring over. He walked over to the map and laid out his strategy with calm, careful precision. Slowly, it became clear that in spite of his minimal experience on the battlefield, he had a solid understanding of how battles were fought and won, as well as extensive knowledge of the Saxon threat. He knew which strongholds were most highly fortified, how healthy their supply of weapons, livestock and crops were, how many able warriors they had, and where the water sources and high ground were. By the time he had finished countering each man's arguments and answering all their questions, which dragged on into the later part of the afternoon, Taliesin considered the day a victory for Arthur. *He's not won them over yet, perhaps, but he's proven himself worth listening to. And he'll have a chance to prove himself in battle once again.*

Taliesin waited until all the men had adjourned to the feasting hall before standing up to inspect Arthur's strategy once again. "Well done, lad," he murmured to himself. "Well done."

Taliesin's gaze strayed, as it always did, far to the north beyond Hadrian's Wall, past Urien's kingdom, past Alt Clud, farther and farther north to where the water and land mingled so much the map became a tangle before it dropped off into the unknown. He ran his finger across the area of the map where he thought Dun Scáthach might be and felt a twinge of sadness in his chest, wondering if Arhianna yet lived up there in that wild land. *Please, Great Mother, let us meet again. Be kind to her.*

"What do you mean you're leaving tomorrow?" Igerna looked back and forth between Taliesin, Uthyr and her son, eyes flashing.

"You asked me to prepare your son to rule," Taliesin explained. "That is what we're doing."

"Not by taking him into battle!" Igerna protested. "I meant for you to teach him the ancient histories—songs, music, art!"

"Am I his teacher, then, or do you wish to be?"

230

The color drained from Igerna's face. She paced in front of the hearth, her face and hands twisted with anger. "I'm so bloody sick of all these battles and those damned fucking Saxons!" She grabbed an ale pitcher from a side table and smashed it into the fireplace, sending flames, ash and sparks flying in all directions. Taliesin had never heard such language from Igerna before, and his mouth fell open in shock.

She turned toward them, face in a wild fury. "Go, then!" She thrust herself toward Uthyr and held up a finger in exactly the same way Taliesin had seen Arthur do on more than one occasion. "But you had better win this battle, husband, and bring my son home. Do you hear me?" She stared at him, eyes widening. "You *win!*"

Arthur did not shrink away or show any sign of shock at his mother's behavior. "I swear it before God, Mother, we shall. I'll not let you down."

Igerna's hair had fallen from its usual braided perfection, pieces of it now hanging across her perfect cheekbones. Her face softened as she regarded her son. "See that you do." She glanced at Uthyr. "And you'd better bring your fool of a father back with you, too!"

"I will," Arthur said, steadily holding her gaze.

Igerna gave them all one last glance, huffed and stormed out of the hall.

Taliesin had never seen Igerna so much as scowl, let alone display such rage. He stared at the destruction she had left in her wake, unsure of what to say or do.

"She's angry," Arthur stated plainly. "She doesn't want this life for me." He shrugged. "But there's nothing to be done for it. God knows I'd love to spend my days painting, or barding—like you— but, like my father, I know how this war must be led—and how to win it."

Taliesin felt impressed and disturbed by Arthur's confidence. He had not known the boy long enough to determine whether it was foolishness, arrogance, or simple truth that fueled his assertions, and it unnerved him. *Only time will tell. Time our Lady Brython doesn't have, I fear.* He stared into Arthur's eyes, hoping the answer might be found within their amber pools, but they provided no immediate answers.

Uthyr broke the silence and moved toward the door. "Come. We've much to do."

231

Arthur walked out with him, leaving and Taliesin followed. He studied the shards of pottery scattered across the floor on his way out, as if, like thrown runes, they might contain an augury of what awaited them.

CHAPTER TWENTY-FOUR
The Battle for Caer Mincip

Thanks to Taliesin's ministrations and the medicine he had brought from Affalon, Uthyr felt well enough to lead his men to the gates of Caer Mincip. Arthur rode by his side, every inch his father's son. The sight of them together inspired hope in Taliesin's heart. *Arthur certainly looks the part,* he thought, regarding the lad's erect posture and noble profile. *He seems to have the sense and wit required of a king. I pray he shows a king's courage and skill on the battlefield.* A victory was essential for Arthur to secure the respect of the other kings and chieftains.

They reached the outskirts of Caer Mincip early the following morning and found the settlement asleep. Either the guards had not noticed them, which Taliesin thought nearly impossible, or else—and this bothered him more—they did not fear them. He itched at the Saxon disregard for their approach. *This is not the sort of victory that marks a future king.*

He rode up alongside Uthyr. "Let me deliver your terms," he offered. "I'll verify whether Octa's within the walls."

"I've a better idea," Uthyr suggested, glancing at Vala perched on Taliesin's shoulder. "Shift into that bird of yours and see what's happening inside. I'll not risk them taking you prisoner."

Arthur's forehead crinkled at his father's suggestion. "What do you mean, Father?"

"Just what I said." Uthyr scowled at his son and raised his brows. "Why do you think kings keep druids in their court? To tell stories and play songs while we drink?"

Arthur, reproached, kept silent.

Taliesin felt both surprised and pleased by the request. Over the past decade, Uthyr had become quite a penitent Christian, and Taliesin had feared he would reject any such tactics. "As you wish, Pendragon."

Uthyr nudged Arthur and nodded in Taliesin's direction. "Go with him and keep watch. The sooner you learn about such things, the better."

Dumbfounded, Arthur dismounted and followed Taliesin to a sheltered area in the woods with relative privacy.

"So, you're going to turn into your falcon?" Arthur asked, his tone incredulous.

"Not exactly. We shall become of one mind. Keep watch over my body."

Arthur did not ask any more questions. Instead, he stared, slack-jawed, while Taliesin settled down beneath a tree, crossed his legs, and leaned against its trunk. He and Vala had become quite adept at merging after so many years of practice. He nimbly threw himself into her, feeling her squawk as sharply as if it had rattled off his own tongue. He was soon flying over the city with her, surveying the scene below through her giant keen eyes. It did not take him long to spot the man he suspected must be Octa. The brute stood in the center of the yard like a bear on hind legs speaking so loudly Taliesin imagined he could have heard him just as easily from outside the walls.

"Great Woden!" Octa moaned in mock despair. "How can we hope to feast in Valhalla if the fates send us nothing but boys and sick old men to fight? It's a disgrace!" The other men laughed as he turned his palms up and looked skyward, as if expecting Woden to answer him. He pointed to a man standing directly beneath where Vala perched. "You there, Cuthbert—you speak their weak tongue. Ride to the sick king and tell him Octa insists he go home to his piss-stained bed!"

Taliesin had heard enough. He urged Vala to fly back to the tree where his body was, traded wings for arms and talons for feet, and opened his eyes to see a shocked Arthur staring down at him.

Taliesin smiled to put him at ease. "It seems the gods have favored us. There aren't that many men within the keep. Once we get inside, it won't take much to capture the fortress."

Arthur stood up, eyes wide. "Then we must attack at once. I'll tell my father what you've seen."

"Look for me in the sky when the battle begins." Taliesin motioned toward Vala, now perching overhead. "I'll keep an eye on things and do what I can to help, but I need you to send someone to guard my body."

Arthur nodded. "I'll send someone, right away."

"Good luck, Arthur. Stay close to your father."

"I will." Arthur ran off.

Taliesin waited for some time, but the man Arthur had promised did not come. He soon saw Uthyr's men moving into position, like Arthur's wooden pieces come to life, and lost patience. He tucked himself deeper inside the woods, merged with Vala, and flew out over the fort. He spotted Octa standing on the ramparts surveying the threat forming around the fortress. He had traded his dismissive banter for a concerned scowl. A man stood beside him, his giant arms crossed over an enormous shelf of a chest. Taliesin noticed the resemblance between the two.

"The gods have blessed us today, Eormenric," Octa said. "Uthyr has brought his son with him." His face spread into a ghastly grin. "His *only* son." He laughed. "Seems he couldn't plow his woman with good seed more than once." He wrapped an arm around Eormenric's meaty shoulders. "This is an opportunity we will not waste—the sick king and his son will die today."

Eormenric nodded, a smile spreading across his face. "And then we move west."

"And then we move west," Octa confirmed. "I hear Uthyr has quite a beautiful wife. I look forward to plowing her. Go light the signal. I'll not take any chances now."

Eormenric gave a nod and ran off. Moments later, he shot out of the back gates galloping at full speed toward a bald, stony hill, torch in hand. Atop the hill stood a pyre. No doubt there were others within view of each other in a chain throughout the countryside. News would spread quickly.

Taliesin flew in pursuit, intent on preventing him from completing his task. He swooped down behind him, talons outstretched, and clutched at Eormenric's shoulders. Unfortunately, his leather jerkin was too tough for Vala's talons to penetrate. The shock, however, served his purpose. Eormenric gave a shout and lost his balance, causing his horse to rear and unseat him. His torch went flying. It landed, unfortunately, in a bed of dry grass. The grass caught fire and the flames began to spread. Eormenric scrambled to his feet and grabbed the torch, looking around for his attacker. Taliesin seized the few moments he had and flew to the pyre, attempting to rip it apart. Eormenric soon arrived and brandished the torch with such force Taliesin dared not risk Vala catching fire. He

235

had no choice but to take to the sky. He watched in defeat as the pyramid of dry grass, pitch and kindling burst into flames.

What to do, now?

Elements were tricky to control; fire most of all. He could only stoke or direct its flames, not extinguish them. Wind would, of course, only cause the fire to spread faster.

It must be water, then.

Taliesin circled the pyre, pulling the clouds toward the hilltop and twisting them into a dark swirling mass. They turned a deep purple, swelling with water, until a great thunderclap shook the earth. Soon after, he felt cold raindrops hit Vala's wings. Within moments, the rain fell in sheets, soaking the flames from the pyre until nothing but sour smoke remained. He took to the sky for a longer view and surveyed the landscape, hoping the flames had not been seen, but, to his dismay, he spotted another orange pyre flowering in the distance. He directed the rain to engulf it as well, but the damage was likely done. *We could soon be outnumbered.*

Taliesin heard the call for the attack. He watched from above as Uthyr's men surged into the formations Arthur had choreographed across the battle map in his father's hall. Before long, a battering ram smashed against the city gates, causing those inside the walls to scurry. Octa's archers picked off their men from above while others attempted to boil tar to pour down upon the men below, but, thanks to Taliesin's thunderstorm, this was proving difficult.

At last, the gates burst open from the force of the ram. Combat turned hand-to-hand, and in this, the Saxons seized the advantage. Their archers continued to pick off men from the ramparts.

Those we can deal with, Vala.

Taliesin pulled the clouds over the fortress, directing lightning bolts to strike the archers' helmets and tips of their bows. All struck fell off the walls like burning sacks of barley.

Arthur saw the opportunity Taliesin had created and cried for their own archers to take over the ramparts.

Triumphant, Taliesin took to the sky to avoid the billowing smoke and saw what no one else could—men on the horizon, riding for Caer Mincip. His heart sank. *The best we can hope for is to sever the head of the serpent before they get here.* He spotted Octa and circled above him, crying loudly, hoping Uthyr would sense his urgency. It was Arthur, however, who looked up and spotted Octa.

Taliesin shrieked again. *Not you, Arthur! Don't be a fool!* But, of course, all Arthur heard were his shrieks, and, to Taliesin's dismay, perhaps mistook them for encouragement.

Arthur surged toward Octa like a wild boar, fierce and without hesitation. Octa laughed, waiting for Arthur with open arms as if intending to embrace him. Once within reach, he slammed him in the chest with his shield. Arthur sprawled backward from the force and landed in the mud. He scrambled to his feet and managed to return a few blows, but was soon on his back again.

Taliesin shrieked at Uthyr who looked skyward, and then drew his attention toward Arthur. Uthyr slashed his way toward Octa, all weakness gone from his limbs. In that moment, he became the Pendragon of his youth, attacking with the strength and fierceness of a bear. He put Octa on the defensive, but not for long. Within four blows, Octa had broken his shield. Arthur came to his father's aid, but Octa merely laughed and soon had him on his back again, this time without his sword and surely a broken arm or shoulder.

As Arthur struggled to get up again, Octa turned all his rage on Uthyr until he, too, fell. He stepped on Uthyr's chest, pushing him into the mud. "You shall live to see your son suffer the fate of my brother, and then suffer the same yourself," he seethed. He smashed Uthyr's leg with his shield, causing him to cry out with more agony than a woman in the throes of childbirth. Octa took off his helmet, perhaps to ensure Uthyr saw his face while he gloated, but this proved a fatal mistake. Taliesin seized his moment, attacking Octa's eyes with Vala's fierce talons. He felt them sink into flesh and clutched with all the strength Vala had. Octa dropped his sword and shield, and Taliesin took off. Arthur seized his opportunity, scrambling to his feet and driving his sword through Octa's heart with a war cry.

Octa bellowed in agony. Eormenric turned to see his father stumble and fall. Like a horse stung by a bee, he went into a violent frenzy, finishing the man he was fighting with two powerful blows. He surged toward his father, cutting through the battle like an enormous plow, face twisted by rage. He threw a spear at Arthur, which would surely have finished him, but some unfortunate soul happened to cross paths with it. Arthur ran to recover his shield, but Eormenric did not run in pursuit. Instead, he remained where he was, shielding his father. He raised his arms and hollered for a retreat.

Cries of victory shook the fortress walls in the wake of the Saxon departure, but the men inside could not see what Taliesin saw. Off in the distance, like a black cloud of locusts rising on the eastern horizon, came Octa's allies.

Uthyr's men were so elated they ignored Taliesin's shrieks of warning. He doubled his efforts, flying down and flapping Vala's wings at Arthur in a frantic plea.

Uthyr realized something was wrong. "This isn't over. Help me up!"

Arthur's grin soured. He looked skyward toward Taliesin's shrieks. As soon as he did, Taliesin grabbed Octa's banner in Vala's beak and dropped it in his lap.

"More are coming," Uthyr surmised. "Alert the flanks!" He struggled to his feet with Arthur's help. "Close the gates!" he bellowed. "Move to defense positions!"

Arthur intervened. "Wait, Father—leave the gates open. Let them think they've caught us off guard. Once they move into the valley to attack, I'll ride out and signal the flanks. They'll be trapped."

Uthyr considered his son's request, grimacing with pain. "It's too risky. They're good fighters, son."

"That's precisely why we must outsmart them. They won't hesitate if they think an easy victory awaits them." Arthur looked up at Taliesin. "Where are they approaching from? Cry once for east or west, twice for north or south!"

Taliesin cried once.

"Once for east, twice for west!"

Taliesin cried once again.

"Give a cry for every hundred men you see…"

And on it went until Arthur seemed satisfied and looked back at his father. "I know what to do."

Uthyr nodded. "Good." He raised his hands and addressed his commanders, now gathered around him. "More approach. My leg's surely broken, so Arthur shall lead our defense. Trust him as you would trust me. I can't ride into battle with you but will join the archers on the ramparts and send as many Saxons to their graves as I can. God willing, the halls of Caer Mincip shall ring with our victory songs tonight."

Arthur looked surprised by his father's deferral but did not hesitate to take it. He turned his attention to the commanders. "We can defeat them, but we must act quickly." He proceeded to lay out his plan for the defense of the city, speaking much the way Taliesin remembered Emrys did—measured and confident. He lacked his father's robust charisma but made up for it with sharp attention to detail. He knew every commander by name, the number of men they commanded, where those men were at that moment, and exactly where he wanted them to be when the Saxons arrived. To Taliesin's surprise, no one objected to his plan.

Once the commanders returned to their men with their orders, Arthur sent messengers to the flanks within the trees with instructions to watch for his signal. "Make no move to attack until you see me ride out with my father's banner." He then took a horse and left through the back gates.

Taliesin knew, with the amount of action soon to reach the surrounding forest, that he had to return to his body. He was also tiring—he had been merged with Vala for some time now, and the bond was getting difficult to maintain. He flew back to where he had left his flesh, praying he would have enough time to come to his senses before the Saxons arrived. He noticed a man standing over him, bow poised, and felt relief.

Arthur sent someone, after all.

He surveyed the scene below once more with Vala's eyes. He shifted back into his body as swiftly as he dared, leaving Vala to fly where she willed. Shaky and damp with sweat, he did his best to rally his senses. "I'm back," he croaked to his guardian, whom he now recognized by his bulk and curly dark hair as Lord Cynyr's son. "Cai, is it not?"

"It is."

"I believe that's the first time I've heard you speak."

Cai sighed. "Speech is like ale. Best not wasted, and too much'll give you a headache."

Taliesin smiled. "Your words?"

"My mum's."

"Wise woman."

"She was, gods keep her."

"Thank you for standing watch."

Cai shrugged. "Arthur told me if I let anything happen to you, he'd kill me."

"Glad to know." The mention of ale made Taliesin realize how thirsty he was. He reached for his goatskin and drained it.

"You any good in a fight?" Cai asked.

"I can hold my own," Taliesin assured him.

"Messenger said more Saxons are coming from the east. The men closer to the city are waiting for Arthur's signal to attack. We're to wait here and finish off any who retreat."

Taliesin smiled, glad to know the plan had been communicated. He surveyed the forest around them and noticed many men sharing the cover of the trees—riders astride silent horses in the dark shadows of the canopy, bowmen perched in the shelter of the limbs, and spearmen, taut as hunting dogs, poised at the edge of the verge. Down below, the gates to the city stood open. The sound of men cheering wafted up over the walls on the late summer breeze, and Taliesin prayed Eormenric would take the bait. Soon the thundering sound of their enemies shook the ground. *They're here.*

Taliesin held his breath, waiting for the flash of Uthyr's red and gold banner. *Great Morrigan, help the boy. He's shown great courage. Grant him your favor.* He prayed for Arthur, moving into the ether, lending his strength to the warriors below. After some time, he felt unsure how long, Cai shook him. "Wake up! You must defend yourself, now. There are too many! I'm taking my men to their aid." Cai's voice seemed extremely far away, as if he were talking to him from across a lake.

"No," Taliesin responded, struggling to wrestle the words from his tongue. "Wait for Arthur's signal." He had a foot in two worlds, straddling the space between them as if precariously poised upon two rafts, each floating in the opposite direction. Cai's interruption had jostled them both, and he strove to restore his vision. He could see Valkyries circling above the field and Arawn's hounds roaming the valley below. He had been watching a great raven circling the fortress.

"We cannot stand by while our men are slaughtered! Cai retorted. "The Pendragon's down in that fortress! We must go!"

"Wait for Arthur," Taliesin croaked. His throat had grown dry again. "Wait for the signal." He sensed no movement around him, so he assumed Cai had agreed to wait.

He moved back into the ether, fully now, watching the raven descend. He soon saw it was not a bird at all, but a woman with black wings. *Morrigan.* He smiled as he saw Arthur ride out of the open gates, banner flying. She flew out over him like a mother bird, her wings sheltering him from arrows and spears as he thundered across the valley.

Taliesin moved back into the physical just in time. Eormenric had called for a retreat, and Saxons were scrambling up toward the trees.

Beside him, Cai dispatched four arrows with such swiftness it took his breath away.

Taliesin gathered his wits and summoned his shadow combat skills, sending men tumbling back down the hill with a mere thrust of his hand.

Cai looked at him in shock.

"Keep shooting!" Taliesin commanded, moving into the fray. He roamed the hillside, casting enemy arrow and sword astray, blasting Saxon soldiers off their mounts and bidding their horses run for the fortress, whispering promises of oats and apples. Horses he had always been able to talk to, long before his current lifetime, and they remained the easiest beasts for him to converse with. They were more than happy to comply.

Taliesin's power emboldened Uthyr's warriors and terrified the Saxons. Cries filled the woods as the enemy dispersed, until nothing but the sound of the wind and moans of the wounded remained.

Taliesin and Cai waited with their brothers-in-arms until they saw the Pendragon's banner thrown over the wall.

"It's done," announced Cai with an exhausted grin. "Caer Mincip is ours."

"She is." Taliesin smiled, squinting in between the worlds to see Morrigan soaring once again over the battlefield, her wings casting shadows in both.

CHAPTER TWENTY-FIVE
Angel of Death

Nothing could dampen Uthyr Pendragon's mood as he spoke to his men in the hall of the newly liberated fort of Caer Mincip. Though every muscle begged for rest, his rekindled hope made it bearable.

"Do you see what we can do when we unite?" he cried. "We cannot be defeated!"

Cheers shook the rafters, and Uthyr's blood raced. "We've taken back our most valued city within Saxon territory, and now, we shall take back all our lands, and send those scavengers scrambling into their miserable boats!"

Again, a sea of cheers filled the hall. Uthyr glanced down at his son with burgeoning pride. "And, if it's not too much to ask, please indulge me in a father's boast." He gripped his son's shoulder. "My son led us well today."

Uthyr looked around the hall at the faces of all those gathered. Most of the men gave a robust cheer, but there were some who merely nodded or gave no more than a few unenthusiastic claps. He marked well who they were. *Before I die, they must be dealt with.* He sat down and leaned toward Taliesin, who sat to his left. "You owe King Urien a debt, do you not?"

Taliesin gave a thoughtful nod. "I regret I do, Pendragon."

Uthyr smiled. "Good. I want you to repay it."

Taliesin raised his brows. "That would require me to spend a year in his service."

Uthyr nodded. "I know. And I'm loath to lose you so soon after your return, but Urien is Arthur's biggest rival, now that Lot has proven himself less than capable. I want to know what he's doing up there in the North. Can I trust you to keep me informed?"

Taliesin sat silent a few moments. "Forgive me, Pendragon, but I feel I can better serve your son's interests by remaining in Caer Leon as his tutor and advisor." He paused. "You realize, as Urien's chief bard, it would be my duty to sing his praises—to do all I can to glorify him, both as a war leader and a king? I don't like to brag, but I fear I must warn you I'm ten times the bard I used to be, and my efforts to that end would surely run counter to Arthur's cause."

Uthyr thought a moment, considering Taliesin's words, then shrugged. "I suppose you're right." He caught Urien's eye. The old king had glanced his way, as if sensing he was being spoken of. "Have you a better idea on how we might keep abreast of the goings-on in the north?"

Taliesin did, and he was quick to offer it. "Why not employ your daughter, Morgause, to the cause? Women, I've found, are far keener than men when it comes to matters of intrigue."

"Oh, she's clever enough, to be sure," Uthyr agreed, "but I'm afraid she'll use her knowledge to further her husband's position, not Arthur's."

Both Morgause's intelligence and ambition had been plain to see from the time she had grown old enough to ask questions. Uthyr had often wished the girl had never been born. She had been a constant reminder of his betrayal of her father. *If only I'd married Igerna when I first had the chance,* he lamented for the countless time.

"Why not send Arthur himself to live in the north?" Taliesin suggested. "Urien wouldn't dare refuse the opportunity to foster him." Taliesin scanned the long hall. "In fact, why not send Arthur to live in a few of your bannermen's kingdoms?" He motioned toward Cynyr. "Perhaps begin with your wife's cousin, as has been discussed. Arthur could train alongside Cai. From what I've seen, he'll receive the best training a warrior could hope for, and he's going to need it. Though men appreciate intelligence, it's prowess on the field they often respect most."

"I agree. His mother insists on thwarting my efforts to make a man of him. He needs to be sent away where she can't continue to coddle him." Uthyr grew more and more pleased with Taliesin's suggestion. "And then," he concluded, "once he's proven himself, you can take him north with you to live with Urien. You can pay off your yearly debt and further our cause at the same time. All you'll need to do is ensure he has plenty of opportunities to show the men of the north he's the better choice for Pendragon."

Taliesin nodded. "I can do that."

Uthyr crossed his arms over his chest and took a deep, satisfied breath. The idea of his son following in his footsteps seemed a true possibility for the first time, and he relished it. "This is good. Now, I must rest." He squeezed the medicine pouch Taliesin had given him, grateful its contents had granted him the day, but their power had waned. He felt a fever coming on and stood up, eager to retire.

243

Once out of view of his men, he relaxed his efforts to disguise his pain and moved gingerly down the hall to his chamber. The relief he felt entering its refuge lasted only a moment. The room darkened as he closed the door, as if storm clouds had suddenly swallowed the sun. The hair on the back of his neck prickled as he turned his head, surveying the room with heightened senses. The flames in the hearth moved strangely, as if underwater, undulating like grasses in a slow-flowing river. His heart thumped. *Lord, preserve us. What magic is this?*

As if to answer, a dark cowled figure stepped out of the shadows, moving toward him through the thick air like a black ship on calm waters. The figure removed its cowl and showed its face.

"Hail to you, Uthyr Pendragon."

"Bran?" Uthyr managed to whisper after a moment.

"I was once known by that name. Now, I speak for Arawn."

Uthyr felt uneasy. *Arawn? What of God's messengers? What of Gabriel? Why, Lord, do you send me a messenger of the Old Gods?*

Bran's ghastly skull tilted to look at him, his dark eye sockets drawing him in like galactic whirlpools. "Your time is coming, my friend. You must prepare yourself."

Uthyr's mind reeled, the fever in his blood running cold. *No! Not now! Not when Arthur is so close!* He stared into the skull of the man he once knew and summoned his courage. "When will it be, then, my friend? Tell me that, if you know—for I've much to do, and must know how much time I have to do it in."

Bran did not hesitate. "You have but two moons. I've come to advise you to use them well."

"No! No, please," Uthyr protested. "I must have more time than this. I must give my son more time—for this, I would do anything. Please, in remembrance of our friendship, please help me, if you can."

"Such requests have a cost, my friend."

Uthyr did not care. "I'll pay it gladly. I beg you, I've much to do yet. So much. My son needs me."

At this, Bran paused. "I know your struggle. I once made such a bargain. I paid for it with much pain and suffering."

Uthyr felt encouraged by the remark. "I already suffer. If I must suffer more, so be it. I have grown accustomed to it. I accept."

Bran gave a slow nod. "I shall plead for you. If Arawn agrees, you shall have your time."

Uthyr held his breath as Bran's ghost spoke, with someone he could neither see nor hear, in a language he did not understand. Yet, from the tone of Bran's voice, he surmised his old friend was arguing on his behalf, as he had promised. After some time, his ghastly skull turned back toward him.

"So be it, Uthyr Pendragon. Your request is granted. Two turns of the moon have been traded for two turns of the sun."

Uthyr felt a wave of gratitude loosen the knot in his stomach. "Thank you, my friend. Thank you. I am in your debt."

Bran's ghost turned to go, prompting Uthyr to cry out. "Wait! You must tell me, what lies beyond this world? Is there a heaven, as the priests tell us? As the Lord, our saviour proclaimed?"

"There are many such glorious realms, and an equal number of horrifying ones, each with their legions of spirits, and a great many beings in between, simply seeking love, adventure and answers. The world holds mysteries far beyond anyone's understanding."

"What are you saying? You don't know if there's a heaven or not? What about the Summerlands? Do they exist?"

"I have glimpsed the Summerlands beyond the Lake of the Dead, which may be the heaven your Lord promised, but I have not entered those glorious hills. Nor will I, until my beloved may join me. Until then, I shall abide in the Otherworld serving Arawn—the one who approved your request."

Uthyr felt confused. "Then Arawn must be the Angel of Death. Do you serve the Angel of Death?"

"Perhaps. He has many names."

Uthyr felt a slight flutter of hope, but it was not enough to quell his unrest. *Emrys, if you can hear me, come and visit me as this dead one has—you, who were far closer to me than he was. Come and tell me of the glories of heaven, I beg you—I must know the pain of this life ends—that the questions shall cease!*

"Do not despair, Uthyr Pendragon. Countless mysteries remain veiled to me. You have been granted a rare gift. Use it well. Farewell, old friend."

Bran's dark figure faded like the last light of day, and Uthyr fell to his knees. Overcome, he prayed until his throat went hoarse and he could no longer feel his body. Not until he heard the cocks crow did he finally collapse into his furs and sleep.

CHAPTER TWENTY-SIX
Return to Gwynedd

Taliesin and Arthur set out with Lord Cynyr and his men early the next morning. It would be a five or six-day journey, depending on how the horses fared—plenty of time for Taliesin to learn more about Cynyr and his son, Cai. He rejoiced that, over the next year, he would be back in Gwynedd, only a day's ride from Mynyth Aur. *It will be good to see everyone and visit the grove. It's been far too long.* He felt shocked to realize that Gareth's son would be a man by now. He even dared to hope there might be news of Arhianna. He thought back to the time she had first returned to Mynyth Aur after leaving her husband and the thrill he had felt upon seeing her enter the grove. It was as if she had brought the very sun itself with her. *Gods, that was long ago.* Their trip to Eire and love affair in Knockma seemed to have happened in another lifetime. *Great Mother, let there be a happy ending to her story…please, lead her home, where she is loved.* He knew it was a fragile, wishful prayer, for even as he set it adrift on the wind, he sensed Arhianna's fate lay elsewhere; far from him, far from their daughter, and very far indeed from their childhood home. Thoughts of that sort occupied most of his time over the next few days, making him melancholy. He felt glad, however, to see Arthur and Cai riding side by side for much of the journey. It seemed Arthur could coax words from his cousin where no one else could. One night in the camp, however, those words turned angry. Taliesin quickly interjected himself. "What's the trouble?"

"Nothing," Cai said, standing up and walking away.

Arthur forced a smile. "Sorry to have disturbed you, Master Taliesin." He got to his feet and motioned toward the large circle of men gathered in the center of the camp. "Are we to enjoy some of your playing tonight? Makes the night pass so much more quickly."

Taliesin would not be detoured. "What was that about?"

"Just a discussion, nothing more."

"About what?"

"I'd rather not say. It's between Cai and myself."

Taliesin respected Arthur's restraint but remained concerned. He stopped in his tracks and lowered his voice. "You know there are many men who would prefer someone else to take your father's place when he dies, do you not?"

Arthur met his gaze. "I do, indeed."

Taliesin nodded. "Then you know how important it is to be watchful of everyone around you, and how careful you must be with your words."

"I do." Arthur looked peeved, as all young people do when they believe they are being underestimated.

Taliesin changed his tone. "All I'm saying is two pairs of eyes and ears catch more than one. The wisest of kings know this. It's why they have advisors. I don't expect you to share everything with me, I just want you to know you can trust me."

Arthur's face softened. "Thank you."

Taliesin left it at that and looked forward to playing his harp. *By gods, I'm much better at that.*

Cynyr's hillfort was nearly as impressive as Caer Leon, with a wide, well-built wall enclosing a good number of roundhouses, a large forge, stable, and an imposing central hall big enough for twelve families to gather.

Once the excitement and bustle of their arrival died down, Taliesin strode out to take the measure of the countryside. Dusk was coming on, and Vala seemed eager to hunt. He stroked her head. "Go on then—get your dinner. I'll find us a tree for the night."

She cocked her head a few times, fluttered her wings and launched off his shoulder.

Cynyr's well-tilled fields unfurled down the hills like a patchwork skirt, its wide hem dampened by the waters of Lake Bala far off in the distance. Taliesin's eyes traced the tree line bordering the river and followed it east, toward Mynyth Aur. His heart fluttered at the prospect of returning to the grove, just as it had at the age of five, when the Sacred Oak had first called to him. *As soon as Arthur's settled, I'll go.*

What a homecoming it would be! He had not seen Gareth or Lucia in over a decade, now. Not in person, at any rate. He had sought Lucia in the shadows from time to time, sending his love or messages of greeting, promising he would return someday. Now, that day was soon at hand, and he rejoiced for it.

The following moon was marked by long training sessions, resulting in nearly daily injuries for Arthur. Taliesin found his healing skills requested more often than his lessons. In truth, Arthur dreaded the latter, often fidgeting or staring into space as Taliesin plumbed his mind in an attempt to determine the extent of his education.

"No more!" Arthur exclaimed one afternoon. "I'm sorry, Master Taliesin, but I should be outside, training. Cai bests me every day. None of this will help me if I can't hold my own on the battlefield. There are only two languages worth learning in the fight against the Saxons—theirs, which I have, and this one!" He brandished his dagger and stabbed it into the table.

Taliesin knew an angry, impatient mind was like a dry field—it could not be sown with knowledge. In truth, he, too, felt burdened by a growing sense of futility. *I'm failing with him.* He let out a long, slow breath. "Very well," he said, motioning toward the door. "Spend your time training."

Arthur's brow wrinkled, looking back and forth between Taliesin and the door. "Do you mean it?"

Taliesin shrugged. "I do. Train until you can best Cai. Then we'll resume our lessons."

Arthur did not seem convinced. "Are you certain?"

Taliesin chuckled. "No. But I can't teach you if you don't want to learn. I'll go to Mynyth Aur for a few moons." He stood up and began collecting his things, feeling a bit ashamed of how relieved he felt. He was not accustomed to dealing with people younger than himself. Then, in a moment of doubt, he hesitated. *Am I doing the right thing?*

But it was too late, even if he were. Arthur stood up, grinning. "Thank you, Master Taliesin. Please know it's not that I don't find your lessons interesting—I do—but this must come first. I swear I'll have beaten him by the time you get back—a few times, at least." Arthur winked.

Taliesin thought, *Gods, there's Uthyr's brazenness, for better or worse.* Resigned, he gave him a nod. "So be it, Arthur. A few moons it is."

Taliesin's heart soared as it always did when he spied the familiar summit of Mynyth Aur on the horizon. "There it is, Vala," he said, pointing at it.

Vala chirped a bit and vaulted off his shoulder, as if she wished to take a closer look.

He imagined again each of the reunions he was looking forward to, beginning with Gareth. *How many children might he and Inga have by now?* With shame, he realized he could not remember the name of Gareth's firstborn. *I've committed generations of poems and songs to memory, but I've forgotten that poor boy's name? No. Please.* After a moment or two, it came to him. *Branok! Yes, that was it. Branok.* He smiled with relief and urged his horse on, for he had reached the stretch of river road where he knew that, if someone were watching, he would be seen.

He looked toward the village with eager eyes but spied no curl of smoke from the forge or the motherhouse. As he rode closer, the muscles of his abdomen gradually grew cold, the way a winter night freezes the surface of a lake. When he spied the gates broken off their hinges, a black panic gripped his heart. A foul smell assaulted him as he rode into the village, confirming his worst suspicions. Bodies lay strewn about, some face down with spear wounds or arrows in their backs next to overturned carts and water barrels. The doors of the stable hung like broken teeth from a jaw, the horses fled or stolen.

Taliesin knelt next to the first man he found, surprised his body had not yet begun to smell. *This happened in the last few days. How could I not have felt it? Or seen it in a vision?* He closed his eyes and blessed the man. One by one, he did the same with the others he found. He soon observed there were no women or children among the dead. He looked up at Mynyth Aur with hope. *Great Mother, let them be safe in the keep!*

He jumped on his horse and galloped up the trail to the fortress. Heart pounding, he pulled at the gates, disappointed to find them unbarred. He ventured in, hoping to hear voices, but nothing met his ears except the sound of his own breath and his horse's tentative hoof clops. He dismounted, lit a lantern, and walked up to the main hall, but still heard no voices. He lit one of the torches on the wall and willed the flames to stretch to the torch beside it, and from that one to the next, one by one, illuminating the entire chamber. "Is anyone here?" He called with fading hope. "It's Taliesin."

The hall was just as he remembered—Bran's throne at the far end, cushions and piles of furs scattered about, weapons on the walls, great stores of wood piled up—but, sadly, there seemed to be no one there. "You've nothing to fear," he called out, hopeful there might be some survivors hiding deeper within the cavern.

Nothing stirred but the flames. He felt confused. *Why did they not take refuge here?* With dread, he realized the answer the moment he posed the question. *They didn't have time.* Still, his confusion remained. For so many years, Lucia had insisted the Oaks be ever ready for an attack; she had demanded caches of weapons be stored throughout the village, that watchmen were always posted, day and night, and every Oak, be they young, old, man or woman, be trained to fight and wield at least one weapon with some skill.

How could this have happened? Were her warnings ignored after so many years? Did Gareth think his mother overprotective? Too zealous and fearful?

He remembered, with a jolt, that Lucia had gone to live in the grove. *Gods—she may not even know.* He swallowed hard and returned to collect his horse, all the while wrestling with questions. *Who did this? Octa's men? Raiders from Eire?* Whoever they had been, they had left no clues. He could not find a single weapon or corpse that did not belong to an Oak. His rage mounted, like water coming to a boil. *Is this to never end? Must there always be wolves circling, hungry for blood?* He exited the fortress, accosted by the horrible sight of the ransacked village below. Overwhelmed, he unleashed a yell curdled with so much agony that it turned the clouds a wounded shade of purple. He reached his hands up and twisted them as if they were rags, sending flashes of lightning flickering across the sky. Thunder followed, causing his horse to whinny and paw the ground in agitation. He galloped to the edge of the forest, fearful of what he might find within the grove. It would forever be the most sacred place on Earth, to him. His body ached with the thought of it being desecrated or finding Lucia unaware of the tragedy that had befallen her clan. Perhaps sensing his distress, Vala appeared overhead, just as he reached the outskirts of the grove. He reached out his arm, grateful for her appearance, and stroked her head a few times before bidding her to his shoulder and leading his horse into the trees.

The rain now fell in sheets, the patter of raindrops on the leaves near deafening. Water streamed down his hair and face, as if the land itself willed him to weep. Hot tears soon ran alongside the cold rain down his cheeks and neck. The trees brought him a feeling of peace, but their regal salve was not enough on a day like today. *Please,* he thought, picturing both Bran and Arawn in his mind, *please, don't have taken them all.*

Like an answer to his prayer, the faint smell of smoke soon filled the air. His heart lightened. *She's alive.* He led his horse through the thickening woods and across the small stream that bordered the grove. A few more steps, and Islwyn's hut came into view—except it was no longer his. It belonged to a new resident.

Lucia stepped out from between the furs covering the doorway and beheld him with a bittersweet smile, as if she had been expecting him. The years had drained the blush from her cheeks and calmed the bounce from her hair, but she still had the beauty of kindness in her eyes. She moved toward him, her face twisted by a restrained sob. "Oh, Taliesin."

Taliesin gave Vala over to a nearby tree branch and embraced her, sending as much love and strength as he could into her heart. "What happened?"

She pulled away. "Come inside." She went to the doorway of the hut and pulled the furs aside. "Your beautiful bird, too." Taliesin extended his arm and Vala hopped on, eager to be out of the rain. Wet feathers made flying difficult. Once inside, she flew to the rafters and perched near the smoke hole.

Lucia had clearly been living in the hut for some time and had improved it immensely. Flat stones lined the dirt floor in a tight pattern, and several shelves lined the walls. Islwyn's small cot was gone, replaced with a larger one piled high with furs. She had kept the apothecary well-maintained. Herbs hung from every place imaginable, filling the hut with an array of scents both pleasant and sharp.

Lucia took a stool by the fire and beckoned him to do the same. He removed his wet cloak and sat down, grateful for the warmth. He had not realized his teeth were chattering.

Lucia clasped her hands, wringing them as she spoke. "I had a vision of the village under attack, so I grabbed my bow and rode to warn them." She shook her head. "I soon learned it wasn't a vision of things to come—it was in the midst of happening. I shot at the attackers, but none of my arrows found their mark, so I jumped from my horse and grabbed at them, but my hands slipped through their bodies."

Taliesin was quite familiar with the experience. "You were shadow-walking."

Lucia nodded and closed her eyes. "I don't know who these people were. They bore no sigil upon their shields. They didn't seem like they were from the same clan. Some were dark, others pale, some thin and tall, others muscular. Their dress and weapons also varied; none of which I've ever seen before, even among all of the strange textiles and goods brought back from Tegid and Creirwy's most distant voyages." She shook her head. "There was nothing that seemed to unify them except their purpose."

"To raid?"

Lucia nodded. "They didn't find the keep, so most of the gold is safe, but they took all that was in the village, and our young men and women, Great Mother protect them."

Taliesin swallowed to wet his dry throat. "What of Gareth and his family?"

Lucia looked at him with tortured eyes. "I haven't been able to find their bodies. I've been shadow-walking since the attack, searching for them, but it's as if they've gone underground or beneath the sea to a place I can't reach—the only mercy is that Bran was here to collect the souls of those who were slain. He assured me neither Gareth nor his family were among them."

Taliesin took her hands in his to stop them from trembling. "What of their leader? Do you remember anything about him?"

She shook her head. "I don't know who led them. It happened so quickly." She paused and closed her eyes, perhaps attempting to recall what she had seen. "One thing I feel certain of—they must have had a mage among them. A powerful one."

252

Taliesin's stomach dropped. "Why do you believe that?"

"The shrouding of the captives would be enough to convince me, but what makes me certain is what happened to me. Once I realized I was in the shadows I tried to return to my body, but some kind of force held me back. I tried with all my will, but no matter how I tried, I couldn't get back. I remember standing over myself, yelling and screaming, trying to wake myself up, but it was no use." She paused, her face contorting as she watched the flames dance in the fire, her composure collapsing. "I wasn't able to return until the dawn broke. By then, of course, it was too late."

Such a thing did indeed sound like dark magic to Taliesin. *Maelwys? Finbheara? But why? Arhianna hasn't been here for years, nor have I.*

Lucia sighed. "I'm an old woman, Taliesin. My body aches. I've lost my husband, my daughter, and now my son and his family. My grandchildren were the only reason I stayed after Bran died. I can't bear to remain here now, not after what's happened. I've decided to go back to the Sisterhood. Maybe they can help me discover who these slavers were and where they've taken our people. But I can't leave the grove without a guardian." She looked at him with raised brows. "Will you stay and watch over it?"

Taliesin's heart sank. He had known she would ask this of him, but he could not break his promises to Uthyr, Igerna or Arthur. He shook his head. "I regret I can't. I've sworn to look after the Pendragon's son. He's here in Gwynedd, training with Lord Cynyr. I had planned to stay here a moon and then return to him."

The wrinkles in Lucia's brow deepened. "I understand."

Taliesin held up a hand. "But there's no need to worry—I can keep the grove hidden and protect it from afar. I'll keep it safe until I can return and take your place for good." His command of magic, especially protective magic, had reached a point where he felt certain of this.

"That will have to do, then. Thank you." Lucia regarded him a moment. "Is that where you've been all these years? Looking after Uthyr's son?"

Taliesin shook his head. "Not until recently."

Over the next hour, Taliesin told Lucia as much as he felt he could about the past twelve years. He wanted, with all his being, to tell her about Morgen — to let her know she had another grandchild — but, of course, he could not do that. *Not yet. Arhianna must know first. Oh, Great Mother, am I ever to see her again? Please tell me I will.* He realized, with a sudden shock, the horrible tragedy awaiting Arhianna if she ever happened to return to Mynyth Aur. His heart sank.

"What of Arhianna? Have you heard from her?"

Lucia winced, as if an old wound had begun to ache. "Arhianna's never coming home," she whispered, eyes glazing over. "I've known that for years. I content myself with shadow-walking when I wish to see her. Sometimes we meet in the spirit, and we speak." She poked at the fire and then looked him in the eyes. "She was there the night of the attack as well. Perhaps she, too, was pulled to it like I was."

Taliesin felt his anxiety deepen. "Is she still living at Dun Scáthach?"

"I imagine so. She's become quite powerful over the years — both as a warrior and a shadow-walker. But I fear where her power comes from."

Taliesin's stomach lurched. "What do you mean?"

"I know she serves Morrigan, which is disturbing enough, but her shadow-wings are the largest I've ever seen. I've tried to reach her, but since the attack, a dark mist shrouds her from me, like a fog or veil. I don't know what to think. Perhaps she can't sense me." Lucia shuddered. "But they can."

"Who?"

"There are strange animals around her. Dragons, perhaps. I don't know. Whatever they are, they pace around her, or crouch at her flanks. I can see their red eyes watching me through the veil, never blinking. They won't let me near her."

"I'll try to reach her," Taliesin proposed, hiding his concern as best he could. "And I'd like to accompany you to Lake Bala, if you'll allow me."

Lucia lit up and smiled, taking his hand in hers. "Oh, I would. So very much. But first, we must care for the dead. I'm so grateful you're here to help me."

"As am I. I can't imagine you facing this alone."

She stood up and gathered her things, few that they were, and they returned together to the village. She did not flinch or weep at the horror within its walls. It seemed she had moved beyond it, somehow.

"Let's lay them to rest in the motherhouse," she suggested, "and burn them together at sunset."

Taliesin nodded. The motherhouse was a fitting choice for a mass pyre. Once its ample wood and thatch were set aflame, all within would be consumed completely. For hours, they dragged the dead inside, grouping families together, and then ministered to each of the fallen in turn. Taliesin closed their eyes, Lucia folded their hands, and together they spoke blessings and invocations over each. The work took all the strength they had, exhausting them in both body and spirit.

At sunset, they raised their torches and invoked the Guardians of the South. They started on the west side of the motherhouse and walked in opposite directions, lighting the roof on fire as they went, until they met on the east side, where the main entrance was. They prayed to the Guardians to engulf and purify all those within the motherhouse with their heat and light, and not to stop until everything had been reduced to ashes. Once the roof was fully aflame, Taliesin took Lucia by the hand. "Come with me." He pointed to the top of Mynyth Aur. "We can watch from above. The smell will be unbearable down here."

Together, they walked out of the village and up the trail that snaked along the side of the great mountain until they reached the summit. They stood side by side at the edge of the mountain, arms crossed against the wind's chill, looking westward. Taliesin spied Vala overhead. He whistled to let her know where he was, and she soon joined them.

Taliesin's eyes looked beyond the terrible sight of the burning motherhouse to the refuge of trees beyond the fields which marked the river's path. He followed its occasional glint through the green valley until his eyes reached the clouds billowing on the horizon, now aglow with the rosy hues of the sinking sun. He took a deep breath and let it out, tasting damp earth and smoke on his tongue.

"The last time I was here was when we burned Bran's body," Lucia said in a cracked voice. "This was the only thing left in the

255

ashes." She pulled *Caledgwyn* from the scabbard buckled around her waist. Its perfect blade gleamed blue in the dying light. "Gareth kept it, from that day on. He would have given it to Branok when his time came, and Branok to his son after that; but I fear there shall be no more sons, now." She gazed into the metal of the blade as if it were a pool of water. After a few quiet moments, she looked up at him. "None but you, Taliesin. You're the closest thing to a son I have left." She slid *Caledgwyn* back into its scabbard and held it out to him. "Bran bid me give her to you."

"He did?"

"He said one day soon, you'll know what must be done with it. Please." She thrust it toward him.

Taliesin took it. "I shall keep it safe. Thank you."

Lucia looked relieved, as if it had been a burden. "And take the gold from the keep," she added. "I won't be needing it where I'm going." She stomped the rock beneath her. "There's enough down there to last the rest of your days. Weapons and furs as well. It's all yours now."

He nodded. "I'll take what I need and seal the mountain as well as the grove. None shall find their way into these places but you and I."

She reached up and stroked his cheek. "Thank you."

They both stood silent a moment, staring down on the smoke and fire below. Taliesin motioned toward a flat, grassy place near the edge of a precipice. "Come and sit with me." He sat down and scooted to the edge, dangling his legs over the cliff, and she joined him. Taliesin noticed her dry lips and handed her his goatskin. "Drink. It's good wine from Lord Cynyr's villa. I'd expected a grand reunion tonight."

Lucia took the goatskin and held it up. "We'll drink it in honor of our departed, instead. Fine wine for their fine souls. May the Great Mother guide them all to the Summerlands." She slaked her thirst and handed it back.

Together they watched the moon rise, passing the wine back and forth until it was gone.

Taliesin reached for his harp. The comfort he sought to impart came forth in delicate strains of notes, his voice and fingers guided by the Great Mother. His voice soared with joy as he watched the music

256

wrap around Lucia in luminous ribbons of gold pearlescent light, lifting the dark mantle of grief off her shoulders. He cast his eyes skyward toward the starry heavens peeking down on them and gave thanks.

Taliesin accompanied Lucia to the shores of Lake Bala, as he had promised. Lucia stopped her horse and pointed to Aveta and Colwyn's old villa atop a nearby hillside. "I can't believe that was my home once," she announced. "Seems a lifetime ago."

Taliesin had fond memories of the villa and the lake from his childhood. Whenever the clan made their annual journey to Gwythno for Mabon, Bran and Lucia had always made a short detour to visit Aveta and Colwyn on the way. As Taliesin always chose to ride in the back of their wagon with Arhianna and Gareth, he had been there many times over the years.

He held nothing but fond memories of it. He remembered them playing hide and seek in the barley field with the children Colwyn and Aveta had taken in. If the sun were shining, they would all go down to the lake to swim until their hands and feet puckered up and teeth took off chattering from the cold. *All of us but Arhianna. Even then, she was fire-blessed, but didn't know it.*

He had always felt intensely drawn to Aveta as a child. He remembered when they first met, and how strongly he had wanted to run and wrap his arms around her. It was only after his ascent to Caer Sidi as a young man that he understood why. There, upon the wheel of Arianrhod, he had learned that she, as well as Lucia, had been mothers to him in other lifetimes. He had kept this to himself, however, for such knowledge was only for the initiated; such a view of the entanglements of one's soul through time and space was disorienting, both a blessing and a burden for those to whom it was revealed.

"Would you like to go up there?" he asked.

Lucia shook her head. "No. Not even that place holds anything for me anymore. Aveta and Colwyn died years ago. I don't know who lives there now."

Taliesin felt a twinge of sadness learning of Aveta's passing but knew they would meet again. That was the comfort of the knowledge gleaned upon the Wheel.

He and Lucia dismounted to stretch their legs and let the horses drink, then walked along the lakeside trail until they came to a small dock with a rowboat.

"Good. It's still here." Lucia untied her belongings from her saddle. She went out on the dock, retrieved an oar from inside the boat, and gave the bottom a few jabs. "Looks like it's still sound."

Taliesin went to inspect the boat for himself. It looked safe enough, but he asked the water spirits to bless it, just in case. He helped Lucia settle in and handed her the oars. She sat there a moment, glancing behind her at the isle with a furrowed brow.

"What's wrong?"

Lucia shook her head. "Gods, Taliesin—what if I can't get there? Or they turn me away?"

Taliesin felt surprised. He had not even considered that possibility. "Why would they do that?"

She sat silent a moment, staring out at the isle. At last, she turned around and looked up at him. "Would you mind rowing out with me? I don't want to steal this boat, just borrow it. You can row it back."

"Of course." Taliesin smiled and stepped into the boat. Vala preferred not to stay and took to the sky. Taliesin took up the oars and aimed for the isle, keeping his strokes even and measured, knowing it would help Lucia drop more easily into a trance. He leant his own energy to the cause, supporting her efforts. As he had supposed, Lucia's fears of not reaching the isle were unfounded. They slid upon the shore with ease and without nearly as much rowing as Taliesin had expected.

Lucia turned around and smiled at him. Taliesin gave her a nod. He set the oars down and stepped out of the boat with a splash. The water came rushing around his thighs, cold and clear, as he pulled the boat up onto the shore. He spied a pair of silhouettes moving toward them through the trees and squinted, trying to make out their faces in the late afternoon light.

"Welcome back, Lucia," the taller one said as she emerged.

"Thank you, Lady Elayn." Lucia kissed her hands.

258

"You've come to stay this time?"

"I have."

Elayn nodded. "We've been expecting you." She turned around and motioned to the other woman, who was still standing within the shadows of the trees. "Come, lass."

Taliesin's heart jumped into his throat as the girl stepped onto the shore. *Morgen?* He blinked and looked again, thinking the light had played a trick on him.

"Master Taliesin! Is that you?"

Taliesin could only stare, wondering how on earth Morgen had come to be there. "Lady Morgen! What are you doing here? Is Nimue here, too?"

"No." Morgen smiled. "I'm alone—she sent me on a moon quest."

"A moon quest?" Taliesin asked. "What's that?"

Morgen furrowed her brow, clearly surprised he did not know what a moon quest was. "When you wander for a moon and see where the Great Mother leads you. I've been wandering for thirteen days, counting today."

"But how did you get here?" Taliesin pressed, doing his best to hide his shock.

"I was walking through the apple grove and came across a path I'd never seen before. I followed it, and it led me to a beautiful waterfall with the most wonderful pools for swimming, and then down into Lady Elayn's village. I had no idea there were other women living on the isle!"

Great Mother, she thinks she's still on Ynys Wydryn. Taliesin glanced at Lucia, who was studying Morgen intensely, as if trying to figure out where they had met before.

"Morgen," he said. "Do you think you're on Ynys Wydryn?"

Morgen fell silent. "Are we not?"

Taliesin shook his head, glancing at Elayn a moment. "No, you're on a different island. One far to the north. In Gwynedd."

"Oh!" Morgen exclaimed, raising her brows and looking at Elayn. "Well, I suppose there's no telling where you might end up on a moon quest. Everything's connected. Isn't that right, Lady Elayn?"

Elayn gave the girl a nod. "Indeed. She sends her sisters where she wills."

259

Taliesin felt taken aback by Morgen's swift acceptance of her circumstances. Morgen, on the other hand, rambled on with an unabated enthusiasm. "They're sisters too, but they have no church. They pray in the open air, like me. Lady Elayn says I may stay here with them as long as I like."

Taliesin gave her a nod and smiled. "Well, that's very kind of Lady Elayn."

"It is." Morgen then looked at Lucia expectantly.

"Oh! Please pardon me." Taliesin stepped aside to present her. "This is Lady Lucia. She was like a mother to me while I was growing up. She lived here with the sisters years ago. Now, she's returned to live with them again."

Morgen smiled. "I see. Welcome back, then, Lady Lucia."

Lucia smiled. "Thank you."

Elayn put her arm around Lucia's shoulders. "Come. The days are growing shorter. We don't have much light left. Taliesin, you'll stay the night and play for us, won't you?"

Taliesin felt surprised and delighted. "I'd be honored." It seemed the strict rules about male visitors had slackened under Lady Elayn's leadership. Either that, or he had come to be considered an exception to that rule, the way Talhaiarn had been.

"Good." Elayn turned to lead the way back to the village, and the rest of them followed. Taliesin and Lucia walked side by side behind Elayn and Morgen. He found it difficult to make eye contact with Lucia. He had longed so desperately to tell her of her granddaughter, and now, they had met—without any effort at all on his part. He burned to tell her everything, but how could he, without consulting Igerna and Arhianna?

To make things more unbearable, Lucia leaned close and whispered, "I don't know why, but Morgen reminds me so much of Arhianna."

Taliesin felt a wave of sadness come over him. "Yes, me too," was all he said.

CHAPTER TWENTY-SEVEN
The Baying of the Hounds

Come. It is time.

Morrigan's voice jolted Arhianna awake. Heart pounding, she kicked off her furs and reached for *Dyrnwyn*, always kept within reach. She stood up, belted it around her waist and left her tent.

It was still dark outside, just the faintest hint of dawn on the horizon. She snaked her way through the hundreds of tents and barracks that made up Morrigan's training camp toward the mountain that loomed over them all. Up its rocky slope, perhaps a half mile, was a gash in the rock that led to the vast network of caverns that Morrigan used as her chambers and hall.

The moment Arhianna arrived at the entrance, torches leapt to life in the darkness, beckoning her inside. Their light danced erratically on the rough surface of the passages, leading her from one cavern to the next, until she was deeper inside the mountain than she had ever been. After a few more twists and turns, she entered a chamber ingrained with a mineral that glittered like stars. Morrigan stood in the center of the chamber, eyes peering at Arhianna like hot coals. Her burnished shield leaned against her thigh, shining like the sun in the center of a strange universe. Cú Chulainn stood some feet away, in the shadows. Her heart skipped as she knelt down and bent her head. "I've come as commanded, Great Morrigan."

"Rise, Daughter of Lucia. Come and watch." Morrigan gripped the edge of her shield and set it spinning in the air, as if she had set it upon the surface of a lake.

Arhianna stood up and ventured closer, watching as a battlefield spread across the shield's surface. Trees sprung up around its edge and clouds rolled in, drifting in the air above the shield and then disappearing at its edges. In the center, grew a camp. Banners flying Uthyr's red dragon sprouted from its tents and flapped in the invisible wind.

Arhianna studied the scene, taking in every detail, until the sky darkened and she could no longer make out the men within the camp. Above the shield, a tiny full moon appeared, casting everything below in a silver glow. She watched, spellbound, as tiny torches and campfires sprang to life. Soon after, she heard a sound that made her blood curdle—the baying of hounds. Within moments, a pair came bounding from the trees, their white coats and red eyes glowing in the darkness. *Father's hounds!* Arhianna watched them run through the battle camp to the largest tent and stand at its entrance, baying to their master. Her heart sank. She knew, from the red banners flying in the night breeze, who they had come for.

The scene faded, and Arhianna stepped back. "Uthyr Pendragon is dead," she concluded. "Or soon will be."

Morrigan took her shield from the air and set it once more against her thigh. "When news of Uthyr's demise reaches Caer Leon, the wolves shall gather. Some will support the boy, but others will side with Lot or Urien. Many will scheme and fight to take the crown, but Arthur is our choice."

"But he's just a boy," Arhianna said, feeling confused. "Surely Lot or Urien would be the better choice?"

Morrigan glanced at Cú Chulainn. "Even so, Arthur is our choice," she repeated, her eyes flaring. "If he is to prevail, he must have a great army at his command—one that will strike fear into the hearts of our enemies and inspire the tribes to rally to his side. You must help him raise that army."

Arhianna felt shocked. She had long ago dismissed the idea of ever returning to the world of men. She felt at ease in the Borderlands, home to outcasts and wanderers. Happy, even. *My life is here. These are my people now.* She looked at Cú Chulainn and felt shocked by the realization of how loath she felt to leave him, in particular. "Are we not that great army?" she finally asked.

"We are but a part of it," Morrigan replied. "Many more must be rallied to the cause. And so, as my sworn servant, I command you to return to Dun Scáthach and convince Scáthach to pledge her warriors to Arthur."

This was the worst blow of all. Arhianna recoiled at the thought, recalling the sting of Uathach's last words to her: *Leave Dun Scáthach, and never return.* She shook her head. "Oh, no—you don't understand. She won't listen to me."

"You must make her listen."

Arhianna almost protested again, but Morrigan gave her a look that froze the blood in her veins.

"Understand this. If the Young Stag fails to win the crown, all is lost—our lands, our songs, our very tongue. Woden's followers shall trample us into dust. I have seen many battles within my shield—many reflections of what may be—and in all of them, a victorious Brython chants the name of only one king—*Arthur*. Under all others, Brython fades into darkness."

Arhianna felt the importance of what was being asked of her. "Perhaps Cú Chulainn could come with me?" she suggested, a glimmer of hope sparking inside her. "They'd certainly listen to him."

Morrigan glared at her. "His path is not yours."

Arhianna wanted to press but instead bowed her head, resigning herself to what had been asked of her. "So be it, then. I shall do as you ask, Mistress."

"Cross the wastelands tonight. They will lead you to the Plain of Misfortune. From there, you know the way."

Arhianna felt confused. "Is there not an ocean to cross?" She knew Knockma and the Borderlands to be in Eire.

Morrigan did not explain. "The waste shall lead you to the Plain of Misfortune. Go, now."

Arhianna returned to her tent and gathered her few possessions. When she emerged, Cú Chulainn stood waiting for her. She looked up at him in despair. "I wish you were coming with me—or going instead of me. I know they'd listen to you."

He shrugged his huge shoulders. "Don't be so sure. Even that isn't certain. For what it's worth, you can show this to Scáthach." He handed her his fir bolg, the weapon Scáthach had gifted him when he left her fortress, so many years ago. "Tell her I now command Morrigan's army in the Borderlands and that I support the Young Stag. She may consent to pledge her warriors. Or, at least, consider it."

Arhianna took the terrible weapon from his calloused hands. "Thank you, Setanta."

Once she had learned his true name, she had never again called him Cú Chulainn when they were alone. They had grown quite familiar, having spent nearly every day of the past ten years training together. At first, she had felt wary of him but, eventually, warmed up to his sense of humor and manner of speaking. Now, though she would not freely admit it, she had grown quite fond of him.

She turned the weapon around in her hands, studying its cruel barbs and wondering how best to transport it. "This nasty thing will need to be wrapped in some thick skins, I imagine."

"It will."

She looked back up at him and saw his eyes hungry for her beneath his dark curls. He had done his best to woo her over the years, and though she had granted him a kiss on occasion, she had never shared his bed. The black horror of her suffering at the cruel hands of Ingvar and his men still haunted her, causing her to push him away whenever his touch became urgent.

"Why do you spurn me?" he had demanded one night. "I know you desire me, Arhianna—I can feel it. And I desire you more than any woman I've ever known. What's wrong? Tell me!"

But she had confessed neither her shame nor her love for him that night.

He had eventually bedded other women, but never stopped trying to win her. His confidence and resolve were forged from a steel as strong as his sword; unwavering.

"I'll miss you," he said in a low voice. After a few quiet moments, he removed his ring from his finger. "Return this to my son's grave. It belongs with him."

Arhianna took the ring. "I shall. With your love." She reached up and wrapped her arms around his shoulders, embracing him like a lover, and kissed him. He kissed her back in a way that gave her hope she might one day overcome the dread of her black past. *But not today.*

She pulled away and set off, feeling the heat of his gaze upon her back like the rays of a hot summer sun.

The night felt like a mantle of starry refuge over Arhianna's head as she rode through the camp to where the green fields of the Borderlands faded into the Waste. Her horse hesitated at the edge of the dry sea of sand, snuffing her displeasure. Arhianna ignored her protests and spurred her onto the plain, keeping to the edges where there were patches of grass and the promise of water. She felt confident she was surely as capable as any warrior at Dun Scáthach now, more so because she had not aged in the years she had spent in the Borderlands. *Perhaps I'm worried for no reason. Maybe Uathach finally met her match on the bridge, and her bones are swirling in the sea below. Even the Scáthach I knew could be dead by now—I might very well find another ruling under her name.* Her confidence grew as she traveled.

When she spied ghostly shimmers moving across the land, she knew she had reached the Plain of Misfortune. She kept her distance, fingers and palms tingling with fire ready to burst from them should any of the Plain Wraiths come near. Yet, to her surprise, they seemed to avoid her as well, turning the other direction whenever she would stretch or flap her dark wings.

Some hours later, Dun Scáthach came into view, its cold grey face and black eyes staring out to sea from its high perch. She galloped toward its terrible silhouette, prepared to meet whatever fate awaited her within its walls.

She left her horse to graze along the river and went in search of the only other entrance into the labyrinth that she knew of besides the grotto. It did not take her long. She had berated herself so much over not having found it before, that its location, once revealed, had remained branded into her mind. She found herself a long walking stick that could serve as both a weapon and torch. She set the top aflame and plunged into the mountain.

The smell of the cold, salt-drenched stone within the mountain brought back a flood of memories. She thought of Niamh, and tears welled up, blurring her vision. *Oh, Lady Arianrhod, if only your feather could wash away memories, rather than bring them back.* She reached into her satchel and touched the feather Taliesin had sent to her, so long ago. She had often wondered if the memories it rekindled would have been better left in the shadows. She had tried, over the years, to bury the memory of her daughter in a deep darkness of her own conjuring, convinced it was best for both of them, but she had never succeeded.

She ascended for an hour or so, until she came to the Great Chamber. All was as she remembered. She went to the tomb of Connla and slipped Setanta's ring back on his stone finger. "From your father. Forgive me for taking it, though I suspect you haven't missed it."

She went to the tomb of Scáthach and returned Arianrhod's feather in a true spirit of penitence. "Forgive me, Great Scáthach, for taking my offering back. I was not ready then," she whispered. "But I am now."

Arhianna found the guardian's cave empty, except for the skulls now stacked a few feet higher than she remembered. She crept cautiously out onto the ledge and up to the bridge, only to find Uathach standing on the other side, bow and arrow poised, just as dreadful as Arhianna had remembered.

Arhianna raised her hands to show she held no weapon. "I come with a message from Morrigan."

"Is that Ronin, who was warned never to show her face here again?"

"It is." Arhianna braced herself to avoid an arrow.

Uathach scoffed. "As if Morrigan would ever speak to a worthless wretch like you!"

Uathach's remarks found no purchase. Arhianna was Ronin no longer. "Nevertheless, she has. And her message is not for you. It is for Scáthach."

Uathach sneered. "I *am* Scáthach, you fool. To whom do you think you speak?"

Gods, no. Arhianna choked on her disappointment. Her worst fear had come true—the Scáthach she had known had passed on, leaving her title to Uathach. *Or she never returned, and Uathach has simply taken it.* Arhianna felt despondent but did not give up. "Forgive me, Great Scáthach," she called out, ignoring Uathach's vitriol. "The message I bring is for you, then."

By now, warriors had gathered behind Uathach. Arhianna scanned their faces and felt disappointed to find no one she recognized. She continued her message, loud enough for all to hear. "The Great Morrigan has foreseen that Uthyr Pendragon shall soon meet his end. In the fight that is to follow in the wake of his death, she bids the warriors of Dun Scáthach declare themselves for his son, Arthur."

"Arthur?" Uathach cried. She let out a "ha!" and spat in the dirt. "I don't think so, Ronin. My mother died fighting Saxons in Gododdin, because the Pendragon couldn't be bothered to send any warriors north to help us. So, I don't think we can be bothered to send any south, can we?"

Resounding barks of "No!", "Long live the North!", and "Lot shall be Pendragon!" echoed off the stone walls of the fortress and floated out over the chasm.

Uathach turned her palms up. "You see? My warriors feel the same. And even if Uthyr *had* come to our aid, do you truly expect us to fight for a boy of sixteen summers?" She shook her head and scoffed. "Ah, little Ronin, I think the more likely story is you've been living down in Caer Leon the past ten years milking all you can out of your girlhood friendship with Uthyr's queen, and she's sent you here to beg me to fight for her weak son, who's never seen a real battle in his life." She shook her head. "He's too young, and Urien is too old. We are for Lot of Gododdin."

Cheers and the pumping of fists and weapons erupted behind Uathach. Arhianna had never expected she would get anywhere with Uathach, but she had to try. "You would disregard Morrigan's command, then?"

"I don't believe you speak for Morrigan. I think you're a fool who speaks for the queen. I told you I'd kill you if you ever came back here. Or don't you remember?"

"I remember it well." Arhianna would never forget that day. It had haunted her nearly as much as the night she suffered at the hands of Ingvar's men. "I also remember you telling me I had not earned the right to train here, because I had not passed the test to do so. I've come to pass that test."

Uathach laughed. "You think you can cross the Bridge of Leaping?"

"I do." Arhianna's heart pounded, every muscle tense with the prospect. Her answer prompted the warriors behind Uathach to chant, eager to watch the fight.

"You'll die before you step foot on it."

In a shocking burst of speed, Uathach notched an arrow and sent it sailing across the chasm toward Arhianna's heart, but it buried itself in nothing but dirt. Arhianna had already dropped beneath the bridge and had begun traveling hand over hand along the lead ropes beneath the planks, where Uathach could not see her. The shouting and noise from above made it easier for her to move undetected, and she had made it nearly halfway across the bridge before the sound died down enough for Uathach to hear her. She had brought a grappling hook and rope in anticipation of such a welcome. She tossed it over the bridge and hooked it into place. Then she waited, silent as death.

"Just like a coward to bring a rope! What's your plan? Hang there until we grow bored and then cross?" After some more taunting and a few curses, Uathach took the bait and walked out onto the bridge.

Like a spider feeling the tremors on her web, Arhianna could sense exactly where her opponent stood. Once she passed overhead, Arhianna continued her journey, quick and silent, to a two-plank gap perhaps ten feet away, taking the end of the rope with her. She raised her head up through the gap, as slow and silent as an adder through the underbrush and waited until Uathach bent down to look beneath the bridge for her.

In a burst of strength, she gave a mighty yell and burst up through the gap. The moment Uathach turned around, Arhianna threw the end of the rope in her direction and kicked her off the bridge. If Uathach managed to keep hold of the rope, she would survive. Otherwise, her time as Mistress of the Fortress of Shadows was over. Arhianna dropped down flat on the bridge and clutched it, waiting for the possible impact.

A hard jolt told her Uathach had managed to keep her wits. Arhianna felt pleased. Though she did not like Uathach, she knew what an enormous asset she would be to Morrigan's army.

Arhianna walked the rest of the way across the bridge toward the warriors who were standing at the edge of the cliff. She could feel their eyes darting back and forth between her and their mistress as she climbed the rope to safety.

Too easy, Arhianna thought, standing on the other side of the bridge. But she knew why—Uathach had underestimated her.

Suddenly, she heard a shriek and felt Uathach's whip wrap around her left foot. *She still means to kill me,* Arhianna realized. She felt the inevitable yank and fell forward onto her palms, landing in a push-up position. She heard the warriors belt out a cheer. Undeterred, she held onto the edge of the bridge and yanked back with her ensnared foot as hard she could. She felt a lurch on the other end and heard the warriors cheer again. She rolled over just in time to see Uathach sailing through the air, hands poised like cat's claws.

She rolled off the edge of the bridge before Uathach could land on her, gripping the short edge of the last plank and swinging as fast as she could out of the way.

"Not this time, Ronin!" Uathach cried. She stood on Arhianna's fingers so she could no longer get away. "Now you can join Niamh down below, along with your old lover, Ingvar. Remember him? Maybe he can rape you again in the Underworld." Uathach aimed the butt of her spear at Arhianna's face and removed her feet from Arhianna's hands.

Arhianna swung away from the inevitable blow, but Uathach was quick to smash her hand instead. Arhianna screamed in agony but did not let go. She grabbed the looped handle of Cú Chulainn's fir bolg and sent its long whip-like strands sailing under the bridge before Uathach could hit her hand again. The moment she felt them wrap around the planks and hook fast, she let go of the plank, gripped the handle of the fir bolg with both hands, and dropped.

The bridge tipped to one side from the shock of her drop and launched Uathach into the chasm. Arhianna watched her fall toward the sea, limbs flailing in shock, until the strands of the fir bolg began to shift. A jolt of adrenalin sent her climbing to safety, doing her best to avoid the sharp barbs woven into the strands of the weapon, but there were too many. Blood streamed down her arms as she pulled herself up onto the bridge and shook the terrible weapon free.

She felt the eyes of every warrior staring at her as she stepped off the bridge and passed under the arch. She strode into the center of the training ring, engulfed in shadow except for the hazy orange bars of dying sunlight stretching through the scores of open chambers. She turned to face the warriors of Dun Scáthach and raised her arms, setting all the torches in the ring ablaze at once.

"By right of combat, I am now Mistress of Dun Scáthach. Any who wish to challenge me, step forward."

No one moved.

Arthur felt his lip split open and immediately tasted blood. Dazed, he did his best to ignore the ringing in his ears and hold his shield. Cai's next blow came swiftly, knocking him backward with so much force, he felt certain the next thing he would see would be the sky spinning above him.

But it was not. *Not today.* He stayed on his feet and willed his senses to come back in line. He kept moving, eyeing Cai with his addled vision, refusing to allow another blow to find its mark. As soon as he felt able, he performed the move he had been practicing in secret—he switched his sword and shield, transferring them to the opposite hands, and delivered a strike with his left.

As he had hoped, the blow took Cai completely by surprise. He lunged into the small gap of opportunity he had created and delivered a deft series of blows that left Cai the one on his back, observing the clouds.

His victory did not go unnoticed. Cheers erupted around the practice yard, and Arthur felt a hot surge of pride. *Finally!* He had been training every day since his arrival, and though he had managed to secure a few hits against some of his brothers-in-arms, not until today had he bested Cai.

Cai lumbered to his feet and grinned, displaying a wide row of bloody teeth. "About time, Lawchwith," he said, smacking Arthur on the back.

Though Lawchwith merely meant 'left-handed,' Arthur felt it was not a compliment. Nevertheless, nothing could dampen his spirits. From that day forward, the nickname stuck. It served Arthur well in terms of keeping his identity a secret, for no one ever asked what his true name was, but it did warn opponents to be wary of his hand-switching tactics. Even so, attacking with his left worked a good portion of the time, and the more he practiced using both hands in combat, the more dexterous and unpredictable he became.

Arthur relished his anonymity so much, he chose to live in the barracks rather than with Lord Cynyr and his family. For the first time in his life, he received the full force of his opponents' aggression in the yard and their crude insults in the drinking hall. He felt he would likely never amount to more than an average warrior, but he had faith that if he continued to train hard, he would gain the skills he needed to stay alive on the field, and that was enough. In terms of battle, he knew his strength lay in strategy, not combat.

Each day after training, which lasted from dawn until the midday meal, the men worked. Some of them had farms in the area. Others had a large flock of sheep or herd of cattle and grazed them in the valley. Some warriors, like Cai, were expert hunters. They, like the shepherds, were free to do as they liked in the afternoons, for they provided the settlement with meat. Arthur, who had no training or skills except his artistic pursuits, spent his afternoons chopping wood, toting water, shoveling out the stables—whatever needed to be done.

In the evenings, he and his fellow warriors without wives spent their time drinking, singing and playing dice. Arthur soon grew bored of throwing dice and took it upon himself to carve a set of game pieces from spare bits of wood. Thanks to him, chess soon became an evening pastime in the barracks, as well, albeit much less popular than dice.

Night after night, Arthur beat anyone who challenged him. Rumor of his prowess at the game spread quickly and soon it became an obsession—*who will beat Lawchwith?* Yet even after a moon's worth of matches, Arthur remained undefeated, and the men began questioning his game pieces.

"I'll bet you carved some kind of enchantment into those pieces," one said, poking an accusatory finger at them.

"What'd ya do, Lawchwith—have a witch hex 'em for ye?"

Arthur denied all wrongdoing. "Bring your own pieces, then," he suggested. "We don't have to use mine."

The next evening, Cai brought his father's fine game board and pieces to the barracks. He also came nightly to play and watch. He set up the first game and sat down across from Arthur. "Now, we'll see if your luck runs out."

But it did not run out. Not that night, or any night after. No matter what pieces were brought for him to play with, Arthur always won. This helped salve his pride a bit, for, even with his surprise left-handed tactics, he lost more matches than he won in the practice yard. The men, in turn, did not grow sour over his nightly triumphs, for they knew they would get their chance to beat him in the yard the morning after.

One night, as Arthur lay upon his pallet, the sweaty stink of a dozen other men hanging heavy in the air around him, his stomach gurgling from sour ale, and every muscle in his body wincing, he breathed a long sigh of contentment and laughed. *Dear God, I've never been so happy.*

A moon passed and Taliesin returned, as promised. Arthur had mixed feelings when hearing of his teacher's arrival. Taliesin was his only connection to his former life, and he no desire to return to it. Not yet, anyway. Summoned from the practice yard, he found Taliesin waiting for him in Cynyr's main hall. Arthur's reluctance soon turned to concern, for the bard looked as if he had not eaten in weeks.

"Master Taliesin?"

Taliesin smiled, somewhat improving his appearance. "Arthur!" He looked him up and down. "You look stronger!"

Arthur returned the smile. "I'd like to think I am."

"Sit. Tell me about your training."

Arthur told him everything he thought worthy of mentioning and then turned the conversation. "But what of you, Master Taliesin? You look unwell."

"Do I?" Taliesin raised his brows and then sighed. "I'm not surprised."

Arthur's curiosity reared its head. "What happened?"

Taliesin tried to smile. "Let's just say my homecoming was not what I expected it to be."

Arthur sat quiet a moment, waiting to see if Taliesin would offer anything else, but it soon became obvious he had no desire to speak of it. Arthur chose not to pry. "I'm sorry to hear that. I'd hoped you were enjoying yourself."

Taliesin sighed and changed the subject. "My time away has helped me realize you were right. The histories can wait. You must learn to fight."

Arthur could not believe his ears. *Am I dreaming?*

273

"To that end," Taliesin continued, "I've someone I want you to meet—someone who can train you better than anyone in all Brython—but the journey is long. She lives far to the north, deep within Pict country."

Arthur's heart soared and thumped with anticipation. He had longed to go north of the wall for as long as he could remember, constantly nagging his father for stories of the men and creatures who lived there.

"When do we leave?"

"As soon as you wish."

"Tomorrow, then!" Arthur cried. He could not believe his luck.

True to his word, Taliesin organized a party to leave the following morning. "We'll go to my father's lands to charter a ship," he explained. "He's sure to have goods to trade. He always does this time of year."

"Your father's lands? Didn't you just come from there?"

"No. I was in Mynyth Aur, where I was fostered by Islwyn." His eyes seemed to go somewhere else for a moment before he continued. He gave Arthur a wan smile. "My father is Elffin, son of Gwythno Garanhir, Lord of Ceredigion. I've not been there in ten years, either. That's where we're going."

Arthur felt satisfied and asked no further questions, thrilled with the prospect of another journey. Over the course of the day, lulled by the rhythmic gait of their horses, he often fell to daydreaming. Fantastic scenes filled his mind about what they might encounter on the open sea and what awaited him at the end of their voyage.

Gwythno rose up in a tide of hospitality with their arrival. Taliesin's homecoming inspired smiles and affection from everyone, and Arthur felt proud to be alongside him. Lord Elffin was as affable a man as could be, ushering them into a warm hall filled with food, ale, song and boisterous company.

"So, where are you off to this time?" Elffin asked after Taliesin propositioned him for a ship.

"North by way of Alt Clud. I thought I could oversee some trading for you if you've got a voyage planned that way."

"I do. In a week. Arvel's leading it, of course."

Taliesin nodded and smiled. "So, he's stayed, then?"

"Best shipbuilder I've ever had, next to Irwyn. Best captain as well. He's not much of a trader, mind you—doesn't really understand the value of things nor does he care to—but I've got others who do." Elffin winked.

Taliesin turned to Arthur and explained, "Arvel's my brother." He looked back at his father. "It sounds like he's happy here."

"He is. Gets on well with the men, especially Irwyn. The women are another story. Bit of a free spirit, that Arvel."

Taliesin chuckled. "I thought he was in love with Creirwy."

"Oh, he is. Helplessly. But he seems to have no problem letting any maiden in the village console him."

"Ha!"

Arthur could not wait to meet this Arvel. Then, as if the heavens had heard his request, two men came bursting into the hall.

"Brother!" cried a man with long dark hair that fell to his waist.

"About time you came home!" admonished the other, grinning widely beneath an impressive, long grey mustache.

Taliesin jumped up from his seat to greet them, grabbing them into a strong embrace. After much back clapping and a bit of teasing, the men came to the hearth where all resettled to make room for the newcomers.

Taliesin wrapped an arm around the dark-haired man's shoulders. "Arthur, this is Arvel, my brother." Then he smacked the other man on the chest. "And this is Irwyn, our master shipbuilder. My grandfather convinced him to come build ships for us rather than the damn Saxons. We've been blessed ever since."

Arthur knew Taliesin could have introduced him as Uthyr Pendragon's son, but he did not, and Arthur felt relieved. He had not been 'Uthyr's son' for moons, now. Here, like in the barracks, he was merely Arthur, worth no more than any other man, and glad of it. He regarded the four men at the hearth with interest, noting the deep crow's feet they all had in the corners of their eyes. *They laugh a lot*, he observed with satisfaction. These were the type of men he enjoyed spending time with; men who enjoyed a good story, quaffing good ale, and laughing in the face of danger or hardship.

"Pleased to meet you all," he said, looking each man in the eyes. He meant it, more than they might know. "I'm looking forward to this voyage."

"Looking to trade, are you?" Irwyn asked.

"No."

"Are you a bard?" Arvel queried.

"I know a song or two, but I'm nothing compared to Taliesin."

"No one is," Elffin said emphatically, shooting a proud glance at his son.

Taliesin came to his rescue. "Arthur is studying with me."

"Ah! An apprentice, then?" Elffin raised his brows.

Arthur nodded. "One grateful for such a teacher."

That satisfied all concerned, and they spent the rest of the evening trading songs and stories while enjoying some of the best food and ale Arthur had ever tasted.

He went to bed feeling certain the wheel of destiny might again be turning in his favor. He gazed into the small fire heating his room and infused the rising smoke with gratitude, as Morgen often did, trusting it to carry his thanks out into the night and up into the heavens.

He suddenly missed his sister so fiercely a pain gripped his chest, as if his heart had been plunged into icy water. He and Morgen had never been apart so long. He hoped she was happy on Ynys Wydryn, and their father had not changed his mind about marrying her to Urien. He closed his eyes and prayed to the Lady on her behalf, as he had done every night since they were separated: *Holy Mary, Mother of God, please keep Morgen safe from those who do not understand her.*

The voyage north was everything Arthur hoped it would be, complete with a storm that electrified nerves and set jaws on edge. Arthur watched Arvel's disposition change from that of a happy, bounding puppy to a fierce alpha wolf, commanding his pack with a capable bark. Thanks to his direction, the ship emerged from the storm with minimal damage and only a few minor injuries.

They arrived in Alt Clud on a sea as placid as a lake, the hull of their ship carving a smooth wake toward a rowdy harbor. Arvel spurred his crew into action, and soon the ship was secured to the moorings of the tarred dock and rocking as peacefully as a baby's cradle in the calm water of the bay.

The sight of an impressive ship docked on the opposite side of the port quickly restored Arvel's playful nature. He let out a whoop, dove into the harbor and swam to it with unnerving speed. Arthur watched the surface of the water anxiously. At last, Arvel's glossy black head emerged from the water next to the other ship. With the agility of a spider, Arvel pulled himself up into the mix of ropes and netting along the side of the other vessel and leapt over the edge of the ship onto the deck.

Taliesin came up alongside Arthur, chuckling. "That's the Ceffyl Dŵr. Arvel's gone to look for Creirwy, no doubt."

Arthur was still puzzling over how a man could do what he had just witnessed. "Who's she?"

"Queen of that ship."

"Queen?" Arthur's puzzlement doubled. "That ship has a woman for a captain?"

"As good as Arvel. And twice as pretty, if you can believe that."

Arthur squinted at the people standing on the deck of the Ceffyl Dŵr to make out their features, craning his neck for a glimpse of the ship's mythical queen. "I want to meet her."

Taliesin laughed and clapped a hand on his shoulder. "You and every other man who draws breath. I'll introduce you, but consider yourself warned, most men fall helplessly in love with her. And if Arvel hasn't managed to seduce her yet, I'm afraid you probably don't stand a chance." He held out Arthur's pack. "Come on. We'll be here at least a few days. There's no way Arvel is going to leave if Creirwy's in town."

Arthur followed Taliesin off the ship and through the harbor's busy fish market, the air heavy with the smell of smoke, brine and tar. The glassy, one-eyed stares of turbot, cod, and striped bass peered up at them from salt-lined planks as they snaked their way through stall after stall of the morning's bizarre harvest. Stout, wind-burned women vied for their attention beneath the shrieking din of marauding gulls, brandishing fresh-baked bannocks, ale, or roasted fish. Arthur's stomach gurgled in response, but the call of the Ceffyl Dŵr was stronger.

Quickly spotted, the two of them were ushered onboard the 'proper' way, up a gangplank and into the middle of a colorful crowd of mariners that made Arthur feel quite plain and shy. He scanned the strange cluster of characters and found the fabled Creirwy in an instant—it could only be her, of course, for there was no other woman on board, yet Arthur felt certain that even if the ship's crew consisted entirely of women, she would stand out like a swan among geese. She wore breeches instead of skirts and a wool tunic belted with the most colorful embroidered sash he had ever seen. Her blonde hair, worn in a spiral of tight braids around her head, gleamed like a pale gold crown in the morning light. Judging from her wrinkles he supposed she had to be near his mother's age, but she had the body of a woman much younger. His heart galloped as her blue eyes shot out over flushed cheeks in his direction. He scarcely heard Taliesin introducing him.

"First time in Alt Clud, then?" Creirwy's eyes widened at him.

Arthur managed to nod and stammer a response he deemed ridiculous the moment it left his lips. A loud growl saved him from his embarrassment, followed by the emergence of the largest head he had ever seen coming up from the ship's hold. It rose out of the darkness like a full moon on a clear night, followed by a chest as round and huge as an ale barrel held up by two legs as thick as tree trunks. Arthur felt his jaw drop.

"Ah, gods!" the giant exclaimed at the sight of Arvel. He let out a long sigh. "You again, eh?" He shook his huge, shaggy beard, sending two shiny gold hoop earrings swinging. "You just don't give up, do ye, lad?" He scanned the rest of the group. His brows flew up and his eyes bulged round the moment his gaze fell on Taliesin. "Good gods! Is that Taliesin?"

"It is."

"Come 'ere, ya wicked bard!" The giant's bellow seemed to shake the ship, causing Arthur to grin at his tremendous presence. *Good God, such men and women exist?* His mind raced with the tales of his childhood; tales of Sídhefolk, giants, merfolk, dragons and selkies.

278

Could they all be true? The idea that they could brought him so much joy, he could scarcely contain his glee. *Wait until Morgen hears of this!*

Creirwy leaned over and murmured in Arthur's ear, gently touching him on the arm. Lightning zipped through Arthur's body from the place she put her fingers. "That's my father, Tegid Voel," she whispered. "This is his ship," she added, much louder.

Tegid heard his daughter and looked over. "Not anymore, t'isn't!" Tegid lumbered over and looked down at Arthur. "Who'er you, then, lad? New to the crew?"

"No, sir, my lord…I'm Arthur." He did not add, 'son of the Pendragon,' but did not know what else to say. He had never been anything but that.

"He's my apprentice," Taliesin volunteered, coming to the rescue once again.

"Ah!" Tegid raised his brows. "You'll be something rare, then, eh? You'll have to play for us tonight!"

Arthur felt as if he were riding a chariot pulled by wild stallions that refused to slow down, no matter how fiercely he pulled on the reins. He had not picked up a harp in moons. He glanced helplessly at Taliesin, who simply raised his brows. "Yes, of course," he found himself saying.

"Good! We'll have a hell of a time tonight, then! Play well an' I'll give ye yer fill o' the best apple wine ye'll ever taste, lad!" Tegid winked at Taliesin, who simply smiled.

All told, Arthur, Taliesin and the crew spent a week in Alt Clud. By the end of it, Arthur had seen and heard more wondrous things than he ever felt were possible in the world. As they left the harbor, he dreamt of sailing to Constantinople, Carthage and Venice; to lands of color and silk and sunshine, with trees that bore fruit he had never tasted. *I'll see them all before I die,* he vowed to himself.

The mood on the ship became progressively somber as they sailed up the coast toward Dun Scáthach. The sky and water grew cold and grey, harassed by a relentless icy wind that never ceased its assault. Arthur's anxiety mounted by the hour. *What if I make a fool of myself?*

"Tell me more about these lands," he demanded of Taliesin, nodding toward the horizon. "What kings rule this far north?" On any map, the area north of the wall was incomplete and vague. It was wild land, uncharted and widely agreed it should be avoided. The men of the sky living there were rumored to be a fierce and bloody lot who could not be reasoned or traded with, who summoned legions of violent spirits to do their bidding.

"Various chieftains," Taliesin said. "They're not much different from us, except that they managed to keep the Romans out. I imagine our people were much like them before the Romans came."

"Wild and uncivilized," Arthur commented.

Taliesin gave him a reproachful look. "Fierce and unconquered. Which is, I believe, what you shall strive to be as Pendragon, is it not?"

Arthur regretted his words. "Tell me more of Scáthach."

At the beginning of their journey from Caer Cynyr, when Taliesin had told him where they were sailing to, Arthur had made the mistake of scoffing at the idea of training under a female warrior. "You want me to train with a woman?" he had cried, incredulous. "No one shall take me seriously!"

Taliesin had immediately reined in his horse and thrown a finger in his direction, rebuking him in a volcanic fury of sharp reprimands highlighting, in painful detail, how ignorant, foolish and ungrateful he was. Taliesin had never so much as raised his voice before then, and the shock of it drove Arthur to quickly repent of his folly. After Taliesin recovered from his anger, he told him about Scáthach and her legendary warriors. Now that they were nearly in her territory, Arthur felt the need to rekindle that knowledge. "What should I know about her?"

Taliesin gazed out to sea, leaning forward on the rail of the ship with his elbows. "You should know she and her warriors have fought many times with King Lot against the Saxon invaders."

Arthur recoiled. "With Lot?" His heart sank. "Then she'll support him for Pendragon, won't she?"

Taliesin stared back at him and frowned. "Why do you think I've brought you here?"

Arthur grew angry. He was not used to feeling like a fool. "Damn you, Taliesin!" He slammed his fist down on the rail of the ship. "I'm tired of being the last to know what the hell is going on!"

Taliesin looked at him, brows crunched. "Then I suggest you ask more questions."

Arthur fumed, and the fire of it burned away his fear. He wished he could bottle up that anger to use later in his training, because, fortunately or unfortunately, his temper abated quickly.

Taliesin softened a moment later. "You must at least prove yourself worthy of consideration, or she will indeed support Lot when your father dies."

Arthur shook his head. "I'm not ready to fight here. You should have given me more time to train at Caer Cynyr before bringing me here."

Taliesin shook his head, dismissing his comment. "I'm sorry, Arthur, but we're running out of time. You'll learn more quickly if you train here, and I believe I can arrange it for you."

At this, Arthur felt a different sort of trepidation. "What do you mean, you *believe* you can? Is this not already arranged?"

"Not yet. But I'm confident I can convince Scáthach to take you in."

Arthur's stomach churned. *We're sailing north, uninvited, to ask one of Lot's allies for a favor. God help me.*

CHAPTER TWENTY-NINE
Windwalker

Morgen spent many evenings in the village with the Sisterhood, learning their rituals and songs. High Priestess Elayn taught her how to ask questions of the Great Mother, and then read her answers in the elements around them. There was nowhere she would rather be than with them in the big roundhouse at night, where they sang songs and chanted to drums or rattles. She liked watching the ribbons of color flow from their hearts and foreheads into the center of the circle, where they swirled with the smoke of the fire and rippled up through the ceiling into the heavens, taking their healing magic out into the world.

She enjoyed being with Sister Lucia most of all. She reminded her of her mother and told her so, one afternoon in the motherhouse while grinding barley by the fire.

"I do?" Lucia smiled. "I'm happy to hear that. Where is she, your mother? Tell me about her."

Morgen had not told any of the sisters in the village who her parents were, but Sister Lucia was special, and she wanted no secrets between them. She glanced over at the other women. They were chattering away, spinning yarn. "My mother is Queen Igerna, wife of Uthyr Pendragon," she whispered. "But please—don't tell anyone."

Sister Lucia raised a brow. "Is that so?"

"Yes. My father wanted to marry me off to some old goat of a king in the north, but my mother saved me—well, she and Archbishop Dubricius. They convinced my father to send me to the abbey on Ynys Wydryn instead."

Sister Lucia frowned. "But you're not at the abbey—won't they be worried about you?"

Morgen shook her head. "My mother knows I'm not there. Only she and Taliesin know where I truly am."

"What if your father asks about you?"

"He won't," Morgen stated with utter confidence.

"How can you be certain?"

"I am." Morgen paused, wondering again if she should share what she was thinking, and then risked it. "Besides, my father will die soon."

Sister Lucia stared at her. "What do you mean?"

"He's sick. I make him medicine from the plants on Ynys Wydryn and send it home, but it can only take away the pain. It won't cure him."

A look of terrible anxiety clouded Sister Lucia's expression. "I fear for all of us, then. Your father is the only thing standing between us and the Saxons. If he dies, they'll move west and raid us all…" Her voice broke. She put her hand to her chest and took a deep breath.

"What's wrong?"

Sister Lucia regained her composure. "They attacked my village. That's why I'm here. I'm the only one left." She stared into the fire.

"I'm so sorry," Morgen stammered, feeling helpless. She did her best to reassure Sister Lucia, wishing now she had never mentioned her parents at all.

Sister Lucia kept shaking her head. "It was my fault. The Great Mother took the Sight from me, as I'd begged her to do a thousand times. So I didn't see it coming. I let them all down."

Morgen felt indignant. "No, you didn't! How could you have known? Don't blame yourself for what those Saxon dogs did!"

Morgen felt a hand touch her shoulder and looked up to see Elayn standing beside her. "Let me speak with Sister Lucia alone, Morgen."

Morgen noticed the other women were no longer there. She got to her feet and left the motherhouse, praying the Great Mother would never take the Sight away from her.

Morgen took the path up to the Sacred Pools and returned to the tree in the apple grove that marked the doorway to Ynys Wydryn. She had showed it to both Sister Elayn and Sister Lucia, longing to take them to Ynys Wydryn to meet Nimue, but Elayn said if they could not see the door, they would not be able to pass through. "You're blessed beyond us, Morgen," Elayn told her. "You can shadow-walk in your own body. We call people like you Windwalkers, for you can go anywhere, at any time. Most of us can only do that with our spirit bodies. I've prayed my entire life for such a gift, but the Great Mother has not chosen to bless me with it. But thank you for showing us where the door is. We shall honor it, and perhaps, one day, it shall appear to one of our own."

The sisters taught Morgen how to tie together long strings of beads, bones and feathers with prayers, and how to weave talismans of protection. These were put into baskets and carried to the tree Morgen had shown them. Together they decorated the tree and placed offerings to the Mother around the base of its trunk. Then they formed a circle around the tree and held hands, chanting praises to the Mother and the gates between the worlds until Morgen could again see the luminous ribbons flowing from their hearts and weaving their way around the tree. They wound around every branch to every leaf, and flowed down the trunk into every root, deep into the earth around them.

When the sky darkened, hinting of twilight, Elayn spoke. "Great Mother, we ask you to protect this gate between the worlds—let no traveler with ill intent pass through."

And so it was.

Marking the tree served Morgen well, for from that day on, she always knew that when she spied the decorated apple within the grove on Ynys Wydryn, she had arrived at the doorway that led to the isle of the Sisterhood. Today, however, she was going the other way; back to Ynys Wydryn, and from there, she would go home. *Father will need more medicine.* She thought of what Lucia had said and felt a knot in her stomach. *Dear Lord, Great Mother—please don't take my father yet. Not until my brother is ready.*

She thought of the prayers they had woven around the doorway between the isles and wished with all her heart they could pray up a wall of protection between them and the Saxons. She pictured it in her mind's eye and filled it with all her will. *Let no one with ill intent pass through,* she murmured, resolving to bolster it nightly against their enemies.

CHAPTER THIRTY
The Selkie Isle

"We're here," Arvel announced, pointing toward an ominous-looking fortress perched upon a cliff. "Dun Scáthach."

Arthur gripped the ship's rail to steady himself against the choppy sea and stared up at its dark form. His trepidation mounted as he studied its cold black walls, slick and shiny as eels in the unrelenting rain.

The sea had roiled most of the day, as had Arthur's stomach, yet despite his strong desire to get solid land beneath his feet, he did not feel comforted by their arrival. To his surprise, they did not sail toward the fortress, but rather in the direction of an island off the coast. "Are we not going there?"

Arvel shook his head. "We go to my people first."

Arthur let out a sigh of relief, grateful for an opportunity to recover from the voyage before facing the warriors of the fortress.

As they neared the island's shores, the heads of several seals bobbed up and down around the wake of the ship. The sight of them cheered Arthur, triggering a golden memory of the day he and Morgen encountered seals for the first time. He could still picture their eyes peering up at them from the deep green sparkle of the Severn Sea. His dark mood lifted as he watched the sleek creatures swim along the side of the ship, escorting them toward the shore. The sea and sky no longer seemed as grim as they had before. The welcoming party started out with perhaps four or five seals, but soon grew to be so many, Arthur could not count them. "Look at them all!" he cried in delight, glancing over at Arvel.

Arvel grinned. "Yes, they're happy I'm home."

Taliesin had come to stand by Arthur and watch the seals, as well. "Arvel was born here," he explained. "He's selkie."

Arthur could do nothing but stare. "What do you mean?"

"He's selkie."

"You mean, he can turn into a seal?"

"Yes. Our mother was selkie. She died just before you were born."

"So, *you're* selkie as well?"

Taliesin laughed. "Not quite. She fostered me. But Arvel is of her blood."

285

Arthur could not believe his luck. *Oh, sister, if only you were here!* He thought about how much she had longed to see a selkie all through their childhood. "I must bring Morgen here," he murmured to himself. He regarded Arvel with new eyes, watching him closely as he commanded the crew to drop the anchors, for it appeared there was no dock on the island. He suddenly felt like a fool, wondering how he could have missed all the signs. Morgen knew dozens of stories about selkies and told them often, describing their characteristics in detail. Arvel had every one of them—long dark hair, big brown eyes, a strong sexual appetite, a playful, canine spirit— and, of course, a deep love of the sea. *I should have known.*

The crew lowered rowboats for those not inclined to swim to shore, which turned out to be a precious few. Arthur soon learned most of them were selkie, as well.

Once ashore, Arvel led the way to a village of driftwood huts. A large fire burned in the center of the village. Around it lounged several selkie females. They were all nude, with long dark hair and soft brown eyes, like Arvel.

Arthur had never seen a mature naked woman before. He tried not to stare, but could not keep his eyes from wandering along the curves of their hips and breasts to the dark hair between their legs. He felt his manhood hardening beneath his tunic. *Oh, no. Please, not now.* He closed his eyes and willed it to soften, but it was no use. Mortified, he adjusted his trousers and tunic, hoping no one would notice.

"Come, we'll cook ourselves some fish," Taliesin said, snapping a few thick branches off a nearby tree. He whittled points on the end of them and handed one to Arthur. They joined the clan by the fire and soon became the focus of attention. A large basket of fish came their way, presented with wide smiles. Taliesin took a fish and Arthur did the same. "Be warned," Taliesin murmured as he skewered it. "They'll eat theirs raw—guts and all. It can be a bit unappetizing to watch."

Arthur felt unconcerned about how the selkies ate but felt glad of an excuse to avert his gaze. He kept his eyes on the fish roasting at the end of his stick, or on the flames dancing in the fire, doing everything he could to avoid staring at the dark patches below the waists of the women sitting cross-legged on the opposite side of the circle.

"We'll row to the grotto of the fortress tomorrow," Taliesin told him after they ate. "We'll stay there until one of them comes down, and then I'll ask them to deliver my message."

"What message is that?"

"That Taliesin the Bard and the son of Uthyr Pendragon are in the grotto and beg an audience with the great Scáthach."

Arthur's manhood softened at last.

The sea remained in a foul mood all night, lurching and swaying with just as much peevishness as she had the day before. Arvel and Taliesin remained undaunted by her temper. At first light, they ushered Arthur into what seemed like far too delicate a craft. Things only got worse as they approached the lagoon. The treacherous rocks at its entrance looked like dragon jaws full of sharp teeth foaming with salty saliva, eager to devour them.

"We should turn back, don't you think?" Arthur cried over the hissing sea.

Arvel grinned at him. "Why would we do that?"

Arthur stared at the rough water churning around the sharp spires and shook his head. *We can't possibly get in there.* Yet, right into that mouth of long black teeth was where Arvel aimed the prow of their tiny rowboat. Arthur cried in alarm as they surged forward, certain the boat would be smashed to kindling. He closed his eyes and braced himself for the impact. *God preserve us!*

Yet no impact came. He opened his eyes just in time to see Arvel guide the bow between a small gap in the jagged wall of sharp rocks and lead it into the calmer waters of the lagoon with the swiftness of a shark, laughing as he went.

Arvel rowed them up to a rock ledge within the shelter of a large grotto and tied the boat to an iron ring that had been hammered into the rock. He waited for a swell, which rose the little craft up a good three feet, and then leapt up onto a rock ledge with the swiftness of a deer. Arthur and Taliesin were expected to do the same, which they eventually succeeded in doing, albeit with none of the grace Arvel had managed.

Once the adrenalin of the voyage subsided, Arthur realized how cold he was. He looked around for a place to take shelter from the sea air. There was none. "Now what?" he asked Taliesin, stuttering each word through chattering teeth.

"Now, we wait for someone."

"How long will that take?"

"Well," Taliesin pondered, glancing up toward a dark passageway. "I'm certain they saw the ship last night. Arvel's quite popular with the women of Dun Scáthach. I imagine they might have missed his, uh…attention. Let's hope so anyway."

Arthur glanced expectedly at Arvel, who smiled. "Don't worry. Someone will come."

"In the meantime, we should start a fire," Taliesin suggested.

Arvel jumped up. "Follow me."

Taliesin and Arthur followed Arvel up into the dark corridor. After a bit, some light filtered in, revealing Arvel's silhouette ahead of them. The light increased as they neared a cavern with an opening that looked out over the sea. All along the walls were candles in sconces, and two pits—one filled with animal furs, and another with burned wood and ashes. There was a large pile of driftwood near the fire pit.

"This looks like a good place to wait," Arthur said with a grin.

"This is a good place for many things," Arvel winked, causing Arthur to immediately feel like a child. He wanted to ask Arvel what it was like to be with a woman. *How are you supposed to touch her?* He had watched plenty of animals mating but thought surely between a man and a woman it must be different.

"The women from the fortress come here to lay with you?" Arthur dared.

"They do."

"How many?"

"Sometimes only one. Sometimes they come together."

"More than one?" Arthur could not imagine such a thing.

"Sometimes."

Arthur stared at him, his curiosity overpowering his embarrassment. "What do you do to them? Where do you touch them? How does it work?" He wanted answers.

Arvel scrunched his nose and eyes at him. "Do you not have women in your village who teach you such things?"

Taliesin answered for him. "They don't follow the old ways anymore, Arvel."

Arthur turned toward Taliesin. "What do you mean? What old ways?"

Taliesin explained. "In some clans, when a boy comes of age, he must prove himself by going into the wilderness and making a kill on his own. When he does, or rather, if he does, an older woman or the clan priestess, if she feels inclined, takes him to her bed and teaches him how to please a woman."

Arthur felt his mouth fall open. "But what of her husband?"

"She may not have one. Or it doesn't matter."

Arthur turned toward Arvel. "You have such women in your clan?"

"Of course. All of them." He laughed. "I could find one to teach you, if you like. More, if you prefer. I know many who would do it. They were watching you last night. I know the look."

The idea of it was too much for Arthur. He found he could not answer, overwhelmed with the idea of himself lounging in the pit of furs he had seen, surrounded by naked women. He turned his attention to starting the fire, striking away at his flint and blowing on the brush beneath the driftwood while he considered Arvel's offer. Soon the fire roared. Arthur and Taliesin gathered close to its warmth and removed their wet clothes. Arvel had worn nothing but a loincloth from the beginning.

"I would like that," Arthur said at some length. "To learn of women."

Arvel grinned. "They are a gift. I shall choose one for you."

Arthur shook his head. "No, I must choose her myself, and not until I prove myself a warrior." He considered what Taliesin had said. If he were to take part in the old ways, he would observe them all—he dared not offend the old gods.

Arvel shrugged. "As you wish."

Taliesin had remained quiet during the conversation, staring at the fire, and Arthur wondered if he disapproved.

When the sun went down, Arvel lit two torches and set them into iron sconces outside the cave. "Someone will come now."

Sure enough, within a few hours, they heard footsteps coming down the corridor. They went to the locked gate and waited. Soon, the flicker of a torch or lantern danced up and down the sides of the corridor. A woman appeared. She held a lantern aloft, illuminating her face. "Welcome back, lover," she said to Arvel. "Who are your companions?"

Arthur looked the woman up and down. She was muscular, taller than most, with half her hair shorn off. The other side flowed free and wild, blowing slightly in the night breeze.

Taliesin spoke. "I am Taliesin the Bard, and this is Arthur, son of Uthyr Pendragon. We wish to speak to Scáthach."

The woman stared at Taliesin and then at Arthur, taking the measure of them. She took a step closer to Arthur. "Son of the Pendragon?" She bent forward and looked deeper into his eyes. Arthur nearly recoiled, fearing she might see things he did not want her to see. He stood his ground, however, and met her gaze.

"Very well," she said at last. "But first, I want what I came for. Go down to the grotto until Arvel comes for you."

Arthur and Taliesin had no choice but to do as she commanded. They gathered an armload of wood and took it to the grotto to build a fire. Arthur spent the next half hour doing his best to ignore the moans of pleasure floating down the corridor.

At last, Arvel came for them. "She's going to take your message to Lady Scáthach. You may come up now."

Relieved to get out of the dampness of the grotto, Taliesin and Arthur followed Arvel back up to the 'love' cavern, as Arthur termed it in his mind, waiting for someone to come for them. They stood in relative silence until the flickering light of an emissary came down the corridor once more. A key turned in a lock, the gate creaked open, and a woman stepped into the cavern. She was as tall as the other woman, but slighter of build, and she had shorn her hair off completely. She had eyes like Creirwy—a shocking blue, the color of a glacier—and seemed to be perhaps no more than a few years older than himself. Her neck torc glittered in the firelight, as did the magnificent brooch on her cloak and the tip of her spear, forming a triangle of golden flashes around her perfect face.

Scáthach. Arthur felt even if he wanted to speak, he would not be able to. He swallowed a few times, attempting to thwart the dryness in his throat.

"Hello, Taliesin," the woman said.

Taliesin stepped forward, as if approaching a king's throne or an altar. *"Arhianna?"*

Arthur felt surprised by the crack in Taliesin's voice and looked over to see his face had gone pale. *Who in the world is Arhianna?*

CHAPTER THIRTY-ONE
Confession

Taliesin could not believe his eyes. Arhianna had not aged since he had last seen her, so long ago, in the strange halls of Knockma. *How many years has it been? Fifteen? Sixteen, now?* If anything, she looked younger, albeit more masculine; she had cut her glorious hair as short as a Roman soldier, and her face and body no longer held any trace of softness. He wanted to reach out and clutch her close, but something held him back. "I have much to tell you," he said instead. "This is Arthur, son of Igerna and Uthyr Pendragon."

Arhianna stepped toward Arthur. "So I've been told." She studied Arthur's face closely. "I see your mother in you."

Arthur felt confused. "You know my mother?"

"I do. Though we haven't seen each other in many years. You resemble her greatly. It will serve you well. People prize beauty." She looked back over at Taliesin. "Why've you come?"

Taliesin felt sick inside, frantically searching the depths of Arhianna's blue eyes for his childhood friend, his fairy love—but he could not find any trace of her. He struggled to swallow back the pain in his throat. "To see Lady Scáthach and ask her to train young Arthur." He put a hand on the boy's shoulder. "The Pendragon's days are numbered. He must be prepared. I know he'll not find better training anywhere else."

Arhianna nodded. "This is true. And I'm Lady Scáthach, now."

Taliesin felt a shiver of knowing flow through him. *Of course, she is.*

Arhianna regarded Arthur anew. "You wish to train here?"

He bowed his head. "I do, Lady Scáthach, if you'll have me."

She considered him a moment. "For what I owe your mother, I'll do this."

Dear gods, Arhianna, thought Taliesin, *if you only knew how much we both owe her.*

"Come," Arhianna said, holding the gate open. Taliesin and Arthur passed through and waited as she locked it behind them. She led them up through the mountain, passing several chambers Taliesin would have loved to explore. It took the better part of an hour to reach the fortress, which they accessed through yet another locked gate. They emerged from the darkness into a training ring filled with warriors engaged in various kinds of combat. Taliesin glanced at Arthur, reading both anxiety and excitement on his face. *As it should be.*

Arhianna led them to a hall with a table long enough to seat forty. She called to a woman who stood over a steaming pot. "Bring these men something to eat." She motioned to the benches, and Taliesin and Arthur sat down. The woman set bowls of broth and a hunk of bread in front of them.

"What training have you had?" she asked Arthur, occasionally meeting Taliesin's unbroken stare.

Arthur looked up from his broth. "Not nearly enough, I fear. I've trained with spear, sword and bow. Of the three, bow is my strength."

Arhianna nodded. "It was mine as well, before I came here."

Taliesin felt a wave of relief as he glimpsed a momentary softness in her manner. She looked at him. "How much time do we have?"

"Only Arawn knows for certain," Taliesin told her, "but I imagine no more than a few years. The Pendragon's health is failing."

She turned back to Arthur. "Then I'll force you to work hard," she warned. "Harder than you've ever worked before. You'll curse my name before you leave this place."

Arthur nodded. "That's a risk I'm willing to take."

"So be it." She summoned the woman from the kitchen once more. "Find young Arthur here a chamber and scrub it out."

The woman gave her a nod. "Right away, Lady Scáthach."

"You'll scrub it out yourself from now on," Arhianna added, looking back at Arthur. "And as you claim to be good with a bow, you'll join the hunting party. We eat a lot of meat here."

"We do indeed!" A huge voice boomed through the air before its owner came around the corner, a doe slung over his shoulder as if it weighed no more than a march hare.

Taliesin grinned. "Gawyr!"

Gawyr's eyes brightened with recognition. "Harp-mauler!" He clapped Taliesin on the back so hard his chest hit the edge of the table. "What are ye doin' this far north? And who's this?" He poked a thumb in Arthur's direction.

"This is Arthur. He's come to train." Taliesin did not volunteer who Arthur's parents were. That was up to him, or Arhianna, to reveal if they saw fit.

"Has he, now?" Gawyr regarded Arthur a moment, clearly taking the measure of him. "I'd wager he hasn't come up the proper way, though, has he?"

"No, he hasn't," Arhianna confirmed.

Arthur, brow furrowed, looked at Taliesin, who explained.

"Traditionally, someone seeking to train at Dun Scáthach must come up the mountain and cross the Bridge of Leaping."

Arthur grimaced and looked back at Arhianna. "So, Lady Scáthach, you've only agreed to train me because of your debt to my mother?"

Arhianna gave him a nod. "I owe her much."

"I can't accept such an arrangement," Arthur said with a frown. "I must earn my place here."

Taliesin shook his head. "You will, Arthur—in time, you will. You must understand this is an exceptional matter." The thought of telling Igerna and Uthyr he was responsible for their only son's death spiked his heart with fear.

Typical of boys his age, Arthur refused to listen. "I can't stay, then. I'll not take something I haven't earned." He looked back and forth between Taliesin and Arhianna, his eyes determined.

Damn it! Taliesin thought. In this respect, Arthur was certainly his father's son.

Arhianna smiled, and Taliesin realized with a pang of dread it was decided. "Take him back to the grotto," she said to Gawyr. "If he can cross the bridge, I'll train him."

Taliesin felt lost, unable to stop the horrible turn of events from unfolding. He knew there was no way Arthur had the skills to cross the Bridge of Leaping. "Please, Arthur—wait a moment—"

"No." Arthur stood up to go with Gawyr. "How am I to be respected if everything I do is handed to me? I must come up the proper way."

Taliesin jumped up. "Don't be a fool, Arthur—"

But it was too late, Arthur was already being led off by Gawyr. Taliesin turned to Arhianna. "He won't make it across the bridge. His training is sufficient to hold his own on the battlefield, but he's no Cú Chulainn..."

Arhianna glared at him. "If that boy is to become Pendragon, I'd think you'd want him to show some courage and honor! When did you become so fearful, Taliesin? Do you have such little faith in the one you believe should take Uthyr's place?"

Rebuked, Taliesin sank back down on the bench. "Arhi—" He paused, remembering her new title. In spite of all his training, he felt as if he were unraveling. "May I call you by the name I know you by?"

Arhianna shrugged. "I'd prefer you didn't." She turned away from him, arms crossed, and watched Arthur and Gawyr cross the ring and disappear through the gate that led down to the grotto.

Taliesin stood up and went to her side, turning her by the shoulders to face him. He hooked his gaze into hers. "Whether you like it or not, Lady Scáthach, Arhianna still lives inside of you. You may have banished her to a small corner of your heart, but she yet lives there, and I love her. I love her with all my heart, and I miss her."

Arhianna stood still as a statue, as if standing on the edge of a cliff. At last, her icy expression cracked. "I've missed you, too." She moved to embrace him, though she stiffened and pulled away when some of the warriors passed by.

Taliesin gave thanks for his small victory. *That will do for now.* He gestured back toward the benches. "Let's sit a while. Please. There's much I have to tell you."

She gave him a nod and led him to the far end of the long table near the cook hearth. She grabbed a pitcher of ale and sat down across from him. Taliesin gladly offered up his drinking horn, grateful for something to wet his throat. "First," he began, pinning his eyes on hers, "do you remember Knockma?"

Arhianna took a deep breath, then reached beneath her tunic and produced Arianrhod's feather. "I didn't, until Gawyr gave me this." She placed it in front of him, fingering its silver quill a moment.

Taliesin felt relieved. *It worked.* He proceeded softly, as if stalking a deer. "And, do you remember the night before I sent you to Nimue?"

"I do."

Now, Taliesin noted, Arhianna seemed the more anxious of the two of them.

"I had a child," she blurted, meeting his eyes for only a moment. "Yours. I thought it was Jørren's. But she was yours." Her eyes darted to meet his a few more times, but she would not hold his gaze. "I didn't know until the feather." She heaved a sigh so weighted with sorrow Taliesin nearly wept. He reached for her hand but she pulled it away, shaking her head. "She's gone, now. I held her only a moment before Scáthach took her away—she promised me she'd be raised here, by the selkies, while I trained, but she lied." Arhianna glanced up at him again, eyes flashing now, the risk of tears conquered. "I don't know where she is. Cerridwen told me years ago she would keep her hidden until she came of age. That time has surely come and gone, yet she's revealed nothing to me."

"Until today." Taliesin had waited years to say what he was about to say, and now that the moment had come, it felt surreal; as if it had already happened a thousand times, because in his mind, it had.

Astonishment froze Arhianna's face. "What do you mean, until today?"

Taliesin gathered his strength. "She's safe in Affalon. She was raised in Caer Leon as Arthur's twin sister from the time she was but a few weeks old."

Arhianna's heartbeat became visible in her throat, a tide of blood rising to the surface of her skin. "All these years? That's where she's been? Down in Caer Leon?"

"She has."

Arhianna bolted from the bench like a startled animal and began to pace. "So, she thinks Igerna is her mother?"

"She does." Taliesin felt the situation begin to spin out of control, all of his rehearsed words flying through his mind like dead leaves in an autumn wind. He gathered a few of them and opened his mouth to speak, but Arhianna ranted over his efforts to calm her.

"We can never be a part of her life, then—she can never know the truth!"

"Of course, we can!"

"How?" Arhianna's eyes grew round, pulsing with emotion. "How could we tell her? Imagine it. 'No, my love. Uthyr Pendragon is not your father, the beautiful queen Igerna is not your mother, and your twin brother is not your brother—you were born to a peasant and a bard.' We can't tell her. It's unthinkable! She can never know…" Arhianna's face twisted with the agony of the impossible situation.

Taliesin could think of no salve for her pain and knew what he was about to tell her would only make it worse. He wavered over the confession he was about to reveal, suspended in time, considering what it would cost him. *I have only just found you, and now I risk losing you again.* But such a thing could not remain concealed if there was to be any hope of reconciliation in this lifetime. He summoned his courage. "There's more I must tell you." His eyes strayed to his hands in a moment of weakness, but he forced them back up to meet hers. "It was I, on Cerridwen's advice, who sent her to Igerna. Forgive me for thinking you did not want her. I knew she was my daughter and felt I had to protect her."

Arhianna stared at him, unblinking. The silence felt strangling, but he held her gaze and committed to wait for her response before he said anything more.

The beat of her heart in her throat quickened. She stood up and struck him across the face. "You bastard!" she seethed in a deep whisper. "You had no right to send her anywhere!" She paced, addled by this information. "Gods curse me, I should have taken her the day she was born and left this place. But I didn't. And now, this horrid place is all I have!" She stared at him as if she no longer knew him and walked out into the ring. "Take him back to the grotto!" he heard her yell.

Taliesin got to his feet and saw two men coming toward him. They gripped his arms and yanked him toward the ring, but he invoked the roots of an Oak and stood fast.

"I am not finished, Lady Scáthach!" he bellowed, projecting a blast of energy outward. The warriors hit the ground like sacks of barley and the clouds shook with thunder.

Every warrior in the fortress fell silent and turned to stare at Taliesin as rain began to fall on the dust of the practice ring. Arhianna looked as shocked as the rest of them.

"I'm sorry, but I have more to say, and it cannot wait." He motioned back toward the hall, blinking at her through the rain.

Arhianna stared at him a moment before yelling at her men to get to work, then walked back into the hall. This time, she did not sit down, nor did she invite him to. "Speak, then."

Taliesin sighed. "There's more sadness I must burden you with."

She stared at him with cold eyes. "Speak."

"Mynyth Aur was attacked," he said, the words feeling like ashes in his mouth. "Your mother survived and has taken refuge with the Sisterhood. Gareth and his family could not be found. Many were killed, but it seems most were taken as slaves." *There. It is done.*

Blood rushed to Arhianna's cheeks. She began to tremble. "Who did this?"

"Your mother saw the attack in a dream and thought the horror was yet to come, but it was happening as she saw it. She said the raiders weren't Saxon, or any clan she recognized; that they varied greatly in both looks and dress, wearing strange clothing she had only ever seen among the wares on Tegid's ship. The attackers bore no sigil or banner and seemed united only in purpose."

Her eyes flashed. "In killing my people."

Her words struck him like barbs. He could take no more. He grabbed her by the shoulders and looked her in the eyes. "Killing *our* people, Arhianna! *Our* people! I loved them, too—or have you forgotten?"

She pushed him away, tears forming in the corners of her eyes, but she quickly traded them for rage. "We must find out who did this and kill them all!"

Taliesin took her hands and refused to let go. "We'll have justice. Your mother has been shadow-walking, searching for your brother, but she said he seems hidden from her. This, and the fact she did not foresee the attack, leads me to believe these raiders weren't men at all, but Fae."

Arhianna's face changed. "Looking for Morrigan."

It was the first time Taliesin had heard Arhianna say the name of their daughter, reminding him that Igerna had changed her name, though ever so slightly, so many years ago. He chose not to mention it. Arhianna had suffered enough for one day. "Looking for her, yes. But she is now on the verge of womanhood, and with her gifts and Nimue's training and protection, she's beyond their grasp. Maelwys will never have her."

298

"Who is Maelwys?"

"Nimue's brother, though they have long been enemies. He serves Oonagh and Finbheara. It was Maelwys they sent to hunt you down and steal your child. And I know, in my bones, it was Maelwys who led the attack on Mynyth Aur. They know our daughter is almost of age, and time is running out. I suspect it was Maelwys who took your brother and his family as bait, seeking to draw us into Knockma."

Arhianna seemed to transform, as if having someone to wreak revenge upon had put her heart at ease. "Then, with Morrigan as my witness, if he's responsible, he shall die for this. I'll not cut my hair until the day I cut his throat!"

"That won't be easy. I tried killing him once," Taliesin told her, producing *Straif* from its sheath. "Stabbed this iron blade through his heart on a beach not far from here and left him for dead."

Arhianna's brow curdled in surprise.

Taliesin smiled. "You think me incapable of such a thing, don't you? Well, it turns out I am. He yet lives. Though it must be through only the blackest of magic. No herb or healer could have saved him."

Arhianna paced a moment and then announced, "I must go to the Borderlands to seek help on this matter."

Taliesin felt encouraged, for her anger seemed to have abated, at least for the moment. "And what of Arthur?"

"He shall have his training. I'll ask Gawyr to see to it." She paused a moment. "I realize now he's been raised as the brother of my only child, so I give you my word, in honor of this, he'll be well-trained." The flash of anger returned to her eyes. "But don't think I've forgiven you." She walked off into the rain, now in a full downpour, leaving Taliesin alone in the hall feeling smaller than he had in years.

CHAPTER THIRTY-TWO
The Training of Arthur

Gawyr escorted Arthur back to the mating cave and instructed Arvel to take him back to Selkie Isle. "And, if I were you, I'd stay there," the giant counseled. "You'll break your mother's heart if you end up in the Bay of Skulls."

Arthur did not know what the Bay of Skulls was, but he suspected it lay beneath the Bridge of Leaping. "I'm not going to Selkie Isle. I'm getting back up that mountain. If I die, I die."

Gawyr shrugged. "Suit yourself." He disappeared back into the mountain and called back, "A dead son on top of a dead husband might be too much for your mother. Think on that."

Arthur and Arvel descended the rest of the way to the grotto where the little rowboat greeted them, bobbing up and down in the swirling currents. "If you can just row me to shore, I'll make my way from there," he cried over the howling wind.

Arvel looked at him intently, brow furrowed. "The giant's right. This is no place for you. Wait for Taliesin and speak with him, first."

"No!" Arthur lanced at him. *They all think I'm a boy! A child! Just like my mother does!*

Arvel relented and motioned toward the boat. "I'll row you to shore, as you ask."

Arthur thanked him and got into the boat. Arvel jumped in after him, untied it, and navigated them back out of the rocks into the open water. Though perpetually grey, the sky had darkened to a deeper shade, signaling night was not far off. The wind off the sea sunk its icy needles into him, jarring his teeth into a clatter.

Arvel rowed them into calmer shallows. He leapt out of the boat with one swift movement and dragged the bow onto the shore. Arthur jumped out, scanning the foreign landscape with trepidation. He had a warm cloak and good weapons, but no plan. The words of warning spoken to him over the past hour came scurrying like rats to feed on his courage.

"Are you certain?" Arvel asked once more, punctuating his doubt.

"Yes." Arthur nodded with feigned conviction. His pride would not allow him to do anything else.

Arvel glanced up at the dark stone cells of Dun Scáthach and frowned before looking back at Arthur. "Good luck to you." He gripped his shoulder. "If you change your mind, build a bonfire on the shore. I'll come for you."

Arthur's anger faded. He managed a smile. "Thank you, Arvel."

Arvel nodded and returned to the boat. He was soon rowing back out to sea, leaving Arthur to contemplate his fate alone. After Arvel disappeared beyond the rocks, Arthur turned and walked inland, gathering driftwood and dry grass as he went. He found a place sheltered from the wind and built himself a fire. Once the cold released him from its painful grip, Arthur fell into his thoughts. He pictured Scáthach's face the moment he had expressed his desire to cross the bridge, remembering the way her eyes had lit up. He had not dared to think much on it while in the fortress, but now, he let himself be excited by the memory of her face and body; her proud manner and fierceness. He had never met a female warrior before, let alone one so powerful. *I must prove to her I'm better than Lot. Better than Urien.* But, most of all, he knew he had to prove it to himself.

Taliesin stepped into the mating cave. Without a word, the men who had escorted him there slammed the gate behind him, locked it, turned around and disappeared back into the mountain. Taliesin felt relieved to see Arvel, who looked at him with brows raised. "What happened?"

Taliesin shrugged. "We had a fight."

Arvel frowned. "Who with?"

"Arhi—Scáthach." Taliesin sighed. "Where's Arthur?"

"I took him ashore, as he asked."

Taliesin shook his head. "This isn't how things were supposed to happen." He rubbed his face and let out a long sigh.

Arvel put an arm around his shoulder. "Don't worry—he's safe. I'll take you to him."

Taliesin shook his head. "No, not tonight. Let him be alone with his thoughts, as I wish to be alone with mine. Let's go back to your people. Tomorrow, I hope, I'll have found the right words to speak to him."

301

Taliesin rowed himself back to the mainland the next morning. He found Arthur's camp easily, but the boy was not there. He tracked him upriver and found him standing at the foot of the Giant's Ladder, looking up at the sheer rock face with his hands on his hips. Arthur heard his footsteps and turned around. "Oh! Master Taliesin!" He smiled and then frowned. "Are you still angry with me?"

Taliesin sighed. "You've made things more difficult than they needed to be, but, no, I'm not angry with you." He motioned toward the Giant's Ladder. "And don't make the mistake of thinking you can climb that. You can't. It was built by giants for their own kind a long time ago, when this fortress belonged to them. Gawyr scarcely made it to the top."

Shading his eyes, Arthur squinted up at the top of the stern cliff face. "Glad you saved me the trouble of trying." He looked back at Taliesin. "So how do you get to the bridge?"

"That's for you to figure out. You're the one who wanted to do things the hard way."

Arthur sighed. "I've been looking for hours. I can't find any other way up, but I know there must be."

"Well, it's not here. I can tell you that much."

"No, it's not," a voice boomed. "Not for scrawny harp-maulers and baby dragons, anyway." Gawyr's large bulk appeared, moving toward them like a bear through the trees.

Taliesin smiled. They had not had time to speak before Arthur had made his rash decision, and Gawyr had been tasked with escorting Arthur back to the grotto. "Have you come to help, old friend?" he called.

Gawyr shrugged. "I have. Thought the least I could do was teach the lad a bit about that nasty bridge. Train him up a bit. Don't want his bones swirling around in the Bay of Skulls." He looked at the two of them and raised his brows. "What the hell are you waiting for? You want help, or not?"

"I do!" Arthur yelled. "I do. Yes. Thank you, Sir Gawyr. Where shall we train? Here?"

Gawyr's face spread into a wide yellow grin. "Hear that, harp-mauler? *Sir* Gawyr. I like it." He winked. "How about you call me that, too?"

"You're not training me to fight, big man."

Gawyr slung a heavy dismissive palm in Taliesin's direction. "Come on, then. We'll train on Selkie Isle. I'm not doing that hike every day." He motioned toward the fortress. "Bump my head on too many bloody rocks going up and down. And I won't ever do this climb again, either. I like my feet on the ground, where they belong."

"We won't all fit in the rowboat," Taliesin pointed out.

Gawyr scowled. "Of course, we won't all fit in that walnut shell, you nitwit! You two row out, and I'll swim. I've done it plenty." He leaned down toward Arthur. "Those selkie women love me." He clapped him on the back and sent him lurching forward. "They'll like both of you, too." He winked at Taliesin. "Plenty of 'em to go around."

Taliesin could not help but roll his eyes. "Are we going there to train Arthur, or to bed selkies?"

"Both. At least, for me. You two do what you like."

Gawyr strode ahead and Arthur and Taliesin scrambled to keep up. They returned to Selkie Isle, where it seemed Gawyr had already made arrangements with Arvel.

"I'm so glad we're going to be together!" Arvel smiled. "Come, I'll show you where you can sleep."

Arvel led them to one of the cone-shaped driftwood huts. Taliesin peeked inside. There were no furnishings, just a sandy floor and some rushes to sleep on with a few furs and blankets, clearly brought from the ship, for the selkies needed nothing but their skins. Taliesin nodded. "This will do fine. We'll need a few more things from the ship, though." He turned to Arvel. "You'll want to be sailing back, I suppose?"

Arvel shrugged. "Another moon will do no harm. I haven't been home in many years. I'd like to stay a while."

Taliesin smiled. "And go to the mating cave."

"Of course! That, too!"

Gawyr wasted no time taking Arthur under his wing. He led him outside the camp to an area that was fairly flat and sandy, and put him through his paces for as long as the meager daylight held out. Taliesin felt glad to see it. *At last, Arthur's getting some serious training.* Gawyr was far more formidable than any warrior south of the wall.

By the time the sun had set, Arthur could scarcely walk or talk. Gawyr looked as if he had simply been out for a brisk walk. "He'll learn. It'll take longer than I thought, but he'll learn." Again, Gawyr slapped Arthur on the back, launching him forward a few steps.

Taliesin put his arm around the boy and led him to the fire, where the selkies had gathered for a meal. "Hope you like fish." He reached down and handed him a fish. "Unless you go ashore and hunt, it's all you'll eat."

Gawyr grumbled. "Too true. I see a bit of bow practice in your training, tomorrow. You have any idea how many of these it takes to fill a man my size?" He grabbed a fish and waggled it. "Besides. You said the bow was your strength. Tomorrow, we'll see how true that is. Be up with the sun."

Arthur ate quickly, not the least bit interested in the women around the fire or anything else, for that matter. He wandered off to bed, half-limping.

Gawyr chuckled. "I went a bit hard on him. Just wanted to see how much he could take."

"And?"

"Baby dragon has promise. Almost caught me with that left hand of his once or twice. He's got the instinct, just needs the brawn. Easy enough for him to get the latter. Not much you can do about the former. But he does. He knows where he needs to be and when. Just has a hard time getting there." Gawyr shrugged. "But that'll come. I'll make sure of it."

Taliesin smiled and handed Gawyr a goatskin filled with apple wine from Tegid's endless barrel. "Thank you, my friend."

Gawyr un-stoppered it and took a taste. His eyebrows raised in approval. "Great Dagda, where the hell'd you get this?"

Taliesin just smiled and held up his flask. "To the young stag."

Gawyr raised his goatskin in tribute. "To the young stag!"

The next morning Gawyr went ashore with Arthur. They did not return until sundown, but they brought back a deer, as promised. The selkies made them roast it on the other side of the isle, far from the camp, for they did not like the smell. Arthur had made the kill.

"Lad's a good shot," Gawyr commented to Taliesin, stabbing a thumb in Arthur's direction. "Making progress with the sword, but let's just say in a battle I'd post him as an archer."

Arthur shrugged. "I would too."

Gawyr grinned. "I like you, baby dragon. Not like those puffed-up cockerels swaggering around the practice ring, thinking they're Dagda's gift to the world." He shook his head. "All the same, when they come in. Keep having to knock them around to remind them they still shit like the rest of us." He eyed Taliesin. "Got any more of that wine?"

Taliesin smiled and pulled out the goatskin Gawyr had returned, full again. Tegid had filled up a barrel for him back in Alt Clud and sent it over to their ship as a parting gift.

"Gods bless you, harp-mauler!" Gawyr grabbed the skin and washed down his venison. "Glad you came back." He held the goatskin high. "More all the time." He took another swig. "Let's have some music, now, eh? I'm aching for some music."

Taliesin found this interesting. Arhianna had always been the first to cry out for music and dancing at every feast and gathering. "You don't have music at Dun Scáthach?"

"We do, we do...but you've got a way with it. Give us something lively."

Taliesin had sung but two refrains when the selkies came wandering over. They gathered around him, shaking their shell rattles and clacking pieces of driftwood together, punctuating pauses in the songs with yips and howls.

Arthur beamed despite his relentless training, his topaz eyes gold and bright in the firelight. He sang perfect harmonies to every one of Taliesin's melodies, weaving his resonant voice into the music with ease.

Taliesin thought back to when he was his age, remembering the thrill of being poised on the edge of the world, yet untouched by disappointment and self-doubt. He smiled. *This is what youth is meant for, lad—adventure! Go to, my boy—go to!*

CHAPTER THIRTY-THREE
The Mountain

Taliesin, Arvel, Arthur and Gawyr spent two moons living among the selkies. In that time, Arthur learned much—both as a lover and a warrior. The selkies were not jealous or possessive, and all the women of the clan were eager to teach him about the dark mysteries of their bodies. Just as eager to learn, he refused none of them—be they fat or thin, young like him, or a bit older—so curious was he to discover how they were all different and the same. Taliesin soon moved to another hut, leaving him to his ardent discoveries.

Arthur's prowess as a warrior grew as well. He felt a jubilant confidence in his chest that he had never known before; as if he had awoken from a murky dream and discovered the truth of the man he was destined to become. He knew he was meant to be nowhere else, with no one else, doing nothing else.

"I know the way up," he announced one morning to Gawyr. The two of them had just arrived on the mainland with their bows, intent on avoiding a fish dinner that night.

"You do?"

"I found it the last time we came to hunt. It's further inland from the Giant's Ladder. Some of the warriors were out hunting as well. I tracked them to the side of the mountain and saw them disappear into the stone. I waited a while, then explored the area and found the passage."

Gawyr nodded, hair and beard dripping with sea water from his morning swim. "And?"

"And, I'm going up."

Gawyr shook his shaggy head. "No, lad. Not yet. You're not ready."

"I am."

"Did you say anything to Taliesin?"

"He wasn't in his hut. I'm not sure where he is."

"He needs to know."

"Go back and tell him, then, if you wish."

What he did not mention to Gawyr was the dream he had had the night before. In it, he had been sitting on the shore of the isle, looking up at the stone face of the fortress, watching its many windows, orange with firelight. He noticed a winged figure fly off one of its ledges. At first, he took it to be a sea eagle but then realized it was far too large to be a bird of any kind. With mounting excitement, he watched it fly toward him, across the sea, until it hovered directly above him, causing him to fall on his back.

He knew it was Scáthach by her face, but she had long red hair made of flames and terrible black wings. "Come up and fight, Young Stag," she had said.

He had awoken in a sweat, full of intense desire, every muscle charged with purpose. Now, there was nothing anyone could say or do that would keep him from climbing that mountain.

Gawyr growled. "At least let me give you some advice, then."

"Please." Arthur was not fool enough to refuse that.

"Listen carefully." He held up a finger. "You want to keep moving straight upwards and stick to the widest passage. If you hear or see anything strange down the side passages, ignore it, or you may end up in places you might never return from, you understand?"

"The mountain's that big?" Arthur glanced skeptically toward the mountain, finding it hard to believe one could get lost inside it forever.

"Nothing to do with her size, lad. Let's just say that, sometimes, she opens up doorways to other places. Or so I've heard. Never happened to me, thank Dagda."

Arthur felt more thrilled than frightened by this prospect. "I see."

"So," Gawyr continued, "the main passage will take you through the Great Chamber and the Hall of Heroes. Don't touch or disturb anything. And I mean *any*thing." He wagged a huge finger in warning. "The passage comes out at a cave beneath the Bridge of Leaping. Scáthach's best warrior guards the bridge from that cave, which, usually, is me—so I'm not sure who you'll find there, but be prepared for the fight of your life."

Arthur gave him a nod and extended an arm. "Understood. Thank you, Sir Gawyr."

"Sir – ha! Never get tired of it." Gawyr smiled and gripped his forearm, then lowered his voice and growled, "Now, don't make me tell the harp-mauler you've gone swimming in the Bay of Skulls."

"I won't. Go to the fortress. I'll be there soon."

Gawyr squeezed his shoulder. "See that you are, lad."

Arthur's breath billowed in front of him, clouding the light of his lantern as he huffed his way up through the mountain. As Gawyr had warned, from time to time, he encountered passages leading off to the right or left. They were far more inviting than the cold stone corridor in front of him, often glowing with the promise of a fire or the smell of food. After hours of refusing his curiosity even the slightest glance inside, he grew weary. *Surely, I must be near the top by now…or have I been going in circles?* Once his doubts got their talons in him, he became increasingly convinced he had somehow gone astray.

Within the next hour, a fresh scent came wafting through one of the side passages, verdant and sublime, like heather-decked hills after a rainstorm. A golden light beckoned from within, as if there were a sunset just beyond. He stopped and took a deep breath, growing light-headed with the clean spring air after so many hours in the dank bowels of the mountain. The scent reminded him of his mother's garden in Caer Leon, and he ached with melancholy homesickness. The longer he stood there, the more he began to notice. He caught the sound of faint music and laughter, which grew in clarity and volume as he listened, as if he were hearing people gather. The scent of the garden then gave way to the smell of roasted meat and fresh bread. Arthur's mouth watered, and he ached for a drink of the wine he could hear being poured. Over the feasting guests, a loud and distinct voice he knew well to be Archbishop Dubricius cried, "All hail, Arthur! Saviour of Brython!" A crowd cheered. "And his fierce and beautiful future queen, Lady Gwynhwyfar, fairest maiden in Christendom!"

Queen? Arthur's heart raced. *What magic is this?*

He stood there in agony, bargaining with himself over whether a single step inside the passageway for a quick peek would be too foolish. After hearing his own voice address the crowd, he could not resist. He allowed himself one step in, keeping his other foot firmly where it was, and craned his neck as far as he could, wishing he were a swan. His efforts granted him a view of the gathered crowd, large iron sconces heavy with candles, garlands of flowers, and servants carrying trenchers of food and jugs of wine.

"On this holy day of their marriage," the archbishop continued, "we ask God to bless them with health and good fortune. May he grant them many children, and may their sons and daughters rule Brython long after them, preserving it from tyranny, until the end of days."

The crowd erupted into cheers, and a woman with a voice as clear as silver bells cried out for music and dancing. "The queen wants dancing!" he heard himself reply.

I must see her—I must see my bride—just for a moment!

Arthur stepped into the passage with his other foot and was instantly dazzled by the vision; a guest at his own wedding feast, surrounded by the beaming faces of a good many people, some of whom he knew, and many whom he did not. Bowers of summer flowers graced dozens of long tables laden with a banquet so varied and generous it could only be Lammastime, but he was not there to admire such details. He scanned the hall with a swift eye until he caught sight of himself at the far end of the hall, seated upon the dais that his mother and father customarily sat upon. *She must be next to me.* He rose up on his toes, hoping to see around the person standing in front of him, but it was no use. He moved in for a closer look, but someone grabbed his arm and dragged him backward, out of the hall and back into the darkness of the mountain.

Gawyr's shaggy beard hung above his head. "You damn fool! Didn't I tell you not to take any of the side passages?" He growled. "I knew you weren't ready!"

Dazed, Arthur rubbed his eyes, feeling as if he had been awoken from sleep. "I was about to see my bride," he croaked.

Gawyr smacked the side of his head. "I told you not to go down any side passages! And besides, don't you know it's bad luck to see your bride before your wedding, you dimwit?"

At this, Arthur had to laugh.

"Glad you think it's funny. Might have been in here another moon if I hadn't followed you. Took me nearly all day to find you!"

Arthur felt confused. "What do you mean? I've only been gone a few hours..."

"That's what you think!"

Arthur felt confused. "I don't understand."

309

"Of course, you don't. I told you, you weren't ready. And clearly, I was right. This mountain holds more terrors and mysteries than any of us will ever be ready for. That's why you don't break the rules. The side passages are only for the initiated."

Arthur remained undeterred. "Initiated by whom? Scáthach?"

"Don't know, don't care—I'm no mage. I'm just here to fight."

"You don't want to go in? See what they have to show you?"

Gawyr scowled. "Great Dagda, no! Knowing what waits for you is a curse!" He squinted and leaned closer. "You don't think so, though, do you, baby dragon?"

Arthur shrugged. "I was taught the future is never certain…it shifts. If I saw something I didn't like, I would change it. It would be like seeing my life on a chess board; allow me to think three moves ahead."

Gawyr sighed and shook his head. "Life's not a game, lad. And those passages are nothing to fool with. Take my word for it." He turned and set a fast pace up the mountain, in spite of having to crouch, warning Arthur when they were about to reach the Great Chamber. "And don't touch anything!"

When they entered the massive cave with its heavy stone sarcophagi, Arthur could not help but ask questions. "Who were they?"

"Former queens of this fortress."

"Not that one." Arthur pointed to the carved likeness of a young man about his age reclining atop the tomb nearest him.

"No, not that one. There lies Connla, son of Cú Chulainn. Sad story, that one."

"What happened?"

"Some other time."

Arthur longed to stay and look at the tombs, but Gawyr pressed on. Once out of the chamber, they passed by dozens of niches carved in the rock on either side of the corridor. Each featured a single skull, some with candles burning inside them, firelight glowing from their eye sockets.

"Before you ask, this is the Hall of Heroes. All of 'em born and trained here at Dun Scáthach."

They soon came to the cave beneath the bridge. Arthur's heart slammed against his ribcage as he peeked over the edge of the cave into the abyss below. Wind howled up at him from the harsh churning sea, hissing salt and snatching at his face and hair. He eyed the bridge, swinging back and forth across the chasm, like a spider's web across a doorway.

"You don't have to do this," Gawyr counseled. "We can go back down and come back when you're ready."

Arthur ignored him and crawled up the steps hewn into the side of the mountain to the edge of the Bridge of Leaping. He looked all around but saw no one anywhere. *Why are there no guards?*

He stepped onto the bridge and walked halfway across it. Still, no one came. He looked behind him. Nothing but trees and rock. Below, the sea churned with fury, blasting him with its salty breath. Sea birds cried out in protest, struggling to ride its unpredictable currents. When he looked up again, he saw Scáthach standing in the archway of the fortress, spear planted in the ground. His heartbeat quickened.

But she did not move toward him as he ran across the bridge. She remained where she was, waiting; watching.

He stepped off the bridge, bewildered. "Why do you not attack?"

"You're a fool if you think I'd send my dearest friend's only son to his death. You wished to come to the fortress across the Bridge of Leaping, like the others. Now you have." She motioned toward the practice ring. "Shall we begin?"

All the warriors of Dun Scáthach were assembled in the practice ring, staring at Arthur.

Arthur's shock turned to anger. *This isn't how it was supposed to be! She was to fight me on the bridge—I've gained no respect among these warriors at all!*

"Well?" Scáthach barked. "What are you waiting for? I thought you wanted to fight! Go fetch a weapon!"

Arthur had no choice but to do as she asked. *Taliesin. This is his fault, damn him! He convinced her not to fight me!* Blood boiling with humiliation, he entered the ring, forcing himself to meet each warrior's glare.

Scáthach pulled out a leather pouch and held it open for each warrior who took a stone from it, holding it up and calling out the symbol. Arthur drew last. "Beith," he announced.

311

"Fitting." Scáthach closed the pouch and tossed it aside. "That's what I drew, before you arrived." She held up her stone, carved with the same symbol on it. "Beith always starts." She threw her chin in his direction. "You still haven't chosen a weapon. What'll it be, *mo phrionnsa*? "Dagger? Spear? Sword?"

Her friendly manner unnerved him. "Sword."

Her blade was unsheathed and against his neck before he could even grip the hilt of his sword. He heard laughter and angry embarrassment erupted once more across his skin.

"You wanted to fight me just a moment ago, did you not?"

Arthur felt as if her blue eyes had pierced his soul and could see everything inside him—his fear of failing, his false confidence, his desire for her—all of it. He felt flayed and exposed.

The warriors cried for blood, eyes full of condemnation. She struck again and he scarcely managed to move away. He turned his anger on himself. *Fight back, you bloody coward! Fight!*

He struck back a different man, one willing to lose, but not without using every ounce of concentration and skill he had— whatever that might amount to. Gawyr had taught him well, and he refused to allow himself to be made a complete fool of. Still, in spite of his best efforts, she made quick work of him. He managed to do nothing but get out of the way a few times before she had him on the ground, her sword at his throat.

I would have died on that bridge today, he realized without a doubt. *I'd be sleeping in the Bay of Skulls right now.*

"Get up," she commanded.

He scrambled to his feet. She put him through his paces again, and again, and again. Mercifully, she demanded the others cease watching and concentrate on their own training. They changed partners every match, but she stayed with him the entire day. She did not dismiss him until night had fallen and the torches had been lit.

"That's all for today. Go eat, lad." She motioned to the long table in the hall where the rest of the warriors had already gone.

Lad? Arthur cringed. *She can't be much older than I am!* He felt helpless, and angry about feeling helpless. He did his best to ignore his frustration, but he did not sleep well. Nor did he the next night, or the following.

312

When he did sleep, he dreamed of the side passages. Since he had glimpsed his wedding, his mind could not seem to break free of the pull they had on him. Every day, that pull got stronger.

Things only got worse over the next few moons, until Gawyr returned from Selkie Isle with news that finally broke Arthur's resolve.

"Taliesin's gone south to serve in King Urien's court. And it's about time, if you ask me. Says he'll be back for you in a year."

"What?" Any meager measure of confidence Arthur had managed to regain since arriving vanished in that moment. He considered Urien the biggest threat to his future—the most capable and perhaps more suitable successor to his father's title. It was true Lot was a strong contender and would surely challenge him when the time came, but Lot was not much older than he was. Urien had been warlord and king for a lifetime.

And now, without a farewell, Taliesin's gone to serve him? Why? Why on earth would he do that?

For days, Arthur stewed over this news, the idea of it chewing at his mind, causing him anguish. It kept him up at night, when he should have been sleeping, and his lack of sleep cost him dearly in training.

Why would he ally himself with Urien? Has he brought me here to keep me out of the way while they forge a plan? He tried talking to Gawyr about why Taliesin had done such a thing, but Gawyr merely shrugged and said he knew as much as he did.

After a week of pondering, Arthur felt convinced he had been a fool to allow Taliesin to divert him from Gwynedd. That was where his parents thought him to be—training with his cousins, close enough to be called home should something happen. *Perhaps he planned this all along—bring me north to this impossible place, leagues from home, where no one knows I am, so he can scheme with Urien to take Caer Leon when Father dies.*

That night, he bundled his things together and crossed back over the Bridge of Leaping, intent on leaving Dun Scáthach and returning to Gwynedd. He found Gawyr waiting for him under the bridge. "Where'dya think you're goin', baby dragon?"

Arthur bristled. "Don't call me that. I'm going to ask Arvel to sail me back to Gwynedd."

Gawyr groaned. "Why? Can't stand being the weakest one in the group? Great Dagda, lad! It's only been two moons!"

Arthur felt his neck and face grow hot. "I won't lie, I don't like it, but that's not why."

"Why, then?"

"Taliesin's gone to serve my chief rival for a year without so much as a farewell or an explanation—I can't just stay up here in this God-forsaken place, days from home, while he glorifies Urien!"

Gawyr's furry eyebrows twisted into each other, like a pair of caterpillars mating. "You think he's betrayed you?"

Arthur felt ashamed. He had not voiced his fear to anyone, and now that it was exposed it sounded strange to his ears. "I pray not. But I must prepare for the worst."

"What you feel is nothing more than your bruised manhood," a woman's voice said behind him. Arthur whirled around to see Scáthach standing at the opening of the cave, nostrils flaring and lips pursed. "That you would so quickly throw away the opportunity that so many have died trying to gain shows how little you value being here. You're not worthy of Taliesin's trust, or the breath I've just wasted on these words." Her eyes flashed with contempt.

Arthur felt stunned, as if she had pulled a blindfold from his eyes and his heart from his chest. His stomach fell to his feet. *I've made a terrible mistake.*

"Yet," she added, "I can only blame myself. I thought you being willing to risk death on the Bridge of Leaping was enough; that for what I owe Taliesin and your mother, I could allow such a thing, just once. Clearly, I made a mistake." She turned away from him and hoisted herself back up onto the bridge, leaving her words hanging in the cave behind her. "Farewell, Arthur."

Arthur could only stare as her form and footsteps disappeared, stunned by the swiftness with which the winds guiding his fate had changed direction. "Oh, God. What have I done?"

Once she was across the bridge, Gawyr let out a long sigh of exhaustion and rubbed his face. "Oh, Dagda. Why'd she have to hear all that? Why?" He looked over at Arthur, shaking his head. "Taliesin's going to kill me for letting this happen. But it can't be helped. You'd best stick with your plan and go back to Gwynedd. I'll send word to him."

Arthur had never regretted anything more in his life.

CHAPTER THIRTY-FOUR
The Melding

Arthur gutted his kill and dragged it up the mountain on a sled of woven willow branches. He had managed to take down a buck that would feed the warriors for days, and prayed such an offering might at last convince Scáthach to hear his apology and reconcile with him.

As he approached the Cave of the Guardian, he called ahead to prevent being killed. "Sir Gawyr!" he yelled, his voice echoing through the stone passage, "It's Arthur! Brought a buck this time!"

"Have you, then?" He heard Gawyr's deep voice behind him and let out a startled cry.

Gawyr chuckled. "Best pay more attention, baby dragon. Could've killed you three times, by now." He winked and took hold of the sled. "I'll take that up. You've dragged it far enough."

"No, I'll do it."

"Nay. I'm looking forward to some meat tonight, and at your pace, it'll be tomorrow before I get any!"

Arthur could not argue. He stepped aside and let Gawyr take the sled. "Tell her I'm still here, and that all I ask is a few words. Will you do that for me?"

Gawyr looked down at him and sighed. "I'll try, but I wouldn't get your hopes up. Wait here."

An hour passed before Gawyr returned, shaking his shaggy head. "No use, lad. She said the only way you'll ever get back into that fortress is if you *really* cross the Bridge of Leaping, and we both know you can't do that. Not yet, anyway. Want my advice? Don't waste any more time here. Go back to your uncle. I'll talk to Arvel for you. Just build a bonfire on the beach when you're ready and he'll come get you. I'll send word to Taliesin."

Arthur felt the embers of hope in his heart start smoking in surrender, but still, he did not give up. "One more moon."

"Why?" Gawyr's eyebrows arched like a pair of question marks. "You're not going to become a warrior sparring with trees."

"I know."

"Go back to Gwynedd, lad, like you planned."

After Scáthach's initial dismissal of him, Arthur had fully intended on doing just that but felt he could not leave without trying his best to make amends. He wanted her support when he became

316

Pendragon. For the past moon, he had slept within the mountain, bringing daily offerings of game, fowl or fish to Gawyr to deliver to the clan along with his request for an audience, as he had done again today. Each time, he had been refused. What he did not share with Gawyr was that it was not only his hope of reconciliation that compelled him to stay, but what he had discovered about the mountain herself.

Ever since he had glimpsed his wedding day within one of her side passages, her mysteries had pulled at him with an ever-increasing gravity. In truth, since that moment, she had steadily become an obsession. Now, with so many hours to himself, curiosity led him to explore her winding passageways, mapping them out on the walls of the cavern where he slept. He visited the Great Chamber daily to marvel at the sarcophagi or gaze down at the violent sea churning far below in the Bay of Skulls, discovering something new about it every time. Most compelling of all was what he had discovered there the night before.

He had given the paintings on the chamber walls no more than a passing glance up until that night. For some reason, on this occasion, he felt drawn to inspect them more closely. Fascinated by the way the figures seemed to rise off the wall, he ran his fingers over them. The moment he touched the stone, a wave of images flooded his mind, so vivid in color and sound he had yanked his hand back in shock. He had stood there, heart racing and hand frozen in the air, gathering the courage to touch them again. Once he did, he had reached up and laid his hand once more over the figures, forcing himself to relax as the images came.

He had learned the figures were the founders of Dun Scáthach — giants, like Gawyr — who had come down from the North seeking game and shelter. He saw a tribe of perhaps fifty, moving over a snow-blown landscape with unimaginable strides, bearskins thrown over their shoulders and immense spears in their hands. Thrilled, he had moved to another painting of a woman with flaming hair and black wings, wielding a long spear. As he had hoped, the same thing happened when he touched it — he learned she was the first Scáthach, daughter of a giantess and a king whose people sailed to the Isle of Skye in strange ships. On he went, absorbing the history of Dun Scáthach through its pictorial murals until the sun came up, surprising him with the realization of how long he had been there. He had left the chamber elated, feeling as if the mountain had shared her own precious memories with him.

If that were not enough of a reason to stay longer, there were also the mysterious side passages. The more time he spent exploring the mountain, the more they called to him. Heedful of Gawyr's warning, he had not succumbed to their siren song a second time, but the temptation had grown.

"Go back to your uncle. It's for the best." Gawyr smacked Arthur on the back.

"Just one more moon," Arthur countered, feeling this was reasonable. Surely, exploring the mysteries of the mountain was a pursuit worthy of a future king, was it not? He felt convinced he would learn things more valuable to him than how to swing a sword.

Gawyr shook his head. "You're as stubborn as a mule. Suit yourself."

"I'll be back tomorrow."

Arthur wandered back down the mountain and returned to the Great Chamber, feeling it was the only place he might find answers about the passageways. He went to the tomb of Scáthach the First, lit a candle, and placed it on the center of her forehead. He watched its melted wax flow over the centuries of candles that had come before it, their hardened supplications streaming down the stony sides of the sarcophagus to the floor like alabaster tresses.

"Great Scáthach, I, Arthur, son of Igerna, wish to become worthy of your order. I ask you to help me cross the Bridge of Leaping." He took his dagger and cut his finger, letting his blood drip into the melting wax as proof of his identity. "In return, I swear, when I become Pendragon, I shall never abandon the people of the North."

He laid everything he valued upon her sarcophagus: his sword and spear, his fur cloak, his gold torc and armband. As he did, the flame on the candle rose up as if the wick were a foot long, and then leaned toward the back of the chamber.

Arthur looked in the direction the flame seemed to point and discovered a painting he had not noticed before. Heart pounding, he walked over for a closer look. *It's the bridge,* he realized.

The Bridge of Leaping spanned the chasm from the Cave of the Guardian to the fortress of Dun Scáthach, just as it did today. Beneath the bridge were figures falling toward the black scrawls of the sea below, its depths filled with the bones and skulls of the unsuccessful. He studied it a long while before reaching up and touching one of the figures. In an instant, he found himself standing behind a man poised at the edge of the bridge, the salty wind whipping his face and hair. *My God! How is this happening?*

The bridge swayed back and forth, creaking a warning. The man took a step onto the bridge, then a few more. Arthur dared to follow him.

The Guardian came running from the fortress, spear poised, and leapt onto the bridge with a battle cry. The force of power released by her jump had to have been augmented by some kind of magic, for it sent the planks arching up like a cobra, launching the man off the bridge and into the air.

Arthur watched him fall into the Bay of Skulls and pulled his hand away. He glanced over at the candle, now understanding. *This is how I'll learn to cross the bridge.*

He knew, now, staying had been the right decision.

Day after day, Arthur went to the Great Chamber to learn from the fallen figures in the painting, until every one of their fatal mistakes was burned into his memory. But he knew it was not enough. The fallen could only teach him what *not* to do. They could not show him how to succeed. He looked wistfully at the opposite side of the bridge, wishing there were successful figures standing there whom he could learn from, but the space was empty.

He fiddled with a stub of charcoal he always kept in his pocket, running it back and forth between his thumb and forefinger, until a piece of it snapped off and dropped to the ground. As he bent to pick it up, a thought came to him.

I could draw one...couldn't I? It might work.

He walked up to the painting, drew himself standing victorious on the far side of the bridge, and, fingers trembling, reached up to touch it.

In a flash, he found himself on the other side of the bridge, just as he had drawn himself, but, sadly, with no memory of how he had

319

managed to get across. He pulled his hand off the wall and paced back and forth between the tombs of Scáthach the First and her son, Connla. He stopped in front of Connla's tomb, watching the light from the flame of his candle dance across his stone face.

"How did your father do it?" he asked the dead youth, knowing Cú Chulainn had managed to cross the bridge.

After a spell of musing, another idea came to him. He went back to the painting of the bridge and drew Cú Chulainn standing at its edge opposite the fortress. Then, hand hovering over the figure, he spoke. "Great mountain, show me your memory of the great Cú Chulainn, son of Deichtine, crossing the bridge, so I might witness his success." He placed his hand over the figure he had drawn and again found himself at the bridge, this time standing next to Cú Chulainn. A woman, whom he assumed to be Scáthach the First, stood at the other end, grinning with menace. He watched as Cú Chulainn started running across the bridge, spear poised, but Scáthach jumped onto the other side with immense force, causing a wave to travel across the bridge. *Seems that's the standard first move.* Cú Chulainn ran toward it and launched himself off its crest, but had made his move too soon, unfortunately. He ended up in a tumble back on the cliff where he had started, his spear claimed by the Bay of Skulls.

Cú Chulainn rested a while and tried again, this time with his sword at the ready. Again, she launched a wave that sent him sprawling into the air. He jumped forward, this time, but not far enough to reach the other side. He lost his balance and nearly toppled into the Bay of Skulls, dropping his sword to clutch the edge of the bridge. He scrambled to safety, cursing all the while, and retreated to where Arthur stood watching.

Cú Chulainn sat down and stared across the bridge for some time. Then, for some strange reason, he took off his boots. Just as Arthur began wondering if he thought bare feet would give him better balance, he did something even more shocking—he stood up, took off pack, unbuckled his belt, and took off all his clothes. The warriors on the other side of the bridge seemed to be as shocked as Arthur was, but began whooping and hollering. Cú Chulainn backed up to allow himself a running start, and then charged toward the bridge. Just before reaching it, he leapt in the air, landed on it with all the force he had, then chased the wave he had caused across the bridge. Scáthach followed suit, sending her own wave against his. The moment the two waves met, Cú Chulainn launched himself off their combined force and sailed through the air like a giant bird of prey, unfettered by weapons or clothing. The warriors cheered as he hit the ground on the other side and rolled to safety, as naked as the day he was born.

Arthur felt both thrilled and despondent. He knew he was incapable of what he had just witnessed. He watched in awe as the warriors of Dun Scáthach cheered Cú Chulainn, and tossed him a cloak.

To Arthur's surprise, Scáthach did not follow the warriors into the fortress. Instead, she walked across the bridge in his direction. He shifted uncomfortably, wondering whether she could see him.

"Not quite what you had in mind?" she called.

Arthur looked behind him to see if she might be addressing someone standing there, but there was no one.

She advanced toward him. "Aye, I'm speaking to you, son of Igerna."

Scáthach the First stood perhaps eight feet tall, with bright copper tresses and eyes the color of spring moss. Her skin gleamed white as salt over muscles as hard as the mountain upon which they stood. She wore a sleeveless tunic of rough wool belted about her waist, tall boots, and leather arm bracers on her wrists. A thick bronze torc circled her long neck.

Awash in awe, Arthur fell to his knees and bowed his head. "Great Scáthach, I'm honored."

"Rise. What is it you seek here?"

Arthur seized his opportunity. "I wish to redeem myself by crossing the bridge. Have you any advice for me?" He had nothing to lose by asking. *And who better to ask?*

"The bridge tests faith and courage, as does the Matron, whom you ignore. What you could not see or hear was Cú Chulainn's prayer to her. It was she who told him to leave all his possessions behind and leap with faith."

Arthur did not know what to say, so remained silent.

"The Matron has beckoned to you from the moment you arrived, yet you refuse to heed the great privilege of her call. Why?"

321

Somehow, Arthur knew she spoke of the mountain. In truth, he had wanted nothing more than to answer her call, but had ignored his instincts in favor of Gawyr's advice. Every answer he thought about giving now seemed ridiculous: *I thought it was a trap. I was afraid. I was told not to.* He realized, in that moment, that whatever the mountain had to show him was far more important than the training he had ostensibly come for. Yet, he had blindly followed the advice of a giant who had made it clear he could not care less about such knowledge.

"Because I've been a fool," he admitted. "I've done nothing but prove it from the moment I arrived."

She did not disagree, and Arthur felt ashamed.

"Yet," she said, "you were wise enough to make a worthy sacrifice to me, and clever and patient enough to learn the history of our people. Those actions were not foolish."

Arthur felt grateful he had managed to do a few things right. "Thank you, Great Scáthach." Again, he repeated, "I would take your advice, if you would bless me with it."

Scáthach gave him a nod. She motioned toward the men standing on the other side of the bridge, Cú Chulainn among them, all awaiting her command. "Remember this: any king can buy, or even force, men to fight for him, but only a beloved king can inspire them to die for him. You don't need to become the fiercest warrior on the field. What you must become is a king worth dying for." She looked at him intently, like an animal on the verge of a kill. "Do you understand?

Arthur returned her gaze. "I do."

She stepped back on the bridge. "Listen to the Matron, son of Igerna."

Arthur found himself standing once more in the Great Chamber. Night had fallen, and his candle had long since burned out, but the moon shone brightly. Full of resolve, he made his way back down into the mountain. As if in response to his willingness, a faint light soon pierced the darkness from a side passage, followed by whispers. He ventured to the opening, heart pounding, and listened to the hushed conversation.

"What will we do, now?" a young woman said.

"Urien will put himself forward. And, you know he'll want more than the title. He'll want the queen for his bed, too, the old badger," answered another.

"How did this happen? He seemed healthy as the sun but a week ago!"

"Seems like a curse, if you ask me. Those Saxons have dark seers they take with them, you know—servants of their evil goddess, Hel. I'll bet you my spring lambs they've cursed him."

"God have mercy. And where's that fool son of his?"

"Probably off singing in taverns with that bard while his father lays here dying. What a disgrace!"

Arthur put one foot inside the passage, straddling two worlds as he had before, and peeked in. He could make out the familiar edges of his father's chamber at Caer Leon, and then he spied the source of the gossip he had overheard standing beside the door—two of the kitchen maids.

At that moment, he heard Morgen's voice call from within his father's chamber, "Arthur? Is that you?"

The two maids shuffled away in the darkness, eyes darting in all directions. His heart quickened. "I'm here," he called, wondering if this were a trick, or if, perhaps, his sister could indeed sense his presence.

"Arthur's here!"

He heard a patter of feet and then saw his sister in the doorway. "Where've you been? Taliesin's been searching for moons!"

What? How can she see me?

Her mother soon joined his sister at the door. "Who are you talking to, Morgen? Do you see Arthur?"

Morgen reached out to touch him, but her hand passed through him. She gasped in shock. "I see him, but..." She tried again, but it was as if he were made of clouds.

"He's in the Shadows," their mother declared. She looked in the direction Morgen looked, but it was clear to Arthur she could not see him as his sister did. "Arthur, if you can hear me, come home at once—our future depends on it. Your father won't last the night." She squeezed Morgen's arm. "Go fetch Taliesin."

Arthur wondered if what he was experiencing was in the present moment, or if it lay in the past or future. Before he could ask, he heard his father croak out his name in a parched voice. "Arthur? Is Arthur here?"

It doesn't matter, Arthur thought. *My father calls, and this may be my only chance to bid him farewell.* He stepped fully into the vision and walked to his father's bedside. To his joy, his father's eyes lit up. "Can you see me, father?"

"I can, my son. I'm so glad you've come home. I can finally die in peace. I know you and Taliesin will make things right." He reached out to clasp Arthur's hand, and, to Arthur's shock, he could feel the warmth of his father's palm.

"You can see Arthur?" his mother asked.

"I can, my love."

Arthur felt the coldness of a dark presence and turned. There, in the corner of the room, stood a dark cowled figure. He nearly cried out in surprise but restrained himself.

"An old friend," his father explained. "Help me up, son." Arthur gripped his father's hand, and felt pleased to see to a younger, luminous self rise from his father's body, as if his flesh were no more than a suit of clothes.

"That's better." His father shot him a grin. "The pain is gone. I can't tell you how relieved I feel. Now, help me get me into my armor." Arthur looked at the armor, wondering how he would manage, but found when he grasped his father's breastplate, he was able to grasp an ethereal version of it. He soon had his father dressed for battle, looking more resplendent than he had ever seen him look. He beamed with pride and admiration.

"Thank you, son. Now, I must go."

"Farewell, Father. I shall make you proud."

"I know you will, son. As will your sister."

Arthur watched his father follow the dark figure toward an archway that appeared in the wall, glowing with golden light, as if from a sunset. The great Uthyr Pendragon turned around and raised a hand in farewell before stepping through. The moment he did, the archway disappeared.

Arthur turned around to see his mother slumped over his father's body, weeping. Morgen soon returned with Taliesin. She gave Arthur a pained look and went to comfort their mother. It was clear to Arthur that Taliesin could see him as well, for he came directly to him, his face slackened with relief.

"Gods be praised, Arthur. Do you know how long I've been searching for you?" He let out a sigh of relief and beckoned Arthur into the hallway, away from his weeping mother. "I must take you back to the day I left Dun Scáthach and save myself three hundred sleepless nights."

"What do you mean?" Arthur felt confused. "How long have I been away?"

"We just celebrated Midsummer. It's been two years since you and I left Caer Leon."

Arthur realized only now the consequences of his decision to enter the side passage. "Wait a moment. I've only been at Dun Scáthach for three moons—are you telling me you've been searching for me for a year?"

"Near enough. As have Gawyr and Scáthach, with no luck, until now. Seems the mountain has finally given you up. I hope she's taught you much. If she has, it may have been worth it."

Arthur felt dizzy, struggling to understand what was happening.

Taliesin continued. "Gawyr told me you believed I betrayed you when I went to Urien's court. I assure you that is not true. But with your disappearance, Urien's position as Pendragon has become undeniable. Until now. Now, we have the chance to put things right."

Morgen came out into the hallway. She had apparently been eavesdropping. "And now you both know when Father will die, so you can be home before he does and set that right, as well."

Arthur envied his sister's ability to always grasp what was happening, no matter how strange or complex. She looked at him and said with a hushed voice, "Please, brother, you must go back and remember to be here before Father passes. Only you can save us from this hell! Half the council has chosen Urien as Pendragon, and the other has chosen Lot. Everyone is at each other's throats."

"All will change now that we've found your brother," Taliesin assured Morgen. "I'll see to that. Go and comfort your Mother. I'll get Arthur back to where he's supposed to be, and gods willing, we shall meet again in a better time."

325

Arthur still did not understand what was happening. "Please—what do you mean, where I'm supposed to be?"

"Back before I went to Urien's court—before Scáthach cast you out. We must meld what you have learned to your younger self, and ensure you're back in Caer Leon well before your father passes. Do you understand?"

Arthur supposed he understood as well as he ever would.

Morgen smiled at him. "Don't worry, brother. You will."

Arthur wished he could embrace her. "I miss you." He looked at Taliesin and glanced toward his mother. "All of you."

"I miss you, too. Terribly. But we'll be together soon." Morgen winked at Taliesin, and Arthur wondered why.

Taliesin looked Arthur in the eyes. "Listen to me very carefully. Do you see this?" He held up a chunk of crystal.

"I do."

"Look inside. I want you to imagine yourself standing within it, as if you were inside a fortress made of glass. Can you do that?"

"I think so."

"Try."

Arthur stared into the center of the crystal, as deep within its facets as he could see, and imagined himself inside. He stared, unblinking, until he felt as if he were drifting into a cave of clear stone, flooded with light. The facets grew as large as fortress walls, filled with scenes of places and people he knew. He floated from one scene to another, too fascinated to be frightened, in what felt like an eternity of dreams.

Had it been a minute or a year when he saw Taliesin's face gazing down at him from above, beckoning...saying something?

Arthur felt himself being pulled out of his dream, waking, forming, then standing within the belly of the mountain once more. "Taliesin?" he whispered in the dark. "Are you there?"

"I am. And if I've succeeded in this endeavor, I'll be departing for Urien's court tomorrow."

Arthur felt shocked. "You're going back to Urien's court? Why would you do that? You're needed in Caer Leon—my mother and sister—"

"Not now, boy! For the first time!"

"What do you mean?" At last, as Morgen had promised, it dawned on him. "Are you saying you've taken us to a day that has already passed?"

"I believe I have."

"Have you not done this before?" Arthur felt an icy apprehension creep into his body.

"I've done it many times as an observer, but I've only melded a few times." The crystal in Taliesin's hand began to glow as if the sun were rising from within its facets, warming the mountain corridor with a summer glow. "Come, we must find our bodies and wait until they go to sleep."

"What do you mean, find our bodies?" Arthur grabbed his arm. "What are these?" He thumped his chest in alarm. "Do we not have bodies?"

Taliesin chuckled. "We do. The flesh body and the breath body."

"Which ones are these?"

"These are our breath bodies."

Arthur's confusion mounted. "Then how can I pinch myself?"

"Because when you're in your breath body, it doesn't feel like your breath body. It feels like your flesh body. This is the body you take to the Summerlands with you. It's also the body you shadow-walk with. Which is what we're doing."

It sounded simple enough, but with each of Taliesin's answers, Arthur's questions doubled. "Can we be seen?"

Taliesin paused. "By those with eyes to see, we can. But that's rare. Your sister is such a one. And I suspect Scáthach has gained such vision, and perhaps those she's chosen to train in such arts. But we aren't going to the fortress until after dark. The idea is not to be seen, but rather to meld."

"How do we do that?"

"We simply wait for our bodies to go to sleep, and then lay down into them. All we know now will meld with all we knew before. Though, truly, there is no before. Not really."

Arthur's head hurt.

They soon reached the fortress. Rather than pulling at the gate, Taliesin simply walked through it. Arthur followed and laughed with delight as the gate passed through his body. "Wait—can we fly?"

Taliesin looked back at him with a cocked eyebrow and a smirk. "I don't know. Can you?"

Arthur closed his eyes and imagined himself rising up, as if floating to the surface of a lake. Soon, he was rising into the air. He let loose a hoot of joy, which inspired Taliesin to join him above the combat ring. "I suppose we may as well enjoy ourselves until dark."

"Until dark? Why not longer? Can't you keep taking us back to the same moment?"

"It's not quite as easy as it sounds." Taliesin looked at him with dismay.

Arthur laughed. "Easy? It doesn't sound easy at all! Who else can do such things?"

"By such things, do you mean travel to moments in the past? Or travel in the breath body?"

"Both!" Arthur's glee had reached a point where he could scarcely withstand the surges of happiness rushing through him. He soared out over the ocean, reveling in the feeling of weightlessness. "It's so beautiful!"

Taliesin stayed by his side. "I travel nightly in my breath body, but moving back and forth in time, with someone else, no less, is a taxing task." He motioned toward a cliff up the coast. "Follow me. Keep your eyes on our destination and think of being there. Don't doubt yourself or you'll sink."

Arthur followed him along the coast toward the cliff, doing his best to stay confident. A waterfall poured over the edge of its jutting black-green jaw, and Taliesin alighted just beside it and sat down on a ridge where Arthur joined him. The sun was setting, casting its glorious death throes of orange and pink across the waves.

"You've made many life-changing decisions since I left you," Taliesin said to him.

"I was a fool for doubting you," Arthur volunteered immediately. "I thought you'd forsaken me for Urien. And Scáthach cast me out for it."

Taliesin nodded. "Yet, you'd not be here with me now if that hadn't happened."

"I suppose not." Arthur considered what he had learned over the past few moons. "And I wouldn't have explored the paintings of the Great Chamber, or spent so many days and nights alone." He shook his head. "I'd never been truly alone before. As children, Morgen was always by my side. Then came endless teachers, advisors, training with my father's men…" He paused. "I discovered a quiet voice inside me I'd never heard before."

"So, your choice has served you well."

"I believe it has."

Taliesin smiled. "The truth is, all versions of our self contribute to our wisdom; most especially the ones that make what seem to be grave mistakes. By melding, you can take this knowledge back to your younger self to enrich your choices."

Arthur's mind teemed with the implications of such power. "This is far more valuable than any combat training. To be able to go into every battle knowing you can return to the day before knowing the outcome? It would turn every loss into a victory!"

Taliesin held up a hand. "I'm not finished. Though I possess such power, wielding it is taxing on both mind and body. When you wake, you'll have knowledge your mind won't know what to do with—you'll think you dreamed not only this conversation, but the death of your father and all that you saw within the mountain as well. Once you meld, your memory of me possessing this power shall seem a silly child's notion. And why? Because a man cannot make sense of more than one story of his past and future, let alone more than one version of himself. Your mind must be melted down and forged anew to master this art. I've struggled many years at it, and still I'm unsure of how many times I've melded. All I know, is my desire to master it has been an ongoing endeavor since Amergin first trained me in the art, so I'm confident I'll continue to at least attempt to send my wiser selves back to my younger. Who knows? I may have melded a thousand versions of myself and only remember a handful of them, but I trust I've gained the benefit of their knowledge."

Arthur felt overwhelmed. "Is it possible you've taken me back to my younger self before?"

Taliesin shrugged. "It's possible. Or, perhaps you've learned to do so yourself, and you don't need my help anymore."

Arthur shook his head. "Stop, no more. I can't…"

Taliesin chuckled. "Let's just manage this meld for now. If I'm worth anything as your advisor, I'll help you recall your 'dreams' in the morning, and you'll remember some of what's happened. If nothing else, I trust you'll wake up without the feeling that I'm going off to Urien to betray you."

"I'm so sorry," Arthur apologized, realizing he had not done so yet. "I should never have doubted you."

Taliesin nodded. "And I should have reassured you before departing, which I won't forget to do this time. Shall we go?"

Arthur felt overwhelmed by the prospect of losing his memories. "I'm afraid to do this."

"Good! You should be!" Taliesin said, standing up. "Engaging great forces should never be undertaken lightly, but nothing worth having comes without risk."

Arthur stood up beside him.

"Now, remember—no doubt."

Arthur nodded.

Taliesin soared off the edge of the cliff like a great eagle and Arthur followed, praying when he woke, he would at least remember the spectacular flight they had shared.

Taliesin woke the following morning having dreamt vividly of Uthyr's death. He knew now, after many years of practice, which dreams were the result of melding, and which were merely the processing of the day's events. This dream was decidedly the former. He took care not to move or let the outside world intrude, waiting with the silent patience of a fisherman for a wisp of the dream to glide near enough for him to catch. He was soon rewarded with a flash of Uthyr's bedchamber, and quickly reeled it in. The dream succumbed, slowly revealing its details, one memory triggering another, until he was able to piece together all that had happened before the meld.

Gawyr had come to Urien's court with news of Arthur's disappearance. Taliesin had returned with him to Dun Scáthach to search for the boy, but with no luck. They soon determined the mountain must have claimed him. Arhianna had taken responsibility. "This is my fault," she had told him. "I cast him out for his ingratitude, hoping to teach him humility. I knew he had the shelter of the mountain and good hunting along the river, so I didn't worry about him. I thought being on his own would make him stronger, as it did me."

"And so it did!" Gawyr had blurted, coming to her defense. "This isn't your fault, Mistress. I told that boy not to go into the side passages—even saved him from them once—but I'd bet my beard that's exactly what he's gone and done!"

Arhianna had gone to the Great Chamber to determine the truth of this and come back with affirmation. "He must be somewhere in the Yet to Come. If he had gone to Days Passed, we would know it."

There was nothing they could do but wait for Arthur to emerge.

Taliesin then remembered traveling to Ynys Wydryn to seek help from Nimue and inform Morgen of her brother's disappearance. The three of them had united forces and searched for Arthur in the Shadows, attempting to discover where he had gone in the Yet to Come. Though he and Nimue were the more experienced shadow-walkers, it was Morgen who came out of trance and said emphatically, "Arthur will appear the night my father dies."

Relieved, he and Morgen had returned to Caer Leon to prepare for the fateful night. He had taken the opportunity to teach Morgen about melding, and how he planned to take Arthur back to Days Passed.

"There are special dreams that mark a melding. You'll know when you have one. They feel different than other dreams. It may be in Yet to Come or in Days Passed. Regardless, your dream marks the moment when the circle began, and the moment you wake is when the circle ends. To harvest the knowledge of a melding, you must connect the two points, which could be very difficult, depending on how many years lie between them."

"This won't be difficult, then," Morgen had assured him. "Father doesn't have much time. Arthur will soon return, and you can take him back to Days Passed. Then all will be well, isn't that right, Master Taliesin?"

She had absorbed everything with a comprehension that thrilled him to be her father. "You are a wonder, Child." He had not been able to resist kissing her forehead. "Take care until we meet again."

CHAPTER THIRTY-FIVE
The Black Star

Arhianna tossed in her sleep, dreaming her baby lay next to the pool on the ledge outside her chamber. The poor thing was naked and wailing, screaming her little lungs out. She ran out to rescue her, but, as always, a sea eagle swooped down and snatched her baby up in its talons before she could reach her.

Arhianna woke up with a gasp, heart thundering. She kicked off her wolfskin, sat up, and rubbed her face. In defiance of the helplessness she felt, she ran out onto the ledge and scooped her imaginary child up in her arms, acting out a victory. She looked up into the night sky, almost expecting to see the sea eagle with its talons outstretched, but the sky held nothing but the moon and stars.

The torture of such dreams had increased since Arthur's arrival, his presence being a constant reminder that her daughter lived. Her mind swam with curiosity. *What is she like? Does she still have dark hair? Is she thin, plump, muscular? Short, tall? What does she like to do? Does she like to sing and dance? Ride horses? Swim? What does her laugh sound like? Is she a good shot with a bow? Can she spear a fish?*

She had learned much without having to ask, for Arthur spoke of his sister often. Many times, Arhianna considered accepting his invitation to return to Caer Leon. *Just to see her grown. Just once.* And then, as quickly as the thought would enter her mind, she would decide against it. This shuffle had happened nearly daily, moon after moon, slowly driving her mad over the past year, but she let no one see her turmoil—least of all, Arthur.

Now, however, his year of training was nearly finished, and she felt hopeful that with his absence, she might again be able to put her daughter out of her mind.

The wind picked up, disturbing her thoughts. She felt it change direction. The temperature dropped, and her every hair stood on end. She felt compelled to look down into the pool. Instead of her own reflection, she saw Morrigan's face staring back at her, eyes glowing red in the night.

She watched the moon move through its phases three times over Morrigan's head. Then a pack of wolves broke through her reflection, tearing and ripping at a kill, blood on their jaws and red flesh in their teeth. When they stepped away, she saw their quarry was neither deer nor boar, but Uthyr's red and gold standard, torn to shreds.

Bring the Young Stag. The time has come.

Morrigan's message was clear. *Uthyr will be dead in three moons. Arthur must be initiated.* Arhianna looked east for evidence of the dawn, but saw none. It would be a few hours before the rest of the fortress awoke.

She cupped her hands to take a drink from the pool, and yet another face greeted her. *Gareth?* Heart in her throat, she seized her chance, desperately trying to read the words on his lips, but the ripples on the water made it impossible. To her despair, he faded away, until all she could see was her own horrified reflection and the stars overhead.

No! She sat back, defeated. This was not the first time Gareth's face had appeared to her in the pool, but it was ever the same—she simply could not determine where he was, or read the message he was clearly trying to get to her.

Where are you, brother? She put her head in her hands and calmed herself. *He lives. Take comfort in that. He lives. You'll find him.* She felt glad of Morrigan's summons to the Borderlands. She could tell Setanta of her visions and see if he had yet discovered who had led the attack on Mynyth Aur, as he had promised. She thought of his parting words to her and felt a thrill.

"I'd do anything for you, but revenge is something I'm especially equipped to deliver. Perhaps, if I can bring your brother home, you'll at last give me what I want."

"And what is that, exactly?" she had asked, expecting their usual sexual banter.

To her shock, he leaned down and whispered in her ear, "Your heart." He had touched her with a tenderness he had never shown before and walked away with a wounded smile that left her stunned and speechless.

She had thought of that moment many times, reliving the emotions he had stirred in her heart. *But it's not to be,* she told herself, dismissing the idea once more. She pushed him from her mind, stood up and stretched her cramped legs, knowing she would sleep no more that night.

333

She went to the hall for a cup of broth and waited for the warriors to rise, watching the fire burn. Arthur was the first one to show up, and she smiled at the perfection of his timing. "Good morning, Arthur. Sit with me."

Arthur did as she asked, brow furrowed. "Is something wrong, Mistress?"

Arhianna shook her head. "Nothing's wrong, so much as changed. I dreamt of your father's death last night."

"Did you?" Arthur raised his brows. "So did I, but I often do."

Arhianna felt intrigued. "Tell me of your dream."

"Very well," Arthur agreed, leaning over toward the fire to ladle himself a cup of broth. "It's always the same. We speak on his deathbed, I dress him in his armor, and then he departs with Arawn through a golden door."

"Always the very same dream?"

"All but the conversation. That changes each time. We speak of many things."

Arhianna felt encouraged by Arthur's reverence for his dreams, as well as the clear counsel he appeared to be receiving from his father's spirit. "This is good, Arthur. A king must heed his dreams well. They tell him things no advisor can impart."

Arthur chuckled. "That's nearly word for word what Taliesin says whenever I mention a dream to him." He looked out of the hall toward the brightening sky. "He should be back soon. His year in Urien's court is almost over."

Arhianna nodded. "I know. So, we don't have much time. I wish to present you to Morrigan before he arrives. Don your finest clothes and meet me by the bridge."

Arthur did as Scáthach had instructed and went to meet her at the edge of the bridge, every nerve pulsing with anticipation. *What does she mean, present me to Morrigan? Must be a ritual of some kind.* The warriors whistled at Arthur as he walked through the ring, asking him where he was going, but Gawyr growled at them and told them to get back to training.

Scáthach gave him a nod of approval when he arrived. She, too, had donned her finest. He admired the polished piece of amber set into the gold brooch she had pinned her fur cloak with. It was enormous and rivaled the ones his father had given his mother. She had also brought her best bow and quiver, and a long spear with a decorated blade.

"Well done. Now, you look like the son of Igerna."

Arthur smiled. "She does have a weakness for fine clothes." He felt intrigued about his fierce Mistress' relationship with his mother. He knew they had met as young women, and that Scáthach had even lived in his grandfather's home for a time, but he knew nothing beyond that. Since arriving at the fortress, he had longed to inquire about their unlikely friendship, but the two of them had never been alone together—not until now. He resolved to ask.

Scáthach led him over the bridge and down through the Guard's Cave. She picked up a torch, and, to Arthur's shock, it burst into flame.

"How did you do that?"

"Do what?"

"Light the torch."

"Ah." She glanced back at him. "I'm a Firebrand."

"What does that mean? You can control fire?"

"I can. You've not noticed before?"

"I'm ashamed to say I haven't." Arthur's respect for her doubled.

"I don't make a show of it."

They passed through the Hall of Heroes and then began the long descent. "How did you and my mother meet, if I might ask?"

"We met in Calleva, at a merchant's shop. Your mother was eyeing some very fine silk."

Arthur laughed. "That sounds like her. But not like you. What were you doing there?"

Scáthach paused. "The merchant knew my father well. I needed lodging for the night."

"Ah."

"Your grandfather was intent on buying a sword. He insisted on a blade of the highest quality, and the merchant brought out one forged by my brother. I took the opportunity to introduce myself, and

335

your grandfather insisted I travel with them to Dumnonia. It was nearing winter, and I was a long way from home. He promised to escort me to my village in the spring."

"So, you lived there for a time."

"I did. And your mother and I became like sisters." She paused, and then said, with uncharacteristic tenderness, "I miss her."

"Come to Caer Leon, then," Arthur quickly offered. "I know she suffers from loneliness. Morgen has always been a comfort to her, but she lives at Glastonbury now."

Scáthach said nothing for a while, but then asked, "What is she like? Your sister? Taliesin says she's a wonder."

"Oh, she is!" Arthur felt thrilled by the familiarity Scáthach was showing him. Until now, she had never said more than a few words to him, and those were typically orders or chastisements for something he had done wrong in the training ring. "Morgen's just about the cleverest person I've ever known. Sometimes I think she knows as much as Taliesin. I don't know if she can summon fire, like you, but she can certainly make it move and dance. She used to make the candles in our room dance."

"Is that so?"

Arthur enjoyed speaking of his sister. It made him feel close to her. "It is. And sometimes I think she can breathe underwater. She can certainly stay under longer than anyone I've ever met."

"So, she's both water and fire blessed."

"She also knows what animals are thinking, or, at least, that's what she's told me. Sometimes, she dreams of things before they happen. Oh! And she knows how to use every herb and plant there is—she says she can feel what they're good for, if that makes sense."

"It does." Scáthach remained silent a while. "I would like to meet her."

"Then it's settled—you must come back to Caer Leon with me. My mother would be so glad of a visit, and you can meet my sister. I'll fetch her from Glastonbury. Truly, Mistress—it would be such an honor." Arthur hoped she would consent. There were many reasons he desired this, some he recognized as selfish; not only would it please his mother and impress his father, but returning home with such a renowned warrior was sure to strengthen his standing among the council.

"I'll consider it," she said as they reached the Great Chamber. "We'll stop here a while. I wish to make an offering."

As the torchlight illuminated the paintings on the cavern walls, a flood of memories assailed Arthur's mind. He felt so overwhelmed by the images rushing in, he nearly crumpled to the ground. Scáthach did not notice. She had gone to the sarcophagus of Scáthach the First to light a candle. This triggered a vivid recollection of lighting a candle himself, as if he had suddenly remembered a dream from the night before. He, too, felt compelled to make an offering. Once Scáthach stepped away, he approached the tomb and began laying his possessions on the tomb. The images increased. "This has all happened before," he whispered. He walked up to the paintings on the wall and reached up to touch them, again prompting a stampede of memories. He laughed from the intensity. "I've been here before!" He called out to Scáthach. "I've touched all of these paintings…they taught me the history of the fortress." He remembered Taliesin's parting words. *"Memories shall come to you. Let them in. They are the keys to closing the circle."*

He turned to Scáthach, who had joined him at the wall. "I remember it all, now—you cast me out. I lived in the mountain for moons, mapping the passages, exploring this chamber…" He trailed off, noting the last bits of memory falling into place. "I took a side passage and found myself standing outside my father's bedchamber. Taliesin was there, and my mother and sister…" He paused. "Taliesin brought me back here—back to the day before he left for Urien's hall." The moment he said these words, his entire body and mind felt energized, as if he had just figured out the answer to an enormously complex problem. "That's why I kept dreaming of my father's death—it was the last thing that happened before we came back." He looked at Scáthach, unable to quell his satisfaction. "Gods, I've done it—I've just completed a melding!"

"Is that so?" He could tell from the look on Scáthach's face that she was impressed. "Well-done, Young Stag. Such an ability sets you apart."

Arthur felt his cheeks flush. "It was Taliesin who took me back. I couldn't have done it without him."

"Even so. It's rare to unlock memories of our travels in other realms unaided by a tonic or an object of power. You have a resilient mind. It will serve you well as king."

"I hope so," Arthur replied. "Who knows where my thoughts might wander now. I feel as if something's been unleashed within me."

"It has," Scáthach confirmed. "You must keep your wits about you." She picked up her torch. "All the more appropriate that we are making this journey. Let's go." She led the way down a passageway that wound north rather than south. On and on they marched, down into the darkness. After some time, Arthur began to smell fresh air full of salt. He could hear the sea as loudly as if he were standing on the beach. Three more twists of the passage, and they arrived at a cavern that opened a mere ten feet above the churning sea. Arthur looked over the edge, and a blast of ocean spray took his breath away. The droppings of sea gulls and tannets lay splattered across the rocks like spilled whitewash. Bones peeked at him from between dark rocks as the sea's veil of swirling foam rose and fell. *The Bay of Skulls.* Movement caught his eye, flashing silver within its black water. *What are they? Fish? Eels?* He thought he saw long, luminous tails or fins, but in the blink of an eye, they became sea foam or trails of bubbles left behind by the crashing of the water against the rocks.

"This way," Scáthach announced from somewhere deep within the cavern. He followed her voice to the dark, gaping maw of yet another chamber. Its black walls glistened like the open mouth of a great beast, salivating at the thought of prey. His body tensed. This passage was wholly unlike any of the others.

"This is the Black Star, Dun Scáthach's most powerful mystery. And her most dangerous." She held out her hand, and Arthur took it. "Whatever happens, don't let go of my hand. Do you understand?"

Arthur wanted to ask what might happen if he did but decided against it. "I do."

Scáthach muttered praise for Morrigan and incantations for protection, invoking the Great Mother and other beings he had never heard of, and then she looked over at him. "Now."

Before he could respond, she pulled him into thick blackness. The chaos that followed threw him into a state of utter confusion. Patterns such as he had seen women weave or embroider swirled

338

around him while his body felt as if it were being invaded by a thousand insects, deconstructing him piece by piece, as if he were made of a million tiny little stars or grains of sand. He tried crying out, but nothing came from his mouth. After what felt like a lifetime in a moment, he sensed himself being reconstructed, and then, as quickly as the overwhelming sensations had seized him, they stopped.

CHAPTER THIRTY-SIX
The Borderlands

Arthur stood at the mouth of a cave, on the edge of a green land with a type of sunlight he had never seen before. Either that, or it was the quality of the colors themselves—so vivid and luminous that they somehow seemed "more" than themselves, like jewels; making him feel as if he had never truly beheld blue or green before in his life. Dizzy, he fell to his knees and vomited until he had emptied the contents of his stomach.

"It will pass," Scáthach assured him.

Arthur took a deep breath, waited for the dizziness to subside, and stood up. Scáthach now stood outside the cave, but much changed. He marveled at her enormous black wings arching up over her head. "You have wings," he croaked.

"I do."

His tongue felt heavy, so enraptured was he by the sight. "Where are we?"

"At the edge of Knockma, where Morrigan grazes her cattle. There's a river nearby, and across that are the Borderlands, where her army is camped. I'm taking you to see her."

"*The* Morrigan?"

"A wise future king would seek her favor."

"Yes, of course." Arthur did not know how he would do so, but he would try his best.

"Can you walk yet?"

He felt weak in the knees, but he refused to admit it. "I can."

"Good. Follow me." She climbed to the top of a hill offering a long view of the valley below. Green foothills dotted with shrubs and trees led to a chain of stark mountains. "See that yellow waste to the right of the foothills?"

Arthur spied it quickly. "Looks like the Plain of Misfortune."

"It is. You can reach the Borderlands by way of the plain as well, but the risks far surpass those of the Black Star if you know how to use it."

"They don't call it the Plain of Misfortune for nothing, I suppose."

"They don't. It can't be mapped. It shifts and changes constantly, like the sea. You can wander out there forever. And if that weren't

340

enough, you have the cursed Plain Wraiths to deal with." She pointed toward an encampment nestled between the foothills and the waste. "That's where we're headed. If we become separated, keep heading in that direction." Her statement alarmed Arthur, but before he could ask her how such a thing might happen, she took off down the hill. Arthur followed as closely as he could, his knees occasionally giving out. He felt grateful she walked ahead of him. He did not want her to see him stumble.

They soon came to a river, flanked on both sides by a vibrant forest with a verdant carpet of ferns and shrubs, much thicker on the side they stood upon than the other. "This river marks the border of Knockma." She pointed to the other side. "Across it are the Borderlands. Once we cross the river, we need to hurry but move as quietly as possible. The Borderlands are home to all manner of creatures of mixed repute. I'd rather not deal with any of them, if we can help it, but we may not have a choice."

Arthur nodded. "Understood."

They found a shallow place to cross the river. Once on the other side, Scáthach began to run with the speed and silence of a deer. Arthur kept up, albeit without the same grace. They had not run long before he began to feel as if they were being watched. He glanced in all directions, eyeing their surroundings, but spotted no one. He suspected it might have been his imagination until they reached an open field and a rider broke from the treeline, headed straight for them. Arthur had an arrow fitted in his bow and was just about to let it fly when Scáthach gripped his arm. "Wait. I think I know this rider."

Arthur kept his arrow pointed toward the heart of their possible enemy as he approached, but soon Scáthach confirmed what she had suspected. "Put your weapon away. He's a friend."

The rider stopped a few feet from them, grinning down at Scáthach. He was broad-shouldered with an impressive build and a thick, dark beard. He looked exceptionally familiar to Arthur. *I've met him before. Where? My father's council?* He stared at the man, unable to recall how he knew him.

"You've been followed," the man announced, nodding toward the forest. Arthur looked behind them but saw no one.

"We have," Scáthach confirmed. "You're a welcome sight."

Arthur noticed how the rider's face lit up at Scáthach's compliment.

"As are you," the rider answered. "Welcome back, Arhianna. Or, should I say, Mistress Scáthach? I like the hair."

Arthur did not like the familiar tone of the man's voice and expected Scáthach to rebuke him, but she did not seem to mind.

"Scáthach will do."

"Scáthach it is, then." The rider winked at her and dismounted. Arthur felt dismayed to see he was a full head taller and a few shoulders wider than him.

"This is my apprentice, Arthur, son of Uthyr Pendragon," she said, motioning toward him. "Arthur, this is the great Cú Chulainn."

The moment she spoke the old hero's name, his memory of Cú Chulainn crossing the bridge at the fortress flooded the space his mind had so desperately been trying to fill. *But Cú Chulainn died long ago. Is the Black Star a portal through time?* He looked to Scáthach for an explanation. "Have we traveled to Days Passed?"

"No," she told him. "I rescued Cú Chulainn from the Lake of the Dead. He commands Morrigan's army now."

Arthur found this even more intriguing but asked no more questions. *I'll save them for later.* He walked behind the pair, listening to Cú Chulainn tell Scáthach all that had happened since they had last seen one another. Arthur did not like the familiar way he touched her.

As they exited the forest and ventured into open land, Cú Chulainn turned around and addressed him directly for the first time. "You must watch yourself here, Arthur. These lands are open to all, which means a good many cutthroats, thieves, spies and assassins roam these hills and forests. Someone surely knows who you are. You'd be a prize worth delivering to the court of Finbheara."

"Finbheara?" Arthur had never heard of this king.

"King of Knockma. Though most agree his queen is more formidable."

Scáthach nodded in agreement. "She's not to be crossed, that one."

"Why do you train here, so close to such neighbors?"

"These lands belong to Morrigan," Scáthach answered. "She'll never give them up. Besides, there's no better place to train an army.

342

Wide open plains for combat, chariot and cavalry drills, a constant source of fresh water from the river, thick forests for hunting and wood. An army must be fed, as well as trained. And they stay forever young. That's reason enough on its own."

"But trained for what? For whom?"

Cú Chulainn looked at him again and scowled. "To defend our people from the hordes of the White Dragon, of course!"

"For Brython?" Arthur did not understand. "But then why has Morrigan not pledged her forces to my father?"

Scáthach answered for him, "Morrigan fights for kings who have married the land, in accordance with the Old Ways—kings who have pledged themselves, body and soul, to honoring the Great Mother and all her creatures, both those who live above the hills and those who live within them. All are her children, and she loves them equally."

"And my father has not."

"No. Nor his brother before him."

"My father has always had a druid advisor," Arthur offered meekly.

"An advisor is not an oath."

Arthur knew now why Taliesin had taken him to train at Dun Scáthach and why Scáthach was now taking him to Morrigan. *They want me to marry the land; to make the oath of the ancient kings.*

The trail narrowed, forcing them to walk single file. Arthur ended up behind Cú Chulainn's horse, pondering his loyalties as the trail wound through forest and along a river.

His mother had always honored both the Old Ways and Christ's teachings, but in her own way. "If the Lord is one of compassion and pure love, as the priests say, then his word is a bridge between all beliefs and all people. He did not come to set us against one another." She believed Christ's message had been twisted by the church to maintain its power. "I know a thing or two about how men create and hold on to power, Arthur. And I promise you, if the church were to preach a message of tolerance and seeking your own path to the Divine, we would have no need of its priests or bishops and the church would crumble. And how do they ensure they grow in power? By destroying all other paths and all other gods! Most cruel of all, they work to burn away the path to the Great Mother by insisting

343

women have no place as spiritual leaders, or in divine rites! Honored priestesses, once revered for their prophetic and healing powers, have been pushed to the shadows and hunted as heretics by a church of men jealous of their power. And, perhaps most ridiculous of all, they insist God is male! God is most certainly both male and female, or neither. But men cannot help but corrupt the message of Spirit. In that, the church is correct—we are all sinners, subject to selfishness and greed."

Arthur and Morgen had often discussed these things and believed as their mother did, weaving together the ancient beliefs of their people with the promise of Christ. They saw no reason they could not inform one another. *So surely, there's a way for me to uphold oaths to both the Lord and the Great Mother. We honor both our father and mother, after all, do we not?*

After crossing the river, the terrain grew steeper and rockier, until they came to an opening in the side of a mountain. Cú Chulainn raised his right hand, and they stopped. He turned around. "She's waiting."

Scáthach motioned to Arthur. "Come."

The cavern was much like the Black Star: wet and cold, with a darkness the eyes could not penetrate. Arthur hesitated. "Is this going to be like the last time?"

A voice issued from within, so loud, it seemed its owner stood in front of them. "Enter without fear, son of Igerna."

Scáthach took a torch from a sconce in the rock and waved her hand over it, causing it to burst into flames. "Come."

Arthur followed Scáthach into the mountain. The flames of her torch danced erratically on the dark, glistening passageway, casting disorienting shadows all around them. Sometimes, from the corner of his eye, he thought he saw faces staring at him, but upon turning his head to look at them directly, they disappeared.

Soon the light within the passage increased. Arthur saw a glow from a chamber up ahead. They entered to find a formidable woman, dressed for battle, leaning over a long table, studying what lay across it. Behind her stood a massive throne constructed of bones, flanked with torches. Again, Arthur felt the weight of eyes upon him and looked up. Several ravens perched overhead, and every one of them had a black eye pinned on him. When he looked back toward

344

Morrigan, he saw she had her eyes on him as well. Only, they resembled fire, not coal. He felt his heart lodge in his throat, and instinctively dropped to one knee. "My queen," he said, not daring to look in her eyes.

"Stand. I want to look at you."

Arthur stood, not knowing if he should look at her or if that might be regarded as disrespectful. He opted to keep his eyes lowered. He felt Morrigan's hand graze his shoulders as she circled him.

"Look at me," she commanded.

Arthur looked up to see Morrigan towering over him and stifled a gasp of amazement. The top of his head came no higher than her ribs. He had not believed the stories the warriors told around the fire at night about their visions of Morrigan on the battlefield, but there she was, exactly as they had described her—tall as a giant, hair as blue-black as raven feathers, and eyes flashing like fire-filled gems.

"You appear to be strong. Look in my eyes, and do not look away."

Arthur met her fiery gaze and felt her dive inside him with ruthless force, surveying his heart like a hawk surveying a field. The things he felt ashamed of tried scurrying for cover like rabbits and mice, but they could not hide from her. She dove in for the kill.

"You have too much doubt in your heart and too little passion. A man without conviction cannot win battles." Morrigan turned and addressed Scáthach. "He is not ready."

Arthur felt as if his clothing had been torn from him. Whatever fury had been missing in his heart now rose up like a bear on hind legs. "I am ready!" he thundered. "Please, don't dismiss me so quickly, Great Morrigan—there's nothing I wouldn't do for my people."

Morrigan turned, a smirk on her face that curdled Arthur's stomach, but he met her gaze with courage. He had spoken true. He would stand by his words.

"You must prove it, then, young Arthur," Morrigan said. "You shall start by fighting Cú Chulainn, tomorrow, at dawn. In the central practice ring."

Arthur looked at Scáthach. Worry creased her brow. *She doesn't believe in me.* His heart sank, but he would not allow himself to feel defeated. He summoned his strength, more determined than ever to prove himself worthy of his father's title and worthy of being Lady Brython's protector.

"Come, Arthur," Scáthach said, leading him by the arm. The moment they were out of the cavern, she turned to him. "Do you have any idea how fierce a fighter Cú Chulainn is?"

Arthur began to feel the weight of what he had gotten himself into. "Do you think it impossible that I should beat him?"

Scáthach hesitated.

Arthur's pride could not withstand it. "That's enough of an answer." He marched off down the trail in the direction of the camp he could see below. It stretched on for miles, tents and settlements spread out along the foot of the mountain to the edge of the plains. Green strips of trees wound along the same edge, indicating where the river flowed.

"Arthur! Wait!" Scáthach ran up beside him. "The truth is, no one can beat him. She simply means to test your courage."

"Then I shall face him and fight until I can no longer stand."

Scáthach nodded. "That's exactly what you should do."

"Right, then. Leave me be for now." Arthur quickened his pace, eager to put some space between them.

Arhianna rushed to Setanta's hall to meet him, anxious for news. At last, she could ask him what she had been aching to ask since arriving. She walked through the large open doors and quickly spied his wide shoulders and dark curls. He sat near the fire trench, sharpening a dagger, occasionally reaching over to quench his thirst from a large mug of ale. She walked over to him and touched him on the shoulder. He turned and gave her a look she had often seen her father give her mother—so like her father, in fact, that her throat tightened. "Have you discovered who attacked Mynyth Aur?"

Setanta sheathed his dagger and turned toward her, pulling a nearby stool over for her to sit on. "For months, I heard nothing, but recently, coins like this have made their way into dice and card games all over the Borderlands." He held up a gold coin bearing the sigil of the Oaks, placed it o the table, and slid it in her direction.

Arhianna picked up the coin. "That's my father's sigil."

"I know. I remember seeing it on his shield."

Arhianna felt a jolt. "So, someone hired cutthroats from the Borderlands to attack Mynyth Aur. Someone who knew there would be gold to pay them with. But who?"

"No one knows. Not yet, anyway. But I'll find out. Someone always talks."

"I thought you'd have found that out by now! My brother's a *slave*, Setanta! It's been a whole year!" Arhianna began to feel helpless, which always fueled her anger. "Enough of this! We must go to Morrigan!"

Cú Chulainn grabbed her hand. "That is the very *last* thing we must do—Morrigan won't risk war with Knockma over a handful of slaves, brother or not! Such are the spoils of war. It's the way of things. You know, as well as I, that's exactly what she'd say. Besides, the Sídhe raid your world all the time. It's been going on since they were sent into the hills, hundreds of years ago."

"Well, I won't stand for it!" Arhianna seethed. "Will you help me or not?"

"Will you please calm down? I can't make a move until I know for certain who hired these men. I promise you I'll find out, but you must be patient."

Arhianna's hatred of the Sídhe thickened like black tar. "If you can find my brother, we can find out who did it. Don't you have a spy who's welcome in the court of Knockma? Someone who can look for him?"

"Funny you should ask. I already have someone in mind." He called to a man on the other side of the hall who came and sat with them. He was clearly a half-breed, and quite a stunning one. He had hair of white gold and luminous skin, but unlike most Sídhe, who were slight in body, he possessed a robust build, much like Setanta's.

"This is Elodir," Setanta announced. "He can charm the words out of any woman he beds, and, the women he beds are mostly Sídhe. They, in turn, can charm the words out of any man *they* bed, and they notoriously bed quite a few. You get the idea."

Elodir looked pained. "I must admit, I've never suffered a more terrible introduction in my life."

Setanta laughed. "Apologies, my friend. But your talents serve our purpose."

Elodir clasped his perfect hands together and looked at Arhianna with a feeble smile that, nevertheless, electrified her. "My lady," he began, "how might I recognize your brother?"

Arhianna felt a glimmer of hope rise in her heart. "His name is Gareth. He was chieftain of the Oak clan of Mynyth Aur, and the most celebrated blacksmith in all of Gwynedd. If he's in Knockma, they'll surely have put him to work in a forge."

"Is he a handsome man? Gifted with beauty like you? Healthy and strong?"

Arhianna found these to be strange questions. "I suppose he is."

"Then I'll find him quickly. Such a man will surely have been urged to breed with Sídhe women."

Arhianna shuddered, thinking of how she and Taliesin were similarly tricked by Fae scheming. "Why's that?"

Elodir explained. "Half-breeds are stronger than full-blooded Fae and can move easily between realms. So, the more half-breeds they have within their clan, the better, and they're shameless in their search for opportunities. They don't prize fidelity, or even understand it. In this, they behave much like animals."

"*Most* animals," Arhianna corrected. "Foxes and wolves mate for life. So do ravens, swans and eagles."

Elodir gave her a nod of deferral. "Very true. Forgive me. I wonder, which of those animals might you be most like?" he asked in a honeyed tone.

Arhianna sharpened the barb on her tongue to answer, but Setanta beat her to it. "Fox."

Elodir clucked his tongue at Setanta, quickly redeeming himself. "Oh no, my friend. Only a fool would mistake a wolf for a fox." He met Arhianna's eyes with a piercing gaze and then raised a finger. "It's important to note not all men and women taken by the Sídhe are unwilling. Many are happy to leave the hardships of their world and are thrilled to take a Fae wife or husband. Who knows, perhaps your brother is—"

"He's not." Arhianna interjected hotly. "He has a wife and children. I pray they're still alive and with him." She turned to Cú Chulainn. "I'm so worried. It's been over a year, now!"

348

Setanta reached over and squeezed her hand to calm her. "In your world, it has, but not here. Stop worrying. If your brother and his family are in Knockma, we'll find them." He stood up, prompting Elodir to do the same. "The moment you know something, come to me, my friend—day or night."

"I will, Commander." Elodir turned to Arhianna and bent his head gracefully in her direction. "My lady."

"Lord Elodir," she responded in kind.

Once Elodir had left the hall, Setanta came and put his hands on her shoulders, looking deep into her eyes. "I swear to you, Arhianna, I'll find your brother before the snow falls, and I'll kill the man who took him—even if it was Finbheara himself. I'll do that, and anything else you ask of me."

Arhianna felt thrilled by his words. "Thank you."

He touched her cheek, sending a shiver down her body. "It's my pleasure. What good is being commander if you can't help those you love?"

His mention of love made her nervous. She averted her gaze. "I must go and find my bed. The Black Star is quite draining."

"Stay and share mine," he murmured. "Or, I can accompany you to yours, if you like."

For a moment, her whole body and soul soared with the idea, but it lasted only a moment. The black demon squatting near her heart yanked her chains, pulling her back down. "I think not." She gave him a sad smile and rushed away.

Arthur ate but could not sleep. Instead, he went out into the camp, seeking to learn as much as he could about Morrigan's army. He wandered through several circles of warriors before a muscular, grisly man with a bald head and a scar across his face called out and beckoned him over. "Who're you, lad?"

"Arthur."

"Fight like a bear, then, do you?"

Arthur did not like the look in the man's eyes. "I'd dare not flatter myself by saying so."

The man grinned. "I'm Hywel. Sit down. Have a drink. Seems you've strayed into the Borderlands, like I did at your age." He took a swig of whatever was in his goatskin. "Best thing I ever did." He winked and laughed. The men around him laughed as well. "You hear all those stories, when you're a wee bairn, about how horrible it would be if you strayed into the land of the Sídhe, but it's all lies. I'd not go back even if I could."

"So, you had no family, then? No wife?"

Hywel laughed again, even louder. "Oh, but I did, lad! Why do you think I'm so happy? Never had to hear her nagging at me ever again!"

Arthur did not care much for the man or his companions, but they were drunk, and he knew words flowed free as a wellspring from the mouth of a drunken man. "Tell me of this army."

"We fight for the Great Morrigan, lad. You, too, could earn the honor, if you've got the spirit."

"How?"

"By fightin' her best. She looks for courage! Fearlessness!"

In the dark, Arthur could not tell how far the camp stretched, but it seemed to him it was far more substantial than his father's army. "How many warriors does the Great Morrigan command? Thousands?"

"Aye, thousands. Thousands you can see, at least—there're thousands more you can't." He winked.

Arthur learned Morrigan's warriors consisted of several companies united either by blood, homeland, or fighting style. Though she had men and women among her ranks, most who fought for her were of a different race.

"Within the forests along the river are the elves. In the foothills are the Sídhefolk who've been cast out of Knockma for whatever reason—thieving, insulting the queen, refusing to obey orders—that sort of thing." The man motioned toward the mountains. "Up there, you'll find the giants and the trolls. They don't come down except when called upon. You don't want to be around when that happens."

"Why?"

"Like a damn thunderstorm! Tree limbs cracking, boulders tumbling—we've lost good men to falling trees and rocks. That's no way to die!"

350

The idea set Arthur's imagination on fire. "But they must be unrivaled in battle! I can't imagine the enemy would think to challenge them!"

"You're clearly new to these realms." Hywel handed him his wineskin.

"Why do you say that?" Arthur accepted it and took a modest swig.

"You think the enemy doesn't have giants and trolls of their own? Gods, that bloody one-eyed Woden has the most heinous giants you've ever seen! And those damn dwarves, as well! Ruthless in battle. And the Valkyries…ohhhhh, gods. They're enough to make you want to join the enemy."

One of his companions slugged him, his eyes shifting all around.

"I don't mean that, of course," he said loudly, then covered his mouth and leaned over toward Arthur. "She's got spies everywhere."

"I've got to fight Cú Chulainn tomorrow." Arthur blurted.

The man's eyebrows shot up. "You *what*?" The other men in the camp fell silent and stared at him.

"I'm to fight Cú Chulainn in the morning," Arthur repeated. "Do you have any advice?"

Hywel let out a lungful of air slowly through his lips, shaking his head. He put a hand on Arthur's shoulder. "I'm sorry, lad. You can't win that match. None of us could. There's no warrior fiercer than Cú Chulainn, except Morrigan herself. The only advantage you have is that you get to choose which weapon to fight with." Hywel paused and raised his eyebrows. "Is it to the death?"

"I don't think so." Arthur felt a jolt of fear. "I hope not."

Hywel shook his bald head. "I hope not, too. Otherwise, it's been nice knowing you, lad."

CHAPTER THIRTY-SEVEN
Wits

Before dawn, Arthur dreamt his father entered his tent. He was dressed in purple robes, his body erect and eyes bright. Arthur sat up and rubbed his eyes. "Father? What are you doing here?"

His father unsheathed his sword, smiled, and laid it in Arthur's lap. Then he walked out, without a word. The moment the flap of Arthur's tent fell back in place, a bell tolled so loudly in his ears that it woke him. He jolted up in bed and saw Scáthach standing in the doorway of his tent.

"It's time. Are you ready?"

"I am," he lied, heart racing.

Scáthach led him deep into the heart of the camp. "You've learned much this past year. He won't defeat you as easily as he thinks. I suggest you choose sword. It's your strength now." She continued giving him fighting tips and bits of advice, but Arthur only half-listened. His thoughts were elsewhere.

Within a half hour, they arrived at a large combat ring, similar in size to the one at Dun Scáthach. Morrigan stood in the center, as tall and strong as a pine tree. Cú Chulainn loomed on the edge, looking like a dark mountain of death. A sizable number of warriors had gathered around the ring, and Arthur felt dismayed. *Why should they care about this fight?*

Scáthach whispered some final words of advice, and Arthur stepped into the ring.

Morrigan looked down at him. "Welcome, son of Igerna. What weapon do you choose?"

Arthur said a silent prayer and met her fiery eyes. "I choose wits," he declared, pulling his gameboard from his satchel. He held it up for all to see.

Protests erupted all around the ring, for those gathered had come to see a fight, not a chess match.

Arthur refused to be deterred. "There are more weapons in the world than sword, bow or spear!" he bellowed, hoping to bolster his position, but his words blew like dead leaves on the crowd.

Cú Chulainn laughed. "There are, lad, but none that serve you better on the battlefield!"

The crowd erupted in cheers and laughter, slapping shoulders and trading grins to the rising chant of, "Cú Chulainn! Cú Chulainn! Cú Chulainn!"

Arthur felt his stomach shrivel but stood erect, eyes pinned on Morrigan, waiting to see if she would agree to his proposal. At last, Morrigan raised her hands and the crowd hushed to hear her verdict. "Wits it is," she announced, a smile curling the corner of her mouth.

Groans of disapproval filled the air until Morrigan raised a finger and added, "but you shall use my table." She turned to the warriors at her flanks. "Go fetch it."

After a chorus of obedient nods, the men turned and pushed their way through the murmuring crowd, now busy placing wagers on who would win. Warriors who had walked away came back, interested in the match once more.

Scáthach came to Arthur's side. "Why didn't you tell me this was your plan?"

Arthur shook his head. "It wasn't, until last night. I walked through the camp and saw many of the warriors playing. That gave me the idea. I'm quite good."

"You'd better be," Scáthach murmured. "Cú Chulainn's the best player in the Borderlands."

Arthur's heart sank. He had counted on Cú Chulainn excelling only in matters of physical prowess. "He is?"

"Afraid so," Scáthach confirmed. "I imagine he's only gotten better over the years. I could never—"

Their conversation was cut short by the men returning with the table. On top of it, sat two leather pouches. The men set the table down in the center of the ring and stepped away.

Arthur ventured in for a closer look. The black squares, with their silvery sheen, looked to be made from the bog oak, and the white were so white, they were surely made from holly. The legs and sides of the table were, like most of Morrigan's furnishings, constructed of bones. Four ravens, carved of black stone, perched on the corners of the table, staring down at the board with life-like eyes of dark amber. Enchantment replaced Arthur's fear as two stumps were rolled in and set on either side of the table.

Morrigan approached the table and slid the leather bags to opposite sides. She reached in and took a single piece from each pouch, which happened to be the queen, somehow, in both cases. She set them down on the board. "As Arthur chose the weapon, Cú Chulainn shall have the first move." She motioned to the side of the table where the white queen stood, bidding Cú Chulainn sit down. He winked at Arthur and smacked him on the shoulder.

Arthur said nothing, his cheeks burning from his opponent's condescending wink. He waited for Morrigan to summon him to the other side and sat down on the stump, only to suffer more humiliation. He felt like a child at his father's banquet table, for the stump was so low the edge of the table was chest-high for him. Not so for Cú Chulainn, of course, who sat like a king across from him. Arthur ignored the laughter of the crowd, balled up his cloak and sat on it.

"Set the board," Morrigan commanded.

Cú Chulainn opened his pouch with a smirk, glancing Arthur's way, and commenced setting up his pieces. "Clever move, lad." He shook his head and chuckled. "Wits, indeed."

Arthur ignored his comments and did the same, first placing his queen in her position. He admired the piece as he reached in for another, and then noticed something astonishing—the piece began to change. Arthur blinked and widened his eyes, wondering if the light were playing tricks on him. He moved closer and watched with rapture as the piece transformed into a shockingly accurate replica of his mother.

"What are you waiting for?" Cú Chulainn asked, eyebrows raised. His pieces were nearly all in place. Cú Chulainn turned to the crowd. "Good thing this isn't a real fight. Lad'd be dead by now!"

The crowd erupted in laughter, but Arthur did not care anymore. The magic of the table and the game pieces held his full attention. Never had he seen anything so remarkable. *If there's any way to possess such a thing in the realm of the living, may I someday be so blessed.* He plunged an eager hand into his pouch, and, one by one, placed each piece on the board and watched it transform. The king became his father, of course. The bishops took the forms of Taliesin and Dubricius, flanking his parents. The knights, to his delight, became Morgen and Cai, brandishing bow and spear astride magnificent horses. In the corners, his rooks turned into the coveted hillforts of Caer Leon and Dinas Emrys. All along his front line stood

354

yet more cousins brandishing swords, some on horseback, some in war chariots. He felt transported by the scene before him, feeling the support and power of all assembled. His anger and doubt vanished, as if the sun had come out from behind storm clouds. *I can beat him.*

Scáthach ventured closer and knelt beside him, inspecting the pieces closely, squinting at each one with deep fascination. "Who is that?" she asked, pointing to Morgen.

"My sister," he announced proudly.

"Ah," Scáthach's brows raised. "So that's your beloved sister."

Arthur could tell Scáthach longed to pick the piece up and inspect it. He wanted to, as well, but feared moving a piece, in any way, would constitute a move. He dared not take any chances with such an important match. He looked up to find Cú Chulainn glaring at him.

"Are we playing a match, lad, or shall we all come back tomorrow?"

"Don't be cross, Setanta," Scáthach chided. "I wish to know who is on the board—on your side as well. I think we all do." Cú Chulainn seemed mollified. He told her who each of his pieces represented, looking at her with an intensity that made Arthur want to beat him even more. He focused his gaze on his opponent, willing him to remove his eyes from Scáthach's face, but they remained as fixed as the North Star. *Well, what did I expect?* He chided himself for thinking he might have had any chance of bedding her. Still, it stung his pride.

"Each move must be made within two score of heartbeats," the Morrigan declared, breaking his reverie. She rapped the table three times with her fist. "Begin."

All the warriors who had come to watch the fight seemed thoroughly placated now and crowded in closer, mumbling and whispering. Arthur turned his attention wholly on the match, knowing he could not afford any mistakes.

Cú Chulainn did not surprise him with his first move, taking the center of the board with his knight. Arthur responded in kind with Morgen, delighted to discover that when he touched her piece, he could feel her energy and counsel. He touched a few of the other pieces and felt elated to discover they all had counsel or possible strategies to suggest.

Cú Chulainn's next several moves were just as hostile, his relentless attack and first-move advantage keeping Arthur ever on the back foot. It did not help that he made comments or crushing sounds with each move, rallying the crowd. At last, Arthur could withstand no more. "Must you do that with every move? I feel as though I'm playing a child."

Cú Chulainn shrugged it off. "They came to see a fight, lad. I'm trying to entertain them." He turned his palms up and looked around with innocent eyes. As ever, the crowd cheered.

Arthur felt Scáthach's breath on his neck and a thrill rushed through him. "You're letting him shake you. Keep your thoughts where they belong."

Arthur centered himself. He was no stranger to rowdy opponents. He chided himself for letting Cú Chulainn get under his hide and resolved to not let it happen again. Now that the game had progressed, he had to concentrate. Within the next five moves, he would know what kind of game his opponent was angling to play. He set his mind to work on creative ways to mislead him, hovering his hand over several of his game pieces for counsel. In the end, though, he took his own. He had devised many mid-game dances, as he called them, designed for different styles of players. He had one in mind, seeing every possible move with a clarity he had experienced only a handful of times. He knew the one advantage he had was that Cú Chulainn seemed to underestimate him. Deviating from standard strategies was risky, but if Cú Chulainn took the bait, it would be a far more satisfying victory. He looked at the board, now dominated by Cú Chulainn's pieces, feeling the pressure build. At last, he moved Morgen into a position that threatened Cú Chulainn's queen, leaving him no choice but to retreat to the edge of the board or lose her. As expected, he did not make the sacrifice. Arthur set the bait with one of his knights.

It did not take Cú Chulainn long to respond. He smiled and shook his head as he took the knight with one of his pawns. Indeed, all would agree it was a bad trade, and Arthur doubted anyone in the crowd would have agreed with his move. He began setting up his attack.

After a few more pawns captured on both sides, Arthur moved his rook into place, threatening both Cú Chulainn's king and bishop, giving him no choice but to retreat and protect his king.

Then came Arthur's riskiest move thus far. Rather than protect his queen, he chose to capture Cú Chulainn's bishop. *Sorry, Mother.*

The crowd moaned in pity for him as Cú Chulainn took her. "Beautiful woman, your queen," he said with a smile, admiring the piece. "Think I'll keep this one!" The crowd laughed as he moved to put her in a pouch hanging at his waist.

"If that piece touches anything but the table, consider the game forfeit," Morrigan warned.

Cú Chulainn gave her an obedient nod and placed the piece back on the table with exaggerated delicacy.

Now, Arthur was left with a few pawns, his two bishops, Taliesin and Dubricius, his two rook hillforts, his knight, Morgen, and his father, the king. Cú Chulainn, by contrast, still had his queen, his king nestled safely between both rook-hillforts, a knight and a bishop. What he did not have, as far as Arthur could tell, was a strategy. Yet, by all accounts, he was winning, and that's what Arthur hung his shield on—that Cú Chulainn felt so assured of victory, he would let his guard down.

In his next move, Arthur checked Cú Chulainn's king, giving him no choice but to move him closer to his useless hillfort, still standing in the corner of the board behind a pawn.

Let me threaten his active rook, Morgen counseled.

That was my plan, he answered, feeling as if she could hear him, and moved her into place. He grew excited, anticipating his win, but calmed himself down. He forced himself to look at the board as his opponent would, seeking a way out of the trap he had laid, but there were no moves Cú Chulainn could make that would gain him any pieces. For the next three moves, Cú Chulainn could do nothing but shuffle his king back and forth between the two squares open to him, waiting for Arthur to make a mistake.

Arthur, however, wasted none of his moves, and soon had the situation he had been angling for. He pushed his hillfort-rook of Dinas Emrys out of the corner and onto the board, putting it face to face with Cú Chulainn's queen. As expected, Cú Chulainn used his next move to protect her.

357

Now! Morgen proclaimed, brandishing her sword atop her horse. *His rook!*

Arthur tried not to smile as he moved his sister into position and took Cú Chulainn's rook. Now, Morgen stood on the same row as his unprotected king, with Taliesin looming large in the middle of the nearly empty board. Arthur's father sat well protected by Archbishop Dubricius and the hillfort of Caer Leon, with two pawns to spare.

Cú Chulainn tried to clear a path for his hillfort, moving his pawn forward, but this, again, was a wasted move.

Arthur knew he had him. It was only a matter of time. He moved Morgen in to threaten the king, forcing another move, then positioned his rooks. Cú Chulainn counterattacked with his queen, but Arthur had planned for this. He moved Taliesin back toward his father, extinguishing the threat, and then slowly chipped away at the defenses around Cú Chulainn's king, forcing him to move where he wanted him to as he built up an impenetrable wall of defense. At last, he maneuvered Cú Chulainn into a position where the rook-hillfort of Caer Leon threatened him head-on, and Morgen stood ready to take him from the squares on either side of him.

"He's done it," Scáthach murmured after a moment.

Victorious, Arthur beamed up at her from his stump, no longer feeling like a child.

Morrigan, too, looked pleased. She held up her hands and announced, "Arthur has won the match. He has proven himself worthy of training with the Warriors of the Borderlands."

The sun was eclipsed by a raucous storm of warriors crowding in around Arthur, congratulating and smacking him on the back while needling Cú Chulainn over his loss. Hywel and the men he had shared ale with the night before cheered the loudest. "Smart lad, goin' for the table instead of the sword!"

"Well done, lad! Well done!"

When, at last, the men dispersed, a smiling Cú Chulainn stood up and offered his arm. "Well done, indeed, lad. I'm impressed."

Arthur stood up and clasped his arm, shocked by the warrior's grace in defeat.

"You've got a king's head for strategy. That's good. Now, we just need to teach you to fight like one."

Scáthach stood by his side, smiling up at Cú Chulainn with a look in her eyes that Arthur had longed to win for himself. She turned her gaze toward him. "I'm so proud of you!" She put a hand on his shoulder like his mother would, wounding him further. "A king who thinks more than he fights brings more men home to their families. But he must still be a terror on the battlefield. Tomorrow, we train."

Arhianna felt surprised to discover Cú Chulainn had ordered a feast to be held in her honor that night to celebrate her return as the formidable new mistress of Dun Scáthach. Cheers erupted as she and Arthur entered the hall, loud enough to shake the rafters. Arhianna smiled and squeezed Arthur's shoulder. "Such accolades shall be yours someday, I'm certain of it."

Cú Chulainn stood up and held his drinking horn high, prompting the hall to quiet down. "To the Mistress of Dun Scáthach and her clever apprentice, Arthur—first man to beat me on the board!"

The hall rumbled again with enthusiastic bellows, and Arhianna and Arthur were shown to seats of honor next to Cú Chulainn.

"You deserve such praise," Arthur said to her as they sat down. "I do hope, one day, to merit such a display of loyalty among my people."

Arhianna squeezed his hand. "I've no doubt you will, Arthur. No doubt at all."

He laughed. "I wish I felt as confident."

"Confidence will come with accomplishment," she assured him.

Friends and fellow warriors Arhianna had not seen in years came to pay their respects, never letting her see the bottom of her drinking horn, and the food was better than she had eaten in some time.

"I've never had beef this fine before," Arthur commented.

"Nor shall you again, anywhere but here," Arhianna explained. "Morrigan's cattle have full privileges to graze within Knockma. No grass is sweeter."

"Music!" Cú Chulainn bellowed. "You've eaten enough, you who can play. Get your drums and harps! It's time for song!"

A dance floor was cleared, and, to Arhianna's surprise, Arthur jumped up and joined the musicians. They launched into something lively Arthur clearly knew well. His voice shocked her with its richness. *Great Mother, the boy is full of surprises!*

"He should have been a bard," Cú Chulainn commented with a smile.

Arhianna held up a finger. "*Could* have been. But he's destined for another path. I'm convinced now, more than ever, that he's our Young Stag."

"Truly? I like the lad, but I don't see it. Not yet, at least."

His arm grazed hers as he reached for her horn to fill it. Her entire body tingled at his touch. *I've had too much ale.* "No more, thank you," she said, tucking her horn beneath her cloak.

Cú Chulainn raised his brows. "Well, if you're not going to drink, you must dance." He set the ale down, stood up, and offered her his hand.

"Oh, I don't think so—I fear I've had too much to drink."

"All the more reason to dance. It will stay the effect. Come. Do me this honor. Don't you see, everyone's looking this way. I've already suffered one terrible defeat today. Don't make me suffer another one. My pride couldn't bear it."

She had to laugh. "I imagine not." Her plan defeated, Arhianna took his hand, triggering an exaggerated show of relief from him. He led her out into the middle of the hall, guiding her through the swirling maze of dancing warriors, until the constant pain she carried with her lifted a bit, letting something she could only compare to sunshine warm a small corner of her soul.

CHAPTER THIRTY-EIGHT
Return to Caer Leon

A pallid dawn struggled through dense fog as Taliesin walked back to Urien's hall. Frost clung to every blade of grass, and no wind stirred the air. *Fitting weather for such a day.*

He found Urien in his customary morning position beside the hearth, staring into the fire. Over the past year, Taliesin had found him a wholly predictable man in every aspect of life. This was both a comfort and a worry, for Taliesin knew both the reaction and the very words Urien would have for him this morning, and they would not be pleasant ones.

"Ah! Taliesin!" Urien's brow furrowed after looking him up and down. "Have you been out all night?"

"I have."

Urien shook his head. "I don't understand why you won't sleep in the hall."

"I prefer the company of—"

Urien held up a hand. "Yes, yes, the blasted company of trees. I know."

Perhaps, I, too, have become predictable. Taliesin joined him by the fire. "Today's the last day of my year of service to you."

Urien frowned. "No, no—that cannot be."

"I'm afraid it is. It's been twelve moons since I arrived." Taliesin smiled. "I trust I've served you well."

"You have, indeed! And my hall has returned in kind, has it not?" Urien narrowed his eyes on him.

Taliesin nodded. "It has, but I must return to Caer Leon."

Urien leaned forward, his elbows on his knees, looking Taliesin in the eye. "As will I, soon enough, from what my men tell me," he said in a low voice. "When the time comes, I trust you'll support me for Pendragon? As well as help me secure Morgen for my wife? Uthyr's made it clear he wishes to unite our houses, and I've been widowed for too long now. I'm ready to marry again, and she's of the right age and breeding."

Taliesin had long ago prepared a response. "The Great Mother shall choose Uthyr's successor. I trust she'll make her will known to us all. If you are her choice, I shall indeed support you."

Urien sat back, looking as if he had smelled something foul. "What has this been, Taliesin, this past year? I suppose you feel you can congratulate yourself on keeping your promise to me, but it was all lies, wasn't it? Your ballads and poems, singing my praises in battle?"

"Not at all," Taliesin responded immediately. "You're a terror on the field. There's no one I'd rather have by my side in a battle." But his praise fell like seeds on frozen earth.

"What a fool I've been," Urien murmured, shaking his head. "I see the truth now. You bear me no loyalty at all."

The look of betrayal in Urien's eyes was the one thing Taliesin felt unprepared for. He had hoped that this time around, he had succeeded in reassuring Urien of his friendship. They had shared many laughs and conversations over the course of the past year, and his songs of praise had been in earnest. But Urien would clearly have none of it. He stood up and glowered at Taliesin, poking a finger toward his face. "Mark my words well, Bard. When Uthyr's time comes, I shall become Pendragon, and I'll remember well who bore me allegiance!" He swatted a hand in Taliesin's direction. "Leave my hall and take your empty words with you!"

Taliesin did not want to leave on such terms, but Urien gave him no choice. Though he prided himself on his ability to weave words, nothing he had rehearsed could change Urien's mood.

"I said, get out!"

Taliesin left the hall of Urien of Rheged with a heavy heart.

Upon arriving at Dun Scáthach, Taliesin felt disturbed to discover from Gawyr that Arthur and Arhianna were not there. "Where've they gone?" he worried aloud.

"Let's get you some bread and ale, and I'll tell you. You look terrible." Gawyr led the way across the bridge and into the hall, barked some orders to the kitchen maid, and motioned for Taliesin to sit down.

Taliesin settled himself near the hearth, weary from his travels. Vala flew up into the rafters, perched on one leg, and tucked her head on her back to sleep. Taliesin envied her. In his eagerness to reach

362

Dun Scáthach, he had rested no more than a few hours a night on their journey. "I need to get Arthur home as soon as possible. His father's time is nigh." *And if we don't make it back in time, this melding will have all been for nothing.*

Gawyr gave him a sympathetic nod. "Don't worry. She's taken the boy to see Morrigan. They'll be back soon. They knew you'd be coming. Why don't we tell Arvel to get the ship ready? He'll be thrilled to see you. Probably thrilled to sail home, as well."

Taliesin agreed. It would feel good to see his brother again, and he could at least busy himself with preparations for the voyage. *And, finally, get some sleep.*

Arhianna and Arthur returned within the week, as Gawyr had promised. "Ho! All hail Lady Scáthach!" he bellowed from the bridge.

Taliesin breathed a sigh of relief. With the voyage preparations finished, he had started restocking the apothecary to keep himself occupied. He abandoned the herbs he had been crushing and rushed outside to greet them.

From the look on Arhianna's face, it seemed she had not yet forgiven him. He had hoped her heart would soften by the time he returned, but the only thing softer about her was her hair. True to her word, she had not cut it. Arthur, on the other hand, grinned and embraced him. "Master Taliesin! I'm so glad to see you!"

"And I, you." Taliesin marveled at the drastic change in Arthur's appearance, finding it hard to believe only a year had passed since he had last seen him. He had grown a head taller, and his jaw had lost the softness of boyhood and now sported a full beard and mustache. Taliesin gripped Arthur's arms, which felt like rock beneath his tunic, and looked him up and down with growing satisfaction. "Gods, you're a man now!"

Arthur beamed at him and glanced toward Arhianna. "We've been training with Cú Chulainn in the Borderlands these past few moons."

"He's won Morrigan's favor," Arhianna added, smiling at last.

Taliesin squeezed Arthur's shoulders, genuinely proud of him. "I'm glad to hear it. Such favor is hard-won."

Arthur chuckled. "It certainly wasn't easy. I've learned much. Feels I've lived an entire lifetime since we left." Arthur's smile melted, and he lowered his voice. "I'm glad you're here. We must sail for Caer Leon as soon as we can. My father doesn't have much time. I don't want to make the same mistake as last time."

Taliesin felt shocked and pleased. "You remember the melding, then?"

Arthur nodded. "I do. And I refuse to waste my second chance."

This was more than Taliesin had dared to hope for. He had expected Arthur to recall the events that had occurred as dreams, at best. *Great Mother be praised.* "You continue to impress me, Arthur." He regarded him with hope, eager to return him to Caer Leon. "Your people will hardly recognize you," he thought aloud, "and your father will be overjoyed to see you so changed. Arvel has the ship prepared. We can sail as soon as you're ready."

Arthur nodded. "Tomorrow morning, then."

Taliesin relaxed fully. They would be in Caer Leon with time to spare. *Time enough for Arthur to prove himself.* "Tomorrow it is. We'll spend the night on Selkie Isle and sail from there."

Arthur turned toward Arhianna. "Please, Mistress—won't you come with us to Caer Leon? For my mother's sake?"

His words kindled hope in Taliesin's heart. *Has he conquered yet another near impossible feat and convinced her to come?* Taliesin held his breath, awaiting her answer, but Arhianna granted them nothing more than a sad smile and walked into the fortress to reunite with her warriors.

Gawyr, Taliesin, Arthur, and, to Taliesin's relief, Arhianna, sailed out to Selkie Isle late that afternoon. He felt grateful for the opportunity to speak to her away from the fortress.

They reached the shores of Selkie Isle by twilight and gathered around the large village fire. After a bit of drink, Arthur nodded in Arhianna's direction, leaned toward Taliesin and said in a low tone, "I think I'm in love with her."

"What?" Taliesin felt equally surprised and disturbed. He lowered his voice. "Are you mad? She's old enough to be your mother!"

Arthur shrugged. "She doesn't look it."

"Well, put it out of your head. Even if you were the same age, and she loved you in return, it's no use. She's the Mistress of the Fortress of Shadows. She'll never give that up. Not for any man."

Arthur's face soured. "She might for Cú Chulainn."

"What?" Hearing this stung. Though Taliesin loved Nimue and knew they were meant to be together, there would always be a part of his heart that belonged only to Arhianna. He knew it was unfair of him, but he cringed at the idea of any other man touching her. "I doubt it," he said, more for himself than for Arthur.

As if she knew she were being spoken of, Arhianna turned and looked at him from across the campfire. They locked eyes for a long moment, and then she got up and walked away. Taliesin saw his opportunity, but discreetly remained seated and finished his ale before going after her.

He found her easily, as if there were an invisible string tied between them. She stood on the rocky shore outside the village, glowing like an apparition in the moonlight. He reached down and dared to take her hand in his. To his relief, she did not pull it away. "Is it true you're thinking of making this voyage with us tomorrow?" he asked.

Arhianna sighed. "It's true I've considered it."

Disappointed, but undeterred, Taliesin put her hand to his lips and kissed it. "Please forgive me, Arhianna."

She remained silent, but he could feel her stifling tears. A long time passed, nothing speaking but the wind and the sea, until he gave up hope she would respond. "Just know I love you. I hope, with time, your heart will soften toward me again." He kissed her hand again, let it go, and turned to walk away.

Before he could take a step, he felt her arms around him. She embraced him tightly, pressing her head into his back. A flood of warmth engulfed his shivering heart. *Oh, thank you, Great Mother— thank you.* He turned around and returned her embrace, crushing her to his chest and burying his fingers in her red curls.

After a spell, she pulled away. "I know from Arthur she's safe and happy. For this, I forgive you. But in the end, it makes no difference."

"What do you mean?"

"Whether she'd been kidnapped by the Fae or sent to Caer Leon by you—it makes no difference, to me. Either way, I've lost her. She'll never call me Mother, and I can never know her—she's forever lost to me. The real fault lies with me. I should never have given her up. I can't blame you. Why wouldn't you think I'd forsaken her?"

Taliesin felt her mounting despair and gripped her hands, looking deep into her eyes. "But she isn't lost to you! She's grown into a strong, powerful young woman. She's safe in Affalon. You *can* know her, and she can know you—let me take you to her—you've only to come with us!"

For a moment, Arhianna looked as if she might consider it, and Taliesin doubled his efforts. "Please…come with us. Let us put this pain behind us and start anew!"

After a long moment, Arhianna shook her head. "No. She can never know I'm her mother. What good would that do? To confuse her?" She shook her head again. "Igerna's her mother. She suckled her. She raised her. I'm nobody to her."

The despair in her eyes nearly caused Taliesin to sob, but he remained strong. "You don't have to tell her—just come and know her, as I have done!"

"I long to, but I know I couldn't bear it." Arhianna wiped away her tears, any trace of the woman he used to know wiped away with them. "I will remain here, where I belong. To watch the north. You and I both know neither Lot nor Urien will support Arthur's claim. I must watch them closely." She unbuckled her sword from her waist and held it out to him. "When the time comes, I want you to present Arthur with *Dyrnwyn*. It shall help secure his position. A great king must have a great sword."

Taliesin regarded the sword with wonder. "How did you come by this? Lucia told me it disappeared with Bran."

"He gave it to me when I met him in the Underworld."

Taliesin felt intrigued and relieved. "So, you were able to bid your father farewell, after all. It eases my heart to know it."

"I was. And for that, I'm grateful."

366

"You'll have to tell me the story."

"I will, one day. Not tonight."

Taliesin took the sword with the reverence it deserved. As legendary as the cool perfection of *Caledgwyn*, the flaming blade of *Drynwyn* was the sword most coveted by warriors. It had slain enemies of both this world and the next.

"Send word when you get to Caer Leon."

"Please, Arhianna—"

Her eyes flashed. "Go! Leave me be!" She turned her back on him and stared out to sea.

Taliesin stood his ground and put his hand on her shoulder. "If you should happen to change your mind and wish to know her, you have only to ask. Find me in the Shadows, and I'll come for you."

She gave him a weak nod, and Taliesin knew that was the last response he would get from her that night. He left her standing on the beach, staring up at the stars, tears glistening on her cheeks.

CHAPTER THIRTY-NINE
The Passing of Uthyr

Taliesin and Arthur arrived at the city walls of Caer Leon to find it much changed. Neither of them knew the guard at the gate. Arthur had to give his name and show his ring to prove his identity.

"Forgive me, my lord!" The guard bowed and backed away, calling up to the guardhouse. "Commander! Lord Arthur's returned!"

An old man poked his head out of a narrow window, then quickly retreated into the guardhouse like a tortoise pulling back into its shell. A moment later, the gates creaked open. Inside, the old man waited for them, already astride a horse, holding aloft a banner bearing the Pendragon's sigil. "Welcome home, Lord Arthur, and greetings to you, Master Taliesin. Follow me, please."

People scurried out of their way as they rode through the crowded streets toward the hillfort. Heads peeped out of windows, curious to know who was being honored with a bannered escort. It did not take long for the news to spread, and soon shouts of welcome came their way.

"Young Arthur's returned!"

"God bless you, Lord Arthur!"

"You look like your father, grown young again!"

By the time they reached the top of the fortress mount, the gates of the fortress stood open to receive them. Once inside, Igerna's white-gold hair and unmistakable figure came rushing their way. "Oh, thank God, you're finally here!"

They dismounted, and Igerna wrapped her arms around her son. "I was so worried my letter wouldn't make it to you in time, or at all. It's a long voyage to Urien's fortress."

Arthur raised his brows and looked at Taliesin, who did not feel surprised. *No wonder Urien was so keen to speak of taking Uthyr's place.*

Taliesin took Igerna's offered hand and kissed it. "I'm afraid your letter didn't reach me, but all's well. We're here, now. Take Arthur to see his father. I'll wait in the hall. Send for me if Uthyr wishes to see me."

"I'm sure he will," Igerna assured him. "Come, Arthur."

She led her son out of the hall, leaving Taliesin in the care of a serving woman. She brought him bread and ale and stoked the fire.

"Thank you." Taliesin settled himself next to the great hearth, grateful for the warmth after such a cold, wet voyage. The wind had been icy and relentless, all the way down, and had not let up on the journey along the river. Even now, the wind howled like a ban Sídhe. *But you'll soon be free of it, my friend, won't you?* He pictured Uthyr standing on the brink of the Summerlands. *Perhaps Bran's with him right now, standing at his bedside.*

No, my friend. But I soon shall be. Bid your king farewell before the sun rises.

Taliesin had grown accustomed to hearing voices, but felt so surprised by the clarity of Bran's, that he turned around to see if he might be standing in the room. He saw no one but the servant woman.

"Might I fetch you something more, Master Taliesin?"

"No, no. Thank you." Taliesin turned back toward the fire. *It's to be tonight, then.* He felt dismayed. He had not expected Uthyr to die for at least another moon. But meldings were tricky, and time a slippery fish. A melancholy came over him, for he loved Uthyr, and Brython would feel his loss deeply. For all his impulsiveness, he had proven to be as strong and inspiring as his brother, Emrys—stronger, in many ways. He bent his head and prayed.

Great Mother, as you have ordained, our beloved king shall die tonight. By your merciful hand, give him comfort and guide him through the Shadowlands; may he rise above the Lake of the Dead by virtue of his righteousness, and cross into the golden hills of the Summerlands where your glory abides…

"Master Taliesin?"

Taliesin's heart jumped at the sound of Morgen's voice. He felt a rush of joy and rose to greet her. "Lady Morgen! I'm so glad you're here."

"And I, you. It's been such a long time. Nimue and I have both missed you greatly."

"And I've missed the two of you. I'm looking forward to a visit to Affalon, once things have been settled in your brother's favor."

Her eyes lit up. "Oh, yes! You may return with me!"

"We shall see."

"My father is asking for you—will you come and join us?"

"Of course."

369

Taliesin followed Morgen out of the hall and down a corridor to Uthyr's chamber, preparing himself to bid farewell to not only a king, but a dear friend. *The world shall be darker in the morning.*

Uthyr noticed him enter and smiled. "Ah, Taliesin. My old friend. Come in."

"Pendragon." Taliesin returned the smile. He went to his bedside. Uthyr's skin had turned the color of ashes, and his eyes had sunken deep into their sockets.

Uthyr shifted and sat up higher, a shade of his former self. "I want you all to listen carefully to what I have to say. I've not much breath to say it with." Igerna sat upon the edge of the bed and took her husband's hand.

Uthyr first turned to Dubricius, also present at his bedside. "Archbishop, honor me in the church here at Caer Leon, that the people might see me, then take me to St. Ambrius and bury me next to my brother. I wish to be buried standing up, facing East, with my sword in my hands."

By the wince on his face, Taliesin deduced Dubricius did not approve of this mode of burial, but he did not object.

Uthyr then turned to Taliesin. "Ask the old gods to bless me, as well, my friend. I need all the help I can get."

Again, the archbishop looked to be on the verge of objecting but remained silent.

To his wife, Uthyr bid, "Invite every lord and chieftain in Brython to my burial, and have Camulos and Aelhaearn organize a council directly following. See they are all housed and fed in the manner they deserve."

"I shall, my love."

"At this council, Archbishop, you will announce that the next Pendragon shall be chosen by God, through trials; trials that demand honesty, courage and cunning; trials that will weed out the cowardly and the devious."

Dubricius raised his brows. "What trials do you mean, my king?"

"That is for you and Taliesin to decide. The two of you are men of Spirit—I'm not. I've fallen far short of it. The Divine speaks to you, does it not?" He looked back and forth between the two of them, challenging them with his stare.

370

"I will pray to the Great Mother on this," Taliesin said, surprised by the turn of events. He glanced toward Dubricius, who looked as if he were in pain.

Uthyr grew impatient. "Well, Dubricius? Will you pray on this? Ask for the Lord's guidance?"

Dubricius raised his brows, looking lamely between Uthyr and his son. "Do you not wish for us to put forth Arthur in your place? This is what I thought you had decided."

Uthyr looked at Arthur. "I love my son and take heart in the new strength I see in him, but he must prove himself to Brython, not to me. That's my wish. If God chooses Arthur, I will rejoice in heaven for it."

From the horrified look on Igerna's face, it was clear she had known nothing about her husband's plan. "And if Arthur should fail? What shall become of us?" She began to shake. "I'll not suffer being married off to some new warlord, and neither will Morgen! And what shall become of Arthur? What if this new king sees him as a threat to his power? What's to stop him from sending someone to murder him? Husband, I think your fever's turned you into a lunatic!"

Uthyr shook his head, too weak to put up a fight. "It must be this way, my love. If Arthur doesn't prove himself, the result will be the same—don't you see? Urien and Lot will challenge him. And, I think you forget, your father is still the most powerful man in all of Dumnonia. If Arthur should fail, you can return to your father's house. You'll be safe there." Uthyr coughed blood into a cloth and became angry. "Enough of this! Now that Arthur's returned, I wish to die in peace."

Taliesin realized, at that moment, that Uthyr's death had never been fixed in time, but rather tied to his son's return. *Of course. How could I not have seen it?*

"Devise these trials and announce them at the council, so that all kingdoms shall know of them. For the last time, do you agree?"

Taliesin responded first. "I swear to do as you ask, Pendragon."

Uthyr looked at Dubricius. "And you, Archbishop?"

After a moment, Dubricius nodded. "I shall, as well, with God's guiding hand."

"Thank you. Now let me speak to my wife and children. I'll see you both in the afterlife."

Taliesin and Dubricius retreated to the back of the chamber while Uthyr lapsed into a coughing fit. Once recovered, he clasped Arthur by the arm. "My son, do you understand why I've done this?"

"I'd have it no other way, Father. You've made a wise decision. I want nothing given to me. I must earn my place."

"I know you will. And I'll be watching, sending you all my strength."

"God bless you, Father. May you find peace."

Uthyr then reached for Morgen, who sat next to him and laid her head on his chest. He stroked her hair. "Morgen, remember what I've told you. You must always be careful."

"I will, Father."

"The two of you must protect one another and look after your mother." He looked toward Igerna, whose face had softened. "Don't be angry with me. We can't part this way. I've no more breath for words, my love. You must trust me."

"I do trust you. I'm sorry..." She kissed his brow. "Forgive me."

"There's nothing to forgive. I love you more than I could ever tell you. I'll be waiting for you in the afterlife."

Igerna sniffed and let out an anxious laugh. "Flowers in hand?"

"Oh, yes. Flowers you've never seen the likes of. Be strong, wife. Be brave."

Those were the last words of Uthyr Pendragon.

Determined to hear the Great Mother's will regarding the trial Uthyr had demanded, Taliesin retreated to the forest outside the city walls. He settled in beneath an oak to fast and pray until she revealed it. He was aware of the first three days and nights passing, until the familiar delirium of hunger and fatigue began unraveling the world around him.

He remained in a strange, dream-like state until the smell of smoke startled him from his trance. He feared a forest fire might have sprung up around him. He rubbed his eyes, now stinging, looking in all directions for flames, but saw only darkness—a darkness far blacker than night.

He coughed, struggling to breathe, and slowly realized, from the echo and moisture around him that he must be in a cave or grotto. *I'm between realms, then.*

He ran his hands around his surroundings, feeling hot stone and powdery soil, soft as ash. He heard water lapping and crawled toward the sound until he felt wet sand. A sudden hot wind came toward him, blowing the smell of sulphur into his face, and he realized where he was. *Great Mother, I'm in the belly of Dinas Emrys!*

He heard the sound of water rippling from somewhere out in the darkness. It grew louder, coming his direction. He stood up and backed away from the water. Heart pounding, he stared in the direction of the lake until eyes of fire rose up and found him.

Bring your young stags to me. I shall choose a king among them.

Taliesin felt a power thrust him from the cave. He gasped in shock as cold, fresh air rushed in around him. Damp with sweat, he felt as if he were suffering from a high fever, and his ribcage buzzed as if a swarm of bees were building a hive inside it. He pulled his cloak tighter around him, teeth chattering, and reached for his goatskin with shaking fingers. He drank its contents and then broke his fast.

So be it, Great Mother. She shall choose him; she, who has lived in these lands for longer than any can remember.

Taliesin returned to Caer Leon and went straight to Dubricius with his chosen trial. To his surprise, the archbishop nodded in agreement. "Only a man with the utmost courage would dare enter that mountain. I don't believe a dragon lives within it, as you tell me, but few who go in come out, so there must be danger of some kind within its stony belly."

Taliesin would not bother arguing with the archbishop about the existence of dragons. It was enough that he did not oppose the trial. "So, you agree, then?"

"It's well-devised for the purposes of eliminating cowards, but a king must possess more than courage." Dubricius leaned closer. "You may think me docile, Taliesin—weak, even—but in spirit, I'm fierce and uncompromising. I'll serve no king but a Christian king. My trial shall ensure the next Pendragon is not only a warrior for Brython, but for the kingdom of Heaven, as revealed to us through our Lord, Christ Jesus."

Taliesin did not feel offended. He had studied the teachings of Jesus and found many of them to be right and good. What he could never do, however, was renounce the gods of his homeland. They, too, deserved worship and respect, and had much to teach. He would never betray them—they had watched over his ancient land long before Jesus was born. But he knew he could not say this to the archbishop. He chose his next words carefully. "I believe the Pendragon must unite all our people, be they Christian, followers of the Old Ways, or someere in between. You and I must win over their hearts, together."

Dubricius paused. He, too, seemed to be prudently considering his next words. "I'm willing to do whatever I must to bring all souls to God. You, and many of our people, call him the Great Mother, for we're all born with a sense of our Creator, but there's a new way of knowing the Creator, through Jesus, and I shall lead our people to this new path until my breath fails me. Believe me, Taliesin—His way offers much more than the old ways." He fingered the cross around his neck a moment and whispered something in Latin. "God has shown me a sword, lodged within a stone. That stone is His word and His promise. Those who survive your trial must then pass God's: he who can pull the sword from the stone shall have God's blessing, and no other."

Taliesin felt grateful for the archbishop's willingness to work with him. It was a quality not often found among the Roman church's authorities. "Did you see, in your vision, where this stone is?"

"Oh, yes. It lies on Ynys Wydryn."

Taliesin could not help but smile. "In a place holy to us both, then."

"It seems so."

Taliesin nodded. "Where, on the isle, is this stone?"

"It rests next to Joseph of Arimathea's thorne tree."

Taliesin felt intrigued. "There's a sword within a stone next to the thorne tree?" He had never seen it.

Dubricius shook his head. "No. The stone is there. The sword must be plunged into it."

Taliesin raised his brows. "How? By whom?"

"By me. I saw it in my dream—God shall plunge the sword into the stone, by my hands."

Dubricius was rising in Taliesin's esteem by the moment. "Which sword do you speak of?"

"One I didn't recognize, but it was magnificent."

Taliesin felt the jolt of fate. In a spell of chills, he realized how, in the past few moons, fate had delivered the two swords held most sacred by their people into his hands: *Caledgwyn* and *Dyrnwyn*. He, a humble bard, had somehow become master of both their fates.

But, how to choose between the two? Caledgwyn, as blue, perfect and cool as the Sacred Pools where it was tempered, or Drynwyn, the blade that flamed and had slain enemies of both this world and the next? It felt like trying to choose between the sun or the moon—water or fire—simply not possible. He resolved to show both of the swords to Dubricius, and then, perhaps, he would recognize the sword from his dream. If so, the choice would be made.

"Archbishop, I must show you something. Please wait." He rushed and fetched the swords from his chamber, presenting them to Dubricius with mounting anticipation. "The sword in your dream—was it either of these?"

Dubricius pulled each blade from its sheath, examined them, and then shook his head. "Each is glorious, but no. The sword in my dream was much different—the blade was luminous and the hilt fine, but they were simple—no jewels or ornamentation." He paused. "Wait—now that I'm speaking of it, I remember there were words etched upon the crossguard."

Taliesin felt hopeful. "Do you remember what they said?"

Dubricius closed his eyes and took a deep breath. After a moment, his fingers began moving in the air, as if he were running them over the pages of a book. Taliesin did not disturb him. At last, Dubricius murmured, "I can't read them…all I can tell you is the letters on one side of the hilt gleam like moonlight, and on the other, they glow like fire."

In a flash, Taliesin understood what must be done. "Thank you, Archbishop. If you trust me, I shall bring you the sword from your dream."

The archbishop raised his brows. "You know this sword, then?"

"I know how to find it. Will you trust me with this task?"

The archbishop paused a moment, then answered, "I will."

Taliesin placed a hand on his shoulder. "Then I shall bring it to you within the moon."

CHAPTER FORTY
Who Wants to be King?

The moment it became known that Uthyr had passed, the arguments that had been happening behind closed doors began raging out in the open. Every powerful lord and chieftain in Brython had an agenda and an opinion, and most were shameless in voicing them. Urien and Lot had both been campaigning vigorously to take Uthyr's place for moons, if not years, forming 'secret' alliances and making promises to any lords who swore to support them in their claim. But who, now, had sided with whom? That, only the Great Mother knew for certain, but Taliesin felt reasonably confident of where each man of power would cast his lots.

As agreed, Uthyr's body was displayed in the church at Caer Leon, and then taken to St. Ambrius to be buried next to Emrys. Every important man in Brython attended Uthyr's funeral and the council afterward. There, Dubricius stood to speak to them not of the Lord's promises, but of their future king, for Uthyr had requested that he be the one to explain his wishes to the council.

"My lords, our beloved king now watches over Brython from Heaven, and a new king must be chosen here on earth." The quality of his voice, usually resonant, but kind, now rang out through the hall as if embodied by a man three times his size. Even Taliesin, who was accustomed to changing the quality of his voice to illicit certain responses from his audience, felt chills as the archbishop spoke.

"But I say he should not be chosen by us, for our judgement is flawed and our hearts impure; I say, rather, he should be chosen by God Himself."

This sent a rush of hushed whispering through the hall. "And how shall God choose this king, Archbishop?" Lot asked, challenge in his tone.

"Through trials. One devised by Master Taliesin, the other by me. Each clan shall choose a champion among them to participate in the trials. The man who passes both shall, by merit, not by blood, earn the title. This was Uthyr Pendragon's final wish and command."

The hall erupted into arguments and discussions about this unexpected turn of events.

"And if no one passes them? Or one man achieves a single task, but not the other?"

"The first challenge shall stand until at least one man achieves it. Only the brave souls who pass the first shall be permitted to attempt the second. In the second, I assure you, only one man shall succeed. He shall, undoubtedly, be God's chosen king."

Questions and arguments rose up like a restless tide until Urien used his booming voice to call for silence. "Tell us of these trials, Archbishop."

Dubricius motioned to Taliesin. "The first is for Taliesin to reveal."

The men fixed their gaze on Taliesin, Urien's particularly hostile.

Taliesin stepped forward to address the council. "He who would be king must prove his courage and cunning by descending into the belly of Dinas Emrys and collecting no less than a five score of dragon scales from the creature's lair."

For a moment, the hall fell quiet, except for the occasional crack from the large hearth fire. It was Lot who first broke the silence. "You can't be in earnest," he scoffed. "You don't expect us to believe a *dragon* truly lives inside that mountain, do you? That's a tale for children!"

Taliesin pitied Lot's ignorance. "I assure you, my friend—it's not. But you don't have to take my word for it. Whoever wishes to become Pendragon will discover the truth of it soon enough."

One of the older lords from Gwynedd spoke up. "Master Taliesin tells true—there be dragons inside Dinas Emrys. At least, there were. I saw them with my own eyes, years ago—two dragons blasted out of the mountain's side and blacked out the sun, tearing at each other's throats. We found their scales in the fields for years afterward."

Lot furrowed his brow. "You're telling me you saw dragons fly out of that mountain?"

"I'd swear it upon my granddaughter's head."

"So why haven't they been seen again?"

The old man shrugged. "No one knows. Some say they burrowed through the earth and now live on the other side."

"I'll bring you her entire hide!" A man shouted from the back. "Fix her eyes onto the ends of my torque and wear them as jewels!"

Taliesin ignored his boasts. "I would suggest, if you value your life, not to try taking them by force."

378

"How else then? Ask her nicely?" Another man yelled and laughed.

"Get them however you choose. But regardless, the price to participate in Dubricius' trial is five score of fresh dragon scales, still glowing. Old ones from the fields will not do."

Urien nodded and looked at Dubricius. "And what of your trial, Archbishop?"

The archbishop held his hand up and the men fell silent, eager to hear. "God has shown me a large stone next to the Holy Thorne on Ynys Wydryn. Into it, by His grace and power, I shall plunge a sword. The man who can pull that sword from the stone shall be God's chosen king."

This sent a fresh wave of exclamations and questions reverberating through the hall. Cai called out this time, "So, the first man who pulls out the sword shall be king? That doesn't seem just. Whoever attempts it first has the advantage."

Dubricius shook his head. "Of one thing, I'm certain. Only one of you shall succeed. He who wishes to be king must also have faith. God has a plan. We must trust Him."

No one dared argue with the archbishop on this point. Satisfied, Dubricius raised his hands. "So now, my lords, all that remains is for us to determine whether we shall carry out Uthyr Pendragon's last wish and choose our king by trial. Otherwise, by blood right, Arthur shall take his father's place as High King. All those who agree to the trials, come stand behind me and Master Taliesin. Those who disagree, move to the other side."

For all their arguing before, the men did not take long to make their choice. After the last man moved, there were very few who were not standing behind Taliesin and the archbishop.

Dubricius turned to address them. "It's decided, then. On the next full moon, the side of Dinas Emrys shall be opened."

The moment Taliesin announced his trial, Arthur had felt excitement shoot through him like lightning. The idea of descending into the lair of a dragon thrilled and terrified him, and his skin bristled with anticipation. Unlike his mother, who remained anxious over his

379

father's decision regarding the succession, Arthur felt grateful for the opportunity to prove himself worthy.

That evening, he cornered Taliesin in his chamber, hungry for advice. "Master Taliesin? I wish to ask you about the Red Dragon."

Taliesin nodded. "You may ask, and I'll tell you what I know, but I hope you understand I cannot volunteer any information."

"No, of course not."

Arthur joined Taliesin at the hearth and launched his questions like a volley of arrows. Though he had been voracious for stories of dragons as a child, and felt certain he had heard them all, he asked Taliesin to recite every ancient story and poem he knew about the Red Dragon. He asked for details about her scales, her wings, her eyes, her tail and appearance; her powers and abilities and where her weaknesses were, if she had any; what she ate, or rather, the better question, what she did not. For hours, Taliesin indulged him.

"Does she have a name? A title?"

"She is Calontân, the Ancient One."

"What can I offer her? What would please her?"

"Gold. Lots of it."

Arthur smiled. "So, it's true, then?"

"That dragons love gold? Oh, yes. Gold, jewels, copper, mirrors—anything that flashes or burns."

Arthur felt a pang of concern. "I'll have to borrow it from the treasury, then." He shook his head. "With the burial arrangements and all of the guests we've been hosting, there's not much coin left."

"That doesn't seem wise."

"Well, what choice do I have? Do you know where I can find a pile of gold?"

Taliesin grinned. "Let it be known, you asked, I didn't volunteer." He stood up, walked over to the large chest at the foot of his bed, and opened it. Arthur walked over, looked inside and gasped. "Whose gold is that?"

"Yours, to use as an offering."

Awestruck, Arthur scooped up a handful of coins and gazed at them in the firelight. He could not peel his eyes away from the firelight glinting off their warm, yellow faces. "Where did you get this much coin?"

"Mynyth Aur. The entire mountain is laced with gold. Be sure to tell the dragon this is but a taste of it. That should compel her to spare your life, if nothing else. Now, you have only to please her with your words. Choose them wisely, or they will be your last."

Arthur's mind whirled with the feat that lay before him. *What does one say to a dragon?*

"In the meantime, do all you can to prove yourself capable of fulfilling your father's role here in Caer Leon."

"Of that, at least, I'm confident," Arthur said. From the age of eight, he had been forced to sit beside his father in the Great Hall while he received everyone from villagers to mighty chieftains, listening to their grievances and settling everything from accusations of stolen livestock to problems of unpaid debts.

"Good." Taliesin nodded. "I don't imagine you'll need my counsel, so tomorrow, I'll go to Ynys Wydryn to see this stone he speaks of. Morgen shall come with me."

Arthur nodded. "She told me this morning."

He had done his best to convince his sister to stay in Caer Leon until he left for Dinas Emrys, but she longed to leave. "Oh, Arthur," she had pleaded with him, "I've been here nearly three moons caring for Father, day and night, and comforting Mother as well. I'm desperate to get back to Affalon. I feel like a fish out of water here. Besides, we'll be together again soon—the second trial is on the island."

"Assuming I pass the first."

"You will. I'll be waiting to watch you pull the Archbishop's sword from the stone."

"Or try to. You know I've not been the best Christian."

Morgen laughed. "Who has? The church has so many rules, they've made it impossible! Don't mistake what men want for what God wants. I'm sure the Great Father wants what any father does— for us to be courageous and fight for truth, and to protect those weaker than us. You've always done that."

Arthur had felt even more sorry that she was leaving. "You've always been so much wiser than I. Perhaps Brython should have a queen instead of a king."

381

Morgen smiled. "It will, again, someday. Powerful queens. But not now. Now, it awaits its greatest king." She had embraced him, and, as always, left him feeling better than he had before.

Now, it was time to prove he was the man she believed him to be.

CHAPTER FORTY-ONE
Excalibur

Taliesin felt glad of the opportunity to travel back to Ynys Wydryn with Morgen. He made the most of their time together, listening to stories of her childhood and answering questions she had about everything, from God to dragons. When they were not sharing memories, he sang to her of the great heroines: fierce Boudicca, who stood against the Romans, beautiful strong-minded Rhiannon, who enchanted the Prince of Dyfed, courageous Branwen, who endured terrible abuse and died from sorrow. He spun them all for her in the spirit of a father for his daughter. The crossing went too swiftly, but they were both glad to reach the shores of Affalon, where Nimue stood waiting by the Willow to greet them.

"There she is," Taliesin announced to Morgen, who looked transformed.

"I'm so happy to be back," she murmured. "I feel like a snared animal in the city."

"Me too, child. Me, too." He leapt out into the shallows, pulled the boat up on shore, and helped his daughter out.

"Morgen," Nimue said, pulling her into an embrace.

Taliesin looked at the two of them in each other's arms, so like mother and daughter, and, for a brief moment, imagined the three of them were a family. Morgen went to the boat to retrieve her things, and he went to Nimue and pulled her close, breathing her in. Her scent had always been a tonic for his weariness.

Morgen took off quickly, walking up the hill, her satchel hitched on her shoulder. "I'm going to walk a while in the grove. Perhaps go and visit the Sisters."

"Of course. I'm sure they've missed you."

"Farewell, Master Taliesin. Thank you for the songs and the stories!" She waved and rushed off, disappearing over the lip of the hill.

Taliesin felt surprised. "She wishes to visit the nuns?"

Nimue laughed. "Oh, no—not those sisters. The Isle of the Sisterhood. She spends as much time there as she does here. The apple groves are connected. She passes through the realms so easily, it's hard for me to keep track of her."

383

Taliesin felt a chill at the deftness of the Great Mother's hand. "Her grandmother has recently gone to live there—did you know that?"

"I did not."

"If Morgen has spent that much time there, they must have met."

"I imagine they have."

Though neither of them would know they were family, Taliesin felt certain they would sense a kinship. *May it heal Lucia's broken heart.*

"I've a special task I need your help with," Taliesin announced, wanting to address it quickly.

"What might it be?"

"I've brought with me the two most revered blades in Brython—*Drynwyn* and *Caledgwyn*. I wish to unite their power; to forge them into a mighty sword for the future king—but this isn't a task for any smith of flesh and blood. Can you help me?"

Nimue smiled. "There's only one smith for such a task—the Lord Gofannon, brother of my mistress, Arianrhod."

Taliesin had hoped she would say exactly that. "Do you think he would consent? And could such a thing be done within the moon?"

"Time means nothing to Lord Gofannon, should he accept. Give me the swords, and I shall take them to Caer Sidi and ask this favor of my mistress. If she asks it of him, I'm certain he'll not refuse."

"Thank you." Taliesin kissed her. "There's one more thing I would ask your mistress to put to the Lord Gofannon, if I might. I seek my oldest friend, Gareth of Mynyth Aur, a revered blacksmith, who I know has worshipped and honored the Lord Gofannon for as long as he's wielded his hammer. He, among others, was taken captive by what I suspect were Sídhe raiders." He did not share that he suspected her brother was to blame, for he had no proof. *Not yet.*

"And you wish to know if Gofannon might know where he is?"

"I would."

She nodded. "I'll go to my mistress and make these entreaties on your behalf." She held out her hands to take the swords.

"If time is nothing to Gofannon, then I suppose this could wait until tomorrow, couldn't it?"

"It could." She smiled, seeing his thoughts.

384

He kissed her again and slipped his arm around her waist, leading her back to the Willow. They spent the afternoon within its sheltering veil, remembering the curves and smell of one another's bodies. Afternoon turned to eventide, and eventide to night, until the blush of morning woke them.

Nimue carefully wrapped the swords and prepared to set off for Caer Sidi. "Farewell, my love. If all goes well, I'll have your sword within the moon."

Taliesin spent the next moon in Caer Leon and returned at the appointed time, praying Nimue had found success in Caer Sidi. To his surprise, she was not waiting for him at the Willow when he arrived, as she usually was. He set Vala off to look for her, enjoying the healing balm of Affalon while occasionally peeking through Vala's eyes. Together, they found her on the far side of the island, sitting upon a large chunk of limestone by the thorne tree the archbishop so revered. *There it is—Dubricius' stone.*

Taliesin aimed himself in the direction of the thorne and soon came upon her.

"Here's where it shall happen," she said upon seeing him.

"Indeed." Taliesin looked around, impressed by the drama of the surrounding country. The tree crowned a wide, golden bluff, with glittering marshland all around, green hills rising up here and there, like turtle shells, dotted with trees and brush. "It's a fitting place for a king to be chosen."

Nimue nodded. "The archbishop is wiser than I first thought."

Taliesin agreed with her. "I find him easier to abide than most of his kind."

Nimue smoothed her hand over the stone she sat on. "I've been here for a full day and night, listening to the stories of this stone. I could sit here for a thousand and still know little."

Taliesin sat down beside her, took her hand and kissed it. "I imagine so."

She smiled at him. "I have good tidings. Gofannon was most gracious. I have the sword you asked for, and also news of your friend, the blacksmith."

Taliesin's chest ignited with hope. "Thank the gods...tell me."

"Your suspicions were right. He's in Knockma."

"I knew it." Taliesin's hatred of Finbheara flared. "Once Arthur is king, I'll deal with that wretched king and his serpent of a queen."

Nimue put her hand on his. "Finbheara's not to blame. At least, not directly."

She hesitated, and Taliesin deduced the truth. "Your bastard brother led the attack, didn't he?" He no longer had to hide his suspicions.

Nimue stared at him without blinking. "I'm afraid he did."

Taliesin nearly flew off the stone, pacing against the mounting fury he felt.

"He's been well-treated," Nimue added, "if that's of any comfort."

"Well-treated?" The clouds began to gather over Taliesin's head. Vala let out a screech from the sky above, as if she, too, were outraged. He did his best to calm down. "Do you call murdering half his clan, enslaving the other, and destroying his village well-treated?"

Nimue stood up, her eyes wide. "Of course not. But it's a blessing, just the same. My brother has only grown in power over the years. He now commands Finbheara's rangers, the fiercest band of Sídhe in Eire—all of them half-breeds, and not only half-man, but half-giant, as well."

"I don't care if they're half-*gods!*" Taliesin held up a finger. "As soon as I've gotten Arthur on the throne, I'll destroy your brother and anyone—Sídhe, man or beast—who rides with him!"

Nimue got up and took his hands. "And I shall help you. But we cannot risk war with Knockma. Promise me you'll not act alone."

"Oh, don't worry. I won't. I'll rally every man and woman of power I know to the cause and crush that damned kingdom so far beneath the hills they'll never see the sun again!"

Taliesin's mind whirled with plans of revenge. *Arhianna shall certainly pledge herself to the task, along with Gawyr and all the rest of her warriors. Amergin will lend his counsel, at least. Lucia can gain the help of the Sisters, and when Arthur becomes king, he, too, can be persuaded.*

"Enough, my love," Nimue coaxed. "We'll act when the time is right. For now, we must wait. Come with me."

386

She led the way back to the part of the island Taliesin knew well, walking along the stream through the apple grove and down the hill on the other side. But there, the shore became unfamiliar to him. They climbed up a saddle of rock to the entrance of a grotto he had never seen before.

"Has it been so long that I've forgotten this place? Where are we?"

"You've not been here before."

"I thought I'd seen every inch of this island."

Nimue laughed. "Oh, no—there are many places you haven't seen. Even I haven't seen them all." She squeezed his hand and pulled him beneath the grotto's rocky upper lip. It dripped with rivulets of fresh water winding their way down its rough jawline through moss and watercress. Taliesin stopped to cup his hands to drink from its dripping veil and then followed her into the green shade of the grotto. After twenty paces or so, he spied sunlight shining down through an overhead fissure onto a waist-high stone dolmen. Something wrapped in fine cloth lay atop it.

Taliesin approached and touched it, smoothing out the folds in the linen. The revealed scenes immediately captivated him, for the figures were clearly himself and Nimue. He beheld himself reaching up to pluck a silver apple from the boughs of the glorious tree it hung upon. Next to that, lay the two of them embraced beneath the veil of the willow, next to the lake. The woven surface of the water tricked the eyes, appearing to ripple along the threads, and the veil of leaves seemed to sway in the breeze. His mouth parted in wonder as he opened the next fold to reveal yet more scenes—a stag leaping through a forest, leading a herd of graceful deer behind him; swans flying across the lake toward the sunset; a spiraling, shimmering ladder of moonlight leading to Arianrhod's Silver Wheel, and the glorious kingdom of Caer Sidi spinning within a midnight sky.

"I wove the linen for you, on the loom of my mistress. I shall sew it as a lining into your cloak. Wear it, and my love and protection shall accompany you always."

Taliesin felt stunned by the fine work and pulled her close. "I'll wear it always," he promised, kissing her cheek.

He then lifted the final fold of fabric to reveal a simple, elegant sword. As Dubricius had described, neither hilt nor pommel were adorned. Its glory belonged to the blade alone. It blazed, full of color and power that one did not need the training of a druid to see. He studied the strange light emanating from the long blade with intense fascination. It distorted the pattern of the weaving beneath it, the way the heat rising from a fire warps the image of things behind it, or water bends the appearance of things within it.

"Behold, *Excalibur*," she whispered.

Taliesin marveled at the sword's perfection, agape at Gofannon's celestial skills. Even the writing Dubricius had described was engraved on the hilt, though he had not told Nimue about this detail from the archbishop's vision. He attempted to read it, but could understand none of it. "What tongue is this?"

"It is of the spirit, in a language not known to this world. In essence, one side says, 'take me up,' and the other, 'cast me away.' Those who would rule well must always ponder both sides." She picked up the scabbard and held it out to him. "I made this as well. Many protective spells have been woven into these threads. As long as the scabbard hangs by its bearer's side, he shall never bleed, no matter how deep his wounds."

Such a gift was worth as much as the blade itself, if not more. Taliesin felt overwhelmed with awe and gratitude for Nimue. He embraced her, his trust in her redeemed thrice over. "Thank you, my love. You've brought a whisper of divine justice down from the heavens, and all men shall be blessed by it."

Taliesin returned to Caer Leon with his precious cargo. He went straight to the church where, as expected, he found Dubricius engaged in his daily duties.

"Greetings, Archbishop," he said as he walked into the chapel.

Dubricius turned. "Ah, Master Taliesin!"

"I've come to deliver what I promised you."

"The sword?"

"Indeed. I think you'll be pleased."

"I'm anxious to see it." Dubricius went to the front pew, motioning for Taliesin to join him.

Taliesin sat down beside him and held forth the blade in its fine scabbard. Dubricius took it and admired Nimue's mesmerizing stitchwork on the scabbard a long moment before studying the hilt. "The words! They're there. But still I cannot read them. What language is this?"

"None of this world. I was told this side says, 'take me up,' and this side says, 'cast me away.'"

Dubricius smiled and pulled the hilt from the scabbard, revealing the glory of *Excalibur*. He gasped and whispered something in Latin, eyes darting back and forth over the silver beauty beneath them. "Truly, my friend, God's hand is in this." He shook his head, brow furrowed in disbelief. "It is every inch and detail the sword I dreamed of." He moved it, mesmerized by the ethereal play of light within its blade. "Wherever did you find it?"

Taliesin smiled. "*Excalibur* is a virgin blade, forged from the two swords most sacred to our people." He did not try to explain where it had come from, or who its celestial smith had been.

"*Excalibur*," Dubricius whispered with rapture. "By far, the finest sword I've ever seen or held, and I know more about swords than most men of the cloth." He sheathed the sword with as much reverence and care as he employed when serving the eucharist. "You've done more than well, Master Taliesin. It's clear to me, now, that God means for us to work together. After today, I shall never doubt it again. Now, I must do my part."

Taliesin bowed his head. "Yes, Archbishop. Soon, Ynys Wydryn shall hold more people than she ever has before—all who seek to be God's choice, and all who wish to witness it."

Dubricius nodded his head. "It shall be a day for the songs."

"Yes. For the songs." Taliesin smiled. "I look forward to it."

"As do I."

Taliesin bowed his head. "Until the day, then. May your work be blessed."

389

CHAPTER FORTY-TWO
The Trial of Dinas Emrys

Arthur woke up and steeled himself for another long day in the Great Hall. Requests for audiences had piled up after his father's death. He had been receiving villagers from morning until night, for the past week. He walked into the hall and indulged a private groan of fatigue at the daunting number of people awaiting his attention. His mother could not assist, as she was fully absorbed in running the household. In addition to the petitions of the villagers, they had been hosting a constant stream of guests since his father's funeral.

The hours rolled on, until, mercifully, twilight fell and released Arthur from his duties. But there would be no rest. He was expected in the feasting hall where several lords and their wives awaited him. Politics and decency demanded he be there, and not only present, but also wise with his words and gracious in behavior.

Weary, he went to visit his mother, hopeful she might have turned a corner. Every day since his father's death had seemed to take a year from her. He knew she had surely been feeling the emptiness of her bed and needed to mourn, but she had been unable to fully do so with all the demands on her time.

Tonight, she looked no better, even though she was dressed in her finest gown and her hair had been plaited splendidly around her head. Her eyes were dull and her skin sallow, despite her maids' best efforts. He went and embraced her with a sigh. "Oh, Mother." He held her close, and, moments later, felt her weeping against his chest.

"What can I do?" he asked, feeling helpless. "Just tell me. I'll do it."

She pulled away, shook her head and mustered a weak smile. "There's nothing you can do." She looked over to her window and gazed outside. "I wish I could just get on a horse and ride until dark, or spend the whole day running around on the moors like I did when I was a girl. I long to go to bed not having said a word to anyone all day." She shook her head and sighed. "I need some peace."

There was a rap at the door, and Arthur and his mother exchanged a glance, surely thinking the same thought. *Peace shall not come for some time.*

"Come in," Igerna called, her tone formal, but she lit up like a star upon seeing the face that appeared in the doorway. "Taliesin! Oh, thank God!"

Arthur felt relieved to see him, too, the burden of Caer Leon feeling lighter in that moment. "I was beginning to think I'd have to travel to Dinas Emrys without you. Everything's prepared. We can leave tomorrow."

"Forgive me," Taliesin said, "but I've come only to wish you luck and to feed and rest my horse. As much as I'd enjoy the company, I must make the journey to Dinas Emrys alone. I hope you understand why I must appear impartial in this matter."

In that moment, Arthur realized how much strength and comfort he gleaned from having Taliesin by his side. He had been looking forward to making the journey together, but he understood. If Taliesin appeared to be favoring or aiding him in this quest, his victory would mean nothing. He did his best to hide the disappointment from his voice. "Of course, I understand. It was foolish of me not to realize this."

Taliesin smiled and put a hand on his shoulder. "Remember everything I've told you. May she find you worthy."

"May she indeed," Arthur replied.

The next morning, Arthur departed with a small company for Lord Cynyr's hillfort. It lay a half-day's ride from Dinas Emrys, and he wished to spend a few nights there before continuing on to the mountain. Not surprisingly, his cousin, Cai, had been chosen to champion his clan in the trial, and Arthur looked forward to reuniting with him before the fateful day.

After a warm welcome, some feasting and formalities, Cai suggested they visit the men in the barracks. Arthur knew why. *They'll be eager to take the measure of me after hearing where I've been this past year.* Now that the lords of Brython had agreed to choose their next Pendragon by trial, and not by blood, he and Cai would stand as equals alongside the other candidates chosen to descend into the belly of Dinas Emrys. As Arthur expected, it did not Cai long to motion toward the practice yard. "Let's see what you've learned up there in the North, eh?"

Arthur knew Cai intended to do everything he could to beat him in front of his men, now gathering around them as if they had been told of the match in advance. He felt uneasy, but he knew he could not refuse the challenge.

"If you like." He forced a smile and took his place in the ring, eyeing the growing crowd with uncertainty. He then spied Cadwallon in the crowd, surrounded by some of his men — Cadwallon, the surly lord who had opposed his father at every turn in the last council. He was not the only man of power present. Many men of influence from Gwynedd were there, and Arthur quickly realized what was at stake. *They wish to see who the better champion is — Cai of Gwynedd or Arthur of Gwent — for that is all I am, now.* He gripped his sword and gave it a few practice swipes. *Lord, grant me victory today.* He had one advantage, thanks to his time away — he knew Cai's fighting style, but Cai no longer knew his. This gave him the upper hand for the first few minutes, but Cai was a swift learner, adapting quickly and putting Arthur through his paces. Soon, it seemed the entire household and every man from the barracks had come to the yard, all of them jeering, cheering, and making bets.

After ten minutes of solid fighting, both Arthur and Cai were exhausted, but neither would cede to the other. Five more minutes, and they were reduced to circling one another, reserving their waning strength for strikes they felt extremely sure of, but none found purchase.

The fight waged on, draining them both, until Arthur felt his lungs would burst. He scanned the crowd, looking for a friendly face, and thought he saw Scáthach standing at the edge of the ring. *What's she doing here?* A rush of adrenaline gave him the boost he needed. He struck anew with such fury and precision that he soon disarmed Cai and had his sword pointed at his throat.

Arthur looked for Scáthach in the crowd, thrilled she had seen him win such a victory, but she was no longer there. To add to his disappointment, the crowd seemed displeased. They had clearly expected Cai to win.

Thankfully, Cai did not spurn him. "Good fight, cousin," he said, grinning through bloody teeth. "Looks like you've learned a thing or two."

Arthur grasped his outstretched arm. "Ale?" he suggested.

Cai nodded. "Ale."

"Well done, today." A man sat down at Arthur and Cai's table in the tavern and set a full pitcher of ale down. He offered his arm to Arthur. "Bedwyr, son of Bedrawt—"

"Of Glwysing," Arthur finished. He remembered both Bedwyr and his father well from the council meetings—his father, for his outspokenness, and Bedwyr, because the serving women in the hall only stopped staring at him long enough to pour the ale. Even then, they often spilled it in their eagerness to get back to feasting their eyes on him.

"Indeed. You fought well, today." Bedwyr nodded in Cai's direction. "Cai's nigh unbeatable. If we survive this dragon challenge, I'd like to come and train with you in Caer Leon."

The chosen son of Glwysing, Arthur thought. "I'd like that. You'd be welcome, by half our people, at least."

Bedwyr's brow furrowed beneath his thick fair curls. "What do you mean?"

"Let's just say the women would bless me, but their husbands wouldn't."

Cai laughed. "I can vouch for that. Get this one out of Gwynedd so the rest of us can warm our beds."

Bedwyr turned red.

Arthur raised his cup to him. "Just the same, you're welcome in Caer Leon. I've no intention of dying at Dinas Emrys, and I'd be honored to train with a warrior of your repute."

Bedwyr raised his cup in return. "Well, then, here's to that. May the husbands of Caer Leon forgive me!"

That night, and for the next few following, people told tales and sang songs in the tavern about the mysterious mountain and its dragons. One man claimed to have witnessed the Battle of the Dragons as a child.

393

"I'd been seekin' one of my sheep that'd run off, and was scramblin' up the side of the mountain when I felt a rumblin' beneath my hands and feet so fierce, I thought the earth would split open beneath me! A terrible blast knocked me to the ground, and when I looked up, two winged beasts burst out of the side of the mountain—one red, and one white. They took to the sky in a rage, nearly tearin' it apart in their wrath, thrashin' the clouds to shreds and shakin' the very stars with their bellows. I should've run, but I couldn't—frozen, I was, crouched on the ground, clutchin' handfuls of grass like a sailor clutchin' ropes on a pitchin' sea. Piercing shrieks split the clouds, causin' rain to fall, 'til the red beast dragged the white to the ground. They say people felt the earth quakin' all the way over in Eire." Someone filled his now empty mug. "The next mornin,' I rode out to see the scars on the earth the beasts left behind. Many of us were there that day, sharin' stories and makin' sure we hadn't gone mad—that we'd all seen it. And we found the black furrow to prove it—a mile deep, and three miles long, and down in the very bottom a black tunnel leadin' to the very pit o' hell itself! We worked for moons fillin' it back up. And in that time, we found plenty of these." He pulled a bundle out of a leather satchel, unwrapped it, and held something up. It was the color of blood and the size and thickness of a plate, sending a chorus of gasps through the tavern. "This, my friends, is a dragon scale."

Some were not impressed. "You're all a bunch of fools!" one man called out. "There's no such thing as dragons!"

"Then what's that?" Someone demanded, pointing to the scale.

He shrugged. "Who knows? Some kind of rock or polished shale? Something found beneath the sea? But it's certainly not a dragon scale! This is just a trick to see who's courageous enough to go into the bowels of that mountain. Just like all these stories. Nothing more."

The man sitting next to him agreed. "There's danger in there, no doubt, but certainly not a dragon."

The stories fueled arguments and wagers all through the night. Some were convinced the mountain held a terrible denizen, others insisted it did not. On one thing, however, all were agreed: the only way to know the truth, was to open up the mountain and go inside.

On the day of the full moon, Lord Cynyr led the journey to Dinas Emrys. Though it lay less than a day's ride away, you would think by the number of wagons, horses and people in their party, that they were traveling to the edge of the world.

Arthur and Cai rode alongside one another, discussing what they knew of dragons. Bedwyr soon found them. "Might I ride with you?" he asked.

"Of course," Cai and Arthur said in unison. He came up and joined their conversation. "Will you be going in, as well?" Arthur asked, though he already knew the answer.

"I shall be. Consider me the patron saint of Glwysing."

"Ha!" Cai guffawed. "Saint, my ass."

They arrived in the foothills by late afternoon, where they encountered a huge encampment. Arthur rode up beside Cai. "Good lord! There must be thousands here!"

Cai shrugged his big shoulders. "What did you expect? They've come to see who'll be king. Or to see a dragon. Surely both are worthy of a long journey."

Arthur looked up the slope of the mountain and felt a flurry of butterflies in his stomach.

"Come, let's explore a bit," Bedwyr suggested.

The three of them rambled through the sprawling camp, which was, in essence, a giant festival. People were selling wares and playing music and, apparently, had been doing so for days.

"I regret we didn't come earlier," Cai lamented, his brown eyes feasting on several young maidens.

Tavern tents had been set up to slake the thirst of the hundreds gathered, and ladies of pleasure roamed in search of lonely men. They soon found Bedwyr, and, before long, the three men had a cluster of women about them.

At sunset, a bonfire was lit on the slope of the mountain, and the sound of a harp rang out in the sky. How they could all hear it astonished Arthur, but he suspected there was much magic Taliesin could manage that he knew nothing about.

"It's time," Arthur said to his companions, now returned from their adventures in the pleasure tents. "Let's go."

The trio made their way through the crowd toward the bonfire, where all the champions would be blessed before being sent into the belly of the mountain.

Taliesin stood like a god upon a rock that jutted out of the mountain above the bonfire. He wore a long white robe, a headdress of antlers, and a cloak of crimson feathers. In his right hand, he wielded a long white staff a foot taller than him, with a vein of something metallic running through it that flashed in the firelight. He looked directly at Arthur the moment he reached the edge of the bonfire, and, somehow, without opening his mouth, Arthur heard him say, *Greetings Young Stag. May the Great Mother guide you to victory.* Taliesin then turned his eyes to the crowd, raised his hands, and spoke.

"Tonight, brethren, the moon is full, and we shall discover who, among your champions, is worthy of the title, Pendragon of Brython!"

A priestess in a blue robe with a crescent moon painted in woad upon her forehead joined Taliesin by his side.

"Come forward, sons of Brython, and receive the Great Mother's blessing from the High Priestess of the Sisterhood. When the time comes, I shall blow the horn and summon you to the Circle of Banners."

One by one, the champions were led up the side of the mountain to the rock, where the High Priestess ministered to each of them, in turn, with the help of an apprentice.

Arthur watched three or four men receive their blessings, and then the apprentice came to fetch him. She led him up to the rock. From there, he saw a sea of faces and a hundred campfires winking beneath the stars. His heart quickened as the High Priestess stepped forward. Her face was painted white, like the moon, and seemed to glow. Black stripes accented her eyes and cheekbones. Other symbols had been painted on her chest and forehead—symbols Arthur did not recognize.

"Will you accept the Great Mother's blessing?" she asked.

"I will."

The apprentice bid him kneel, and the High Priestess raised a torch in the air. "For fierceness."

She circled him, blowing flames in his direction. They licked his cheeks face and arms, burning them, but he did not cry out. She completed the circle and handed the torch to the apprentice. The apprentice exchanged it for a shell, filled with a smoldering mix of herbs and resins.

The High Priestess lifted the shell high in the air with both hands, offering it to the moon.

"For clarity."

She brought the shell level to her chin and blew thick blue smoke into his face three times. He breathed it into his lungs, each time feeling the world around him intensify. Sounds became clearer, colors more vibrant, and smells more pungent.

The apprentice took the shell and handed the priestess a skullcap filled with dark liquid.

"For courage." The High Priestess dipped her fingers into the liquid and smeared it on his burned cheeks and bottom lip. It felt thick and sticky, and tasted like boar's blood.

"Rise, Young Stag."

Arthur stood up and the apprentice led him back down and moved on to the next man.

The blood had quelled the pain from Arthur's burns somewhat, but his thoughts felt strange to him. As there were many others still awaiting their blessing, he sought out a place where he could be alone. He spied a small clump of trees down the mountainside and sat down beneath their branches to pray. He had been there for perhaps a quarter hour when a voice startled him from his meditation.

"Are you afraid?"

He looked up to see a young man with pale eyes staring at him from beneath a dark hood.

"I am," he admitted.

"So am I."

Arthur felt surprised. *What does he mean?* From his height and the sound of his voice, the lad could not have been more than thirteen years old. He did not want to insult the boy, but if his clan had truly chosen him as their champion, they were guilty of sending a child to his death. "I'm sorry, but you seem too young to be the champion of your clan."

The boy laughed. "Oh, I'm not our champion! I've paid someone to let me into the mountain. I want to see the dragon!"

Arthur's concern mounted. "I don't think you understand how dangerous this is—you could die in there." He glanced toward the massive crowd gathered on the slope. "Where are your parents?"

The boy ignored his question. "Once I saw a dragon, I could die happy."

Arthur suppressed a chuckle. "You say that now, but you might change your mind once you see her. I might, too."

The lad shrugged. "I'm ready to find out."

Arthur stood up, intending to learn the boy's name and warn his father about his son's intentions, but before he could ask, the blast of a horn came sailing down the mountainside, reverberating across the foothills.

"It's time!" The lad exclaimed, rushing off with a wave. "Good luck!"

"Wait!" Arthur called, but the boy ran off and did not look back. Realizing there was nothing he could do, short of running the boy down, he left the child to his fate and turned toward his own. He hiked up the mountain to the gathering place, where banners bearing the sigil of every champion's clan had been erected on tall poles. Maidens in blue robes, holding torches in both hands, stood behind each champion, creating a circle of color and fire.

Arthur spied the red dragon of his father's house flicking her pointed tongue into the night and felt a wave of pride. He took his place beneath her raised talons. *One thing's for certain—there can surely be no better sigil for such a quest.*

When every champion had found his banner and taken his place beneath its wing, Taliesin went to the center of the circle and raised his hands to the sky. "It is time, blessed men of Brython!" he bellowed, turning as he spoke. "Each of you has been chosen the most noble son of your house; the pride of your kingdom; the champion of your clan. Some of you who descend into the darkness this night shall not emerge to see the dawn, but you can die knowing you shall forever be revered as men of courage!" He looked into the eyes of each man, and then said, "Those of you who accept the first challenge for the title of Pendragon, follow me."

398

No one refused. The torchbearers escorted their champions along the thin trail that led up the eastern side of the mountain, lighting their way. Arthur's banner had been closest to the trail, so he and his torchbearer went first, behind Taliesin. Arthur glanced back at the chain of men trailing behind them, their locations on the slope marked by the flickering torches of their escorts.

Taliesin moved with the agility of a goat up the rocky trail to the old rift, now reopened. It looked like a dark stab wound between the mountain's ribs. The disturbed rocks, now scattered about, had been smothered by years of moss and ferns that thrived on the warm sulphuric air coming from within. Nothing could be seen inside.

Taliesin turned to him. "Are you ready, Arthur, son of Igerna?"

"I am," Arthur replied without hesitation.

"May the Great Mother protect you." He looked at him as a father would and squeezed his shoulder.

The maiden who had escorted him handed him her torches, one lit, one not. He bowed his head to her, took them, and plunged into the black gash in the mountain. He put the unlit torch into his belt, intending to save it for the journey back up. He calculated he would have perhaps four hours to complete his task, but if something went awry, he had also brought several candles and a lantern.

The darkness was viscous and thick; a choking warm blackness that smothered. Arthur held his torch aloft, hopeful of a better view, but he could scarcely make out anything but the torch itself. He heard others entering behind him and moved in further, one hand against the rock to his left, feeling his way along a muddy drainage trail that tumbled steeply down into the bowels of the mountain. He lost his footing a few times, so forced himself to slow down and choose his steps with care. At last, the pitch eased a bit, as well as the steam and smoke in the air, but it had taken him quite a long time to reach that point. He took advantage of the reprieve, scanning everything around him, waving his torch in all directions, but saw nothing but rock, moss and mud.

After some time, he came to a series of caverns where tunnels forked off in different directions. He had learned much by mapping out the mountain at Dun Scáthach, and employed all his tricks—visualizing the shapes of the turns he made, marking the tunnels he chose with charcoal before going in, leaving cairns at critical points—

and he prayed they would serve to lead him back out again. *It'll all be for nothing if I get lost.* A few more twists and turns led him to the largest cavern he had seen yet. He held his torch aloft and gasped at its size. Occasionally, the light from his torch triggered the reddish flash of a scale. He found a few score in such a way and began to think the trial might be easier than he had anticipated. But after another hour of searching, he had still found no more.

Five score? I'll be in here for days, at this rate.

He continued downward, following drainages and pools until he came to what seemed to be a large lake. Sulphuric steam made his eyes water, obscuring what he could see. He moved out onto a flat section of shore, where the mist moved in erratic patterns. It granted him moments of clarity, in which he could see out over the lake's surface, but those moments did not last long. He waved his torch over the surface of the shallow water and saw several fiery flashes in the sand. Thrilled by his luck, he scooped up the glowing scales in handfuls, counting them as he dropped them into his bag, until screams of agony and terror caused him to freeze.

His mind reeled with horrible possibilities. He ran in the direction of the screams, intent on delivering help in whatever way he could. He slipped and stumbled along the way, cursing the darkness, following the cries of agony. The mist mercifully cleared for a moment, allowing him to spy several torches in the distance. He rushed toward them until he could make out figures and faces. He felt relieved to see Cai among them, alive and uninjured. "What's happened?"

"She..." Cai shook his head, struggling to catch his breath. "She ate someone and pulled another in...I don't know who. But he's not surfaced."

"Did you see her?"

Cai shook his head, brows curled in confusion. "You can't see anything in this darkness. I think something from the lake got him and dragged him in, but no one saw what."

Arthur held his torch aloft, struggling to see through the shifting steam, and spied several men on the other side of the lake up to their waist or knees, collecting scales. He shook his head. "With such easy prey—who could blame her?" He called out over the lake. "Get out of the water!"

400

Some of them looked in his direction, but soon went back to what they were doing before. Arthur scanned the lake, his anxiety mounting. "We have to warn them. Come on."

"They know." Cai waved a hand toward them. "They saw the whole thing."

It took Arthur a moment, but he realized the men were likely taking advantage of the fact that the beast had just attacked and was likely busy feeding.

"Look, Arthur—the water…"

Arthur looked where Cai had pointed and saw the water parting as if the prow of an invisible ship were carving its way toward the men.

"Get out of the water, you fools!" Arthur called again, scrambling in their direction. He raced as fast as he dared over the slippery terrain, intent on forcing the men to heed his warning, but they refused to move. Cai came running up behind him. "It's no use. They won't listen."

In desperation, Arthur called out, "Oh, Great Calontân!"

In a bold and perhaps foolish move, he did not yet know, Arthur opened his two satchels of gold and emptied them out onto the rocks.

"What are you doing?"

"It might be her. You should hide. No reason for both of us to die."

Cai drew his sword instead.

Arthur knelt next to the pile of gold pieces and let them run through his fingers, over and over, hoping the clinking, metallic sound would attract the beast. Heart pounding, he called out again. "Hear me, Great One! I've brought you a gift! Come and claim it!" Again, he picked up handfuls of coins and clattered the pieces together.

Arthur saw the invisible prow turn away from the men and move toward him. *God save me.* "I mean it, Cai—find a place to hide."

Cai stood next to him, legs planted in the ground like two trees, sword and shield poised. "I'm not going anywhere."

Out of the steam, the head and wings of the creature Arthur had summoned emerged. She loomed over them, tall as a mighty fir tree, water running down her snout and teeth, dripping on them like black rain. Her great leathery wings arched up over her triangular head

401

into the darkness above and flapped, blowing away the steam until Arthur could see her in terrifying detail. She tossed Cai aside with a flick of her talons. He cried out and Arthur heard the clatter of metal against rock. Arthur thought of the piles of bones he had seen in the nearby cavern. *Oh, Great Mother.* Every instinct urged him to flee, but he did not. He bent down on one knee, clutched two fistfuls of gold, and held them up. "For you, Great Mistress of Fire! I've brought you gold in exchange for the scales we've gathered!" Belting out the words somehow made him feel less frightened—for the moment, at least.

The Red Dragon's great head moved down toward him and hovered above his own. His torchlight glittered across her eyes and glistened off the blood and saliva on her teeth. He choked on her foul breath and felt its heat on his face as he gathered handfuls of gold and poured them out again in front of her. "For you, Great Calontân. I beg you not to attack any more of us!"

Her eyes flashed in the dark like a cat, both of them pinned on Arthur. Her head rose up tense and arched, like a snake about to strike, and he felt his bowels turn to water. *I'm going to die.* But she did not strike. Instead, he heard her talons scrape the ground, raking the gold pieces into the water.

"This was all I could carry, Great One—but I know where to get more—much more—thick veins of it, deep in a mountain not far from here. If you agree not to kill any more of us, I shall tell you of this place."

Any who challenge me shall die. Any who remain here when next the sun sets, shall die.

Her words rumbled like thunder through his body. Everything in him wanted to flee, but he felt unsure of whether she had agreed or not. He licked the boar's blood on his lip for courage. "If we leave you in peace, do you agree we can gather scales until the next sundown?"

Where is this mountain you speak of?

Arthur saw her talons beneath the water, squeezing coins and sand between them. "A few days' ride to the east," he stammered. "Known as Mynyth Aur, it rises up from the village which sits at the western edge of the forest which holds the Sacred Grove. The village was attacked. None live there now."

402

If you have lied to me, I shall fly to Caer Leon and burn it to ashes.

Arthur bowed his head. "I swear it's true. I'm at your service, Great Calontân. If there's something else you desire, please tell me."

The dragon moved closer, and Arthur quelled a surge of panic. She reared her head back and Arthur felt his knees buckle. *She's going to strike.* Yet, instead of belching the fire Arthur was expecting, she turned around and sank back into the depths of the lake.

Arthur let out his breath and collapsed on the sand, heart pounding, until he remembered his cousin. *Oh, God. Cai!* He scrambled to his feet and ran to his side. "Cai?" He shook him a few times. "Cai!"

Cai mumbled and Arthur let out a sigh of relief. "Thank God. Can you stand up?"

Cai sat up and let out a yelp.

"What is it?"

"Few broken ribs, I think. Shoulder feels dislocated."

Arthur looked and saw his arm hanging limply by his side.

"It looks to be. I'll push it in."

"Watch the ribs, please."

Arthur took the wrist of Cai's injured arm, pulled it forward and straight out in front of him. Cai cried out in pain but let out a sigh of relief as Arthur guided the ball of his arm bone back into his shoulder socket.

"Thank you." Cai groaned to his feet. "My ankle feels sprained, unfortunately. Get your scales and let's get out of here."

Arthur went to the water's edge, where dozens of scales flashed. He gathered them up, counting as they went, until he had enough. "That's it. Let's go."

Arthur led the way back out of the mountain, but Cai's injuries slowed their pace. After another half hour, Arthur noticed Cai looked dangerously unsteady on his feet. "You don't look well, cousin."

"I'm fine."

Arthur knew he was lying. "Sit. We're safe here. You should drink something."

With some coaxing, Cai sat down. Arthur helped prop him against a rock and soon Cai had fallen asleep.

Arthur feared staying in the mountain and suffering the Red Dragon's wrath, but Cai needed rest. He made sure he had his flint and put out his torch. If there was one advantage to having a dragon in the mountain, it was that the temperature inside was quite warm. He, too, soon fell asleep.

Arthur felt unsure of how long they had slept but everything in his body told him they needed to move on. "Cai?" He lit his torch and roused his cousin. "Cai! It's time to move on. How do you feel?"

"Stiff, but I can move."

"Good." Arthur helped him to his feet. "Let's get out of this place and get some ale, eh?"

This solicited the laugh Arthur had hoped for. He did his best to keep things light-hearted, checking on his cousin often without letting on that he was. A few hours later, they arrived at the long narrow climb up the wash to the top. "We made it," he whispered to Cai. "You go first."

Cai moved ahead of him, and Arthur held his torch high so Cai could see. It was a painfully slow ascent. Cai often slipped in the mud and had to rest, but, at least, he did not have to be carried.

Arthur knew one foot in front of the other would inevitably lead them out, so he kept his focus on this and nothing else. After a few hours, they spied the beckoning flicker of torches overhead and took heart that the ordeal was nearly over.

Once at the top, Cai recounted the scales he had collected and handed the bag to Taliesin, who stood waiting outside. With much care and strategic movement, he slipped through the gap back into the outside world.

Arthur opened his bag and counted his scales as well, but to his astonishment, found he was short.

This can't be. He counted them again, but it was undeniable. He was short by three. *How could I have lost them?*

Cai called to him from outside. "Arthur? Are you coming?"

Arthur sighed and accepted his fate. "I have to go back down. I don't have enough. Some must have fallen out."

"How can that be?" Cai sounded as astonished and defeated as he felt.

"I don't know."

"You can't go back down there, Arthur—the sun's about to set!"

"I have to!" Arthur snapped, his temper flaring. "Just hand me a fresh torch!"

He heard talking outside, then a long silence. Then, to his surprise, Bedwyr squeezed into the mountain with two torches. "Let's go," he said, handing him a torch. "You're not going back down there alone."

"I am."

"Like hell you are! I'd be dead if it weren't for you. She was headed straight for me down by that lake. Cai would come with us, but he knows he'd only slow you down. He says he'll make it up to you when we get back."

Arthur did not waste any time arguing. It was clear Bedwyr was set on going. "Thank you." He took the outstretched torch and began making his way back down to the lake, praying the dragon had eaten enough for one night. He and Bedwyr had been descending for no more than a quarter of an hour when Arthur heard someone coming up the wash. "Hello?" he called.

A breathless voice came floating up. "Why are you coming down? You should be going the other way!"

"Somehow I've lost a few scales."

"Take some of mine, then. I can't become Pendragon, and I don't need this many. I just wanted a few to remember this night."

Arthur held up his torch and, to his surprise, saw the young lad he had spoken to before hiking up the side of the mountain. "Ah, it's you! I'm glad to see you're still alive."

"I'm careful."

Arthur turned to Bedwyr. "I don't know if I can take these from someone else…"

"Dammit, Arthur! Don't question a blessing from the gods! Take the damn scales and let's get out of here!"

"How many do you need?" the boy asked.

"Three."

The boy opened a leather satchel filled to the top and gave him ten. "Just in case. You don't want to take any chances."

Arthur felt impressed. "You must have gone all the way to the lake to have collected that many."

"I did. And I saw you with the dragon. I've never seen anything so brave. When the time comes, I'm certain it shall be you who shall pull the sword from the stone."

Arthur felt surprised. "You're well informed."

The boy shrugged. "Not really. Everyone knows about the trials."

Arthur grew suspicious, wishing he could get a better look at the boy's face and clothes. "What's your name?"

The boy paused a moment, which only deepened Arthur's curiosity, but then blurted out, "Gwydion."

"Gwydion?" Arthur nodded. "Fine name."

"Thank you. My father's fond of the old stories. Speaking of my father, he doesn't know I'm here. I need to get back in my tent before he wakes."

They climbed together for some time, until Gwydion stopped and announced, "There's the gap! We're almost there."

Arthur craned his neck around the boy and spied a long strip of white light up above. "Won't need this anymore." He threw his torch over the edge of the narrow lip and Arthur watched it sail down into the blackness below until it went out.

Bedwyr, too, threw his over. "Easier to climb with both hands."

Arthur felt uneasy about throwing away their last torch but could not argue with Bedwyr's logic. He tossed his over, as well.

They had not climbed more than twenty feet when Arthur heard something that made his entire body shiver with dread. "Stop," he called to his companions, listening.

It came again from below. A low growl, like terrible heavy doors creaking open, echoing through the air from the blackness below. Arthur leaned over the edge of the wash and looked down. A blast of fire lit up the enormous cavern below, and a burst of hot air came rising up towards his face.

"Run!" Arthur cried. "Run!"

Gwydion shot up the wash, leaping with the lithe strength of a young deer, and Bedwyr pushed Arthur ahead of him. They scrambled madly over the rocks, the sound of the dragon's wings

406

flapping growing ever louder. Arthur kept his eyes on the gleaming white gap beckoning from above, wishing desperately it were closer.

The Red Dragon came into full view. Gusts of hot air hit their faces as she flapped her huge wings, whipping the smoke and steam into shreds. She arched her head back and belched a torrent of fire at the white gap. Cries of terror came from outside the mountain as the dragon clawed at the gap, raking stones and rock down in front of it. The world soon went black.

"We need to hide until she's gone," Arthur yelled to his companions over the sound of falling rock, some of which sounded frightfully close. He felt for his rope. "Hold on to this. I saw a place we can hide not far down." He tied the rope to himself and passed it into Bedwyr's hands, trusting he would pass it to Gwydion. He felt his way back down the wash as quickly as he dared, feeling for the side passage.

The sound of wings and gusts of hot air came their direction, and Arthur tried not to panic. *It's here. It's here. I know it's here…*

A blast of fire came toward them, lighting up the inside of the mountain and blinding them with its brightness. Thankfully, she had miscalculated their location—or else thought to toy with them a while—and the fire hit the wash some thirty feet above them. The light gave Arthur a good look at where they were and how far down the side passage was. He aimed straight for it, tugging at the rope, knowing the dragon would not miss them with her next volley of flames. Luckily for them, a section of the wash was obscured by a pile of rubble that had slid down in the dragon's fury, shielding them somewhat from the abyss the dragon hovered in. Still, she hurled her flames at them, and though they could not reach them directly, the heat in the air caused them all to cry out.

Arthur tugged at the rope. "There it is!" He yanked them toward the passage and ran in. They hid in its cool refuge, peering blindly into the darkness and listening as the dragon clawed at the rubble. Arthur heard her snuffing, and soon could see her red eyes glowing in the darkness. They illuminated enough of the passage that Arthur could see it stretched further in. *Great Mother, please don't let it collapse.*

He jumped up and pulled at his companions, tugging them away from the opening and deeper into the cavern.

Seconds later, the dragon let loose a blast of flames directly into the passage, scorching it with heat and smoke, but the flames did not reach them. Tree roots and other bits of plant matter smoldered in the aftermath. Bedwyr took a candle from his satchel and rushed to take advantage of the flames, coming back to them with his hand arched around the flickering light like a new mother cupping her infant's head. "Now what do we do? We can't get out that way."

"No. We must find another way." Arthur felt grateful for the small lantern he still had tied to his belt. The glass around it had cracked, but the candle had not fallen out. "Light this and blow that out. We can't burn more than one candle at a time. We should save the torches for when we need more light."

They explored the passage with the modest light of the lantern, seeking a way out.

"Might we dig where the tree roots poke through? The trees can't be far behind," Gwydion reasoned.

Arthur reached a hand up and touched the roots. "These are dead. Who knows how long they've been buried, or how far beneath the surface we are. If we loosen the soil above, it could collapse."

"We simply wait, then," Bedwyr said. "There are a thousand men down in the camp. You know they must be trying to clear the rubble from the gap. We should climb back up there and start clearing it away from this side."

Arthur shook his head. "We have no idea where the dragon is. She could be perched by the gap, waiting to burn us to cinders. There's nowhere to hide up there, and no cover. It's too risky."

"What do you suggest?" Bedwyr demanded.

"We follow fresh air, if we find it, or flowing water."

Gwydion spoke up. "I know another way in. There's an underground river that flows from the lake out of the mountain and emerges several miles from here. I had planned to come that way with a guide if I couldn't find someone willing to let me in the gap."

"No," said Bedwyr, shaking the ashes from his blonde curls. "We should wait for them to reopen the side of the mountain. They won't let us rot in here."

"They could easily assume we're dead," Arthur countered, turning to Gwydion. "Are you sure of this other way out?"

"Sure enough."

408

"Then we should make our way to the lake and find the river."
Bedwyr's lip curled. "You mean the lake the dragon lives in?"
"Yes."

"The dragon waiting to kill us?"

"Yes."

"How about this," Bedwyr suggested, lighting one of his candles on a burning root. "You two stay here, and I'll climb up to let them know we're alive. If you hear me scream, I've failed, and the two of you can go and try to find this other way out." Bedwyr walked off before they could answer.

"Bedwyr!" Arthur scrambled after him, but Bedwyr did not get far. He let out a yelp just as Arthur caught up to him. He stepped back from the edge of the passage, holding his candle aloft. Arthur peered over the edge and saw what he did—nothing but black space.

"She clawed away the whole wash!" Arthur murmured. He held his lantern up, inspecting the walls all around the edges of the tunnel. They were unclimbable. He kicked some rubble off the lip of the cliff and heard it fall into nothingness.

Bedwyr let out a string of curses that would make a soldier cringe. "We're going to die in here."

"Not if we can find that river."

Bedwyr's green eyes flashed in the candlelight as he looked all around, at last accepting there was no way out of the passage. "Seems we must." He stepped away from the now sheer cliff edge and followed Arthur back to where Gwydion stood.

"We can't go back that way," Arthur announced. "Let's find your river."

Gwydion seemed strangely serene. "We'll find it. I'm sure this passage will meet up with the wash eventually. It was made by water, like all these passages, and water always finds a way out. If we keep heading downward, I'm sure we'll find it."

Arthur turned to Bedwyr. "How many candles do you have?"
"Six."

"I have eight," Arthur said, feeling relieved.

Gwydion opened his bag. "These glow as well, you know." The faint light of the collected dragon scales illuminated their faces.

Arthur opened his satchel and a reddish glow burst forth, like a bed of coals after a bonfire. "I'd forgotten that!" He laughed, relieved by their stroke of luck.

"Ha!" Bedwyr exclaimed, opening his bag of scales. "I thought they only looked this way because the firelight was shining on them."

Arthur felt wholly optimistic now. He blew out his candle and grabbed a handful of scales. "Let's go. If you smell or hear anything, speak up. Otherwise, keep quiet."

The trio descended through the dank passage. After a few hours, Gwydion spoke up. "I smell water. And fresher air. It's coming from this passage."

"I don't smell anything," Bedwyr said, after a moment. "And this way doesn't seem to head downward."

"No, but still." Gwydion reached in his pouch and pulled out a hunk of bread, tore off chunks for Arthur and Bedwyr, and then took a piece for himself.

"Oh, God bless you," Bedwyr cried, mouth full. "I was just wishing I had something to eat."

They chewed their bread in silence, evaluating the passages, and then Gwydion took a swig of his flask and handed it to Bedwyr. "My father's wine. Try it."

Bedwyr took a swig, let out a satisfied 'ah,' and passed it to Arthur, who took a few swallows. He had drunk enough wine at his father's banquets to know it was of high quality. "Who's your father, again?" he asked.

Gwydion ignored his question. "What do you say? Try this way, just for a while? If I'm wrong, we just turn back. Arthur's marking the way."

Bedwyr was now completely agreeable. "Sounds good."

Arthur chuckled at the boy's cleverness. He had often seen his mother work the same tactics on his father.

They followed the passage which led back upward for a bit, but then it curved sharply downward. The moment they reached the crest of the small hill, cool air met them.

"He's right," Arthur announced, breathing in the wet, mineral-soaked air.

"You have a nose like a hunting dog," Bedwyr commented.

"I don't smoke," Gwydion mentioned, glancing at the pipe in Bedwyr's pocket. "Ruins your sense of smell."

They kept moving in the direction of the cool air until Arthur thought he picked up the faint sound of running water. "Stop! Do you hear something?"

They froze in place.

"It sounds like a stream," whispered Gwydion after a moment.

"But small," Arthur said. "Not like a river."

"Maybe it leads to the river. It has to flow somewhere."

They moved toward the sound, coming to a small stream that ran down a steep, stalactite-studded cavern into darkness below. "We can at least fill up our skins," Bedwyr said, stooping to fill his.

"I say we follow it," Arthur suggested.

No one had a better idea. They scrambled down the steep cavern floor, staying as close as possible to the ground as slipping was inevitable on the slick muddy rocks. Arthur went first, followed by Gwydion, with Bedwyr in the rear. The ground at last leveled out to a muddy bank and Arthur felt hopeful it might be the riverbank they had been searching for. He held up his scales for a better look. Water stretched out in front of him for at least a mile, steam rising off its surface. With mounting dread, he realized where they were.

Behind him, Gwydion cried out. Arthur heard the sound of rocks falling, followed by a splash that sickened his stomach. He ran back to where the sound had come from and found Gwydion in the stream, holding his ankle, Bedwyr leaning over him with concern.

It was not long before a burst of flames lit up the cavern.

Bedwyr scooped Gwydion up and ran for cover behind a large boulder, where Arthur joined them. They were covered in mud from the climb down, and Arthur felt thankful, knowing it would help conceal their scent. He crouched at the edge of the boulder, watching the dragon sniff the air. She roamed the edge of the lake, stabbing her snout in between the rocks and tossing them aside. Eventually, she tired of this, and dove back into the lake, giving Arthur the opportunity to speak with his companions.

"I'll find the river and come back for you."

He gave them no chance to protest and ran off, intent on his quest, knowing it was their only chance of salvation.

CHAPTER FORTY-THREE
The Silver Wheel

Morgen closed her eyes and breathed in the celestial scent of her beloved Ynys Wydryn. She never tired of wandering through the apple trees or marveling at their silver boughs, heavy with beguiling fruit. She plucked a few apples to take as gifts for Lady Elayn and Lucia, whom she had visited every week since returning from Caer Leon.

She found the tree that served as the doorway to the Sisterhood's apple grove and made her way to the village. She found Lucia in the motherhouse and discovered she had been left in charge of the settlement.

"High Priestess Elayn has traveled to Dinas Emrys with a company of our initiates to preside over the Mother's blessings in Taliesin's trial," Lucia explained.

"How wonderful! My brother's among the champions," Morgen announced with pride. "He promised to bring me some of his dragon scales when he comes to Ynys Wydryn for the second trial."

Lucia shuddered. "May the Great Mother protect him. I hope he realizes how unpredictable dragons can be. I'll never forget when your father talked my husband into following a dragon down into the earth. Taliesin was just a boy, then, and they took him, too! The fools were nearly eaten! All I can say is, it's a good thing I didn't know where they were. I would have died from worry. I thought they'd simply been delayed in Emrys' court."

Morgen laughed. "Arthur made my father tell that tale a thousand times. He loves dragons."

"I fear he'll have changed his mind by the time he emerges from that mountain. Let's pray he doesn't take any unnecessary risks."

Morgen thought of Arthur and felt a jolt of worry. "Perhaps I should look in on him."

Lucia raised her brows. "I'm surprised you haven't, already."

Morgen felt a pang of guilt. She had felt so certain Arthur would succeed that she had not considered anything else. "Will you help me?"

"Of course."

The two of them sat down cross-legged near the fire, and Lucia picked up a drum and mallet. Lucia beat it softly while Morgen

412

appealed to the spirits who guard the ways to open them for her. As always, she invoked the power of her ancestors for protection as she entered the shadows.

Leaving her body was easier whenever Lucia or Nimue was with her. She felt safe and watched over. Fearless, she rose out of her flesh and went forth in her luminous body, thinking of her brother.

In a flash, she felt him beside her. He was breathing hard, clambering over rough terrain in near darkness. She smelled sulphur in the dank moist air and knew he must be within the mountain.

"Arthur," she said, putting her hand on his shoulder. He stopped walking and looked around.

"Arthur, I'm here."

"Morgen?" Arthur's breathing changed and she could see him smile.

"I'm here, brother."

"Thank God," he whispered. "I've been praying you'd hear me. The way out of the mountain has collapsed. Can you help me find the river? We think it might lead to another way out."

"I'll try."

Morgen sailed ahead of him and came to a fork with two passages. She took the one on the right first, sensing her way through the darkness, until she arrived at a deep pool. She could hear water draining out of the pool on the far side but could find no way through—not one a person in their physical body could take, in any case. She dove into the pool, feeling where the water flowed, but the openings in the rock were too small for anyone to fit through—even a child.

She returned to the fork and took the left passage. It led through a series of small caverns that eventually opened up into a cavern so enormous, she could not see its end. A large body of water stretched out across it. Steam rose from its surface, and the smell of sulphur filled the air. *A hot spring?* She moved along the edge of the water until she spied a wide ribbon of water flowing down a slippery, algae-covered wash. She followed it through a series of caverns, some of which had no dry way through. They would have to be waded. Others had only a small gap between the surface of the water and the ceiling of the cavern, but the openings seemed big enough for a person to swim through.

413

After much searching, she spied stars and flew out into the night. The water flowed out of the mountain and cascaded down into a mossy pool surrounded by ferns, clearly used for rituals and bathing by the locals, and then continued on its way through the terrain until it flowed into a larger river.

She flew higher, surveying the landscape below, and spied campfires glittering in the foothills. More winked into view as she flew toward them. *There's the encampment.*

She thought herself back to her brother's side and reported her reconnaissance.

"Arthur? Can you hear me?"

"Yes, sister. What have you found?"

"The river's more of a spring, but it's not far. When this passage forks, keep left. It will lead you to a large lake. If you stay close to the water's edge and follow it straight on for about a quarter mile, you'll find the spring. You'll have to wade or swim through some of the caverns, but it will lead you out. From there, the encampment lies to the northeast, perhaps five miles as the crow flies..."

"Thank you, sister—you've saved us. If I become High King, you shall always have a place by my side."

"Just come back to us, brother. Nothing else matters."

She was about to depart when a cold feeling of dread came over her. She rose up, looking around for its source and spied a creature's head rising up out of the lake.

"Hide, Arthur! Hide!"

But there was nowhere for her brother to hide. The shore was sandy with nothing but small rocks where he stood. A terrifying voice filled her being.

You were warned, Young Stag. You have failed.

The dragon arched her head back. Morgen flew in front of Arthur as the torrent of flames came down. Using all her fire-bending will, she forced the flames to flow around them.

When the dragon saw Arthur still standing on the shore, unburned, she lowered her head and turned it slightly to regard him with one of her eyes.

He kneeled. "Great Calontân, forgive our trespass. We wish to leave you in peace."

The dragon turned her eye to Morgen.

414

Who are you, child, who bends fire?

Morgen bowed her head and kneeled beside Arthur.

"Great Calontân, I am Morgen, Arthur's sister, and your humble servant. I beseech you, be merciful and spare my brother and his friends. I have told them the way out—they shall leave and never suffer any to open your mountain again."

The dragon's eye seemed to pull her whole being into it, as if it were a tunnel into another world. She felt suspended somewhere outside time, unable to think her own thoughts.

You, child, are a Daughter of Dragon Mistresses. I shall grant this if you and your brother swear to defend me against all enemies, and suffer none to make a prize of me.

Before Morgen could answer, Arthur stood up. "I swear to do so, Great Calontân, if you agree to honor peace in return."

You have grown bold with your sister at your side.

"We are each other's strength."

Morgen's heart soared at her brother's words, for they were true for her as well.

The dragon parted her great mouth. Her eye-tooth was as long as Morgen's leg.

I swear to honor peace, if I am left in peace. This mountain, and the one you promised, now belong to me. Any who enter are mine to do with as I wish.

She turned her eye to Arthur.

Farewell, Young Stag.

Then she turned her eye on Morgen once more.

Farewell, for now, Daughter of Dragons. You and I shall meet again.

The Great Calontân slipped back into the lake, and Morgen rose in the air to watch her glide gracefully away, her scales gleaming red and gold beneath the water.

Morgen returned to her body and opened her eyes to see Lucia across from her. She stopped drumming. "Did you find your brother?"

For a moment, Morgen forgot how to speak. She waited until she could summon words from her tongue again. "I did. He's safe."

415

Lucia handed her a cup. "Drink. You've been shadow-walking for hours."

Morgen took the cup, drained it, and then told Lucia all that had happened.

"You're both a Windwalker *and* a Firebrand?" Lucia seemed shocked.

"What's a Firebrand?" Morgen had never heard the term before.

"Have you ever caused something to catch on fire?"

Morgen did not think so. "I used to make flames dance to entertain my brother. That's all."

"Are there others in your family who can control fire as you do?"

Lucia seemed concerned, and Morgen wondered why. "No. Mother said I need to hide it, so I don't frighten people. Just like she said I must not let others see how long I can hold my breath underwater."

Lucia stared at her, as if seeing her for the first time. "So very special you are, Morgen, blessed by both fire and water, and so skilled at shadow-walking at such a young age." She paused a moment, her stare growing more intense. "When you invoke your ancestors, do you see them, by any chance?"

Morgen shook her head and suddenly became dizzy. She put her hand on the floor to steady herself.

"Forgive me. You should eat something," Lucia said. "You're still halfway between the worlds." She went to the pot hanging over the fire, ladled some broth into a bowl, and handed it to Morgen. "Sip this. I'll fetch you some bread."

Morgen blew on the hot broth, feeling its steam against her face, and thought of the dragon.

Lucia sat down near her and handed her a disk of bread. "Such gifts are often passed down from our ancestors," she told her. "You may wish to ask who they are, and see if they might speak to you."

Morgen thought that sounded like a good idea. "I'll try."

Lucia smiled at her in a curious way and stroked her hair.

Once High Priestess Elayn and the other sisters came back from Dinas Emrys, Morgen decided to return to Ynys Wydryn. "I want to be there before everyone arrives for the second trial," she told Lucia.

"Of course, you do," Lucia agreed. "Your brother may be our next High King. You, of all people, must be there to witness his moment of triumph."

The following morning, at sunrise, Lucia accompanied Morgen to the Crossing Tree, as it had come to be known. There, they said their farewells, and Morgen windwalked into Ynys Wydryn.

Once in Affalon, Morgen took a deep breath, as she always did when first arriving. It seemed to infuse her entire body and soul with knowledge of where she stood, and brought on a feeling of deep contentment. She headed for the Willow, thinking Nimue might still be sleeping. As she reached the bottom of the tor and neared the water's edge, however, she heard a voice. She held her breath and listened.

"Morgen..."

She turned around, looking for the owner of the voice. "Are you my ancestor?" She had been asking to meet her ancestors, as Lucia had suggested.

"Morgen..."

She spied a dragonfly hovering in the air above her head. It flew up and down, back and forth, almost teasing her.

"Follow me!"

Morgen had never once refused a call from any animal, bird or insect. They always had something wonderful to show her. She followed the dragonfly, who flew along the water's edge. Then, strangely, it dove in!

"Wait!" Morgen protested.

"Follow me!"

Curious, Morgen took off her shoes and cloak and dove in. She often swam at dawn when the world was at its quietest. Beneath the water, the dragonfly looked like a queen's brooch of sapphire and gold. She swam in pursuit, her eyes wide open so she would not lose sight of him.

The dragonfly led her down into the mouth of a cave, and Morgen felt a creeping fearfulness.

"Have no fear. Follow me!"

417

Morgen knew she could hold her breath for much longer, so doubled her strokes and surged after him. His body glowed so brightly, it lit up the cavern passage around her. Crystals in the cavern walls reflected the dragonfly's light, flashing beautiful colors through the water. She nearly let out her air gasping at its beauty.

The dragonfly then swam upward, and Morgen followed, kicking her feet as hard as she could to keep up. They emerged in a huge crystal cavern with a circular hole at the top, flashing colors in all directions. "Oh, Dragonfly! How beautiful!" Morgen's voice echoed through the chamber. Her heart felt so light with happiness, she whooped with joy.

The dragonfly zipped around the cave, his blue and gold body flashing back and forth, adding to the wonder. Morgen noticed the water felt warmer here, like a wonderful bath, and she swam around and around, floating on her back and looking up at the glorious crystal temple around her. "Thank you!" she cried to the dragonfly. "Oh, thank you!"

The dragonfly zipped around some more, sometimes soaring up into the sunlight through the opening overhead and then darting back down into the cave.

Morgen enjoyed the cave so much, it took her quite some time to realize there was another opening in its crystal walls. She swam to the edge of the pool where she had noticed another source of light, and, sure enough—there was something beyond the cavern the dragonfly had shown her. *Where does that passage lead?*

Morgen hoisted herself out of the pool by gripping two large crystal points. She walked through the passage toward the light. It led to yet another cavern with a wide opening. She spotted long grasses and tree branches around the cave's mouth, and beyond those, something splendid and luminous spiraling up toward the sky.

The dragonfly hovered in front of her face and then zipped out the mouth of the cave. She followed and emerged in a place she felt certain she had never seen before. *Where have I crossed into this time?* The trees and flowers were different than any she had ever seen on Ynys Wydryn.

She looked at the dragonfly, still hovering nearby. "Where have you brought me, little friend?"

She approached the spiraling column carefully, looking to the dragonfly for guidance. He seemed wholly unintimidated by the strange structure, darting and zipping around it in a playful fashion. Morgen ventured closer and saw it was a spiral staircase, whirling up to infinity. She whimpered at its beauty. "Where does it go?"

"To Caer Sidi, child," a man's voice said.

Morgen whirled around, her heart in her throat, to see a man dressed in dark blue robes. He had tattoos of the same color all over what she could see of his chest and arms. Around his neck, he wore a magnificent torc, and woven into his long silver hair hung leather thongs tied with beads and feathers, much like the ones she and the sisters had made for the apple tree.

"I'm glad you chose to follow my messenger. I am Myrthin Wyllt." The man bent his head.

"Myrthin Wyllt?" Morgen did her best to look at him and not the luminous spiral to her left. She did not want to be rude. "Are you a friend of Nimue?"

"Oh, yes. Yes. We've been friends, among other things, for many lifetimes. And we shall continue to be for many more to come."

Unlike her, Myrthin Wyllt seemed completely undistracted by anything around them. He regarded her fully, as if he had a thousand eyes and ears, all trained wholly on her. Morgen felt certain if he and Nimue were indeed good friends, as he claimed, she would have mentioned him. *Wouldn't she?*

"Have you always been here? I've never met you before. Why has Nimue never spoken of you?"

"I'm sorry to say, we've had a bit of a disagreement, Nimue and I."

Morgen's wariness spiked. "You have?"

"Yes."

"Over what?"

"Over you."

"Over me?" Morgen furrowed her brow. "I don't understand." She considered running back to the cavern and swimming back. She felt more worried about offending Nimue than offending this man. *Or spirit. Or god. Or whatever he is.*

"Well, I want to take you to meet Finbheara, King of the Fae, but she insists you must stay here. She was so angry with me for even

419

suggesting it, that she trapped me here. Now, I can only leave this place in my spirit body."

Morgen's mind lit up like a torch with the idea of meeting any of the Fae—let alone a king—but she did not want this man to know it. She proceeded carefully. "Why does she not want me to meet him?"

"She fears he'll imprison you in his kingdom. But I don't think he could, do you? You're a woman now, come into her full power—a Firebrand and a Windwalker, no less. And you've proven yourself a Doormaker, as well."

"What's that?"

"Exactly what it sounds like. You created a doorway to the Isle of the Sisterhood, did you not?"

Morgen felt confused. "I didn't create the doorway—I merely found it."

"Oh, no," Myrthin disagreed, shaking his head. "You created it. It wasn't there before." He stepped closer. "The Isle of the Sisterhood is your destiny, child. You'd know that if I were your teacher. There's much you should know that Nimue is hiding from you. Ask her. Tell her you spoke with me and you'd like to know the truth about your parents."

Again, someone had urged her toward her ancestors. But, unlike her trust in Lady Lucia, Morgen felt uneasy around this man. She backed away, fearful of his knowledge about her, yet, at the same time, unable to resist the temptation to ask him questions. *What does he mean, the truth about my parents?* She also could not deny her eagerness to meet a king of the Fae.

"Even better," he suggested, "don't ask Nimue about any of this. She might not tell you the truth. But her mistress, the Lady Arianrhod, will." He motioned toward the moonlit spiral. "She utters nothing but truth."

Morgen stared at the first step on the spiral and noticed there were patterns and markings upon it. She moved closer and bent down to study them. They moved in geometric patterns, beckoning her to touch them.

"Go to her, child. See what she has to say," Myrthin whispered. "You've nothing to fear."

Morgen looked up through the spiral, disappearing into the stars, and felt dizzy. "I can't climb that high!"

Myrthin laughed. "Windwalkers don't have to climb! You can fly, child! You know that! Ah, you have so much to learn."

Morgen knew this was true. She felt as if she were becoming lighter by the moment. Soon, her feet left the ground, and she found herself hovering above the step, as if she were treading water. She looked down at Myrthin, who gazed back at her with smiling eyes, encouraging her. She turned her eyes back up the spiral, and in a burst of will, surged skyward along its luminous coil into the heavens.

CHAPTER FORTY-FOUR
Return to Earth

Morgen felt like laughing and crying all at once, so overwhelming was the beauty around her as she burst out of the spiral.

Suspended in the violet blackness of space, engulfed in an indescribable silence she could only compare to being underwater, Morgen hovered above the glorious whirling spiral she had ascended through. She saw it was but one of thousands being pulled into a grander spiral, expanding ever outward. Towering at its center stood a tremendous being of light, hands upturned, hair and robes swirling in the ether.

The Lady Arianrhod!

Senses charged and fearful of it ending, Morgen willed her entire being to absorb the glory of the galactic majesty around her, memorizing every detail she could perceive and overflowing with gratitude for such a blessing. She tried to do the same with the luminous queen but could not bear to look at her without feeling overcome.

Figures and scenes began emerging from the spiral beneath her, rising and bounding toward her like a dog who hears his master has come home. They entered her body with an energy so powerful she felt terrified.

On and on, the parade of souls came, drowning her with their memories. Every choice she had ever made or not made arced together in a strange tapestry of light—every lifetime she had ever lived—on Earth or in other worlds—all of it converged on her, filling her with tremendous energy she simply could not assimilate. The being known as Morgen disappeared, taken over by all the beings and choices she had made or been.

Stop! Please! Mistress Arianrhod! Please, Lord, please, make it stop!

All became golden light, and she knew nothing else. No thought. No senses. No fear. Nothing but light.

Then, in the most painful moment of her life, she felt pulled from the light back into the spiral, feeling as if she were sinking into the depths of a cold black ocean.

"Oh, Myrthin! What have you done?"

Morgen heard Nimue's voice and, like a child longing for her mother, moved toward it. Soon, she heard the crackle of a fire and felt the scratchy warmth of a wool blanket on her skin.

"Why do you rebuke me, woman? She was called! You, most of all, should understand that!"

"Don't play me for a fool, Myrthin Wyllt! I know you better than that!"

Morgen could do nothing but mumble. She felt hot. So hot, she longed to kick the heavy blanket off her body, but she could not move.

"Morgen?" She felt Nimue's cool hand upon her forehead. "Speak to me. How do you feel?"

Morgen could not open her eyes. Struggling to control her panic, she whispered, "Too hot."

Mercifully, Nimue removed the blanket.

"I can't move," she murmured through heavy lips.

"But you can breathe. You'll be fine," Nimue rubbed some leaves together between her palms and put them beneath Morgen's nose. "Breathe deep."

Lavender and rosemary.

"That's it...and again..."

After a few minutes, Morgen could move her fingers and toes. With a few more breaths, her arms and legs. "Thank you."

"Now, child," she heard Myrthin say, "tell us what you saw."

Morgen did her best to describe her experience, but knew no amount of words could ever do it justice. She grasped at a few of her memories, picking out the details she could remember. She discovered that, by describing them, she could recall more, as if everything she had experienced were connected by tiny threads. Then, as if a dam had broken, she felt overcome by images so strong, she gasped. The room around her disappeared.

"Don't be afraid," she heard Nimue say. "Where are you?"

Morgen looked around, heart pounding from shock. She rode upon a beast the size of a horse with a huge hump on its back. She was with a large number of people, all of them riding donkeys or strange beasts like hers, moving through the hot land toward a settlement in the distance. "I'm in a yellow land, full of sun and

423

strange trees I've never seen before. It's so hot. I've never felt heat like this before. The people here are wearing white robes and sandals, like the Romans. I have bracelets around my arms and wrists, and necklaces made of coral and blue stones."

A young man walking beside her poured her a cup of water from a decorated bladder. She took it gratefully, gulping it down and handing the empty cup back to him. She forgot about Nimue for a moment, dropping into the vision and talking and laughing with the people around her in a strange language she did not know she could understand or speak, yet she could. They arrived at the settlement as the sun dropped low in the west, turning the sky pink and then orange.

A dragonfly zipped in front of her, and she became lucid again. She heard Nimue's voice in the sky. "Morgen, what's happening? Stay with us, if you can."

Morgen straddled the two worlds with her senses, holding each in her awareness with a delicate touch.

"Night's falling," she murmured. The sky turned purple as the last curve of the sun sank below the horizon. The air remained warm, but now, pleasantly so. Morgen could not believe night could ever feel as warm as day, yet it did—warmer than the hottest summer day at home. "I smell flowers in the air," she told Nimue. "They smell like honey tastes, thick and heavy."

This seemed to excite Myrthin. "What else, lass? What else do you see?"

Nimue caressed her forehead. "Move as if you were approaching a small animal or bird you don't want to startle. Quietly. Softly. Rest in the smell of the flowers and the warmth. Rest, until something happens."

Morgen smiled and closed her eyes, content to feel the warm night air on her skin and breathe in the sweet scent of the flowers, listening to insects chirp into the night. After a time, she heard a faint sound in the distance.

"Drums," she whispered. "Many drums."

She floated toward the sound over undulating hills of sand now silhouetted against the dying glow of the sun. A tremendous crowd of people had gathered in front of an imposing stone temple held up by massive columns. They danced to the drums around tall bonfires,

424

the women occasionally letting loose high-pitched, undulating wails into the coming night. The smell of roasted lamb, strange spices and hot bread filled the air.

The people danced hand in hand, moving in serpentine patterns between the cones of fire. Morgen felt an overwhelming urge to dance with them, and, with that thought, she was in the crowd, grasping the hands of two dancers on either side of her. Even though she did not recognize their features, she knew the man on her right was her brother, and the woman on her left was her mother. It did not seem strange to her that they had black hair and dark eyes and skin, she knew them just as well, and loved them just as much.

She stopped trying to straddle the worlds and let go of 'Morgen' once more, dropping wholly into the lifetime around her. *I want to stay here. I'm so loved.*

The drumming stopped, and the dancers stopped spinning. A man's voice rose up over the crowd, chanting.

He must be a priest.

The dancers dispersed. For the first time, through the opening gaps in the crowd, Morgen saw the body at the center of the temple. It was wrapped in linen, with an amulet over its heart. The priest beckoned the people forward. They gathered up offerings of flowers, food, and jewelry, and placed them around the body.

Morgen desperately wished she had an offering to place around the body. Instantly, the thick smell of the honey flowers engulfed her. She looked down to find her arms full of white blossoms. Smiling, she walked up to the body and laid the flowers across its chest. Her mother and brother did the same. She looked up to see the priest staring straight at her, his eyes benevolent.

"Her Ba is here among you," she understood him announce to the crowd. "Our beloved High Priestess is present, rejoicing with you. She shall live on in the afterlife, and ever be a blessing to us."

The crowd cheered as Morgen felt herself pulled away, back up into the night. *No!* She felt her soul lamenting as the world below faded away and the sound of voices replaced the revelry.

"We could lose her, you fool!" Nimue said.

Myrthin laughed. "You're the fool, my love. She's far more powerful than you think."

I'm still here, Morgen wanted to whisper, but she feared doing anything that might break her trance. She felt hungry for more. She forced her way back down toward the temple, lay down on one of the cushions in its vast refuge, and fell asleep, dreaming herself into yet a deeper dream.

She awoke in a different temple, this one built upon a jutting plateau surrounded by mountain peaks. A wide road paved with hundreds of small stones zig-zagged the face of the temple mount. Worshippers moved along its cobbles, succumbing to or waiving off the petitions of the many people selling wares or services along the way. The noise and bustle increased as the worshippers made their way up, up, up; eyes ever fixed upon the long, rectangular temple at the top.

This temple, too, had impressive columns, like the first, though of a completely different style—these were tall and white, with scrollwork at their tops. Both the columns and the people she saw upon the road looked Roman to her, but they were not speaking the language of the Romans.

Not far from the temple flowed a large spring, fed by several bronze spouts in the shape of strange beasts, coming out of the side of a mountain. A large bathing pool had been carved out of the mountain rock, with stairs leading into it. Some people were simply washing their feet and hands, but others were disrobing and fully submerging themselves. The green water sparkling in the sunlight looked so welcoming—so cool and inviting, she felt herself drawn to its edge.

The moment her foot touched the water, her clothing fell away, as if made of mist. The water welcomed her, cool and clear as she had imagined, and she let herself grow heavy and be cradled in its green embrace. It felt good to wash the sand of the desert from her body and hair. She floated in the water on her back, looking up at the clouds overhead, letting her feet bob up and down occasionally to move herself this way and that. She watched the clouds a long time before tilting herself upright again. When she did, none of the other bathers were there. She was alone in the pool. Three women in white robes stood at the pool's edge, waiting for her. Two of the women came down the first steps into the pool to meet her and guide her out. They sang a song in a language foreign to her while the first woman dried her skin with clean linen. She noticed she had fuller breasts and hips, and her hair felt heavy around her shoulders. The second clothed her in a short white robe, and the third placed a crown of laurel leaves upon her head. The women led her to the temple. The one who had crowned her walked in front, and the ones who had dried and dressed her flanked her left and right, walking slightly behind her.

People bowed as she passed, whispering prayers. As before, she began to feel who she was in this lifetime.

She stopped to drink from the holy waters of the Cassotis, which flowed near the temple. Now purified, she walked with her women to a great colonnade which marked the outside of the temple. They opened the large bronze doors for her and bowed their heads as she entered. The comforting aroma of a pinewood fire filled the air. In the center of the temple was a sunken space where a golden statue of a god presided alongside a large, rounded stone.

She became lucid for a brief moment. *This is the house of Lugh, God of the Sun, but here in this land, he, like me, is known by another name.*

A wide chair awaited her, placed over a crack in the floor, out of which vapors rose into the air. She touched the rounded stone, whispering words in a tongue her ears did not recognize, but her soul understood, and sat down in the chair. Laurel leaves were placed into her left hand and a dish of fresh water in her right. She shook the leaves as she drank the water, closed her eyes, and breathed in the vapor rising through the crack beneath her sacred chair.

She knew the vapors came from the breath of a serpentine dragon far beneath her feet, banished there by the sun god who had claimed dominion over this place.

Remember me, child? We have long been allies. It is because of you that I spared your brother.

Tethered between worlds, she honored the dragon with every drought she took if its breath, knowing it was the source of the ancient knowledge the supplicants craved. Though they believed she spoke the words of the sun god when she uttered answers to their questions, she knew the truth—she and the dragon. She suspected the sun god knew as well.

She felt one world give way to the other, pulling her toward it. Hungry for more knowledge, Morgen resisted, ignoring the voices of

Nimue and Myrthin when they came floating up on the vapors between her feet.

No, I cannot return. Not yet. I must go deeper.

She remained seated over the dragon's breath, breathing in her dark, fiery secrets, until the dragon had no more to tell her. She closed her eyes yet again and fell asleep, dropping into an even deeper dream.

She felt a jolt and gripped the arms of her chair, leaning forward to avoid being thrown from it. She opened her eyes to find herself no longer in the chair of a priestess, but in a horse's saddle, thundering across a sea of long golden grass blowing in the wind. She was surrounded by other riders, all women clad in colorful trousers, deerskin boots and gold bracelets in the form of snakes wound around their arms. She looked down and saw she, too, wore such bracelets, as well as a thick collection of beaded necklaces. She felt heavy earrings swinging against her neck and long braids snapping in the wind as she galloped alongside her kinswomen. Her body felt lithe and muscular, capable of anything.

Before long, they reached a circle of round tents made of animal hides. They all dismounted. She knew the moment her foot touched the ground why she was there, as if the earth itself had told her. She untied a leather pouch from her saddle, took out her crown of antlers, and set it upon her head. More knowledge came.

Wholly inside herself, she entered the largest tent. The man she had come to help lay in a pile of furs, wet with fever. His wife held his head in her lap and whispered her thanks, over and over, before leaving him in her care.

She knew the man's fever had not come from food or drink. It came from a predator lurking in the shadows, breathing its foul breath upon him from behind the veil of night; a predator whom none of the man's hunters could find, nor arrows could kill.

But She will. You cannot hide from Her, Dark One. Her holy fire shall burn you from your lair.

Murmuring protective mantras taught to her by the shaman mothers who had come before her, she blessed the tent, circling nine times in the direction of the sun before sitting down where the man's wife had been sitting before her. She reached into her pouch and took out her healing stones. She placed them upon the man's heart, mouth,

428

eyes and forehead. Then she took out the sacred red and white mushrooms that would reveal the unseen. She blessed them with fire and water, put them in her mouth, and took up her drum.

You cannot hide.

She beat her drum, chanting the words that would drive the dark spirit out of the man's body and into her healing stones. She saw its black form rise and beat her drum louder, forcing all her power into her words. It hissed at her, gnashing its teeth, lunging its claws at her face, but he could not touch her.

Tabiti shall burn your darkness from the world!

She heard the demon scream as white flames ignited his hair and skin, feeding like ravenous white wolves on his darkness, for fire grows stronger as it consumes. Yet still, the demon fought, his shrieks deafening.

Hail, Great Tabiti! Hail your holy fire!

She beat her drum louder, yelling her chants, filling the space with the holy words. She heard the women of the tribe all around the tent, chanting with her, forming an impenetrable circle. The demon had nowhere to flee.

The flames doubled, filling the tent with blinding light, until, as she had sworn to do, Tabiti burned the demon's darkness from the world, and its shrieks stopped. Light filled the tent, as if a star hovered at its center.

She gathered the light into her hands until they glowed like the moon. She rubbed them vigorously and placed them on the man's body. Like all light, it rushed to the dark places, until there were none left.

Great Tabiti, it is done. By your grace, it is done. She collapsed from exhaustion and fell into a deeper dream; one she could not wake from.

She could no longer remember which name or body she belonged to. She was no one.

Morgen woke to find herself in a hut she did not recognize, with Nimue by her side. Nimue's face lit up upon hearing her stir.

429

"Myrthin!" she cried, her voice croaking as if she had not spoken in hours. "Myrthin!"

She looked at her as if she had risen from the dead. "Oh, Great Mother be praised—at last, you've come back to us! Welcome back, child."

Morgen's memories slowly returned, as if she were piecing together a dream. She felt different; much different.

Myrthin appeared in the door of the hut. "She's come back to us?"

"She has."

The beads and bones decorating his robes clattered against one another as he came and knelt beside her. "You journeyed deep in the dreaming, child. So deep, we feared you'd never come back."

Nimue took her hand. "We tried to stay with you; to ensure you could find your way back, but you left us behind."

Morgen remembered. "I had to know more."

Nimue helped her sit up. "Drink this. You must stay awake now."

The brew was bitter, and Morgen knew it would do just that. The moment she had finished it, Nimue put bread in her hand. She ate it dutifully, feeling herself come into her body.

Nimue caressed her brow. "Myrthin's right. You're far stronger than I thought. You are but remembering your power from many lifetimes before. It belongs to you, this great power. Perhaps it always has." She squeezed her hand. "Know this, however: though your gifts are needed much, by your brother and others, you shall not be honored for them like you have been in your lifetimes before. You may even be reviled for them. There will be those who shall call you a witch, a sorceress, or a concubine of the devil. The gifts you have, if not tamed by the church, shall be the cause of your persecution. Yet, for your brother's sake, if you wish to help him become the Pendragon, you must endure it. Do you understand?"

Morgen already knew this and had made peace with it long ago. "Let them call me whatever they like."

Myrthin looked down at her, eyes stern. "You may find in time that even your brother may grow fearful or envious of you."

430

"Never," Morgen said, growing angry, for she now knew how timeless her bond with Arthur was. "There is nothing I wouldn't do for him, do you understand? *Nothing.*"

CHAPTER FORTY-FIVE
Queen of the Sídhe

"Let me train her, Nimue! You know nothing of the world, and her brother shall soon be Pendragon—she must be prepared!"

"I know plenty of the world! All I need to know. Or care to."

"You don't."

Morgen could hear Myrthin and Nimue quarreling again outside the hut. They had been arguing a good deal over the past three days. Morgen longed to return to the peace of Ynys Wydryn, but her journey through Caer Sidi had left her so weak she could not stand. Nimue had stayed by her side while she recovered, brewing tonics and broths for her. Myrthin, too, had been there, but offered nothing but questions. *So many questions.*

"She was chosen as much as Arthur was! She was meant to rule the underworld, and Arthur the upper! Sun and Moon! Brother and Sister! Dark and Light! Don't you see? How can you be so blind? It's her destiny, Nimue!"

Nimue remained silent, and Morgen felt frightened. *What is he speaking of? What does he mean, rule the Underworld?*

"You will stay away from her, Myrthin Wyllt. You're not to call her here again, do you understand? Your ambitions ruined my brother and nearly cost me my one true love. I don't trust you. I shall train her, and you, by the power of Arianrhod, shall remain here."

Myrthin chuckled. "Until I can summon one more powerful than you to free me. Why you would choose to imprison me so close to the source of all knowledge, I don't know. Could it be that *I* am your one true love? That you secretly desire I find a way to escape, and so become your equal?" He then murmured something Morgen could not understand. Something meant for Nimue's ears alone.

"Don't flatter yourself. Just because you've discovered how to make your skin smooth and your muscles hard again, doesn't mean I desire you any more than I did when you were withered and old. My eyes see beyond the flesh. I see the ugliness of your ambition."

Morgen heard footsteps and then the sound of the skins over the door of the hut being thrown back. She turned her head to see Nimue in the doorway. "You're awake! Good. How do you feel?" She rushed to a cauldron hanging over a fire and ladled something steaming into a bowl. "Drink this."

Morgen sat up and took the bowl, blowing on the liquid to cool it. "I think we can leave today," she whispered. In truth, she still felt weak, but she feared what might happen if they remained with Myrthin any longer. "I'll drink this, and then we'll go."

The wrinkles in Nimue's brow relaxed. "Good, good." She reached over and stroked Morgen's cheek. "I'm glad you're feeling better."

The silence in the hut felt heavy as Morgen finished her tonic. She felt pleased to discover it lent her a good measure of strength, and she dared to think she might actually feel as well as she had led Nimue to believe. She finished it and stood up. She wobbled a bit but took a deep breath and willed her body steady. As soon as she felt stable, she took Nimue's hand. "Let's go. Swimming's the easiest thing in the world. Surely easier than carrying the weight of this body around on land."

Nimue smiled. "Very true."

They emerged from the hut to find Myrthin in their way, arms crossed and eyes unblinking. He pinned his gaze on Morgen. "You can come back whenever you like," he offered, shooting Nimue a defiant glance. "Here, you can discover who you truly are and what you're meant to do in this lifetime." His tone sounded desperate to Morgen and she felt a sudden repellence toward him.

"Come, Morgen." Nimue grasped her hand and led her back toward the crystal cave.

"But what did he mean, rule the Underworld?" Morgen could not forget Myrthin's words.

Nimue sighed. "He believes you could rule the lands of the Sídhe."

"But how?" Morgen struggled to understand. "Why does he believe that?"

Nimue gazed toward the setting sun a moment. "You know you have gifts, Morgen. Like I do. The king and queen who rule the Sídhelands of Connacht would love to have you serve them with those gifts. This is why Myrthin wants to take you to them."

"But if I go there, I might never return, isn't that right?" Morgen had heard scores of cautionary tales about the Sídhe. Every family had lost someone to the hills.

"It is. So, if you wish to see your mother and brother again, and I know that you do, you cannot go. The Sídhe are powerful, and in their own realm, more powerful than you can imagine." She turned and gripped Morgen's hands. "Promise me you'll never return to the Crystal Cave without me. Believe me when I tell you, Myrthin's not to be trusted. It's why I've imprisoned him there."

Morgen did not want to swear. The idea of never seeing Caer Sidi again made her soul wither with sadness. "But I must return— there are so many things I haven't finish learning—memories I've not visited yet—I want to go back."

"Perhaps one day, Morgen—but as you are now, it's too dangerous. You could barely move for three days. I almost lost you. What would I tell Ta—" She left off. "What would I tell your mother? When you're stronger, I'll take you back, but you're never to go there on your own. Do you understand?"

Morgen could not bring herself to say anything.

"Please, Morgen. Try to understand, there are things you're not ready for yet. You will be, in time, but not yet."

Later that night, as Morgen rested beneath the Willow, her mind wandered back over all the things Myrthin had said.
Could it be true? Am I destined to become Queen of the Underworld? Queen of the Sídhe? She pictured herself wearing gossamer gowns of spider webs and flower petals, like the stories said the Sídhefolk wore, riding on the back of an owl beneath a full moon. *What if it's true? It would mean that I, too, am destined to rule a kingdom, like Arthur.*

This idea appealed to her far more than becoming a nun or a wife to some lord or king, like Morgause. Yet those were the only two roles open to her in the world she had come from.

She succumbed to sleep, and sometime in the night, she dreamt Myrthin came and stood outside the veil of the Willow. She could see him there, through the swaying leaves.

"Morgen," he said in a warm, low voice.

Her heart quickened and she sat up. "What are you doing here? How did you get out of the cave?"

"My spirit's not imprisoned. Just my body. May I come in?"

Morgen remembered what Nimue had said: *Myrthin is not to be trusted.*

"May I come in?"

"No. Go away. I don't want to talk to you."

He chuckled, and the sound of it reminded her of a cat purring. "You summoned me."

"No, I didn't."

"Oh, but you did."

Morgen felt confused.

"I know you're scared, so I'll tell you why."

"I'm not scared!" Morgen snapped hotly.

"You are. And that's to be expected. But you'll grow out of your fear, just as you'll grow out of your hesitation, because you're meant to become someone greater than sister to the Pendragon, or wife to an old, rotting king. You know it. I know it. Nimue knows it. I can tell she loves you deeply, perhaps because you're the only child of the man she thinks is her one true love. But I can teach you so much more than she can, child. I was *her* teacher. She means well, but she cannot offer you what I can." He parted the Willow's veil without moving his hands. "I'll not come in against your wishes, but I must look you in the eyes as I invite you to become Queen of the Sídhe."

Morgen had scarcely listened to anything he had said after *you're the only child of her one true love.* "What do you mean, I'm the only child of her true love? Is she in love with my father?"

"She is. But your father is not Uthyr Pendragon. Has Nimue not told you that?"

Morgen felt dizzy.

"You're a grown woman now. You deserve to know the truth. Do you want to know the truth?"

She clutched her stomach, fearing what she might learn, yet unable to say anything but, "I do."

Myrthin smiled. "Courageous, as always. The truth is, you were conceived in the Hollow Hills of Knockma. This is why you can both see and create doorways between the worlds, and wind-walk and shadow-walk with such ease. Your father is Taliesin the Bard, born of

Cerridwen, Mistress of Darkness and Consort to Arawn. Your mother is Arhianna of the Oaks, Firebrand and Mistress of Dun Scáthach. She was born of Lucia, granddaughter of the powerful priestess Rowan, blessed by the Sight, and Bran of the Oaks, now Guardian of the Otherworld. These are your ancestors, and believe me, no one with more powerful ancestors exists."

"You lie," Morgen protested, her mind fighting against what he had told her. "Nimue's right—you're not to be trusted."

But, try as she might, she could not keep his words from embedding themselves into her whole being like seeds, destined to grow. She wanted him to leave so she could wake Nimue and demand the truth, but he remained where he was.

"The Sídhe have been seeking you since before you were born. They would have stolen you away to Knockma long ago, were it not for Taliesin. To protect you, he took you to Queen Igerna, who had just given birth to Arthur. The queen raised you as the twin sister to her own son, telling nobody her dark secret—not even her husband, Uthyr Pendragon. Only she, Taliesin, Nimue, and I know the truth. So, the question remains: will you sit in your father's court, reviled and misunderstood, or will you be worshipped as the Queen of Magic that you are? Your kingdom is not here, Morgen of the Sídhe. Would you not see the land of your beginning? Speak with your true people?"

"Liar!" Morgen lanced the word at him like an arrow from the bow of her mouth. The force of her anger and fear caused her to wake up, heart thundering. She took a deep breath.

It was just a dream. Just a dream. It's not true.

She lay still a long time while her heart calmed, watching the moonlight dance on the leaves of the Willow, but found she could not sleep. She left the tree to get a drink of water and stepped on something sharp that pierced her foot. She cried out and bent down to see what it was. There, tangled in the grass, lay a leather thong tied with broken shells, bones and beads. Her hand trembled as she picked it up.

"Nimue!" she called, but Nimue did not answer.

She went back into the shelter of the Willow and looked on the other side, where Nimue usually slept. She was not there.

436

Morgen went in search of her, desperate to learn the truth. She found her sitting on the log by the lake, watching the first blush of dawn light up the sky. Nimue turned at the sound of her approach and smiled, patting the log beside her.

Morgen instead walked in front of her and blurted, "Is Master Taliesin my father?"

Nimue stood up and looked at her with a pained face. "What happened? Did you dream of him?"

Morgen shook her head. "I had a dream, but not of him. I dreamed Myrthin told me this."

Nimue sighed and took Morgen's hands in her own, gripping them tightly. "Please forgive me, Morgen. He didn't want you to know. He didn't want you to feel confused or hurt."

"Who?" Morgen demanded, growing angry. She pulled her hands away.

"Master Taliesin."

Morgen backed away, eyes filling with tears. "It's true, then?"

"Yes, child. It's true. Master Taliesin is your father."

"And who is my mother?"

Nimue's face looked as if someone were twisting a dagger in her ribs. "The woman who gave birth to you is Arhianna of the Oaks, now the Mistress of Dun Scáthach."

Morgen shook her head to rid her mind of this knowledge, but it was no use. *My mother, Nimue, Taliesin—they've all been letting me believe a lie!* Her world crumbled around her. "How can this be? How could you have kept this from me?"

Then, the most painful realization of all pierced her heart, like an arrow loosed from a bow.

Arthur's not my twin. Oh, God. He's not even my brother!

This realization, far more disturbing than anything else, sent her into a panic. Eyes wide, she collapsed to her knees and wailed, unable to stop the pain engulfing her.

Nimue dropped to her knees and tried to comfort her, but Morgen shoved her away, falling forward onto the shore. She sobbed until her throat felt raw and her stomach muscles cramped from soreness.

Nimue did not attempt to touch her again but stayed nearby. Though Morgen felt intense anger toward her, she nevertheless felt glad Nimue had not abandoned her to her sorrow. But she could not stay with Nimue any longer. *Not now. Not after this.*

At nightfall, Morgen slipped quietly away from the Willow and swam back to the crystal cave. Myrthin stood waiting for her when she surfaced. She pulled herself out of the pool, walked over to him and held out the string of beads she had found by the Willow. "Teach me everything."

Myrthin smiled and took back his beads.

"And then take me to Knockma."

Myrthin's eyes lit up.

She held up a finger. "But I must be able to return—my brother needs me." Her throat tightened. "I mean, *Arthur* needs me."

"I cannot promise that," Myrthin said. "Once you enter the realm of the Sídhe, things change."

"What things?"

"Time. Distance. Colors. Feelings. Music. Everything."

Myrthin's words did nothing but stoke her interest. She looked up the spiraling staircase of moonlight that led to Caer Sidi, a mere dozen feet from where they stood. Even during the day, the spiral was visible, twisting through a permanent column of night into the stars. "Is that how we get there?"

Myrthin shook his head. "Oh, no. The kingdom of the Sídhe lies within the earth, not above it. The Sídhefolk are spirits of nature, not of the heavens."

"Then how?"

"Through the hills, of course." Myrthin pointed to a long chain of purple hills, far to the west, that Morgen had not remembered seeing there before. "A doorway must be created. But we know you can do that."

Morgen knew Nimue would disapprove. She hesitated. "How long will it take us to get there? Do you have horses?"

"We don't need horses." He pointed to the tallest hill. "All you must do is picture the two of us standing at the foot of that one, there. The tallest. Do you see it?"

"Yes."

"Imagine standing there, with me by your side, just as we are now." He took her hand.

Again, she hesitated.

"What holds you back? What do you fear?"

"Not seeing those I love again."

Myrthin laughed. "Where you're going, you'll learn to master time and space—nothing and no one shall be beyond your grasp! Fear is for the small-minded, my child. And you are anything but. Cast it aside and remember the powerful being you are!"

In a sudden surge of confidence, Morgen's hesitation vanished. She looked toward the tall mountain, imagining the two of them standing at the base of it, looking up. The next moment, that is where they stood. She looked over at Myrthin and smiled.

He grinned at her, eyes sparkling, and took her hands in his. The intensity of his stare frightened her. Instinctively, she pulled away, but he held her hands fast. He turned them over and examined her palms, left, then right, tracing their lines with a long, graceful finger. His touch felt strangely soothing, as if she were a babe being rocked to sleep, and she relaxed.

"Such power in these hands," he whispered. "The hands of one who has wielded great magic in many lifetimes." He looked up at her again, his grey eyes gripping hers. "You shall rule a kingdom as surely as your brother shall." He held her hands tighter, pulling her closer to him. She resisted, holding her ground.

"We've been together before. Do you remember?"

She did not answer. She knew they had. She had seen him many times while exploring Caer Sidi, but had not wanted to admit it. She feared encouraging him. She looked away, again, trying to pull her hands from him. "Let go."

"Look at me."

She did not.

He gripped her hands tighter. "I said, look at me! You must know me if I am to teach you. Look at me, or I'll take you back to Nimue!"

Morgen looked. Before her eyes, Myrthin's face and body changed, morphing into the various men he was in the lifetimes they had shared together: in Egypt, in Greece, in Scythia; as lovers, as brother and sister, as father and daughter, but most often as priest

439

and priestess. She felt stunned, unable to move, hypnotized by his changing forms. With each one, memories came to her, reminding her of her overwhelming journey in Caer Sidi. She felt as if she were choking on them. "Stop!" she managed to cry. She yanked her hands from his grip and shoved him away from her. To her utter shock, he sailed some twenty feet in the air and slammed against a tree.

Terrified, Morgen's hands flew to her mouth. *Oh, dear God! Great Mother! What have I done?*

Before she could run to see if Myrthin was dead or merely injured, she heard a horse galloping in her direction and whirled around to see a well-armed man with sleek features and pale skin staring down at her from his mount. She marveled at the length of his fingers, ears and nose, but his most captivating feature was his upturned eyes—an intense shade of icy blue that nearly glowed from his eye sockets.

He pointed a sword at her chest. "Name yourself."

Morgen felt dizzy from the adrenalin racing through her blood. She blurted out, "Lady Morgen of Caer Leon."

The rider's expression stretched into a smile; whether joyful or wicked, she could not decide.

The rider pointed toward the lifeless lump at the base of the tree. "And who is that?"

"The Great Druid, Myrthin Wyllt."

"Not so great at the moment, is he?" More teeth joined the rider's grin. Three other rangers soon arrived from different directions, encircling her. One scooped up Myrthin as if he were made of straw and laid him across his saddle.

"If you don't want to travel in the same fashion, I suggest you climb up. In front, please." He held out his hand to help her.

Morgen backed away, scanning her surroundings for the best direction to run.

The smile disappeared from the rider's face, replaced with a thin cold line that reminded her of a snake. "As High Ranger of Connacht, I demand you come with me."

In a panic, Morgen tried to 'think' herself back to the Crystal Cave the way she had 'thought' herself to the foothills. She closed her eyes, hopeful of success, but try as she might, she could not concentrate. Upon opening them, she found she was still there, at the foot of the rider's horse, his glare growing ever more frightening.

"So be it," In a swift flash of strength, he reached down, grabbed her, and threw her over his saddle. "Ride on!" he commanded. "Back to court!"

"As you command, Lord Maelwys!"

The strange man named Lord Maelwys slipped her belt over the pommel of his saddle. "So sorry, child, but I did give you a chance to ride comfortably. Seems you prefer to learn the hard way. I do hope you'll be more cooperative at court."

Morgen had wanted to spit in the face of her smug captor every moment of the uncomfortable journey to court, but now, standing within its glory, she wanted to kiss him for bringing her there. The trees that formed its cathedral-like edges, the flowers that served as its carpets, the sky overhead—all were ablaze with colors more vibrant than she had ever seen in the world she had been born into. She felt the urge to weep.

"My queen, this is young Morgen, whom I promised to bring to you. We've also brought you Myrthin Wyllt, though he cannot speak at the moment. I imagine he'll recover soon enough, the old mule."

The queen seemed a vision from a dream. She peered down at Morgen with wide, incandescent eyes from beneath a living crown of butterflies. "Welcome home, Morgen. We've been waiting for you."

From all sides, creatures moved toward Morgen bearing gifts—resplendent bouquets, gowns so light they seemed woven of mist or moonlight, flutes fashioned from river reeds, delicate baskets full of fat red and white mushrooms—all were laid at her feet.

"You shall be our salvation."

Salvation? Morgen felt confused. "I don't understand."

"You shall open the doors of the hills for us, so that we may roam freely between the worlds once more. An age of magic shall begin!"

Morgen had no idea how she would accomplish such a thing—or even that she should. "I'm sorry, oh beautiful queen of the Sídhe,

441

but I know nothing of these doors—Myrthin Wyllt brought me here. Only he knows."

The queen stood up. "He knows very little."

Morgen saw the queen's wings for the first time. They were reminiscent of Myrthin's dragonfly, blue-green and purple, shimmering in the soft sunlight as they carried the queen aloft, filling the air with a warm hum. "Very little," Queen Oonagh repeated. She floated down to where Morgen stood. "And you know more than you think." The queen smiled down at her. "Together we shall do great things, child." She stroked her cheek with a long cool finger that felt like a soft breeze.

CHAPTER FORTY-SIX
From Stone to Throne

Nimue secretly followed Dubricius to the Thorne tree and watched him from the shadows as he prepared the trial that would determine the next High King.

For three days, she watched him fast and pray, sleeping only a few hours each night with the sword *Excalibur* upon his chest as if he had been laid in a tomb with it.

At the break of dawn on the third day, he awoke and began to speak in a strange, incomprehensible language. He looked up and fell to his knees as if shot by an arrow. Nimue soon realized why.

Descending from the clouds came beings with three sets of wings. They were more beautiful and terrible than Fae; more glorious and fiery than dragons. The creatures enfolded Dubricius in their many wings, and the sword within his hands burned as bright as the sun. His strange words grew thunderous. The wind changed and picked up, blowing so forcefully around the stone that Nimue could no longer hear the archbishop's cries. Then, with a mighty heave, he plunged *Excalibur* into the stone as if it were as soft as the earth after a good rain, and there it stayed.

For the first time in her life, Nimue became curious about this God of the Christians.

The sisters from the abbey soon came to witness the miracle. From that moment on, *Excalibur* was never left unattended. Prayers were ceaseless, day and night, as the order prepared for the arrival of the men who had been victorious at Dinas Emrys. Nimue, too, went to prepare, for she had much to pray about, too.

The next full moon arrived, and with it came not only all of Brython's champions from Dinas Emrys accompanied by their households, but hundreds of travelers intent on witnessing who would become their next king. Who among them, all wondered, would pull *Excalibur* from the stone?

Unable to bear crowds, Nimue watched from the shadows as Dubricius and Taliesin led the champions up the hill to the Holy Thorne and the stone beside it.

Dubricius raised his hands, and all fell silent. Even the wind seemed to die down.

"My dear brothers and sisters in Christ, we have gathered on this holy isle today to witness God choose a king for us."

Nimue watched in awe as the clouds parted and the sun came out, illuminating *Excalibur*'s stunning blade. People began murmuring, some whispering and pointing, some crossing themselves, others bowing their heads to pray.

Dubricius raised his hands to the sky. "Praise be to you, oh Holy God, for you are mighty in spirit and righteous in purpose; you know the number of the stars and give to all of them their names; abundant is your power; beyond measure, your understanding. You are a strong fortress, eternal and unbounded; an everlasting rock."

The archbishop sprinkled holy water upon the stone while three monks walked around it, swinging braziers of burning incense.

Dubricius then reached down and gripped the hilt of *Excalibur*. "Almighty God, let only he whom you deem righteous and worthy release this sword from the stone in which it rests, thereby revealing your will. We ask this in the name of Jesus Christ, your only begotten son, born of the blessed Virgin Mary. Amen."

A resounding chorus of "amens" rolled through the crowd.

The archbishop crossed himself and raised his hands again. "Those who have emerged victorious from the lair of the dragon, step forward."

Perhaps a dozen men approached. Upon their shields, Nimue recognized the sigils of several great clans, but none were as terrible and majestic as the red dragon emblazoned across that of the young man she knew had to be Arthur, son of Uthyr. She studied him closely, watching his every movement. *Is he truly to be our High King, Mistress?*

As much for his family, as for himself, this choice has been made.

One by one, the archbishop summoned the champions forward to grip the hilt of *Excalibur*, and one by one, they failed to pull it out.

When Arthur stepped forward, however, the blade began to glow, as if the sun shone on it alone. Arthur made the sign of the cross, fell to one knee and whispered a prayer, then approached. To everyone's astonishment, before he had even wrapped his hand around the hilt, the sword leapt up into his hand.

It was at that very same moment that Nimue heard an unearthly shriek fill the sky.

She comes. Nimue threw her eyes into the clouds, searching.

Another shriek shook the sky and the crowd grew restless.

"What in God's name was that?" a man asked. "That was no hawk's cry!"

A woman wrung her hands. "God is angry we are testing him!"

"No, you fool!" said another. "It's Satan who's angry! A righteous king chosen by God shall now rule Brython and drive his heathens from our shores!"

Cai of Gwynedd was the first to drop to one knee and cried, "All hail Arthur Pendragon!"

Bedwyr quickly followed suit.

Those who had witnessed the miracle did likewise, but those farther down the hill, who had not, had no such vision to calm their fear. They clutched at one another, stumbling about as they shaded their eyes and searched the sky for the source of the terrifying shrieks.

Nimue burst from the shadows and spoke with a voice that somehow reached all ears, "Bow your heads, people of Brython! The Red Dragon approaches!"

The crowd churned into a panic, running to take cover where they could. Arthur, Taliesin, Dubricius and most of the champions stood their ground, along with some of the more courageous onlookers. Nimue especially admired the archbishop's courage, again surprised by his character, for he had not run nor cowered, but watched with awe, transfixed, on his knees beside the stone which had held *Excalibur.*

Nimue made her way to the stone, for this was the moment she had been anticipating. The dragon arrived with the fierceness of a storm, blocking out the light of the sun. Her wings stirred the wind so forcefully as she landed atop the hill, that anyone brave enough to still be there fell to his knees, unable to withstand the force.

A fresh wave of pandemonium broke out on the hill. People screamed and scrambled in all directions. Most of the champions took cover as well, except for Cai, Bedwyr and a young man from the crowd who crouched some twenty feet from them, peeking at the sky from beneath his cloak.

"Gwydion!" Arthur yelled to the boy. "Come here!"

The boy stared up at the dragon with eyes round as hen's eggs. As soon as he ventured closer, however, Nimue knew it was not a boy she beheld but rather a maiden in trousers. *Now there's a bold lass.* In a flash, she saw a wedding at Caer Leon and smiled. *A future queen is she, Mistress?*

But Nimue had no time to listen for an answer. She stepped forward and knelt before the Red Dragon, basking in the coppery light cast by the afternoon sun on the magnificent creature's scales. "Great Calontân, welcome to Ynys Wydryn. You honor us with your presence."

The dragon bent her head toward Nimue, who stroked it with her lithe, white fingers.

Nimue turned to face the crowd, the Red Dragon's head at her shoulder, and beckoned to Arthur. "Step forward and kneel, Arthur, son of Igerna, if you would be king."

Arthur came forward without hesitation and knelt.

Nimue noticed the crowd creeping back toward the scene, too curious to stay away or remain hidden. She addressed them once more. "*Excalibur* was born of Brython's two sacred blades, *Dyrnwyn*, blade of the sun, and *Caledgwyn*, blade of the moon. It was forged in Caer Sidi in the breath of the Red Dragon by the great god of all blacksmiths, Gofannon, brother of my mistress, the Lady Arianrhod." She looked Arthur in the eye. "It has leapt to your hand, son of Igerna, but you must marry the land to wield it. Do you accept?"

Dubricius glanced toward Taliesin with a look he could not quite decipher, but before either of them could say anything, Arthur spoke.

"I do."

Nimue smiled. The dragon's head flashed in the sunlight as she tilted it back and snorted fiery sparks and smoke into the now clear sky. Nimue turned to the dragon, who dug her talons into the earth creating deep, black furrows. Nimue bent down and gathered up a handful of earth.

"Do you, Arthur, son of Igerna, swear to take this land as your pure and virtuous bride; to protect her from all enemies, within and without; to husband her and respect both her glories and terrors?"

"I do so swear."

Nimue gave him a nod of satisfaction. "Open your hands and make the oath."

Arthur offered her his cupped hands and she poured the earth into them. He turned to the now gathered crowd.

"I, Arthur, son of Uthyr Pendragon and Igerna of the Summer Country, swear unto death to defend this land against all enemies; against all who would crush her beauty with their blasphemous feet, or plow her curves with their poisonous seed. No longer shall our enemies kill her children or take her treasures. She is now my precious bride, and is, as she has always been, your eternal queen."

He turned to address the of champions who had come to the hill. "Will you fight for her?" he asked them. "Will you swear spear and sword to defend her alongside me? Will you ride beneath the banner of the Red Dragon? For, my brothers, as you can see, she has awoken!"

Nimue watched, with deep satisfaction, as every champion there kneeled before Arthur. She touched him on the shoulder. "Now, my king, you must ride her."

The look of confidence drained from his eyes.

"Let all witness your courage as you ride her back to Caer Leon."

Arthur turned to the beast, and, after a conversation only they could hear, it seemed they reached an understanding.

Then, in the greatest act of courage any man, woman or child assembled had ever seen, Arthur Pendragon climbed astride the neck of Calontân and let her bear him into the sky.

The crowd forgot everything else, craning their necks and shielding their eyes as the great beast sailed the winds above.

Nimue sensed Taliesin by her side and felt his breath in her ear. "It is done, my love," he said, staring up at the sky with as much wonder as any of them. "And yours, dear Nimue, was the greatest trial of all."

Nimue smiled. "There are always three, you know."

"It is the sacred number." Taliesin kissed her hand and looked with satisfaction at the massive crowd, knowing all would carry their own fantastic accounts of Arthur Pendragon back to their villages, taverns and halls where their magnificence would only grow. *Arthur*

Pendragon, who pulled the sword from the stone and rode a dragon to his throne!

The bards of Brython would feast on such a story for thousands of years.

Nimue squeezed his hand. "Now that Arthur has succeeded, we must turn our efforts toward Morgen."

Taliesin now looked at the crowd with different eyes, scanning it for his daughter's face. *How could I not have noticed until now?*

"Oh, gods. Where is she?" The look on Nimue's face drained all the satisfaction from his chest. "What's happened?"

"Morgen is no longer a child. She's a woman, and her power has grown obvious. She found the crystal cave, and there met Myrthin Wyllt, who could see the truth of who she was and told her. She feels betrayed by us and has freed him. By now, I imagine he's convinced her to go with him to Knockma."

Deep down, Taliesin knew this day would come, no matter how hard he tried to prevent it, so he did not allow himself to grow angry. Instead, he focused on possible actions to take while the crowds left the shores.

Once all of the skiffs and boats had departed from the island and none remained but the nuns of Glastonbury, Taliesin and Nimue passed back into the hidden realm of Ynys Wydryn to speak of Morgen. Taliesin had thought of nothing else over the past few hours and had made a decision.

"I must return north and tell Arhianna the Sídhe have taken not only her brother captive, but also her daughter. Where she hesitated to act before, I doubt she will now."

Nimue took his hand. "I thought that would be your decision. And I wish to go with you."

Taliesin felt both pleased and surprised. "Are you certain?"

"I am." Nimue gave him a strong nod. "We should seek Amergin's help as well. And, of course, that of our new king. He cannot stand by."

"No, he cannot." *And Arthur must be told the truth as well. It won't do to have Morgen reveal it.* "I must tell Igerna what has happened, and together, she and I must tell Arthur."

"Yes, that is wisest, my love."

Taliesin regretted the sorrow and betrayal he would have to lay on the shoulders of their new king, but the time for dark secrets was over. A new day had dawned—a new hope—and Arthur deserved to begin his reign in the full light of the truth, however painful it might be; Arthur Pendragon, who, Taliesin felt sure now, would become the greatest king Brython had ever known.

Character Reference

AMERGIN (AM-ergin) - bard, druid and judge who battled the Tuatha de Danaan alongside his brothers to avenge their murdered uncle; one of several foster-fathers to Cú Chulainn, beloved hero of ancient Ireland

AMLAWTH (AM-loth) - Igerna's father, a powerful lord of Dumnonia

ARAWN (AIR-oun) - Lord of the Otherworld/Underworld

ARHIANNA (ahr-ee-AH-nah) - daughter of Bran and Lucia, gifted with the power to control fire; twin sister to Gareth

ARVEL (AR-vel) - son of Elffin and Ula

BEDRAWT (BED-rawht) - Lord of Glywysing, one of the landholds east of Caer Leon

BEDWYR (BED-weer) - son of Bedrawt of Glywysing

BRAN – servant of Arawn, former chieftain of the Oaks, husband of Lucia, father of Arhianna and Gareth, now a servant of Arawn in the Underworld

CADWALLON (cad-WAH-len) - nicknamed Cadwallon "Long Hand" Lawhir, a lord of Gwynedd

CARADOC FREICHFRAS (KAIR-a-doc) - also Caradoc "Strongarm" Freichfras, lord of Gwent, son of Igerna's sister, Tywanwedd

CEFFYL DŴR (KEFF-il-door) - Tegid Voel's ship, now captained by his daughter by Cerridwen, Creirwy

CEREDIG (KAIR-ih-dig) - lord of Alt Clud, a kingdom in the far north located in modern-day Scotland

CERRIDWEN (KAIR-id-wen) – goddess of the Underworld, keeper of the Sacred Cauldron, initiator of Gwion, mother of Creirwy, Morvran (deceased) and Taliesin, grandmother of Morgen

CONNLA (KONN-lah) – son of Cú Chulainn and Scáthach the First

CREIRWY (KREE-wee) - daughter of Cerridwen and Tegid Voel, now captain of the Ceffyl Dŵr

CÚ CHULAINN (koo KULL-an) - "The Hound of Ulster," beloved hero of Ireland, son of Deichtine and Conchobar mac Nessa; the only warrior capable of matching Scáthach the First in combat

CYNWAL (KUHN-wal) - Queen Igerna's eldest brother

CYNYR CEINFARFOG (KON-er kain-VAR-vog) - Lord of Caer Cynyr, cousin of Igerna, known also as Cynyr Wledig (the Imperator) and Cynyr Goch (Connor the Red)

DAOINE SÍDHE (DEE-neh SHEE) – "people of the hills," supernatural beings descended from the Tuatha Dé Danann, also referred to as fairies or fae

DUBRICIUS (doo-BRIH-shus) - archbishop of the early Roman Christian church in Brython

ELAYN (ee-LAYN) - High Priestess of the Isle of the Sisterhood in Lake Bala

ELFFIN (ELL-fin) - son of Gwythno Garanhir, foster father to Taliesin, Lord of Maes Gwythno or the Cantre'r Gwaelod (Lowland Hundred) known as Cardigan Bay in modern-day Wales

EIRE (ehr, or –EHR-eh) - Irish/Gaelic name for Ireland

ELODIR (eh-lo-DEER) - half-Fae associate of Cú Chulainn

EMRYS (EM-riss) - son of Constantine, the Romano-British emperor; known also as Ambrosius Aurelianus

FEIDHLEIM (FAY-lim) - head of Amergin's order in Ireland in his absence

FINBHEARA (FIN-varra) - king of the Daoine Sídhe of Knockma, located in modern-day county Connacht, in Ireland

FIONN MAC CUMHAILL (finn ma-COOL) - legendary hunter-warrior in Ireland

GARETH (GAH-reth) - current lord of Mynyth Aur, son of Bran and Lucia; twin brother to Arhianna

GAWYR (GOW-er) – giant who once served as companion and bodyguard to Taliesin, arranged by Urien of Rheged; now a warrior at Dun Scáthach

GEREINT LLYNGESOC (GAIR-ent LIN-geh-soc) - husband to Queen Igerna's younger sister, Gwyar; one of Arthur's many cousins

GWYDION (gwid-ee-ohn) – a youth Arthur meets at Taliesin's trial on Dinas Emrys

HYWEL (HOW-el) - one of Morrigan's warriors

IGERNA (ih-GERN-ah) - daughter of Amlawth, widow of Gorlois, wife of Uthyr Pendragon; mother of Arthur by Uthyr, mother of Morgause by Gorlois, foster mother to Morgen, daughter of Taliesin and Arhianna

ILLTUD FARTHOG (ILL-tewd VARTH-og) - Igerna's nephew by her elder sister, Rheinwylydd; cousin to Arthur

INGVAR (ING-vahr) - Jute chieftain loyal to Hengist, enslaver of Arhianna and her former clansisters, murderer of Arhianna's husband, Jørren

IRWYN (IR-winn) - Saxon ship-builder brought to Maes Gwythno by Garanhir, good friend and ally of Bran and Elffin

JØRREN (YOR-en) - Jute chieftain and former husband of Arhianna, murdered by Ingvar

LUCIA (loo-CHEE-ah) - clairvoyant granddaughter of High Priestess Rowan of the Isle, wife of Bran, mother of Arhianna and Gareth

LOT (Welsh: Lludd) - Lord of Gododdin, a kingdom in the far Northeast in modern-day Scotland; husband to Morgause

MAELWYS (MALE-wiss) - powerful apprentice of Myrthin Wyllt, brother of Nimue

MYRTHIN (MEHR-thin, English: Merlin) - arch-druid and advisor to Emrys and Uthyr

NIAMH (NEHV) - steward of Dun Scáthach

OISIN (UH-sheen or O-sheen) – famous Irish bard; son of Fionn Mac Cumhaill, a renowned warrior of Ireland

OONAGH (OO-nah) - Queen of the Daoine Sídhe, wife of King Finbheara

SCÁTHACH (SKAH-tagh) - queen and warlord of Dun Scáthach on the modern-day island of Skye in Scotland

TEGID VOEL (TEH-gid VOLE) - giant who fathered Creirwy and Morvran by Cerridwen

TUATHA DE' DANANN (TOO-ah day da-NAHN) - ancient gods of Ireland and ancestors of the Daoine Sídhe

ULA (OO-la) - selkie foster mother to Taliesin; mother to Arvel by Elffin

URIEN OF RHEGED (OO-ree-en of REH-ged) – lord of Rheged, a kingdom in the North

UTHYR (OO-ther) PENDRAGON – chief warlord of Brython

Location Reference

AFFALON (AHV-uh-lon) - meaning "land of apples," Affalon is the ethereal island realm of Nimue, Lady of the Lake and priestess of Arianrhod; known also as Ynys Wydryn

ALT CLUD (alt CLOOD) - kingdom in the western part of Scotland that later became known as Strathclyde. Its main fortress sat upon Dumbarton Rock, known in the Iron Age as Alt Clud or Alt Clut

AMBRIUS (AM-bree-us) - ancient name for a town in modern-day Wiltshire on the eastern edge of the Salisbury Plain where Stonehenge stands

ARMORICA (ar-MOR-i-kah) - "place by the sea," ancient name for Brittany, known also as Gaul at the time; Armorica was part of Gaul that lay between the Seine and Loire rivers, as well as what is now known as the Brittany peninsula

CAER LEON (kair le-ON) – fortress and main residence of Uthyr Pendragon

CAER LIGUALID (kair lih-GWAH-lid) - fortress of Urien of Rheged; former name of the settlement now known as Carlisle, in Cumbria, near the modern-day Scottish border

CAER LUNDEIN (kair LUN-den) - ancient Welsh name for London

CAER MINCIP (kair MIN-cip) - ancient Welsh name for modern day St. Albans, located on the northwestern outskirts of London

CAER SIDI (kair SIH-dee) - fortress of the goddess Arianrhod located within the constellation of the Corona Borealis

DUMNONIA (doom-NO-nee-ah) - ancient name for modern-day Cornwall, in southwestern Britain

DUN SCÁTHACH (doon SKAH-tagh) – the "Fortress of Shadows," on the modern-day Isle of Skye in northwestern Scotland

DYFED (diff-UD) - kingdom in southwest Wales

EXETER (EX-eh-ter) – ancient Roman city in modern-day Devon county in Britain

GODODDIN (ga-DOH-thin) – kingdom north of Hadrian's Wall, on the eastern shores of modern-day Scotland

GWENT (gwent) - kingdom in modern-day southeast Wales, where Caer Leon is located

GLYWYSING – kingdom neighboring Gwent to the west

KNOCKMA (nock-MAH) – kingdom of Queen Oonagh and King Finbheara of the Sídhe in the kingdom of Connacht, in Ireland

MAES GWYTHNO (may-ess GWITH-no) – ancient name for the kingdom that now lies underwater off the Ceredigion coast in Cardigan Bay, Wales, often referred to as the "Welsh Atlantis"

RHEGED (REH-ged) - kingdom of Urien, in modern-day Cumbria, the most northwestern county in England

STRATHCLYDE – kingdom in western modern-day Scotland, where Alt Clud is located

YNYS MANAU (innis man-OW) – the Isle of Man, Britain

YNYS WYDRYN (IN-ess WID-rin) – "the isle of glass," also known as Affalon, the ethereal island realm of Nimue, Lady of the Lake and priestess of Arianrhod

ULAID (oo-lay-EED) – ancient kingdom in modern-day Northern Ireland

VIROCONIUM (veero-CONE-ee-um) - Roman settlement in ancient times where modern-day Wroxeter lies

ABOUT THE AUTHOR

 J.M. Hofer writes in Salt Lake City, Utah, where she can seek the solace of the American desert whenever it calls.

Her first novel, *Islands in the Mist*, was one of five semi-finalists out of 2000 in the fantasy genre of the 2013 Amazon Breakthrough Novel Award Contest.

If you enjoyed *The Young Stag*, she humbly invites you to post a review on Goodreads or Amazon, and thanks you for your readership and support.

Visit her world at www.jmhofer.com, where you can sign up for her mailing list, the Chieftain's Circle. Members will always be the first to know about giveaways, promotions, book signings and author events.

Islands in the Mist Series
Book I: Islands in the Mist
Book II: Across the Sea
Book III: Rise of the Pendragon
Book IV: Into the Shadows
Book V: The Young Stag

Made in the USA
Middletown, DE
28 September 2022